THE DUSK REAPERS

CURSEBREAKER
BOOK ONE

JT LAWRENCE

FIRE FINCH

About the Author
JT Lawrence

JT Lawrence is a USA Today bestselling author
of 30+ books, and a Kindle Unlimited All-Star. Mother to a
menagerie of chaos, voracious reader, gin fan, and urban
farmer.

*Stay up all night
with USA Today bestselling author
JT Lawrence.*

www.jt-lawrence.com

amazon.com/author/jtlawrence

tiktok.com/@stay_up_allnite

instagram.com/authorjtlawrence

facebook.com/JanitaTLawrence

x.com/stay_up_allnite

bookbub.com/authors/jt-lawrence

pinterest.com/stay_up_all_night

linkedin.com/in/janita-thiele-lawrence-56533610

SPECIAL THANKS

*Immense gratitude to my readers
whose loyalty, support, and generous reviews
give me the courage to face the blank page
over and over again.*

I wouldn't be able to do this without you.

I hope you enjoy this new magical adventure!

- Janita (JT Lawrence)

PROLOGUE
- THE LITTLE GREEN-EYED GHOUL -

THE HAUNTED FOREST, JOHANNESBURG, 1998

The forest breathed in. Green, umber, brown. Hard black branches, leaves soft as skin. Sunlight cascaded through the canopy, speckling the dead leaves below, dappling the carpet of decay.

"They say this forest is haunted," said the man in a cheerful way. He was slightly out of breath from the exertion of the walk, and his cheeks were lightly smudged.

The woman pulled her thin cardigan tighter, adjusting her scarf against the unexpected chill in the air. She smiled at him, her eyes alight, teasing. "You don't believe in ghosts, do you?"

The man shrugged, palms facing the hidden sky. It was a receptive gesture; he was open to the idea. He was open to most things. It was one of the reasons the woman was in love with him. She took his hand and loosely linked his fingers with hers as they made their way past the tree trunks covered with lichen and moss. *Such beautiful patterns,* she thought. *Such delicate shades of blue and teal. Lichen should be the name of a paint color.* Of course, she knew it would be impossible, because lichen came in all shades, including gold. She had seen it on river rocks and dead oak stumps.

Liquid Amber was the name of the trees that surrounded them. How wonderful that sounded, how rich and royal, something out of a fairytale. As they wended their way through, the couple could hear the beat of birds' wings, and the busy work of beetles. They could feel the spring of humus underfoot.

The woman stopped to swat at a mosquito needling her calf. She had an irrational hatred of mosquitoes, and was perversely pleased when she looked at her palm, freshly dabbed with the flattened remnants of the delicate pest and a small smear of crimson blood. She rubbed her hands together. "Is it much farther?"

The weather had been beautiful before entering the woodland —a bright clear sky full of promise—but once the trees outnumbered them, the ceiling of branches and leaves kept that happy brightness out.

"We're almost there," the man replied, giving her an encouraging look.

The woman regretted wearing her new sneakers. When the man had suggested a picnic in a forest, she had envisioned the romantic notion of a few trees and a bottle of champagne. Now she sighed at her previously pristine shoes caked in mud. *Not that it really matters,* she told herself, instantly feeling guilty for focusing on the negative instead of appreciating her healthy heart and strong legs. Stained sneakers were certainly a First World Problem.

In the distance, an animal cried. The howl was so full of sorrow it stopped the couple in their tracks. They frowned at each other. It had sounded like a wolf, but there were no wolves in South Africa, and certainly none in Johannesburg.

"Dog?" asked the woman. She didn't want to say it sounded like a wolf; it would have been a silly thing to say. Still, the cry had possessed a definite lupine quality.

The man exhaled a smoky plume of breath. "Must have been."

They continued walking. The man patted his chest pocket without meaning to, like a smoker checking for his pack of Camels. He was worried that he would lose the tanzanite ring. He was more worried that the woman would turn down his proposal, but not losing the ring would be a good start. What was that well-known saying? *Grant me the serenity to accept the things I cannot change, courage to change the things I can, and wisdom to know the difference.* Already he was questioning his decision to bring the woman to this forest. He didn't remember it being so … so, well, spooky. He knew people whispered that it was haunted, but that's what bored people did, didn't they? Make drama where there was none? Lack of drama silently called people to action like an empty glass at a party.

Anyway, *spooky* wasn't the feeling he had been aiming for. He thought he'd tell a joke to lighten the atmosphere, but as he opened his mouth, another howl reached their ears. The animal was closer than before. It sounded like a wolf, but he wouldn't say that out loud. Who would marry a man who seemed afraid of wolves in the woods, especially when the "woods" happened to be in a city sprawl historically free of wolves?

"Are you all right?" the woman asked. He nodded and resisted the urge to tap his pocket again. The ring would surely still be there since the last time he had checked, all of six seconds ago.

Finally, they reached the small clearing he remembered from his previous—spook-free—visit.

"This is it," he said, and pressed his lips together. It wasn't as picturesque as he had built up in his mind, and his cheeks burned with self-consciousness. He pushed the hair out of his eyes, imagining the woman wondering what on earth she was doing here, with him.

Still, there seemed to be more air to breathe in the circular clearing, and the leaves were greener. There were snatches of blue sky. In the distance, a stream twinkled.

"It's beautiful," she said.

The man's shoulders relaxed. He swung his backpack off, leaned it against a boulder and unzipped it. He pulled out a weatherproof camping mat which he laid out on the ground, covered it with a picnic blanket, then began to unpack the food he had brought: strawberries, salmon, cream cheese, rye bread in consideration of the woman's gluten intolerance and a still-cold bottle of Brut. White napkins. Plastic champagne flutes. The woman turned away from him to hide her glee, and her nerves. She crossed her arms and pretended to admire yet another shade of lichen. When she turned back to him, he was gone.

I won't panic. Of course, I wouldn't panic, she thought, as fear gushed through her like ice water. He probably just stepped away to gather kindling, or to pee. She could hear her heart beating, could feel her lungs forcing the clammy green air in and out. Even if he had voluntarily gone into the dense forest that surrounded them, it didn't necessarily mean he was safe. That wolf-animal could have attacked him, could have crushed his windpipe with those giant lupine jaws. The woman's stomach began to ache; bitterness climbed her throat. She tried to control her breathing, tried to stay calm. The pattern of the picnic blanket—red and white checks—

jumped out at her as her adrenaline pumped through her body. She blinked the pattern away and looked for a clue as to where he could have gone. Candles, fruit, bread. *He probably just nipped away for a pee*, her thoughts repeated. God knew she needed one now, too, with her nerves jangling like this. The air around her became colder, darker. She strode over to his backpack, searching for a flashlight, but as she reached into the darkness, she found the bag empty.

"What are you doing?" the man asked.

His voice, though friendly, made the woman jolt. She looked up at him open-mouthed and saw that his hands were full of wildflowers. Relief mopped up the fear. He had left to collect flowers. He had been gone less than two minutes. Why had she almost lost her mind with worry? It was the damned forest, the ghosts in her head. She exhaled a feverish laugh and doubled over, holding her aching stomach.

"You gave me such a fright," she said, still laughing, then standing upright. Her near-hysteria made her eyes water.

"Sorry," he said, concern on his face, his arms still full of wildflowers. "Are you okay? I didn't mean to frighten you. I wanted to surprise you." He put the beautiful blossoms down on the blanket and approached her. Worry creased his forehead. The woman was extremely pale.

She laughed again and swiped at a tear. "You surprised me, all right. I thought you'd been taken by a dingo or something."

"A dingo?" he asked, and his concern melted into amusement. Their mutual self-consciousness faded as they laughed together, and then he held her for a long time. With their senses heightened and completely surrounded by nature, it felt to them both a beautiful moment. The engagement ring seemed to blaze in the man's pocket. When they finally released each other, he motioned grandly to the blanket.

"M'lady," he began, not without trepidation.

She hesitated for a moment, taking a deep breath to steady herself.

Honestly, at that point, if she wanted to hightail it out of there, he would have completely understood. He'd be right behind her, literally and figuratively.

Instead, she looked into his kind eyes and smiled generously, as if her whole body and mind were saying *I'm ready for you. I am yours.*

She sat down. It wasn't the romantic date she'd expected. It was better. More real, more visceral. She felt closer to the man than ever, and when he lowered himself down next to her and began tearing the foil off the top of the bottle and untwisting the loop of the cork's wire cage, she felt that they could make love right there. Not the kind of love driven by lust and primal need but instead an intimate, highly focused co-worshipping of each other in this cathedral of trees. But something stopped her from unbuttoning her blouse. It was the eeriness, the mist.

The invisible forest eyes watching her. The warmth she felt evaporated.

"Can you feel that?" she asked, and pulled at her cardigan again, wrapping it as tightly as it would go. The cork popped —a muted sound—and the man poured the rose-copper liquid into the flutes.

"What?" All he could feel was his damn heart hammering against the damn ring in his damn pocket.

"Eyes," the woman said. A shiver shook her spine.

He glanced at her, puzzled. "Eyes?"

"Like someone is watching us."

Cold mist continued to roll in, and the sky's tint deepened.

He looked around, the hair on the back of his neck rising. "Why did you have to say that?"

She looked at him apologetically, but he nodded. "I feel it, too." His whisper was conspiratorial as he tipped his untouched wine out onto the ground beside them and wiped his hands on his jeans. "Let's blow this joint."

"I thought you'd never ask," she joked, jumping up, relief splashed across her face. When she glanced at the man to see if he'd registered her humor, she was met with a face as pale gray as the moon. She gulped. *What is it?* she wanted to ask, but no sound came out. Instead, she turned to look at what had transfixed the man.

A very young child stood at the edge of the clearing. Was she three, or four? The woman had never been good at guessing children's ages. The child was naked and dirty, and her long black hair was a black spiderweb of knots. When you looked at her brilliant eyes, the rest of the picture faded to a blurred background. They were an impossible color, a light green with a flush of ocean, and their intensity was difficult to look away from. The very energy of the forest swirled up and around them, through them, till they were all connected by the color of the child's eyes and the spirits of the trees and the soil and the stones and the dead leaves.

The woman wanted to ask questions.

Hello, little girl, she wanted to say. *Where are your parents? Where do you live? Are you lost? Are you scared? Can we help you?* but her mouth was frozen. It became clear to them that this was no powerless little girl, nor was she lost. If there was any power in that circle, it belonged to the fearsome feral child. If anyone should be gripped by terror, it should be the man and the woman. Not taking their eyes off the apparition, they blindly grabbed each other's hands and began trampling backwards. The child's demeanor darkened, and fear clutched at the couple's bellies. Her nest of dark hair began rising, and there seemed to be a glow around her and through her. Her whole body lifted, floating above the ground, her hair on end, her eyes as bright as a twin green suns. When the girl opened her mouth in a terrifying silent scream, the couple felt as if they would disappear into the vacuum.

They turned and ran. Unbeknownst to the man, the tanzanite ring lifted out of his pocket and went spinning in the air, catching a sliver of light as it fell to the forest floor. The couple smashed through the forest as fast as their legs would take them, away from the abandoned picnic and the cold mist and the nightmarish green-eyed ghoul.

They escaped, and the forest breathed out.

A SPELL
- EQUINOX STITCH -

[To be chanted in your or your coven's chalk circle to celebrate Equinox and The Wild. Required: Chalk, four candles, and one smooth hagstone per person, to be held in the left palm. Optional: Herb and flower confetti from your potion garden.]

She burns whole forests green to black

Turns hand-shaped leaves to dust

She caps oceans with her smoking ice

Moves mountains with fearsome gusts.

Power erupts from her like lava

Flames race along burning roots

As she knits the future with her fire

From the ashes grow green shoots.

All that burns will soon flourish

and all that flourishes must burn

Death is not the end, no, no—

The world just turns and turns.

All sleeping seeds she wakens

The rainbow is her token

The destructor's power is taken

In love, all curses are broken.

As the seasons all blow through

Our fragile destiny's sealed

Everything lost is always found

Everything hurt is healed.

This is the orbit of the wayward woman

Who knits with stars and stones

The Wild, the wanderer, the wasp, the witch

This is the course of the wayward goddess

A flame, a stone, a stitch.

CHAPTER 1

PEACOCK OF PAIN

ASHA

MORNINGVALE HOSPITAL, SEPTEMBER 2022

It hurt to blink.

I tried to close my eyes against the brightness. The white lights overhead seemed to cut into my skull, but the dark was filled with looming terror. So, I had to choose between the fear and the glare, and in between was stuttering pain as my brain restarted and my neurons resumed firing.

My life hung in the balance: the taut tightrope of a flatlining heart.

Soul teetering, I gasped. It was a desperate, ugly sound.

I cried out, tried to fight, but I found my limbs shackled. I was unable to reach for my knife. I railed against the padded cuffs. I shouted in a language I didn't recognize. I felt sparks along my veins until my arms were burning, then a welcome release. Immediately a steel tray smashed against the wall, the sharp instruments it had held clattering to the floor.

As I moved, sensations streamed back into my wasted body. Pain seemed to stitch my organs and skin with thick red nylon cord. Then the voices crept in.

What the hell was that?

The speaking in tongues?

That wasn't tongues. That was Latin.

I mean, what the hell was THAT?

The tray fell.

The tray FELL? That isn't what I saw. I saw it flying across the—

Hey. Focus. Her heart rate is spiking.

Watch BP. Watch it. Worried about that BP.

That tray flew across the room! Did no one else see that?

Forget about it. We don't have time. Give her a tranq. And pethidine.

She's pulled her IV out.

Get it back in.

I can't.

Get it back in or she'll arrest again.

She's fighting too much. I can't get the needle in.

Did anyone else see that? The sparks? What the—

For God's sake, shut up and give her that shot.

I heard paper tearing, vials tinkling. The voices were soft at first, distant, like in a dream. Then I felt the bee-sting in my thigh, a pinch to let me know this was no nightmare. The sharpness of the cold needle biting into my clenched quadricep stood apart from the other pain, which was mostly a dull ache originating from my scalp and traveling down my spine and throughout my body. It was how I would expect quicksilver poisoning to feel: a cool, slow, lethal ache as the mercury coats your cells. The dullness of the pain did not persist. As I thrashed around, fighting the darkness, the ache became more active, more acute, as if it had been waiting for me to wake up to present, unashamedly, its full glory. A dancing, shimmering peacock of pain. I thought I might die.

Oh.

The tranquilizer was working. My limbs fell to my sides, resting on the sweat-drenched sheets. Sweat, or urine, or blood, it seemed to matter less and less.

And then the painkiller kicked in. Blessed painkiller.

The liquid opioid warmed me right through, dissolving any thought of poisoning, trauma, conflict, or pain. My thoughts dissolved into one another and, finally, the darkness won.

Again, the white lights. The pain. The voices.

When I surfaced this time, things were clearer. The people wore stethoscopes and nurse scrubs. Name badges flashed on their chests, but I couldn't read them; my brain was not yet taking calls.

The voices were trying to help. I clenched my jaw to stop myself from fighting them. It wasn't easy. I was conditioned to fight, I knew that much. I didn't know much of anything else. I felt the sparks again, flaring through my veins. A golden green current under my skin, balls of invisible fire in my palms.

She's coming to, one of the people in the room said. There was surprise in her voice. She had obviously not expected me to survive.

Took her time, chipped in someone else.

All it took was two weeks.

Two weeks of restraints and crash carts.

Two weeks from flatlining to conscious.

That's about the same amount of time it takes you to play nine holes, so I think she did pretty well.

Sure. Coming back from the dead can't be easy.

There was forced guffawing and idle chat, tired attempts at worn-out jokes. What else did one do, working one punishing shift after another, dealing with bloody life-and-death situations more often than deciding what to eat for breakfast? Tired attempts at humor beat no humor at all.

I swallowed, wincing. My throat was dry and swollen.

Was this a hospital? It looked like it, felt like it. Antiseptic colors and scents. Monitors beeped and purred around me in symphony with the voices. I wanted to ask them what had happened to me, how I had ended up so unceremoniously on their ER gurney.

Then I realized it wasn't just the prior circumstances that I couldn't remember. I bit down harder, till my skull threatened to light up again. I tried to coerce my limbs to relax. I forced my arms down alongside me. I didn't have to guess whether it was blood, urine, or perspiration. This time the hospital bed was dry.

It's the small victories that count.

Dry hospital sheets: check.

(Mostly) survived unknown trauma: check.

Sanity: to be determined.

Now all I had to do was remember my own name.

CHAPTER 2

ROOK

ASHA

I was having a dream about wolves running in a dark forest when I heard a tapping on the door. I remembered I was in the hospital. I had gotten used to the door being open wide at all times, with medical staff striding in and out at will. Now that my room was empty and quiet, I guessed it meant I was out of immediate danger, maybe even out of ICU. More gentle knocking reached my ears.

Come in, I tried to say, but my voice was less than a croak. The handle turned. The door opened, revealing a woman in a white lab coat. She had fabulous fiery red hair and stylish black-rimmed glasses. A laminated ID card hung on a blue lanyard around her neck. I squinted, then closed one eye, trying to get the letters on the ID to focus. "PSYCHIA" was all I could make out.

She came over and lifted a plastic cup for me to drink from. The straw felt thick against my lips and the water tasted cool and sweet in my desiccated mouth.

"Ah," I said, sweeping my teeth with my reconstituted tongue. "Thank you." My voice still sounded decidedly amphibian, but at least I could communicate. If I was lucky, I might be able to get some questions answered.

The redhead gave me a perfunctory smile and wheeled a chair toward my bed. When she sat down, I caught a ribbon of scent: sandalwood and rose hand cream. She was holding a digital clipboard with a neat gray stylus at the ready.

"Right, Ms. Rook," she said. "I've been waiting for you to wake up. Rather impatiently, I might add." She smiled again, but this time it seemed more genuine.

I didn't know what to say. *Rook?* Really?

"Rook," I said aloud, feeling the sound of the short word, and the sharp *K*. "Rook," I said again, and then closed my mouth as I realized I must sound like a preschooler with a rather alarmingly low IQ.

PSYCHIATRIC UNIT said her ID card. Doctor T. Gilbert. University of Witwatersrand.

"Call me Taryn," she said. "All my patients do."

"I'm your patient?" I asked, blinking. My heart was a stone sinking to the riverbed. "This the ... psychiatric unit?"

"Oh," said the doctor, her lips turning up at the corners. "Oh no, don't worry. You're in a regular hospital ward—"

I sighed, and my muscles automatically relaxed.

Gilbert gave me a skewed smile. "I'm here to chat with you about your near-death experience and recovery. It's standard practice to help you prepare to cope with integrating back into society."

My head was spinning. Maybe they had injected something into my IV line. "What now?"

She adjusted her glasses. "You suffered major head trauma. You almost died. Although I understand that your body has healed exceptionally well, you can't just go back to your regular life and expect everything to be the same."

Questions buzzed like black bees inside my brain. I had to close my eyes for a moment. "I almost died," I echoed.

"Yes," Gilbert nodded, smoothing her flaming hair away from her face. "And believe me, post-traumatic stress is not something you want to mess around with. It leaves you vulnerable to all manner of sub-optimal mental states, especially anxiety and depression, and the inflammation the distress causes is certainly not good for healing."

Healing. The word stood out for me, although I didn't know why.

"I have a more pressing problem than PTSD," I said.

The doctor stopped scribbling on her clipboard and lifted her gaze.

I rubbed my eyes. "I ... I can't seem to remember anything."

Doctor Gilbert didn't try to hide her surprise. "*Anything?*"

I spent a moment looking around the room, searching for a clue, for a shred of anything. I came up blank.

"Asha Viridian Rook," stated the psychologist. Instead of waiting for me to babble on about my foreign-sounding name like before, she plowed ahead, reading my medical file to me. "You're twenty-eight years old. Previously in excellent health, although you do have a rather curious hospital record."

I frowned at her. She turned the file around to show me the multiple entries, but my eyes weren't doing a great job of reading yet. I shook my head.

"Five years ago, you came in for a dislocated shoulder; a few months after that, a broken collarbone. The next year it was your ribs. Cracked. Then a broken finger and a chipped kneecap." I must have looked horrified, because she stopped reading and looked at me. "Were you in an abusive relationship?" she asked. "*Are* you in an abusive relationship? Because I can help you with that. We have resources."

I shook my head. "No," I said. "I mean, I don't know."

"You're just really clumsy, then?" she suggested. "Or maybe

regular injury is a career perk. Perhaps you moonlight as a stunt double."

Moonlight.

"What?"

"I was just kidding," she said.

"You said '*moonlight.*' What's my real job?"

Taryn scanned the file the hospital staff had put together. "It just says self-employed."

Hmmm. "Anything else interesting in there?"

"There's no next of kin listed. You know, a friend or relative to notify if—"

"Oh," I said, feeling suddenly bereft. "That must happen sometimes, right? Someone's in a hurry to fill in the admission form and they leave some details out."

"Sure," said the psychologist, then looked uncomfortable. "Actually, that never happens. I just didn't want you to feel bad. The truth is, we searched and searched for someone to call when they brought you in."

It was my turn to fib. "That's okay," I said, but my body felt hollow. The worst thing about the feeling of stark loneliness was that it was achingly familiar. I looked away from her, and when I glanced back, I saw she was staring at me. "What?" I asked. "What is it?"

The psychologist was hesitant, but her curiosity got the better of her. "I have questions," she said.

I ground my teeth. "I have more."

"Well, maybe we can work it out together. I can help." The psychologist glanced backwards at the door, which was still ajar, then leaned forward and whispered, low and slow. "But first, I need to tell you something."

CHAPTER 3
SKULL SPLINTERS
ASHA

I glanced at the door, too. *What?*

Doctor Gilbert's voice streamed at full volume once more: "We can begin our session by discussing how you got here." At the same time, she passed me her clipboard, on which she had typed THERE IS A DETECTIVE OUTSIDE, LISTENING.

I frowned at the message, then nodded and handed it back. "Okay," I said. "I'm ready."

Why a cop would be interested in my condition puzzled me, but I didn't have anything to hide—or did I?

"I understand that your recall is poor at the moment," the doc said, "but I'm confident that your memory will return when the swelling has gone down and you return to your regular schedule."

I couldn't imagine having a "regular schedule," I couldn't even imagine what I looked like, apart from my arms, which I'd had plenty of time to stare at. Long, slender, and inked with flowing botanical illustrations of vines, leaves, tendrils, and flowers. A particularly beautiful bloom on the crook of my arm was covered with Band-Aids and transparent tape where the IV fed into my bloodstream.

Doctor Gilbert followed my gaze. "Let's start with what you *do* know."

"Er," I said, looking around the white-walled room for clues, or inspiration. It was empty apart from a single floral arrangement.

The doctor waited patiently.

"I know my name," I said. "Because you told me."

"It was on the ID you were carrying," she said. "We cross-referenced it with your hospital records, of which there are plenty, as we previously discussed."

"I know I almost died. I felt it. And then I overheard the staff saying so afterwards."

"Yes," she said, pushing her glasses up the bridge of her nose. "You were found on the pavement in the inner city, half dead —mostly dead—in a pool of your own blood. You had a catastrophic skull fracture."

Which explained why my head had felt like it was the eye of a vicious tornado.

"No one expected you to make it. The neurosurgeon's prognosis was so bleak that the surgical team hesitated to work on you. But you were a fighter, literally. You've been smashing things since you arrived, including an intern's nose. You also smashed the prognosis, which saw you, at best, in a permanently vegetative state. In the end it was an eleven-hour operation during which you technically died. Twice." She took a breath. "The good news is that you've regained eighty percent of your brain function, and from what I've seen, I'm guessing you'll be out of here in a couple of weeks."

"I'm lucky, then," I said. "Apart from the part about getting my head smashed in."

"Thirty-six stitches," Gilbert said. "They had to pick skull splinters out of your soft nervous tissue." She tapped her stylus on the clipboard. "And yet here you are, having a perfectly pleasant conversation with a stranger."

"I don't know if I'd call it pleasant," I replied.

"You don't understand. You shouldn't be conscious," she said. "You should be sedated and hooked up to a ventilator."

I lifted my hand and tentatively touched the back of my head. It was padded with a thick layer of bandages. It felt tender, but not painful.

"I was found on the pavement?" I asked. "Did I fall? Was I hit by a car?" The rest of my body didn't seem hurt.

Doctor Gilbert hesitated. "This isn't going to be easy to hear."

Sweat beaded on my upper lip and prickled under my arms. "I'm listening."

"You were attacked."

"Attacked?" I repeated. "Mugged?"

"Your wallet was found on you, as was your jewelry. It didn't look like a mugging."

Dread crept up my legs. "Was I—?"

"Apart from your head injury, you weren't assaulted in any other way."

"How do you know?"

"Security camera."

"What?" I asked. "Can I see it?"

"Yes," she said. "But not yet. There's a process to these things." She motioned to the detective hovering outside.

"So you saw the attacker?" I asked. "Has he been arrested?"

The psychologist shook her head. "He or she was wearing a black robe with a hood. It was impossible to make out any distinguishing facial features."

A black hooded robe? That sounded scary as all hell. I exhaled, my nerves scratching at my insides.

"The color has drained from your face," said the doctor. "Would you like to rest? We can continue tomorrow."

"No!" I said. *Please don't leave me.* "I need to know more."

She stood up, and the artificial light set off the red in her hair. "I don't have much more."

I sat up a little bit straighter and groaned with the effort. My muscles were sleepy and stiff. "Earlier, you said you were waiting impatiently for me to wake up. Why?"

Doctor Gilbert smiled. "Because I'm nosy, and you're an interesting case."

I felt the sparks again. What was happening to me?

"Because I recovered?"

"Because your recovery was pretty close to miraculous. Except that I don't believe in miracles."

I looked at her. "What do you believe in?"

She smiled again. "Science. Humanity. The third law of thermodynamics."

"You said there was no next of kin listed on my medical records."

"Yes," she nodded. "I can show you."

"Then who are the flowers from?"

Maybe there was someone who cared about me, even if he or she didn't exist in ink on a hospital admission form.

"I don't know," Gilbert replied. "None of them had cards. Which is a shame, because I'd love to know which florist they came from. They've stayed fresh for weeks."

They've stayed fresh for weeks.

The tissue paper was black with a logo I couldn't quite make out.

"You did come in with a ring on," said the psychologist. "It looked like an engagement ring. Tanzanite. I thought you might be engaged, especially when the flowers arrived. But when no-one showed up to visit—"

Ouch.

"—I figured my assumption was wrong."

"Can I see it?" I asked. "The ring?"

It was optimistic, but I wondered if seeing the ring might spur some kind of memory.

"Sure," said Gilbert. "It's in a bag with your other personal belongings. I'll get it from the nurses' station."

"No need," said a gruff, masculine voice from behind Doctor Gilbert. The detective was tall, strong, and annoyingly good looking, and he was holding up a transparent plastic bag marked *ROOK*.

CHAPTER 4
FLAT WHITE OCEAN
ASHA

"I'm Detective Armstrong, from the Parkview Police Station."

I noticed he didn't show his badge, and took it as a good sign.

He lifted a transparent clamshell container with bright green grapes inside and dropped them unceremoniously on my side table. When we both raised our eyebrows at him, he said, "What? My mother always said to take grapes to hospital patients."

The detective was attractive, albeit in a weathered kind of way. I liked the timbre of his voice; it made me feel comforted, even embraced. He came across as masculine, but not macho. I think he'd be my type, if I knew what my type was ... and if he weren't a cop.

I looked him straight in the eye with confidence I didn't feel. "I'm Asha Rook, apparently."

"Hello, Asha Rook," he said. He wasn't smiling, but his warm brown eyes were full of light. "Just the person I came to see."

I shifted a little against the hospital sheets and it felt like the temperature in the room had risen. It appeared safe to say that the part of my brain that controlled sexual attraction was A-okay.

Detective Armstrong faced the doctor. "If you've finished your session, I'll take over."

"We're finished," replied Gilbert, "but I'll stay for the interview."

"No need," said Armstrong.

"Detective Armstrong," said the doctor, folding her arms in front of her. "Ms. Rook is my patient. She's extremely vulnerable right now. I will not allow you to question her alone."

There was an awkward silence where the cop seemed to be summing up the psychologist while she stared at him, standing her ground. He broke the standoff with a shrug. "That seems fair," he conceded, and offered her the only chair in the room. She waved away his offer and proceeded to perch on the wide windowsill on the other side of the room, her lanyard swinging in front of her.

"I appreciate you coming to see me," I said. "But I'm afraid you're wasting your time."

"Why is that?" asked the man, lowering himself into the visitor's chair.

"Severe post-traumatic retrograde amnesia," said the psychologist. "Due to the brain injury caused by blunt force trauma."

"What she said," I answered, indicating Gilbert. I took another sip of water from the plastic cup.

Detective Armstrong rubbed his finger on his chin, as if he were considering this for the first time. "In my experience, most people know more than they think they do."

"Do they?"

"Always."

We looked at each other. His energy was intense, and there was definitely a connection between us. He may have felt the same way, because he broke eye contact first and scooped his fringe away from his tanned forehead. I couldn't help but notice his hands, which were strong and elegant.

"Ask me anything," I said. "I want to find answers as much as you do."

"Do you know the person who attacked you?"

I shook my head. It hurt. "No."

"Do you know anyone who might want to harm you?"

"No."

"Do you remember anything at all about the night of the twenty-first of September, 2022?"

I gasped. "It's *2022?*"

The cop threw Gilbert a worried look.

"I'm only joking," I said, and he exhaled. He wasn't impressed. I may have acute amnesia, but it looked like he had an acute sense of humor failure. Maybe he wasn't my type, after all. Or maybe my joke was just lame, which was entirely possible. They both blinked at me, and I realized they were still waiting for an answer.

"No," I said. "I don't know what happened on the twenty-first of September. But I'm guessing it was the day I was attacked."

The detective narrowed his eyes at me. I could tell he was trying to work out if I was faking the memory loss. I wished I were. I'd much rather be trying to hide something than be marooned in this flat white ocean of zero personal history.

Suddenly, I knew what I needed to do. I eased back against the bed and closed my eyes.

"I'm feeling very tired now."

I heard the chair wheels track along the tiles as the cop scooted forward. "I have a few more questions."

Join the club, buddy.

Doctor Gilbert stepped forward. "I think it's best to let her rest."

"I can't leave yet," said the detective. "I don't have anything."

"Neither does she," the doctor said. "You'll have to take my patient's statement another time."

"I'm not here for a statement," he said, which made my eyes click open. "I came here to arrest her."

CHAPTER 5

RETROGRADE

ASHA

All of a sudden, I wasn't tired anymore.

"Er, what now?" Perhaps the gruff detective's sense of humor had miraculously risen from the dead and he was trying to get a laugh out of me.

"Ms. Rook," said the detective. "On the twenty-first of September, you killed a man."

The flat white ocean that had previously surrounded me seemed to rear up and pour into my head, fizzing and sparkling and dissolving my thoughts. A bright bubbling liquid panic.

"What?" My mouth was suddenly cotton. It became difficult to swallow, and there was no more water in the plastic cup on my bedside table.

"Don't say it like that," scolded doctor Gilbert. "Don't make it sound like it was her fault. Like it was premeditated."

"It could have been premeditated," said the cop, shrugging. "The video—"

"Oh, please," replied the annoyed psychologist.

"There's a video?" I asked. "A video of me ... killing someone?"

Anxiety grabbed me by the throat. Perspiration prickled. This couldn't be true.

"She was attacked," Gilbert said. "She was defending herself."

"Was she?" asked Armstrong. "She didn't look like a victim in the video."

The doctor's skin flushed in frustration. "It was clearly self-defense," she said.

Armstrong shook his head. "There's nothing clear about the clip."

I looked at the detective. "Clear enough for you to want to arrest me."

I felt an odd sensation then, like fire traveling through my veins. As if my limbs were detonation cords and only I could hold off the explosion. I squeezed my eyes shut until the feeling faded. When I opened them again, he was gazing at me.

"Look," he said. "You've been through hell. I understand that. I don't usually make a habit of arresting hospital patients. But you killed a man and don't remember doing it. You're not cooperating, so I needed to get your attention."

I stared at him and spoke past the constriction in my throat. "You have my attention."

"You need to remember what happened that night."

"It's not a switch you can flip," said Gilbert. "Post-traumatic retrograde amnesia of this severity takes time and therapy to treat. Even then, we're not guaranteed a comprehensive or accurate memory retrieval. It may take months, or years."

The detective stood up to leave and checked his watch. "You've got a week."

After Armstrong skulked away, doctor Gilbert turned to me. "Are you thinking what I'm thinking?"

"That Detective Armstrong should go eat a bag of dicks?"

She laughed out loud. There was disapproval in her expression, but delight in her eyes. I thought then that she reminded me of someone. A friend, perhaps, or a sister—of which I apparently had none.

"What are you thinking?" I asked her.

"We need to fast-track your therapy. We need counseling, hypnotism, neurogenesis. There's no way I'm letting you go on trial for self-defense."

"Okay," I said, scrambling out of bed. I yanked the IV out of my arm. It stung more than I expected it to, and tears sprang to my eyes.

"Stop!" said Gilbert, eyes wide with shock. "What are you doing?"

"I'm getting out of here," I said. "No way I'm playing sitting duck."

"You're safe here," said the doctor.

"Apparently not from cops."

I may not remember much about myself, but I knew for certain that I would not be able to stand being locked in a cell. For me, it would be a fate worse than death. Perhaps my core value was freedom. Perhaps that's why I killed a midnight attacker on some inner-city sidewalk.

The locker was empty. "Where are my clothes?" I demanded.

"The police bagged them up. They've been sent in for testing."

"Hex them," I said.

"Excuse me?"

I shook my head. "I don't know why I said that."

Hex them! my thoughts repeated.

There was that weird language again. I didn't know where it came from or what it meant.

"You can't leave," said Doctor Gilbert. "You're not well enough. You sustained a major brain injury. Technically, you shouldn't even be able to walk."

"I can walk," I said, still searching for something to wear.

She wore that look of disapproval again, then undid her belt. "Untie your gown and turn it around," she said. "So that the flap is in the front."

I did as she instructed. She tied the knots so that they did a better job of covering my front than they had my behind, then used her belt to cinch them in place. Then she handed me her silk scarf, and her cardigan.

I stopped scrambling for a second. "Thank you. I'll return these to you."

She shook her head as though it didn't matter. "Where will you go?"

There was only one place I could go. "I want to go home, but I don't know where that is."

Doctor Gilbert blinked at me. "I do." She took a business card out of her pocket and copied my address from my medical file.

When she handed it to me, her face was stern. "You need to check in with me."

"Okay," I agreed.

"I'll meet you anywhere you like for a session. Just call me, okay? We'll get you better."

I thanked her again and ran out of the room, down the antiseptic passage, almost bowling over an old man wheeling his oxygen tank.

I sprinted through the VIP ward, where the wealthy patients were treated. It had real art on the walls, automatic glass sliding doors, a five-star kitchen, and gold name plaques on the doors. *Miraphine, Herlamin, Taranath.* They sounded like elves.

I couldn't face the claustrophobia of an elevator so I ran down the stairs. It occurred to me that my body was holding up pretty well. Wouldn't most brain injury patients be leaving in a wheelchair? When I reached the ground floor, I jogged past the long reception counter where the staff ogled my fancy outfit. As soon as I burst through the automatic glass doors and into the fresh air, I felt my anxiety dissipate. I congratulated myself for dodging what would most certainly have been a—

I felt his hand on my arm before I saw him.

I had dropped my guard. I had been distracted by the sunshine on my skin—something I hadn't had for weeks—the shimmering green leaves, the smell of fresh lawn clippings. My body yearned for these things just as I felt the vise of his palm and knuckles clamp down on me. It felt like slow motion as I turned to look at him, energy sparking under his rough grip. There was a neat metallic click between us, and when I looked down, I saw that he had handcuffed me.

"If I look ill," the detective said to me in a low voice, close to my ear, "it's because I've just finished eating that big bag of dicks."

CHAPTER 6
TANGLEWOOD MANOR
ASHA

"You can't arrest me," I hissed.

He looked amused, which I found infuriating. "I'm not arresting you."

I delivered a pointed look at the silver cuffs glinting on my wrists.

"I'm *escorting* you," he said, and slid on his shades.

"Escorting me?" I said derisively. "In handcuffs?"

He glanced down at them. "For your own protection."

I felt my energy sparking again—a high, aggressive energy, turning my limbs to air—as if I were preparing for a fight. I curled my fingers into fists to hide the balls of fire I felt in my palms.

"You're an interesting one," he said. He hadn't looked me up and down, but I got that feeling anyway.

"What's that supposed to mean?"

He shrugged. I was getting sick of his shrugs. I realized that he was a shrugger, which was another reason to dislike him.

"Your appearance," he said. "It's misleading."

This time I couldn't argue. Apart from my tattoos, I had no idea what I looked like.

"Petite," he said. "Pretty. Covered with more flower tattoos than a hippie festival."

I glared at him. So I didn't know what I looked like, but how attractive could someone be with a bandage wrapped around their head, wearing a creased hospital gown the color of well-chewed gum?

"Definitely pretty," he said, as if he had heard my thoughts. "But underneath that Peace-Love-Forever, you're a real little fighter."

I remembered how I had fought with the doctors, kicked the intern in the nose, sent steel trays flying. I knew deep down he was right, could feel it in my muscles and bones. When it comes to fight-or-flight, you'd better stand clear.

Detective Armstrong pulled me along to a gunmetal gray Toyota Corolla sedan which was baking in the sunny parking lot. He installed me in the passenger seat, careful to not touch me inappropriately as he strapped me in. The cabin smelled like sunburned leather seats and mint chewing gum.

Once the key lit up the engine, he turned to me. "So? Where are we off to?"

What was this? A spontaneous road trip in handcuffs?

"I thought you were taking me to the station," I said.

"Nope," he replied, shifting into reverse. "I told you. I'm escorting you. Where do you want to go?"

I crimped my lips together. Did I trust the man enough to tell him my home address? And then I realized he must already know it. He already knew more about my life than I did.

"Look, Ms. Rook. I knew you were going to break for it. I could see it a mile away. I don't know what you're hiding, but I'm going to find out. In the meantime, I thought I'd take you where you want to go. It's not like you'll get far in your ... predicament."

"I'm feeling fine," I said.

"I didn't mean that. I meant no wallet, no phone. How were you planning on getting home?"

I glanced at the back seat, where my bag of personal belongings lay.

"You could just give them back to me," I said. "This place is buzzing with Ubers."

"Ha," he replied. "You're not getting away from me that easily."

Twenty minutes later, when Armstrong killed the engine, I leaned forward in the passenger seat and stared, my mouth agape. The street was shaded by scores of jacaranda trees, and the house we had parked in front of was a huge Herbert Baker house on a double stand. *Tanglewood Manor*, the sign said. Almost every surface was covered in leaves. Trees reached for the sky, climbers scrambled up stone walls. Every surface was covered with creepers, vines, shrubs, wild grasses, and flowers, matching the ink on my skin. The walls looked alive. It looked like my dream house. How was this possible?

I peered at the number on the wall and double-checked it against the card Doctor Gilbert had given me. The address was correct.

I wouldn't know where to begin breaking into this place, but with his line of work, the detective might have a few pointers. When I tore my eyes away from the house to ask him, he was holding a small bunch of keys in the air next to his head, and looking amused. I couldn't help but smile back, but we both immediately recognized the error of our ways and wiped the friendliness off our faces. I reached for the car door handle.

"Hang on," he said.

I turned back to him, and he motioned for me to raise my wrists. He freed me as deftly as he had cuffed me. As I climbed out and made my way to the front gate, I felt his presence behind me. He was coming in. Of course he was. Unlike a vampire, a detective does not wait for an invitation.

CHAPTER 7

RUPTOR MALEDICTUM

ASHA

Sliding the silver key into the lock felt at the same time novel and familiar. It was as if my body knew the feel of the metal sliding in, muscle memory knew how far to turn until the bolt gave way. I recognized this ritual, this rigid dance of metal parts amidst the lush green foliage. My body had done this hundreds of times. Once we crossed the threshold I stopped in my tracks, my mouth hanging open again—in what was becoming a rather unattractive habit.

What, my inflamed brain said. *No way.*

The house was indeed a manor. More than the architecture, seeing all the different plants and trees made my heart beat stronger.

In the front garden grew a massive peach tree, three different apple varieties, pecan, almond, foxtail red amaranth. Citrus, lemongrass, and ginger guarded the west corner, spiky Sea Buckthorn, the east. I could smell lemon zest, catnip, rosemary, and sage. There was a sea of blue-green society garlic scapes, pink pom-pom onion flowers, bright yellow fennel umbels. Bees and butterflies whirled around us, joined by damselflies, midges, and slow-buzzing fruit beetles plated in speckled-banana patterned armor. A mossy pathway overrun by creeping thyme and clover beckoned us to the front door, but I wasn't yet ready to go inside. I was basking in the richness of the unexpected suburban food forest. I couldn't tear my eyes away from the abundance of leaves; my feeling was that we were watching them actively grow as we stood there. The trees seemed to move molecules right then, absorbing sunlight, inhaling carbon, drawing water up through their advanced networks of roots, all the while manufacturing and sending sugars and starches where they were most needed. I felt an intense connection to the earth, to the soil, to the mycosphere beneath me. And it wasn't a one-sided relationship: I had the feeling that they had been waiting for me to return. That was how I knew I had come home.

Because Armstrong gave no indication of leaving, I decided to just be honest about how I was feeling. It was too overwhelming to keep to myself. I thought I might cry if I didn't say something. "There must be some mistake."

"There's not," he said.

"It's the most beautiful thing I've ever seen. This can't be mine."

"It is," he said, in his gruff way. "Congratulations. Can we go inside? My feet are killing me."

The red front door looked familiar, and the sun-warmed round brass knob felt right in my palm. *Is this how it would be?* I wondered, never getting my memory back but rather rediscovering my life, piece by piece, in these small ordinary moments. The front passage was dark, the floor a polished puzzle of pine. We moved forward, toward the light, and were rewarded with a large open room flooded with sunshine and the scent of the back garden, which seemed to be waiting impatiently outside, tendrils scooping the air around them, grasping for their next beam or branch to climb. A boho farm-style kitchen was on the left: solid scrubbed timber counters, dozens of serving boards, vintage bottles, and a retro bread box. On the right were wing-backs and a handsome oak bookshelf groaning under the weight of hundreds of books. I felt my eyes light up. *Books!* But before I could reach out to take one off the shelf, I heard a sound at my feet.

A small black shadow was circling my ankles, and then another joined in. Forgetting about the detective altogether, I sat right there in the middle of the room, in the path of golden afternoon light, while the beautiful black cats jumped on my lap, meowing and purring and dragging their cheeks against me as if my hospital gown was made out of catnip. Tears sprang to my eyes, but I didn't cry. We stayed like that for a while, then a cat jumped onto Armstrong's lap, who was now sitting on a wingback, while the other cat settled into mine. I blinked at the animal, who started to purr.

"I have cats," I said, more to myself than to him.

"Of course you have cats," he said.

I'm not sure what he meant by that, but I took it as a compliment. "I don't even know their names."

"Circe and Odysseus," said the cop.

I frowned at him. "How do you know?"

"Mad detective skills," he said, then looked pointedly at the silver food bowls in the corner of the kitchen, which were labelled Circe and Odysseus.

I smiled at him; I couldn't help it. Maybe he wasn't as bad as I thought, though I did wonder why he was still in my house. Was he trying to get me to trust him? Trying to make me feel so comfortable in his presence that I would let down my guard and tell him everything I knew, even though that was nothing? Maybe it was nothing more than a coldblooded attempt at drawing me out, but a small part of me admitted that it wasn't horrible having company on such a strange day. "Tea?"

"I thought you'd never ask," he said, rubbing Circe's ear.

I found the kettle without much trouble, but the array of teas was mind-boggling. The tea cupboard looked more like a traditional medicine stall in a Hong Kong market than a beverage station.

"Uh," I said. "Coffee?"

"I love coffee," he said.

I would explore the rest of the house later, on my own. After the promise of the forest at the front, what I really wanted to see was the back garden. We took our steaming mugs out, leaving the cats to lounge on the sunny windowsill. If the front was a forest, then the back yard was a jungle. Not a brick nor square inch of plaster was exposed. Even the playhouse in the corner was blanketed in leaves. Vegetables were interplanted with dazzling flowers, pumpkin vines twisted up trellises, fruit trees were espaliered on the back wall, berry bushes thrived in colorful clay pots. A mature grapevine covered the lathes shading the terrace, and ripe grapes hung down as if they were placed there for decoration. All kinds of citrus scented the air around us as we walked along a path carpeted with Penny Royal. To the right was a large conservatory, a gothic clear-glass greenhouse veined with lead.

"I've never seen a garden like this before," said Armstrong.

Before I could answer him, half a dozen hens appeared from behind what I had thought was a playhouse, but then realized was a chicken coop.

"Hello," I said. "Hello, chickens," because what else do you say to six hens you never knew you had? I automatically reached up and picked some mulberries, and they squawked in delight when I scattered them on the ground. My palm was stained by the purple juice, and I had that feeling of déjà vu that I was starting to get used to. Two snow-white pekin ducks ran past me, honking as they chased one another. An unusual wind chime made of old silver keys tinkled alongside us. I was amazed at the garden, the animals, the house. I must have had the most wonderful, peaceful, fulfilling life there. I felt like I was in a magical garden.

Detective Armstrong lowered himself onto his haunches and stretched his hand out toward a fallen log. Without thinking, without hesitating, my hand shot out and collided with his, almost sending him falling backwards.

He recovered his balance and looked at me, his forehead creased in question.

"Amanita phalloides," I said, glancing at the pretty toadstools he had been about to touch. "Death Cap. It's the deadliest fungi in the country."

"What's wrong with you?" he muttered.

"What's wrong with me? I just saved your life!"

"What's wrong with you that you feel the need to grow poisonous mushrooms? It's in your vegetable garden, for heaven's sake!"

I didn't have an answer. It seemed crazy and risky, especially with the animals underfoot.

It's none of your business, I wanted to say, but I knew it was. My disregard for human life seemed to be a recurring motif, and he was paying attention.

Magic spell broken, we returned to the wrought iron table on the terrace and began to drink our coffee in earnest.

"Thank you for escorting me home," I said. I was ready for him to leave, ready to tackle the rest of the house on my own … after maybe making a sandwich and lying on the parquet floor in the sun with my felines. If I felt brave enough, I might even look in the mirror.

"We have one more thing to talk about," said the detective, looking at his watch, then at me.

I put my mug down. "Yes?"

He fetched the bag of my personal belongings and deposited it on the table between us. I waited, the dappled sun playing on my inked forearms as the breeze fluttered the grape leaves above us. His gaze was curious and intense. From what I had experienced in the hospital, few people, especially men, could keep eye contact with me for more than a moment, but this cop had no problem doing it.

"You can have your personal effects back," he said. "Necklace with vial, tanzanite ring ... it's everything except for the knife. We had to hold on to that."

"The knife?"

"I have pictures of it, if you want to see. If you're not squeamish." He watched my every minuscule movement, waiting for me to twitch.

The next thing I knew, I was looking at pictures on his phone. A black-handled blade the size of a hunting knife was stained with dark blood. It looked delicate, carefully created and honed, like an antique. There was a close-up shot. Engraved on the knife was a decorative line: *RUPTOR MALEDICTUM*.

"That's the knife that...?" I asked, not finishing the sentence.

"That's the murder weapon," he said, and watched me flinch.

Oh my hex, I STABBED someone? "My fingerprints?"

"Yes, not that we needed them. We have the footage, after all."

Yes. The footage.

"And we kept your clothes," he said. "They went to the lab."

"Doctor Gilbert told me."

Hellions. There was self-defense, and there was being a psycho.

"We have everything we need to charge you."

I didn't like this power play. If he wanted to arrest me, he should get on with it. I didn't appreciate his idle threats. "So why don't you? Why play games?"

"Because I don't think it's that simple."

I looked away, annoyed, and folded my arms. "Right."

"The more I learn about this case, the more I want to know. And honestly? I think things will reveal themselves faster if you're not in custody."

After the detective left, I looked in the fridge. It was empty. I would need to gird my loins and go shopping. But not today. Instead, I grabbed a bunch of grapes and sat in a sunny spot in the jungle, watching the bees ruck the rosemary blossoms, the wild rocket flowers, the white lavender. I watched them fill their pockets with pollen until their baskets were overflowing, then make their way back to the beehive that I had not noticed before, nestled among the jasmine hedge. I did a quick mental inventory.

Two cats.

Half a dozen hens.

A colony of bees.

A food forest.

A psychologist's business card.

A curious detective.

Poisonous mushrooms.

A dead man with my knife in his chest.

I closed my eyes and pictured the glinting blade and the inscription on my knife.

RUPTOR MALEDICTUM.

Without knowing I knew any Latin, my old self translated the phrase easily for me. I opened my eyes.

THE CURSEBREAKER.

CHAPTER 8
A SKELETON WEARING A HAT
ASHA

I had been putting off looking in the mirror since I arrived home. Armstrong had called me "pretty" but I was sure he was being generous. I had noticed in the hospital that my bathroom mirror had been removed, and that staff avoided eye contact with me, so I had assumed the worst. Eventually I took a deep breath and walked up to the brass-framed antique looking glass that was hanging in the passage. What I saw startled me. Staring back at me were a pair of the clearest green eyes imaginable. They gave me a jolt when I saw them—no wonder the nurses used to look away from me. Straight jet-black hair cascaded from below the bandage that wound around my head like a mummy turban.

I unwound the dressing slowly, my scalp still tender. The ER staff had shaved a band most of the way around my head, and that—combined with my proliferation of tattoos—gave me a punk rock look. I turned my head to try to see the stitches on the back, but all I could see was the side of the waterproof dressing that remained in place.

I stripped off my hospital gown and examined my tattoos. They were expertly drawn and elegant, and I may have been imagining it but they seemed to change color with my mood. I looked at my reflection again. My body was petite, but strong, and looked more feminine than I felt. Good muscle tone, good boobs.

"Could be better," I said, cocking my head. *Could be worse.*

I had a shower, then made myself another cup of coffee and wandered through the house, trying to avoid tripping over Odysseus and Circe as they wound themselves around my ankles in an animated infinity sign. I made slow progress, because there were so many interesting things to look at. The clock struck midnight. The walls were crammed with art and posters, the corners full of plants in containers, and there was a bookshelf in every room. It would take days to acquaint myself with everything in the house, which I quite liked the idea of. I wasn't in a rush to get back to work. I didn't even know what I did for a living.

I moved in front of a black and white painting of a naked woman looking into a pond. Her reflection was a skeleton wearing a hat. I liked the painting, and understood that in my previous life I had embraced my dark side. Pentagrams and other strange symbols took pride of place in many of the posters and book covers. Illustrations of the solar system, too, with special attention paid to anything lunar. Majestic wild animals—wolves, ravens, rabbits, and foxes—peered from paintings and shelves. I seemed to love the color black, judging by the clothes in my closet and the general décor, including furniture, lamps, baskets, pots, and frames. Black, copper, gray and chlorophyll green was my chosen color scheme. I put down my empty mug and made my way through to the conservatory, which I had been saving for last. The clock struck midnight. It was late, and I knew I should be sleeping, but my curiosity got the better of me.

The conservatory was vast and, as I had guessed, brimming with plants of all kinds. I loved the look of the space: clear windows held in place with black lead to form a Victorian-style greenhouse with a steeply pitched roof, Gothic arched glazing bars, and a curved bay front offered me a panoramic view of the garden beyond. The floor was checkered black and white, and baskets hung from above with delicate stems trailing down the side. I admired the ornate ridge details, intricate cresting, finials, and decorative glass. Inside, rare orchids sat shoulder to shoulder with carnivorous plants and strange lilies, and the air was humid and perfumed.

I did feel as though I belonged there, that it was my perfect home, but I also couldn't help feeling that I was trespassing in someone else's house, someone wealthy and more intelligent than I was, because how could I possibly have all of this? The queue of exotic plants went on and on, all around the room.

Where the leaves stopped, there was yet another bookshelf, which I gazed at suspiciously. Everyone knows you can't keep a bookshelf in a conservatory, right? The humidity would destroy the paper. So I lifted my hand and touched one of the books—and saw that it was a timber block, painted and glazed to look like a book. I took out another one, and another. They were all the same. *Why would she do that?* I wondered, and then corrected myself. *Why would I do that?*

An odd sensation kindled in my stomach, a secret thrill. There was obviously a hidden passage, all I had to do was find it.

CHAPTER 9

TOXIC FUMES AND FURY
NICKY

The chaos spiked my blood, over and over. It was in every muscle as I ran, every nerve, every fiber, neuron, cell. It was nighttime in the city and my mind confused the streetlights with the stars. All kinds of lights popped through the dark, a long-forgotten idea that we are being observed by the being who pricked those breathing holes into our sky.

Run, run, run!

Colors swirled in psychedelic spiral spikes. Car lights, traffic lights, carbon monoxide burned my lungs. Suburbs and spires. I lost my shoes and my way. No one was chasing me, unless you count the voices in my head.

Keep running, keep going. It will be over soon.

My blonde hair kept getting in my face, sticking to sweat-soaked skin. Two bright moons zoomed toward me and there was a squealing sound. Hot rubber in the air; brake fluid. The twin moons knocked right into me, taking me down. My arms dug up tarred gravel and the stones remained under my skin, slippery with weeping red oil. There was something broken in my hips, but I could still get up. I was confused, and more voices—different voices—shouted at me. Toxic fumes and fury.

What are you doing?

You ran right in front of me!

You need an ambulance!

But the other voices—the deeper humming voices—were more in tune. *Run,* they said. *Run, run, run.*

I loped off, unable to jog with the broken thing. The broken bone thing in my pelvis. But I could keep moving. I didn't know why I was there.

Are you crazy?

You almost killed us both!

You need to stay here while we get help.

Someone grabbed me. I grunted and wrestled the insistent hands off my slippy-slide arms. They let go.

Call the ambulance.

Call the cops.

Yes, I thought. *Call them all. Because they are part of this. We are all part of it.*

More moons came at me, swerving and honking. I finally made it across the bubbling river of black tar and speeding stars and planets. Mars blinked at me. I was almost there. I tried to run again because I knew the grabbing hands would get me if I didn't hurry, but the hip bone was jutting and my legs didn't work. *Almost there,* I told myself, joining in with the chorus of voices.

Almost there, Nicky. You can do it. Keep going.

I stood on an island, cars whizzing by, galaxies ever-expanding around me. People don't understand the position we're in, always getting smaller in space, even though we're not shrinking. A metal shell stopped in front of me, my reflection in the glass rolled down.

Are you okay?

No.

What is your name?

My name is Nicky, but that doesn't matter anymore.

The driver looked at my hand with its wedding ring.

Can I call someone for you?

My husband's name is Derek. But that doesn't matter anymore, either.

Do you need help?

I didn't need help from metal shells or twin moons. I needed to get to the bridge. If I reached the bridge over the highway, everything would fall into place. Run, limp. My cheeks were wet, my arms slick, dripping blood from fingertips. The pain wouldn't last long. The bridge would take my pain. Hip clicking, feet burning, I resisted the urge to crawl. I was close now, close to the final answer my body had been begging me for.

I made it onto the bridge and it felt right. Air is better on a bridge. Cars still zooming, shrieking around me like animals trying to escape a flooding zoo.

It's not just me, we're all trying to escape.

I will help them escape.

I climbed up the concrete side of the bridge, still warm from the afternoon sun, scuffing the edges with blood. Standing at the highest point felt good and right. I was ready. But then the wailing behind me made me pause. Blue lights flashed. Men in uniform. I needed to hurry, needed to escape before they could stop me. I looked down at the streaming traffic below: white lights on the right, red on the left. So many metal shells, so many people who needed to escape. I spread my arms wide and closed my eyes, ready to swan dive into the stream of oblivion.

Go, said the voices in my head.

Now is your chance.

This is what you're supposed to do.

What are you waiting for?

I took a deep breath and moved my weight forward. Just one more step and it would all be over.

"Ma'am," said a voice from outside my body. It was a gentle voice. I kept my eyes tightly closed. "Ma'am."

Ignore him, said the voices. *Finish what you came here to do.*

I shuffled the last inch forward and took a deep breath, lungs full of city smog and broken promises.

"Ma'am," said the man again. "I'm going to help you to climb down."

I looked at him. I couldn't help it. I needed to see if he was real. He had a badge, and a gun nestled in a leather holster against his hip.

"I'm not climbing down," I whispered, and leaned into the fall. But the man was a bolt of lightning, catching me from behind before I could fly. He held me tightly, thinking I would fight him, but I couldn't. I was broken, and teetering on the edge of a bridge.

"I've got you," he whispered, and feeling his secure embrace made me go limp. But then I looked into his eyes and saw that he needed to escape, too.

"I'm going to carry you down," said the kind stranger. "We'll get you a blanket. Some tea while we wait for the ambulance."

We swayed on that edge, that razorblade between life and death. He realized that I wasn't going anywhere.

"Come down with me," the man in uniform said. "I'll take care of you."

When I refused, he set his jaw. I could tell that he didn't want to use force, but there was no other way to remove me from the precipice. His arm stiffened against my shoulders, and he grabbed my left wrist, twisting me toward him. Apology in his eyes, and something else.

Don't let him stop you, Nicky, said the voices.

You're so close.

You're right there.

One small step forward and you've done it.

The man in uniform was never going to let me go. I had no

choice. I understood what the other emotion was that I saw in his eyes. It was fear, and I knew that I could set him free.

With my right hand I quickly grabbed his revolver. His eyes and mouth opened wide in shock.

"Death is not the end," I told him, and pulled the trigger.

The explosion was deafening. In slow motion, a black hole opened up in the policeman's chest. The kickback from the revolver made me reel backwards, and he fell back, too. The bullet had split us apart, slamming me into safety and sending the man tumbling off the side of the bridge to fall to the traffic below. The cars on the busy highway screeched and shrieked and crashed into one another. The explosions as they collided burst in my head. Shattered glass like diamonds on the ground. Vehicles rolling, smashing, cartwheeling until finally they all came to a stop.

"Hands in the air!" shouted another uniformed man, who was pointing his gun at me. His colleague was talking into a two-way radio. I heard "Massive pile-up on the M1"; "Get all EMS out here"; "It's a freaking circus."

"Hands!" he shouted, and then it was kind of like waking up. Everything that had happened before seemed nebulous, dreamlike, impossible. I realized I was barefoot, and my dress was torn. Pain flared up from my fractured bones and lacerated skin. Police lights spun and flashed as I looked at the barrel of the policeman's revolver. I was shaking hard. I raised my arms, but I wasn't sure why I was doing it. Why was there a policeman pointing a gun at me? Why was I standing on a bridge? Why was I hurt? The whole evening was an obscure blur. The flashing blue lights hurt my eyes. A spotlight came on, pointed directly at me so that I had to shield my eyes from the glare. A gun lay on the tarmac. I squinted at the policeman who was now just a silhouette with a weapon.

My mouth was cotton and bile. "What happened?"

CHAPTER 10

THE BOOK OF SHADOWS

ASHA

In the conservatory, I began pulling the blocks off the bookshelves. A dozen, two dozen, more, all painted exquisitely to look like books. When I touched a turquoise block it felt different from the rest. I slowed down, pushed my hair out of my face, then gripped the book as hard as I could and pulled it. There was a groaning sound, and an invisible bolt shifted.

Then, just as I knew it would, the entire case rotated on its center pin, opening up an Asha-sized entrance to what lay beyond.

I stepped through the doorway and stood with my arms at my sides, taking in the room that had opened itself to me. It was the polar opposite of the conservatory. Where the greenhouse was bright, airy, and full of living plants, the hidden room was dark and filled with dead things. Bunches of drying herbs hung from nails in the wall and the room was scented with a heady mixture of their fading perfume. I recognized rosemary, sage, yarrow, vetch, thyme, and lavender. There were others that I didn't know, some spiky, some soft. A piece of heavy furniture stood in the center, made of dark wood and etched with a copper border to match the prep sink and tap. It was more like a kitchen island than a table, and in the middle of the island was a large leather-bound book on a bronze recipe book stand. I looked at the hundreds of jars and bottles on the shelves, at the framed frog skeleton and the taxidermy bat; I stared at the hundreds of crystals of all shapes and colors and the cast iron cauldron on the floor.

What the actual.

The room was totally weird in every way. What was even more weird was the fact that I felt completely at home. None of the dead things made me uncomfortable; none of the unusual scents bothered me. Instead, the sensations swirled around me, comforting me in a way I hadn't felt since waking up in the sanitized ICU. When I regained my consciousness after the attack, I didn't know who I was, but standing in that room—a room inside a house, inside a jungle—I understood that I didn't need a memory to know myself. *This* was who I was. I walked up to the large book in the center of the room. The cover was thick old leather, the title embossed in gold.

THE BOOK OF SHADOWS.

I opened it, expecting to see printed words, but instead there were pages and pages of handwritten notes and drawings in iridescent ink. The handwriting changed every two hundred pages or so, which made me think that the book had been passed around.

I wanted to read every single word, but it was almost two a.m. and my energy was ebbing. Instead, I flipped through to the last few pages, where the last style of writing began. *Asha Viridian Rook,* it said. *Potion Mistress. Healer. Green Witch. Cursebreaker.* I slammed the book shut, releasing a puff of glittering dust.

Excuse me, but what the WHAT now?

I mean, the clues were all around me, but really? *A witch?*

Mind blown, I dropped to the floor. I laughed out loud, or maybe it was a sob. The intricate herb garden, the two black cats, the pentagrams and paintings—of course I was a witch … not that I knew what that entailed. And what was this about breaking curses? And making potions? I guess I'd learn as I went along. Circe—or Odysseus?—padded in and wound herself around my legs, tail in the air. I stroked her soft black fur as if she were a genie's lamp, wishing I knew what this was all about.

You'll understand soon, came a soft wave of a thought, as if someone had whispered it in the far recesses of my mind. Circe's eyes and mine met, green to green, and for a moment I thought the voice must be hers. Then she stuck her bottom in my face.

Lying in bed later, hemmed in by my feline familiars, I again felt that sensation of peace and belonging. I imagined it would feel odd sleeping in a bed I did not recognize, but the four-poster seemed to recognize me. The memory pillow was gentle on my healing wound, and the mattress knew my body well. Exhausted, it took all of a minute to fall into the stiff arms of a restless sleep.

My peace was not to last. I heard something, or someone, outside the house. Perhaps it was more of a feeling than a sound, but it was enough to wake me and get my adrenaline flowing. I lay there, frozen. I told myself I was being paranoid. It was just the wind. A falling branch. A wandering cat. I had a security system, I reassured myself. No one could enter without setting off the alarm. I looked at the security keypad to make sure the red light indicated it was set, but there was no light. I tried my bedside lamp, no dice. Perhaps there was a power failure, or a power cut—silly me, I hadn't paid my bills while comatose in the hospital. Or load shedding, or a simple tripping of the circuit breaker. I maneuvered myself out of bed, careful not to disturb the sleeping cats. Again, I felt something, like a ripple in the atmosphere. Something was happening, but I didn't know what. My heart began beating hard and fast, my chest tightened. My fingers began to tingle, and I had that odd feeling of sparks running through my veins again. In the emergency room, it happened because my life was in danger. Suddenly, Circe and Odysseus were at my side, and I found that I could see quite well in the dark. I wanted to go down the stairs and inspect the circuit board, but I didn't want to be that person who everyone shouts at in the horror movie.

Don't go down those stairs!

Instead, I clicked my bedroom door closed as quietly as I could, and locked it. I pressed the panic button, but, as I feared, it was as dead as the security beams. I had lost my phone in the attack and had not yet bought a new one. I didn't know what to do. I began shaking. The next ripple I felt came from just outside.

Holy hex, holy hex, holy hex, I thought. *He's standing outside my bedroom door.*

I knew it was a "he" by then because I could feel his presence, his menacing energy. My intestines melted. I couldn't hear past my galloping heart. One of the cats hissed, and I knew they could sense him, too. The smell of burning metal was so subtle that I thought I was imagining it, but when I looked at the bedroom door handle, I saw it was slowly starting to glow.

The wood around it darkened and the scent of molten steel swirled with the smoke of charring timber. My lungs constricted with panic, and my veins flared. I was unarmed and scared as hell.

I knew without a doubt that the man was there to kill me.

CHAPTER 11

A HAIRLINE FRACTURE

ASHA

The first thing I had to do was get my body under control, because I couldn't think straight while my chest was on fire. I tried to control my breathing, tried to quieten the buzzing anxiety that was shutting off my brain. The steel glowed hotter, and I knew I had seconds to come up with a plan. I picked up Circe and Odysseus and ran to the bathroom, locking the door, hoping it would buy me more time. The window there was tiny, and if I managed to climb out of it, there would be no soft landing on the paved driveway a story below. I heard the bedroom door being forced open. The cats hissed again. The man was in my room.

Despite my head injury, I decided I'd rather take my chances with the paving bricks below than succumb to the violence of a man. I climbed up onto the lid of the toilet and wrangled my body, arms first, through the small square space. The metal edges scraped my ribs and hips as I squeezed through, but the pain was distant, most of it drowned out by fear. I found my body quite flexible and was grateful for it as I scrambled to shift my legs out while holding on to the inch-wide ledge above the window. There was nothing to climb down on, and nothing to break my fall. I would have to just jump and hope for the best.

I heard sirens approaching, but they were blocks away and I was fast losing my grip on the concrete wall. I looked back into the bathroom, watching the handle glow as the bedroom one had done before. The sirens were close, but still not close enough. I wondered which bones would break, mostly because I needed to be able to run after the fall. I breathed in and out, my eyes trained on the melting handle, trying to work up the nerve to fracture more body parts. Circe and Odysseus jumped up on the windowsill, then took their places on my shoulders. As the security company's squad car squealed to a stop a few meters away, followed by another car—one I recognized—the bathroom door was kicked open. There stood a man in a black hooded cloak, his eyes ablaze with malevolence. As he caught sight of me he flicked his wand in my direction, but I had already let go. The plummet took my breath away. Expecting to crash into the hard ground, I closed my eyes, said a little upside-down prayer, and hoped for the best. A sprained ankle, perhaps, or a hairline fracture somewhere that wouldn't hurt too much.

But instead of the expected collision, I felt my body slow down right before it was due to collide. It was as if someone had, right at the last minute, pulled the toggles on an invisible parachute, allowing me to float down for the last couple of feet. I felt like Mary Poppins. The only pain I could feel was the cats' respective claws in my shoulders. Heavily armed security guards ran toward me. I looked up at my window. It was empty.

"Rook. What the hell just happened?" asked a gruff voice, grated by both irritation and concern. I swung around, my body still on high alert.

"Intruder," I gasped. "Bedroom."

He motioned for the security guards to enter the house. They obeyed, despite the cop's lack of authority over them. I stared at him, looking so different in his—crumpled—civilian clothes.

"What are you doing here?" I asked.

Detective Armstrong shrugged. "Got a call."

"From who? I couldn't even phone *them*." I motioned at the security company's truck.

"Your alarm system was compromised," he said. "That sends an automatic panic signal to the desks. Then they couldn't get hold of you, so they treated it as an emergency."

"And you know this how?"

"I put myself down as a contact. I was worried about you."

"You don't even know me," I said.

"I know that someone tried to kill you three weeks ago and their plan failed."

"Mostly because I killed him," I said.

He looked amused. "Yes," he said. "Mostly that." Then his smile vanished. "And after what I've seen tonight, I accept that it was self-defense. And I suspect you're still in danger."

Anger rose like a rattlesnake between us.

"You could have warned me."

"What was I supposed to say? I had a *bad feeling?*"

"Yes," I said. "That's exactly what you could have said."

The guards came out of the house, hands twitching on their AK47s. "All clear," they announced.

"There was someone in there," I insisted. "I saw him. He burned my door handles."

The guards looked quizzically at each other. "There was no damage to any handles," the taller guy said. He showed me the photos on his phone, required for the debriefing. There was no damage.

"But I saw him," I said. "I felt him."

The guards were polite, but their body language made it clear that they thought I had wasted their time by the way they climbed back into their vehicle. I felt like I should offer them a thermos of coffee, but the engine growled and they sped off before I could articulate my thoughts. I was still in shock.

"I don't want to invade your space," said Detective Armstrong, "but I can stay here tonight, if you like. That couch downstairs looked pretty cozy."

I was feeling so vulnerable that my gratitude bubbled up as tears. I wiped my eyes on my pajama sleeve. "But you're off duty," I said. "And what about your family?"

He didn't miss a beat. "I have no family. And if I did, I'd still offer to stay. In fact," he said, scratching his stubble, "I don't even need your couch." He glanced at his sedan. "My car will do."

"No," I shook my head. "You'll stay in the guest room."

"Okay," he said, pulling a half-jack of whisky out of his pocket. "But ... first, a drink. We need to talk."

CHAPTER 12

DAY OF THE DEAD

ASHA

Armstrong cracked open the bottle and poured us two fingers each. I added ice.

He took the now-familiar bag of my personal belongings from the crime scene and dumped them on the table between us. The wires of the mains had been cut, so we looked at each other over the halo of light dispersed by six black candles in a silver candelabra. Six tubes grew out of a Mexican skull—*Día de los Muertos*, Day of the Dead—the design of which pleased me and apparently bothered the detective in equal measures.

"Why?" he asked. "Why the fascination with death?"

I blinked at him. "What's not to be fascinated by?"

He shook his head. "I don't get it."

"You will," I said. "One day." I meant it as a joke, but he bit his lip and looked somber, downing his whisky and then immediately topping up both our tumblers, despite my not having had a sip. I took a long draught to make up the difference, and also because the shock was still vibrating in my bones. Almost immediately I felt a warm calm traveling through my body.

Armstrong was clearly worried, the way he kept looking at me. "Are you going to tell me what just happened?"

"What? You know what happened. There was an intruder."

"So you jumped out of the window."

"There was nowhere else to go."

He didn't break eye contact, and his cheeks were beginning to show the warmth of the whisky. "You landed on your feet."

"I know! I was so lucky, right? I was expecting a broken leg."

"What about the cats?" he asked.

I automatically glanced down at them. They were snacking on kibbles.

"Well, I couldn't leave them behind, could I?"

He looked at me for a long time. "There are things about you that do not add up."

"Agreed," I said. "Like strange men in black hooded cloaks trying to kill me."

"How do you know he wanted to kill you?"

"Why else would he be breaking into my house in the middle of the night?"

"Good point," he said, not without humor.

I decided I liked him again. Temporarily.

He rubbed his face, and I could see the exhaustion in his expression. I finished my drink and placed the tumbler on the table. "We should probably get some rest."

"Probably," he said, nodding, his hand massaging his neck. "Or we can talk some more. Try to figure this thing out."

It was three a.m. I poured more whisky, this time from my own cabinet. After tasting it, I inspected the embossed copper label, which said it was home-distilled at The Copper Cog & Ale, a local gastropub. I had the immediate urge to visit.

"Okay, Detective," I said, sighing. "How does one go about *figuring this thing out?*"

"Well," he said, scratching at his stubble. "Seeing as it's late, we're drinking, and I'm staying the night, perhaps we should start by calling each other by our first names."

"I don't know your first name."

"Sam," he said.

"Sam? You don't look like a Sam."

"What do Sams look like?"

"I don't know. Friendly hobbits."

He laughed out loud.

"I'm not kidding, I said. "You're way too tall to be a Sam. And I don't want you calling me Asha. I like it when you call me Rook."

"All right," the detective said, his lips curving up. "I'll stick to Rook and you can call me whatever you want."

"Deal. What's next?"

Sam played an invisible piano on the table while he gathered his thoughts. "Usually, I'd ask the big questions first. Who is trying to harm you? And why you?"

I nodded.

"But we don't have the answers to that yet, so we'll have to ask the smaller questions. The ones that don't seem important."

"Like?"

"Like who are you? Where did you come from?"

"I don't know the answers to those."

"We could also look at what we do have." He eyed the transparent plastic bag that he had brought along. My personal items from the crime scene.

I took a breath. "Okay."

He unzipped the bag and began placing the items on the tabletop between us. I watched, nervous and fascinated. Who knows what incriminating things I had in my possession that night—not that anything could be more incriminating than that bloodstained knife? The first thing the detective laid down was a phone.

"Thank goodness," I said. "Now I can—"

"It's been fried. Wiped and deactivated. We wanted to trace your contacts, but no such luck."

Maybe it was for the best. Who knew which photos and WhatsApp messages I had on the thing. Next up was a thin silver stick, which I quickly guessed was some kind of wand.

"I don't know what that is," I mumbled, avoiding eye contact.

Next, Armstrong brought out a silver chain with a large amulet and passed it to me. It was beautiful: a purple vial encased in a spiral of silver. It glowed in the candlelight. The vial had a lid, which I dared not open in Sam's presence. Next was a hip flask, which I really liked the look of. Again, I couldn't be sure what was inside it. Cinnamon whisky from the Copper Cog, or any number of potions from my newly-discovered favorite room. Seeing my anxious expression, the detective assured me it was empty. I relaxed. Maybe things would be okay, after all. There was one last thing in the bag.

"Your clothes," said the cop. "We got them back from forensics."

"Oh," I said. It made sense that the fabric was black, because that seemed to be my favorite color. Thinking it was a dress, I stood up and shook it out, blinking in the candlelight to figure out what it was. When I did, I looked at Sam, who was watching my reaction very closely. It wasn't a dress. It was a long black hooded cloak.

CHAPTER 13

DAMN THIS DISLOYAL FLESH

ASHA

"I wasn't expecting this," I said to Detective Armstrong, holding up the black hooded cloak.

"Weren't you?" he said, watching me with his hawk eyes.

My mind flashed to the potion room. The frog skeleton; the bat, frozen in time. Then the more immediate reality of the objects on the table between us, including what may or may not have been a silver wand.

"Look," I said. "A lot of weird things have happened in the last twenty-four hours. I'm not sure of anything."

He didn't break eye contact. "That's understandable."

"I mean, I wake up, clueless, in the hospital, and next thing I have this—" I gestured to the house around us. "This amazing —albeit rather odd—house. Garden jungle. Hens. Cats."

"And you discover you've killed a man," Sam said.

"I keep forgetting that part," I said.

He blinked. "I don't."

"Well, it's your job to keep that in mind, I guess. Especially when you're sitting across the table from a purported murderess."

"I'm starting to think it was self-defense," Sam said. "Even though no one else witnessed tonight's intruder. And there's no proof. And no apparent reason. And—"

"I get the idea." I sipped my drink. It burned my throat and felt good. Another part of my body was warming to the detective, but I ignored it. There was no way I could get romantically involved with a cop, especially the lead detective on the case in which I was the prime suspect.

"I'll figure you out eventually," he said, and I saw a flash of hunger in his eyes that made me interpret his words in a slightly different way.

There was a subtle adjustment in my breathing, like my body had changed gears. As if in slow motion, I sensed that Sam's breathing was in sync with mine. I had to snap out of it. *Damn this disloyal flesh.*

"Maybe it's time we called it a night." I downed what was left in my glass.

Sam nodded and finished his drink, too. "Probably wise." He stood up, taking the tumblers to the sink and washing them out before arranging them on the drying rack. Something about the way he did it, so comfortable and familiar, made me imagine a life with him. A dozen rather pleasant second-long scenarios played out in my head.

"Sam," I said.

He looked at me, drying his hands on the tea towel hanging next to the back door. The burglar bars over the window were covered in a climbing plant that looked like a green curtain. It had purple blossoms on it.

"Do we know each other? I mean, did we know each other before now?"

He frowned. "No," he said. "Definitely not."

"You sure? I feel like I know you."

"Believe me," he said, coming back over to the table. "I would have remembered."

I showed Detective Armstrong the spare bedroom. It seemed well equipped enough, if not a little feminine for his bulky frame. When I looked in the en suite bathroom to check for a fresh towel, there was a pink toothbrush and moisturizer. I wasn't sure who they belonged to. A lover? A sister?

"Good night," I told him, and spent the next hour wide awake in bed, feeling his presence downstairs, which was comforting and unnerving at the same time. Finally, I heard him get up and ascend the stairs toward where I lay. My heart began to hammer. Despite wanting him, I pretended to sleep. I heard him step tentatively into my bedroom, as if to check I was safe, then pad across the hallway to the room there, where he laid down on the couch. I waited for my heart to slow down, and only then did I manage to fall into a deep and healing sleep.

CHAPTER 14

THE NURSE WITHOUT A FACE

NICKY

There was the scraping of the metal bolt, a jolting clang, a humming vibration of the iron bars, then a nurse darkened the doorway. She carried a tray in her shadow-hands and I knew what that meant.

A snake strangling my arm until it gives up with a long, satisfied exhalation.

A pistol held to my head until it beeps a green light, allowing me to live another six hours.

The pinch of the needle piercing my already perforated skin.

The nurse had no face.

I swallowed my bile and tried to swirl enough saliva in my mouth so that I could speak. The snake squeezed and squeezed until my upper arm went numb. My hip bones ached.

Hissssssssss.

"Where am I?" I asked.

The nurse without a face ignored my question.

"Please," I moaned. Salty tears stung my swollen eyelids.

She aimed her white pistol at my temple and we waited for it to beep. It took longer than usual and my lungs burned from holding my breath. Finally, there was the electronic chirrup, and the green light blinked. When she reached for the syringe, I tried to lunge for it, but the old restraints held me back. I smelt sweat and leather. She watched me until I fell back against the stretcher, then attached the needle to the syringe and drew liquid from a small vial, flicking the tube with a fingernail.

"Don't," I begged, but it was too late. She jabbed my right arm; a silver prick traveled deep into my muscle, and I felt the effects immediately. My spine gave way. My neck melted. My head lolled, and my lips parted in a sigh. My brain turned into cold gray dough.

The bright memories stopped knocking, and I surrendered to the dark.

CHAPTER 15
OCCULT FRIDGE MAGNETS
ASHA

When I woke up, the detective was gone. I couldn't help feeling disappointed. I tried to piece together the night before: the intruder, the undamaged door handles, the attraction I was feeling to the man whose job it was to find enough reasons to arrest me. I bristled at the idea. Freedom was everything to me. No dalliance was worth that. I needed to reign in my desire, which had surprised me the night before with its sharpness.

I made my way down the stairs, tying my black robe around me. It was comforting, as robes can be. I narrowly survived death, almost tripping over one of the black cats, who I still couldn't tell apart. I switched on the kettle, ready to face the uncertainty that was the tea cupboard. Waiting for the water to boil, I mooched around my kitchen, sternly avoiding the tumblers on the drying rack and the images they conjured. The plants on the windowsill turned out to be some kind of pea. I snipped a pod off and snapped it open, popping one into my mouth. Fresh and sweet.

Thank you, Nature.

I didn't know where it came from, but it seemed a habit if I ate something from the garden. An automatic thank you to the Great Wild—not that I knew what the Great Wild was. I closed my eyes and opened my mind to any other phrases or ideas that may come to me, coaxing my memories back.

When the kettle snicked off, my eyes clicked open, and I was staring at the fridge door, which hosted the lunar cycle, an old, splattered kombucha recipe, and a chocolate ice cream emoji. Among the pagan and Wicca symbols and occult fridge magnets there was a note scrawled for my attention: a reminder to go to yoga every Tuesday at nine a.m.

I grabbed a glass jar of dead leaves from the cupboard, twisted it open, and gave it a tentative sniff. It occurred to me how bizarre the concept of tea was.

Little finger in the air. Excuse me while I sip my hot brew of dead leaves.

I poured the hot water over the sticks and leaves. It didn't smell altogether unpleasant.

The doorbell rang, making me jump and almost drop my tea.

Who could it be?

I felt anxious imagining the possible answers. Apart from Detective Armstrong, it felt like I knew no one, that I was alone in the world. And while the loneliness made me feel hollow, the idea of someone outside my house, wanting to come in, filled me with dread. I tried to peer out of the kitchen window, but the view of the pedestrian gate was obscured by the many shrubs and brambles between us. I put down the steaming mug and hesitantly made my way to the front door. Once I arrived at the gate, I saw an older man in an unusual brown hat waiting there for me. He had white sideburns and a matching beard, and he was wearing an obscenely cheerful Hawaiian shirt, which made my hungover eyeballs smart. In his hand was a carrier bag. He gave me an upbeat generous smile, took off his hat, and I couldn't help smiling back.

"Hello," I said. There was just enough awkwardness in my tone and my manner to convey the uncertainty I felt.

He beamed at me. "Hello, Rookie. Been a hell of a long time. You hiding from someone?"

The smile froze on my face. I didn't know what to say. "What?"

His grin faltered. "What's wrong?" he asked, forehead creasing in concern. "Asha?"

I stood in silence, watching him. I had no idea who he was. He looked friendly enough and judging by what he carried, he came bearing gifts, but for all I knew he could have been a suburban serial killer.

"It's been long, but not that long," he said. "I mean, I know I need a haircut."

It was an attempt at a joke, but I felt so tense I couldn't smile. I realized the sooner I was honest, the better.

"I don't know who you are," I stammered. "I'm sorry, I mean it's clear that we know each other, but—"

"What do you mean?" His cheer evaporated. "What do you mean you don't know who I am? Asha? What's wrong? What has happened to you?"

I swallowed hard. "There was an accident," I said, and then shook my head. "No, not an accident. Something happened to me. I have a head injury."

"What?" demanded the man. "What do you mean something happened to you? What the hell happened?"

I felt suddenly tearful. "I had thirty-seven stitches in my head."

"What?" he yelled. His face contorted in confusion. "Why didn't you call me? I've been worried sick! And you haven't been answering your phone!"

"Why would I call you?" I asked.

"Asha!" he cried, thumping his chest. "It's me! Merlin!"

The name meant nothing to me, apart from conjuring up images of happy wizards in fairy tales.

I blinked and shot him a look of apology. "I'm sorry," I said again. "I don't remember anything, or anyone. Retrograde amnesia, apparently. Don't take it personally."

Circe and Odysseus padded out the front door and up the path, stopping on either side of me. I looked down at them and added, "I didn't even know that I had cats until yesterday."

The man was visibly shaken, and I felt disturbed, too. He was clearly a friend of mine, and he had brought me something, so I decided to let him in. Things were awkward enough without us having to stand on either side of a wrought iron gate. The felines stuck to my ankles like glue as if they were unsure of our new visitor, but they didn't show any hint of aggression, which I took to be a good sign. When we reached the kitchen, I poured another mug of the mystery tea, handed it to Merlin, and we sat at the wooden table—uncomfortably—regarding each other through the steam.

"Well, then," he said, and a very subtle smile returned to his lips. "I suppose I'd better introduce myself." He took a sip of the concoction I had served him and pulled a face.

"You don't like the tea?" I asked.

"Nope," he said. "Nope, it's not that." He cleared his throat. "It's just a little hot."

"You can be honest," I said, "no need to be polite. I'm trying to get the hang of the tea cupboard."

He looked relieved. "It's terrible," he said. "What is this stuff?"

I shrugged. "I have no idea." The labels were all in Latin.

I suppose it was rude to serve visitors mystery dead leaf brew, but this was all uncharted territory.

"My name is Merlin," he said, and I thought of the happy wizards again and thought that this man may easily have been a wizard in a previous life, or perhaps Papa Smurf, because every time I looked at his bushy white beard and kind eyes, that's who I thought of.

"How do we know each other?"

"Mushrooms," he replied.

I was about to laugh, but it appeared he was being serious. "Mushrooms?"

I thought of the poisonous fungi in my garden, and the beautiful illustrations in my potion room. There may have even been some interesting dried mushrooms in the tea cupboard. So, it was safe to say that I was most likely a fan of fungi.

"I'm a mycologist," he said.

Ha, I thought. *Merlin the Mycologist.*

"You're a mushroom dude?" I asked.

"I prefer the term *scientist*," he said, eyes twinkling behind his small round specs, "but yes, I am the Mushroom Dude. I write books, teach courses, do lectures, run workshops, and consult."

"Consult? Who do you consult for?"

He grinned at me. "Funny you should ask."

It took me a while to figure out what he was suggesting.

"Why would I consult you about mushrooms?" I wondered out loud.

"The world of mushrooms is vast, majestic, even magical," he said. "There are twenty-five thousand individual species and every mushroom has its own superpower. Over the years, I've been teaching you which mushrooms would be best for certain ... mixtures you make."

"Mixtures?"

He sat back a little in his chair and rolled his shoulders. "Tinctures, ointments, that kind of thing."

The man was clearly alluding to potion-making, but perhaps he didn't want to spell it out. How much did he know? How much did he know I knew? It was a minefield. He was playing it safe, not wanting to spook me.

"When I discover a new mushroom that I think you would be interested in, I bring it to you. And if you were working on a specific project and had questions, you would call me."

"Okay," I said.

We locked eyes. "But then it became more than that."

I choked on my tea.

"Oh," he said, showing his palms, looking apologetic. "Oh, I didn't mean that at all. Our friendship has always been platonic. Extremely platonic."

I nodded, still coughing the tea out of my lungs.

"Our relationship is warm and wonderful," he said, his face lighting up. "We used to joke that I would walk you down the aisle one day, wearing this hat." He glanced at the odd brown hat on the table at his right elbow, and put it back on. "It's made out of mushroom leather, you know. It's fireproof."

I laughed out loud. I couldn't help it. Here was this eccentric man sitting in my kitchen wearing a fireproof mushroom hat and saying that we were great friends. Closer than friends.

"What do you know about me?" I asked. "What do you know about my parents?"

Merlin's eyes burned and the edges of his mouth turned down. "You really don't remember anything, do you?"

I shook my head, feeling my stomach harden and sink. A black stone in a cold river.

Merlin rubbed his cheeks with the palms of his hands and exhaled a short, sharp breath as if preparing to break my heart. "There's no easy way to say this."

"Just tell me," I said. "Just get it over with." I had already assumed the worst.

"Your parents are dead." He flinched as if the phrase physically hurt him. "What I mean to say is you thought they were dead. That's what you told me."

"Why did I think they were dead?"

"I don't know. I never asked. It seemed too personal. I knew you would tell me when you were ready."

"But how could I have not been certain either way?" I asked. "How can anyone live like that? Not knowing?"

"It's complicated," he said. "You had a rather ... unconventional childhood."

"What?" I put my empty mug down. "What do you mean?"

He shifted in his chair again and finished his tea, which was now lukewarm. "Look," he said. "You never liked to talk about the past, and I never pushed you. I have always been here for you to talk to you, but you've always been very good at ..."

"Yes?"

"You're very good at pushing people away."

"Well," I replied. "That makes sense."

He pushed his glasses up the bridge of his nose. "Why do you say that?"

"At the hospital," I said. "I was there for weeks, but there were no visitors and just one single bunch of flowers."

"Rookie," he said, shaking his head. "If I had known you were in the hospital, I would have been there every day. I would have brought you banana pecan muffins!"

"No family, they told me. No friends. There was no one to call."

"They could have called me," he insisted, slamming a fist onto the table and making me jump. "They could have bloody well called me."

"Anyway," I said, shaking my head and trying to dismiss the new tension that had arisen. "Anyway, it's over now. We've been through the worst."

Of course, that wasn't true, because there had been a man in my house the previous night who tried to kill me, but Merlin didn't have to know that.

"I have to go," he said, and jumped up from the table.

"No, please," I said. "I have so many questions."

He looked at me and sucked in his lips. "Of course you do. I'll be back." He glanced at his wristwatch and frowned. "I was just supposed to drop this off. I'm late for a lecture."

"But—"

"I'll call you," he promised, looking over the top of his specs at me.

"I don't have a phone," I said.

His smile returned. "Yes, you do."

He pushed the carrier bag he had brought toward me. Before I could thank him properly, he was out the front door and opening the pedestrian gate, which he had apparently used his own key for. If I had given Merlin a copy of my house keys, I must have really trusted him.

I stood in the front garden with Circe and Odysseus by my side, and looked around at the leaves and blossoms and insects in the air. This was my old life, I thought, but it felt like a whole new world.

I felt strangely comforted by Merlin's visit. Since I had woken up in the hospital I had felt extremely alone, but Merlin made me feel that I had someone who would help me if I was in trouble. He closed the iron gate without slamming it, and then look back as if he had remembered something.

"Rookie," he called.

I looked up at him, and he grinned.

"You used to call me Papa Smurf!"

When I wandered back into the kitchen, the fridge caught my eye again.

Yoga every Tuesday at nine a.m. Sun Salutation Studio.

I looked up at the clock. It was 8:45.

Doctor Gilbert had said I should try to keep my routine as much as possible as a way to coax my memory back. Also, I felt restless after Merlin's visit. Going to yoga would be a good idea. I hurled myself up the stairs, pulling my hair into a messy ponytail, and brushed half my teeth. I jumped into some neon-pink leopard print yoga pants I couldn't ever imagine choosing, a sports bra, and tank top. I zoomed back down, dodging the Grim Reapers on the stairs—AKA Circe and Odysseus—and opened the entrance to the garage. What I saw there made me stop. I had expected a car, but instead there leaned—rather elegantly—a midnight blue Vespa.

After hesitating for a second, I assured myself that if the Vespa was there, I must be able to ride it. I eased on the helmet and wondered why people say *it fits like a glove*, instead of *it fits like a helmet*, because nothing, I thought, fits more snugly than the right size helmet. I jumped on and opened the garage door. Sunshine flooded in. I punched the magic words into the GPS and took off, arriving at the Sun Salutation Studio two minutes before the practice was due to begin.

Hot and flustered, I rushed into the timber-floored hall. Everyone looked up at me with wide eyes and dropped their towels.

"Asha?"

"Asha!"

A dozen women of all ages, skin colors, and hairstyles flocked to me.

"We were so worried about you!"

"We heard you were in an accident!"

"We thought you were dead!"

I was dead.

"Did you get the flowers?"

That stopped me. "Those were from you?" I asked. The woman who had spoken had a beautiful bob of silver-gray hair. She wore a black turtleneck and a look of easy eternal wisdom. "Of course they were. You didn't see our Starfall insignia?"

I frowned at her, then my eye caught a poster on the wall, which had a symbol on it that I was sure I had seen before. When I looked on the ground, I saw a circle of black yoga mats, all printed with the same sign. Of course, it had been on the black tissue paper of the bouquet, but it was an easy detail to overlook, especially when you wake up with thirty-seven stitches in your head.

"Insignia?" I said, still trying to make sense of it. "Of the yoga studio?"

I'd never heard of a yoga studio sending someone flowers in the hospital. How much was I paying for this membership, anyway?

"Yes, Asha," said the woman, gesturing to another yogi to close the blinds. "We are so glad you have come back to us."

Another woman lit incense and a dozen candles, and set them in the middle of the circle of mats. The elegant silver-haired woman looked at me expectantly as an eerie calm settled around us.

I cleared my throat. "This isn't really a yoga studio, is it?"

CHAPTER 16

THE STARFALL COVEN

ASHA

The other women stared at me in the dim light of the yoga studio.

"What?" exclaimed a young woman with short, wavy purple hair. "You don't remember us? *At all?*"

"I don't remember anything," I said. "Amnesia, from the head injury."

"But you remembered to come back to us," said the leader.

"I had a reminder on my fridge door," I said. "But I probably won't be doing headstands for a while."

There were a few tentative smiles.

"When you say you don't remember *anything*," said a pretty, petite woman with dark eyebrows and long hair. "Does that mean ...?"

"Did you really think you were coming to a yoga class?"

I shrugged. "Yes?"

The women seemed shocked, horrified, but also fascinated. No one spoke for a while.

There were posters on the walls that—despite their beautiful backgrounds of oceans, forests, and mountains—were distinctly not yogi.

Smash the Patriarchy.

When you hit a woman, you hit a rock.

She Persisted.

Blessed be the STRONG for they will right every wrong.

The elegant woman, clearly the leader, sighed and put her hands on her hips. "All right, then. In that case, we'll do some introductions."

The eleven women went to stand at the front of their yoga mats. I automatically stepped forward, joining in and completing the circle. The silver-haired woman nodded at the one beside her: she had a tall, willowy frame with pronounced cheekbones.

"I'm Ivy," she said. "I've been a part of this coven for four years."

The blonde woman next to her piped up. "I'm Esmeralda. I'm the familiar whisperer and veterinarian."

"I'm Boston," said the next woman. "I'm a futurist."

The purple-haired woman smiled at me. "I'm Forsythia, and I'm the travel agent and events coordinator."

There was also an ER doctor, a hacker, a lawyer, a healer, and a spellcraft mistress.

And so we went around the circle and I tried as best as I could to remember the names of the coven members, all the while thinking how familiar but surreal it all felt. Dream déjà vu.

"I'm Soleil," said the leader. "I'm the high priestess of the Starfall Coven. We meet every Tuesday at nine a.m. under the guise of a yoga class so as to not arouse any unwanted attention."

I nodded. I was the only one who hadn't introduced herself. But that made sense, because everyone already knew who I was. I went ahead anyway.

"My name is Asha Viridian Rook, but I've forgotten who I am."

Soleil took a step toward me and her glittering eyes arrested mine. "You have not forgotten your essence, Asha. Your core cannot be forgotten. You are a wild woman. Weird and wonderful. You're a magic-maker, a spell-slinger, a wise young witch."

I had seen my home and the clues therein. I had discovered the potion room and the books on spellcraft, but it was still a shock to hear the word said out loud.

Witch.

I was a witch.

"I don't really know what that means," I said.

"You will remember," said Soleil. "And we will help you."

The women gathered around the burning candles in the center of the studio, forming a neat circle and holding hands. Ivy— the willowy hacker—and purple-haired Forsythia stood on either side of me, giving me encouraging glances as I took my place. I felt a combination of strangeness and familiarity, and self-conscious about my clammy hands.

"*Evoco et excito, nunc et semper, res ac mortales,*" said Soleil, and whipped her wand in front of her, a wand I'd only noticed right then. I felt my yoga pants loosen, my sports bra unravel from my ribcage. Instinctively, I grabbed at my clothes, only to see, when I looked down, that I was wearing a long black cloak in place of the pink leopard-print leggings. Glancing around, I saw that we were all wearing the same thing. It felt spooky as hell, especially with the candlelight playing on the women's solemn faces. My eyes teared up from the incense smoke. Suddenly I wondered what I had gotten myself into.

One of the witches whose name I had forgotten mumbled, "Isis, Astarte, Diana, Hecate, Demeter, Kali, Inanna." She repeated it over and over again, like a mantra. The witches let go of each other's hands and turned their palms up, open for reception.

Soleil shook her hair back. "May the element of Air blow out the old and usher in the new." A brisk breeze fluttered the hems of our cloaks. "Let us not resist the change that the Mother knows we need." The flames of the candles flared, and the hot wax hissed. "May the element of Fire burn away our egos and instead ignite a furnace of passion and guiding light. May the element of Water cleanse and quench and purify. Finally, may the element of the Earth nourish and support our roots so that we may thrive. So mote it be."

The witches echoed the high priestess. "So mote it be."

Solcil opened her arms and inhaled deeply. "Ancestors, witches and wise women who have gone before us, hail and welcome. May Mother Earth work through us and guide us in everything we do. May we re-commit ourselves daily to righting the wrongs we see in the world around us. So mote it be."

The witches replied: "And so it is." We all sat down cross-legged on our black yoga mats. Soleil looked at me. "Now we do our witch work."

"What is witch work?" I asked, and a few of the women smiled at me.

"A witch's work is to take back our power," said Soleil, "so that we may restore balance to the rest of the world."

It sounded like gibberish to me. "I don't know what that means."

"It's imperative that the multiverse be kept in balance. Light and dark, good and evil, life and death."

"There is no light without the dark," I said. I didn't recognize the thought; it came from somewhere inside me.

The high priestess's eyes lit up. "Yes," she said. "Without death, life would be meaningless."

"You are a reflection of nature," said Boston. "A power source."

Soleil nodded. "As a magical woman, you are able to tap into the Void and become a conduit for good or evil."

"I don't know how," I said.

"I have no doubt that you'll soon remember. We need your expertise in this coven. We count on you a great deal to get the work done. You are one of our most important assets."

"Assets?" I couldn't imagine being an asset or an expert at anything with my swollen brain. "My expertise in what?"

Soleil smiled again; her gaze was warm and intense, and I felt it penetrate my whole body. "Dearest Asha," she said. "We are a curse-breaking coven. And you're our cursebreaker."

CHAPTER 17

THE CURSEBREAKER

ASHA

We did a group meditation and some foreign incantations, which I found quite fascinating. Just when I thought the meeting was over, Soleil regarded Forsythia, the friendly witch with the wavy purple hair. "What is on our agenda this morning?"

We all sat around in the circle, candles flickering, incense fragrant. My fellow witches' eyes gleamed in the warm light. Forsythia opened her hand, and a glittering notebook appeared. She took a matching pencil out of her hair that I was sure had not been there before.

"We have a backlog," Forsythia said. "They've been piling up since Asha's been in the hospital."

Soleil switched seamlessly from maternal witch to businesswoman. "Triage all the open curses. Ivy and Esmeralda will take what they can. The rest of you can help."

"So mote it be," the women chanted.

The high priestess knitted her fingers together. "What is our main concern?"

"I apologize for interrupting, Soleil," said Boston. "But is it wise?" She angled her head very slightly and raised a pierced eyebrow to indicate my presence.

"I understand your reservations," said the high priestess, "but we don't have a choice."

"Rook has only just been discharged from the hospital," she said.

Technically, they hadn't let me out. I had run away, but the coven didn't need to know a small detail like that.

"If she's forgotten everything—"

"I am here, you know," I interjected. "In case you'd like to talk to me instead of about me."

Boston glared. "Well," she sniffed. "I see that despite your amnesia, you haven't forgotten your attitude."

"That's enough," Soleil said sharply. "Boston, while I appreciate your concern, I'll ask that you keep it to yourself. The sooner we can get Asha to remember what she needs to know, the better."

"With all due respect …" began Boston.

I looked at her. I don't like it when people start sentences that way. I was beginning to think that Boston may be a bit of a bitch.

"With all due respect," she said again. "I worry that Rook won't know vital things. Like how important it is to preserve the veil."

The veil?

Soleil reacted slowly, with patience. "Asha. It is of paramount importance that we, as touched people—"

"That means magical people," explained Ivy.

"Touched people have a duty to uphold the Masquerade. What that means is we have to keep our powers a secret. Untouched people stopped believing in magic centuries ago, and it made everyone's life a great deal simpler. A huge amount of pain has been avoided. Do you understand?"

I nodded. In any case, I was in no hurry to blurt out to anyone that I was a witch. Their secret was safe with me.

"I'm still concerned," said Boston, who was starting to get on my nerves. "And, honestly, I don't see the point in involving Rook in this meeting. If she has amnesia, then how will she be able to help? She won't know any spells. She won't know how to make any of her potions."

Esmeralda, the animal whisperer, chimed in. "But how will she ever remember if we don't include her?"

The rest of the coven nodded in agreement.

"We need to tell her everything," said Forsythia.

Soleil cast her eyes at me. "Perhaps not everything." Her lips curled into a ghost of a smile. "We don't want to scare her away."

"There are two urgent priorities," Forsythia said, glancing down at her notebook which shimmered in her hands. "The first is, well, Asha's case." Soleil nodded for her to continue. "The second is that we've found incontrovertible evidence of a werewolf attack in the city. We've had four separate sightings, and there is an untouched human recovering in ICU. Critical but stable. Ivy managed to go undercover as a nurse to surreptitiously test him, and the swab came back positive for *Canis lupus*."

My eyes gave away my incredulity. Being a witch was one thing, but mythical creatures running around the city was ridiculous. And witches undercover as medical professionals? I scrutinized their faces. Were they joking? Was it some kind of sanity test? Apparently not.

Ivy smiled at me. "What? You don't think I'd make a good nurse?"

"I, er ..."

Maybe a Halloween nurse, I thought, with her long dark hair and pale skin. She was especially attractive and I could easily imagine her in one of those short-skirted blood-spattered horror nurse outfits.

"I used one of the apothecary's glamours," Ivy said. "It wasn't as good as yours usually are, but it worked well enough."

"Glamours?" I felt hundreds of questions popping into my head, as if I had Pop Rocks on the brain. I felt like an idiot when Boston rolled her eyes, but it didn't stop me from blurting out my next question. "What does a werewolf have to do with curses?" It's a sentence I had never expected to say, but there you go.

"Most werewolf cases are curses," explained Forsythia.

"Contagious curses," said another woman. "That's why they always take priority. They can be spread by even the smallest injury via tooth or claw."

"Also," said Ivy, "werewolves are very tricky to explain away to muggles."

Soleil cleared her throat as if to scold Ivy.

"Erm ... I mean *non-magical humans,*" she said, flashing me a naughty smile.

"That's not good news." Esmeralda bit her thumbnail. "What about vampires?"

If I had been drinking tea, I would have launched it out of my nose. Instead, I coughed to cover my surprise and avoided eye contact.

Forsythia shook her head. "Still lying low. Now that Baldassare's gone, they seem a bit aimless, to be honest. We've had an attack here and there, but their criminal activity remains minimal."

"We must watch them," uttered the high priestess, and the witches nodded. "They may seem as if they are drifting, but keep in mind that vampires are the most ambitious species in the Realm. They'll be up to something. They always are." Her words seemed to echo in the yoga studio, and the coven nodded solemnly, shadows passing over their faces. I wondered who Baldassare was, and what the vampires had done to be so feared. Soleil blinked as if to clear the memories that had clouded over the room and adjusted the hood of her robe. The witches whispered amongst themselves and gathered their things. "Before you go, there's one more thing."

CHAPTER 18

THE DUSK REAPERS

ASHA

"It's a new case. An urgent one. I received a phone call late last night from an old friend." The high priestess had our full attention. "There's a woman who needs our help."

"Who?" asked Forsythia, pen poised, ready to add it to her list. "And what kind of curse is it?"

"It's only the suspicion of a curse, for now," replied Soleil. "We'll need to meet her to be sure."

I wondered who "we" were until I turned my gaze to Soleil, who happened to be looking right at me.

Me?

"But I don't know anything," I said. "Boston is right. I'll just get in the way."

"You're the right person for this job," said Soleil.

"Maybe in the past," I replied. "Maybe before the head injury. But now ... I wouldn't know where to start or what to do."

"You have to start somewhere," said Ivy.

Soleil nodded. "You are supported. The Void will guide you. Your instinct will direct you. You need to learn to trust yourself again."

I wouldn't even have known my own name if it hadn't been on the hospital chart, and now a secretive coven of witches wanted me to investigate a questionable curse?

I shook my head. I had my own healing to do, my own investigating into who I was—or who I used to be. It felt like they were asking me to give them something I didn't have.

Soleil blinked at me. I could tell she wasn't used to being refused. I felt guilty and uncomfortable, but how could I agree to help them when I was this clueless? I was restless, and wanted to leave. I could feel the disappointment hanging in the air like thin gray smoke.

"I have to go," I said, rolling up my yoga mat and slipping on the carrier. I couldn't wait to escape the candlelit studio which seemed cloying now with its sweet incense.

"Asha, wait," said Soleil.

I pretended I hadn't heard her and ducked outside, leaving the other witches to murmur about me. I slung the mat on my back and squeezed my helmet on, noticing my pink leggings were back. I was about to slot the key into the ignition when there was a warm flash in my hand that sent the keys flying into the foxgloves in the adjacent garden bed. I gasped and looked up to see Soleil staring at me, her wand outstretched. I looked at my empty palm and then at her again. She muttered something under her breath and whipped her wand backwards, as if it were a fishing rod, and the silver keys came sailing toward her for an easy catch.

"Asha," said the high priestess. "You know as well as I do that you can't avoid your destiny."

I didn't have an answer to that.

"But, of more immediate concern," she said, coming closer, "while you remember your magic, you're going to need protection. You don't yet understand what you're up against."

"Tell me," I said.

Soleil hesitated, as if she didn't know how much to divulge.

I grew impatient. "I know I'm not safe. First, this,"—I waved vaguely at my head injury—"then, last night, a man broke into my house."

The blood drained from her face, leaving her lips pale, and her eyes more intense than ever. "They're moving quickly," she muttered, mostly to herself.

"Who?" I asked.

"That was no ordinary man," uttered the high priestess. Before I could reply, she stepped closer and grabbed my arm, the grip of her cold fingers making me jolt.

"Listen to me. You know Ivy is a hacker," said Soleil. "She helps us by taking down dark magic apps, fake news, and other dangerous sites. One of the things she does for us is check the dark web Dusk Reaper list for any names we recognize, anyone we might want to warn, or—"

"Dusk Reaper?" I repeated. It sounded weird but familiar at the same time.

"The Dusk Reapers are an underground group of anonymous paranormal bounty hunters."

"I'm sorry, what?"

"Wizards, mostly, although there are some other cretins involved. They're paid assassins—" she looked at me sharply when she said the word, although I didn't know why—"who use their magic to murder for money. They're everywhere in our society, and there's no way of knowing who they are, or who the head hunters are."

My stomach turned to stone as I absorbed what Soleil was

saying. There wasn't one man trying to kill me, there were hundreds.

"You need to re-learn how to defend yourself," said Soleil. "We need to practice your fighting skills—"

"Fighting skills?"

"And your protection spells. Your attack magic. Are you well enough to begin lessons tomorrow?"

"Tomorrow?" I repeated, like a braindead Barbie.

Soleil sighed. "Asha, I understand this must be overwhelming for you. But the threat is very real, and we need to prepare ourselves."

Shocked and upset, I zoomed out of the yoga studio's parking lot, my hands and arms shaking as I controlled the Vespa beneath me.

We'll help you, Soleil had said when she handed my keys back. *We'll protect you.*

But how would a coven of weird women in conjured witch cloaks save me from the unseen enemies that surrounded me? The threat seemed too large, too ubiquitous, to fight against. What was the point of even trying? They had almost killed me once. Now they were just waiting to finish me off.

As I raced along the road, giving the cars around me a wide

berth, my mind was sparking with everything I had heard at the meeting.

I couldn't help looking around at the drivers and passengers in the cars around me, wondering if any of them were magical creatures. Eventually I arrived home, looking forward to a cup of dead leaf brew. I imagined myself pouring the hot water over the strange herbs and sticks and going to sit in the back garden to watch the hens pecking around, with Circe—or perhaps Odysseus—on my lap. I needed some time out. Things were happening way too quickly, and I needed to be able to spend some time processing it and planning what I was going to do. When I hit the button on the remote to open the garage door, nothing happened.

"Damn it," I swore, pressing the button harder and harder. The remote light flashed, telling me it wasn't a problem with the battery. I shook the remote and banged it against my palm, then tried again. Nothing. I gave up with a sigh and parked in the driveway, jumping off my scooter and taking the house keys out of my jacket pocket so that I could unlock the front gate. While I was looking down at the bunch of keys in my hand, I heard a rustle to my right. My heart knew something was wrong before my brain registered anything, and it sprinted in my chest.

A man's voice whispered: *"Fiat fulgur."*

Before I had time to look up, a bolt of electricity hit me in the back. It burned through my body. It twisted me and threw me to the ground, where I was just able to put my hands out in time to save my face from planting into the pavers. My house keys flew out of sight. Had someone just tased me? I lifted my head to look at my attacker. It was a man with a waxy face, wearing a long black cloak. He smirked, then held his wand out in front of him, ready to strike again.

CHAPTER 19
COLD EVIL INK
NICKY

Bolt. Clanging. Footsteps. The nurse without a face.

"I'm sorry about last time," I said — I had been rehearsing the speech. "I wasn't thinking clearly. I'm just scared. I don't know where I am or what has happened."

It wasn't one hundred percent true, but my fractured memories were equally unreliable. The surreal recollections couldn't be true. I felt her disdain for me, her judgment.

The snake began its strangulation.

I gulped down my terror and resisted the intense urge to grab her arm. I was perspiring from the pain. "Please. Talk to me."

Hisssssssss.

"All I know is that I was at home, waiting for Derek. My husband."

Pistol. Beep.

"And the next thing I know I'm in this r-room."

Locked up. Strapped down. Brain vacuumed.

"I just keep thinking this is a bad dream. That I'll wake up. You know?"

I was desperate for a human connection. Just a word. A look of understanding. But why was I even asking her? How could she answer, without ears or a mouth? Despair overwhelmed me, and I cried. Ugly sobs crashed out of me, mourning the new darkness I carried inside. The cold, evil ink that now frothed through my veins. *Murderer,* it fizzed. *Murderer.*

"No," I replied, shaking my head. "No."

I was no murderer. I was a blonde suburban housewife and a mom to a dear Labrador named Sebastian.

"My husband's name is Derek," I repeated. "Derek Landau. Can you contact him?"

The nurse sighed, though I was not sure how. She pushed the needle in with more force than usual. I flinched, tensing the muscle, which made the injection sting more.

"At least tell me why you are keeping me here."

I needed to know why I was being held prisoner in this bleak cell or I feared I'd go mad. Before I could ask any more questions, the drug hit, and my body dissolved into nothing.

. . .

I had a plan.

The next time the needle-bearing nurse entered the room, I'd be ready for her. I spent the early hours of the morning slowly extricating my right hand, millimeter by millimeter, from the old leather wrist cuff. There was no clock on the gray walls; the hours shifted and paused, shifted and paused, like a heavy corpse being dragged in a tarpaulin. The only sounds were my gasps and groans of effort, and the occasional clanging of bars elsewhere in the building. Finally, I managed to dislocate my thumb and pull my hand out of the restraint. The injury was painful, but the freedom was worth it. With an aching hand I was able to unbuckle the remaining cuff and then release my ankles, too. I searched in the dark for something I could use as a weapon, but came up empty-handed. There was nothing apart from the stretcher that served as my bed. I wondered for the first time where my clothes were, my car keys, my wallet, and wondered for the thousandth time where my husband was. How would he find me here? In this strange new world of plain gray cells. He'd call the police. He'd hire a PI to investigate my abduction. But I knew I couldn't wait to be rescued; I needed to find my own way out.

It soon turned to early morning. I had no windows to see the sky flame with sunrise, but I could hear the building waking up. Large levers for the fluorescent lights banged down, water rushed through pipes, shuffling footsteps of guards with silver keys jangling from their utility belts. My thoughts were smoggy and disconnected, but I knew I was in trouble. I knew I had to get out of there. I didn't have a weapon; I'd have to use my body. I had never taken a self-defense class and what I knew about hand combat was scary, but I rearranged the pillow and bedding so that it looked like I was still asleep under the covers, then glued myself against the wall next to the door, and waited for the faceless nurse to return.

CHAPTER 20

BARE HANDS AND A BLANK BRAIN

ASHA

Was this the wizard who had broken into my house the night before? I didn't know, and it didn't matter. I reached instinctively for my ritual knife, but instead of finding the leather holster around my thigh, there was pink leopard-print lycra.

Hex! I thought, making a mental note to never be caught unarmed again. I didn't have my knife, I didn't have my wand, but the worst thing was that I didn't have my memory. How would I be able to fend off this magic mercenary with bare hands and a blank brain? My hands were still shaking, my heart ready to rip through its cage. I looked around desperately for help. The sunny suburb was usually thrumming with joggers, dog-walkers, kids on bikes, and babies in strollers. Where was everyone?

I was still splayed out on the sidewalk beneath the jacaranda, breathing heavily, palms on fire from saving my head from crashing into yet another concussion. The man loomed over me, a sick, satisfied look on his face. His wand glinted in the dappled sunlight. I felt completely helpless and hopeless, but despair did not set in. The ICU doctors had given me another chance to live, and I wasn't going to let this magical murderer take it away from me. I jumped up and landed perfectly, surprising both of us. Without thinking about it, my body spun around, leg extended, kicking the wizard's legs from underneath him and making him fall. As he collapsed—it felt like slow motion—I jumped again and landed with both feet on his chest, forcing his breath out of his shocked lungs. His eyes bulged. His cheek capillaries bloomed. I saw a tattoo behind his ear: a golden scythe. With a practiced movement, I stiffened my right hand and brought it down hard on his inner wrist. He exclaimed in pain as his wrist bone fractured, forcing his fingers to open and release his wand. As soon as I grabbed the wand it may as well have been a sword, as I used two hands to reach it high and then bring it down to his chest in a stabbing motion.

"*Aversum,*" he choked out.

Just before the wand penetrated his breastbone, someone called my name, making me freeze, blink, and wake up.

I say "wake up" because from the time my body first reacted to the attack it had been like moving in a dream. My body had known exactly what to do even as my mind floundered. My limbs had become light and strong and moved instinctively. A kind of combat muscle memory I'd never have guessed I had. But when I heard my name being called, I snapped out of it just in time to not drive the wizard's wand into his black heart. I looked for the person who had called me, but the street was empty. Too late, I understood that it had been a trick of the wizard's to distract me, and now that I was no longer in stealth mode he was easily able to fling me off and grab his wand back with his uninjured hand. He didn't hesitate to send a bolt of lightning my way — *Fiat fulgur!* — which I managed to dodge, but his second one got me in the thigh, and I cried out. It felt like a flaming spear had been imbedded in the muscle. I almost collapsed again, but I knew if I did that it would be game over. Instead, I hauled together every ounce of energy I had and stepped toward the Dusk Reaper. There was discomfort on his face, most likely a result of his shattered wrist, but it was overshadowed by a grim smile. This wasn't just a job for him; I could see that he enjoyed hurting people. He pointed his wand at me for the last time, and fear flowed through me like a bucket of cold water. My muscles stiffened, and my eyes fell to the ivy that carpeted the wall.

Suddenly, words flowed from my mouth. I recognized my voice but not the foreign sounds. The wizard's smug expression faded as he felt the magic swirl between us.

"Hedera augescis," I uttered. The leaves on the wall began to expand and multiply, and the rustling tendrils snaked toward

us. Within seconds the foliage and the stems had doubled, and the runners were at our feet.

The wizard stepped back. "*Impedio!*" he yelled, and one of the hundreds of stems froze, just to be immediately covered by the rest of the advancing parts.

"*Volas,*" I said, and whipped up the air in front of me. The ivy rose off the ground, as if it were growing upward. He took another step back and murmured some more spells which did little to discourage the proliferating plant. It reached him, pulling at his cloak and his arms, trapping his ankles so he could no longer retreat.

Quietly, I uttered his death knell. "*Rumpis.*"

The stems went for his chest and his face, curling around his neck. The wizard dropped his wand and screamed, trying to prize the plant away from his throat, but more and more shoots wound around him until his breathing became shallow and his skin turned scarlet, then purple, then blue. He toppled over into the bed of wildflowers and copper grass as the ivy slithered, stifled, and strangled him until his body no longer moved.

I was left breathless by the magic and the violence. I hadn't understood the ancient words I had used but the power singing in my veins told me everything I needed to know. The tattoos made sense now, and the ambitious garden. I had a connection with plants and soil that I could feel but not explain. I watched as the form of the wizard's dead body began sinking down into the earth as if being digested by the plant's hungry suckers and the microbes in the soil. It got smaller and smaller until it had disappeared altogether. The ivy retreated, winding its way back onto the wall it came from, while the wildflowers and irises spread happily to cover the patch of dark soil left behind. My heart still thudding, I tried to make sense of what had just happened.

What had my shadow book said?

Potion Mistress. Green Witch. Cursebreaker.

I guessed that my plant-whispering ability was part of being a green witch, whatever that was. Then, if I had these magical green thumbs, it would follow that I could grow all the ingredients I'd need for potions, so that part made sense, too. As for curse-breaking, I was still a little in the dark. I supposed potions were part of it, but I suspected there was a lot more to curse-breaking than plant whispering and dead leaf brew. Whatever it entailed, I'd have to think about it later, because I felt like a sitting duck standing in front of my house with no way to get in. I had no phone, and no keys since the attacker had sent them flying. As far as I could tell, there was only one option open to me. I took a deep breath and began to run.

CHAPTER 21

SKUNK SMOKE AND RAW ONION

ASHA

My body was jangling with adrenaline and my limbs felt disconnected from my mind. There was no logic to running, apart from the fact that I would no longer be a target stuck outside Tanglewood. I ran and ran, my shocked body relieved to expend its nervous energy. My right thigh that had been struck by the wizard burned and ached, but there seemed to be no major damage done as it still worked well enough to keep me moving forward.

I thought I would be tired after what had happened, but the opposite was true. I was thrilled by what I had learned about myself and my power. It felt like a wonder and a gift. Yes, I needed my ritual knife and my wand, but now I knew I could defend myself without those things, too. It would be smart to brush up on my Latin and my spells, and to practice my fighting skills as Soleil had suggested, but deep down I had an inherent power that no one could take away from me, even if they had been able to take my memory.

I ran as if on autopilot, and began to enjoy trusting my body. It seemed to know more than my troubled mind. I let myself run for a mile down the road before I realized where I was heading. I was on my way to Detective Armstrong at the police station. I thought he'd be able to help me get back into my house. I had a vague idea where the station was. I heard a car racing down the street ahead and was glad to have activity around me again after the spooky silence of before. Huffing, I turned a corner, and ran straight into a huge, bulky man in a black suit. I practically bounced off him. I was about to apologize, then I heard the screeching of tires on the road beside us, and felt his strong arms around me, one around my torso, the other clamped over my mouth. The air smelled of burnt rubber and hot asphalt. Wide-eyed, I tried to launch myself away from him, away from the black SUV with tinted windows.

This can't be happening, I thought. *I've just fought for my life—*

I screamed for help, but no sound came through the man's meaty paw. I stomped hard on his foot, but it soon became clear that the mountain of a human didn't feel pain. Looking up at him, I shuddered when I saw his face. Was he even human? He was impressively ugly, with boulders for shoulders and a greasy, stilton-like skin. I couldn't help pulling a face, especially when I got a whiff of him, which was a stomach-turning odor of rotten pumpkin, skunk smoke and raw onions.

"Holy hex," I moaned. I almost retched, then tried to breathe through my mouth to mitigate the stench, but my lips were covered. I wondered if this man's superpower was suffocation by stink.

What a horrible way to die, I thought, as my throat constricted. Death by Stench. *I should have let the Dusk Reaper fry me when I had the chance.*

The terrible smell didn't stop me from struggling. I was still stomping and kicking as he lifted me up and moved toward the SUV.

"No!" I shouted. "No!" and launched into a new frenzy of fighting. There was a tree nearby, and a hedge, and I quickly wondered if I'd be able to get them to intervene, but the combination of the man's baseball mitt–sized hand over my mouth and the lack of fresh oxygen zapped my brain, and before I could muster any kind of spell, my mind floated away, and my body collapsed against the ogre's fetid mass.

The man bundled my half-conscious body into the black SUV. With the few brain cells that were still functional, I wondered why he was bothering with taking me somewhere to kill me instead of just doing it right there on the quiet street. Perhaps the bounty fee was higher if you dragged the hit somewhere before putting a bullet in their brain. By "their brain," I meant my brain, of course, but the whole scenario had taken on a strange dreamlike quality, probably because of the lack of oxygen. The door slammed behind me as I fell, flaccid, on the seat. He climbed into the driver's seat and there was a decisive click as all the doors around us locked, and a hum as the vehicle glided forward. I exhaled hard, trying to clear my lungs of the stench, and then took a deep lungful of the cabin air, which was slightly less revolting than the close-up odor of my abductor's blue-veined skin.

With the fresh-ish oxygen washing away the insult in my lungs, and being able to breathe freely without his paw mashed against my mouth, the sharpness of my vision returned, and I was able to lever myself into a sitting position. I thought I was alone, but across from me sat an attractive brunette in a black suit. She had a shiny bob, London bus red lipstick, and red-bottomed stilettos so sharp that they could literally blind a man. She was petite and very put together, a bold contrast to my exhausted, wounded, sprawled-out body in pink leopard print leggings. The way she sat with her legs elegantly crossed, commanding the space, told me that she was definitely the boss of something.

"Asha Viridian Rook," she said, taking off her shades. "Where the hell have you been?"

CHAPTER 22

RIVERSIDE
NICKY

I heard the nurse coming, could recognize her strident steps down the corridor. My pelvis, which I guessed was fractured—and certainly not used to standing—ached for the medicine I was used to her bringing. Her injections killed the pain in my body and the pain of my existence by knocking me out for hours. My hand was throbbing as I pressed my spine against the cool cell wall. Mind scrambling, thinking of what I'd do when, in a few seconds, she'd lever open the security gate and unlock the door. All I knew was that I had to overpower her and slip out of the room. I didn't know what was waiting for me on the other side, but I was willing to risk it to get back home to Derek and Sebastian.

She approached the gate and the clanging sound made me jump, even though I had been expecting it. Adrenaline ignited my body . I curled my fingers into pulsing fists, ready to fight.

The door beeped and opened and the nurse stepped into the dark room. I waited, holding my breath, until she closed the door behind her. As she reached for the light switch to her left, I jumped. She gasped in surprise as I tackled her and pinned her to the floor, sending the medical equipment clattering. It turned out that she had a face, after all. I smashed my palm over her mouth to stop her from screaming for help. Injured and unarmed, I had only the element of surprise on my side, so I had to work fast. I scooped the syringe off the floor.

Without looking at it, I stabbed it deep into the nurse's neck and released the drug. She was fighting me, trying to yell, terrified eyes wide, but soon I felt her body relax under mine as the tranquilizer hit. She stopped fighting, and her eyes rolled back. I climbed off, panting, my atrophied muscles exhausted from the brief exertion. I caught my breath, then searched for her access card and keys, which I quickly found and stashed in my robe pocket. I spent a moment looking at her face, which was new to me. It wasn't unpleasant; not like I'd imagined in my dreams. I realized that this was not the same nurse as before. This one had luminescent light brown skin and wore an old-fashioned nurse uniform, like something out of the Victorian era. I was admiring her when suddenly her eyes shot open and she gasped as if she were drowning. I screamed.

She lunged at me, taking me down, my elbow cracking into the floor, my pelvis on fire. I gritted my teeth and fought back with all the energy I had, sure that the nurse would soon lose consciousness again. She held me down with her left forearm across my chest as I fought to shove her off. The nurse reached into her utility belt, bringing out a compact black tube-shaped device. By the time I realized what it was, it was too late. She stuck the taser into my chest and pressed the button. A blue thunderbolt roared through my ribcage, lighting my skeleton on fire, and short-circuiting my heart and lungs.

When I woke up I was back on the stretcher, back in the leather restraints which were now reinforced with tight black cable ties I knew I'd never be able to squeeze my way out of. My entire body flared and ached in never-ending waves.

I closed my eyes, clenched my jaw, and swore under my breath.

There was a soft clicking sound to my left. When I opened my eyes again, I saw that the lamp had been switched on, and the nurse sat in a metal chair in the corner, watching me. She wore a flesh-colored Band-Aid over the injection site on her neck, and I immediately felt guilty when I caught sight of it.

"Sorry," I said. It came out as a whisper.

She didn't reply.

"Sorry. I was desperate. I don't know why I'm here and you wouldn't answer my questions."

She lurched up, fury in her face, neck veins protruding like cables running under her skin. "You want to know why you're here?"

"Yes," I said. "Please."

She turned to me, and despite the dim light I saw she already regretted her decision. She knew she should knock me out and disappear, but something made her stay. The nurse retrieved the chair from the corner of the room and placed it next to me, the steel legs scraping the concrete floor as she adjusted it after sitting down. She was close enough that I could read her badge: Sister Devka. I watched her expectantly—anxiously—because I knew the answer wasn't going to be pretty. The neon nightmares I had every time I slept had been slowly revealing what had happened prior to my incarceration. Running in the city night traffic, getting hit by a car, climbing up onto the bridge above the highway, and a cop trying to talk me down. An explosion emanating from my hand.

"You had a psychotic break," said the nurse.

I frowned at her. There was no reason for me to snap. I had a wonderful, easy life, a loving husband, a beautiful house, and a golden-haired Labrador that I loved more than most people loved their children.

"That doesn't sound right," I said.

"You were catatonic for a while," continued the sister. "When you arrived here you weren't walking or talking. You weren't responding to stimuli."

So much for being abducted. "Who brought me here? What is this place?"

"The judge agreed to forgo the trial."

"The judge?"

"The evidence was clear. There were plenty of witnesses. You were deemed incompetent to stand trial. That's why you're here instead of prison."

I closed my eyes and rubbed them. I wanted to cry. "So the nightmares are true," I said. "I shot someone."

"Yes," nodded the nurse. "A policeman risked his life to save you. He climbed up on the bridge to talk you down. You fired at him, point-blank."

This can't be true.

This can't be true.

This can't be true.

This is just part of the nightmare. When I wake up, I'll be safe and warm in bed with Derek and I'll laugh about how frightened I was about a dream.

"No," I said. "I wouldn't do that. I've never killed anyone. I don't own a gun. I wouldn't even know how to fire one. You've got the wrong person."

But then how did I remember the crime so clearly? It was like I had been in someone else's body.

"Mrs. Landau," said the nurse. "It was you. It was definitely you. You were brought straight here from the crime scene."

"Where is *here?* What is this place?"

"Riverside," she replied, and I saw the small logo on her badge.

"Riverside," I echoed. *Riverside.* I had heard of it before, seen it in a news article. "A mental asylum."

"For the criminally insane," said the nurse, causing me to flinch.

"That's ridiculous."

The nurse shifted in her seat.

I stared at her. "Criminally insane people are serial killers. Sexual predators. Cult leaders who spike the Kool-Aid."

"I admit that you don't fit the profile," said the nurse. "I've been reading your file, trying to figure you out. I agreed that you didn't seem the dangerous type—until you attacked me." Her hand traveled subconsciously to the dressing on her neck.

"I'm so sorry," I repeated. "I thought I had been abducted. I was trying to get home to my husband. He must be so worried about me."

"Mr. Landau knows where you are."

"Oh, thank God," I said, feeling an unfurling of relief in my chest—a blossom opening. I sighed and put my hand over my heart. *Oh, thank God.*

My whole body relaxed. Derek would be doing everything in his power to get me out. I no longer needed to fight or escape. He'd take care of me, arrange an expensive lawyer. A day in court.

But then a thought hit me and the blossom faded and shriveled. Did I deserve to get out? I had killed a man.

"What was his name?" I asked in a low voice. "The policeman who tried to help me?"

The sister took out her phone and scrolled to the document she was looking for.

"Joseph Molete," she read out loud. "Husband. Father of three."

I blinked at her while it sunk in, then buried my face in my hands. Hot tears. A stone ached in my throat. I sobbed loudly and without restraint in a way I'd never wept before. I knew it was true; I had the gunpowder-scented memory to prove it. The full weight of what I'd done closed in on me, squeezing my ribs like an iron vise. I wanted to die. How could I live with this knowledge?

The nurse let me cry unimpeded, and when I finally surfaced, she was still by my side, and I had the feeling she was holding my hand to comfort me, even though she wasn't.

CHAPTER 23

MOONLIGHTING

ASHA

I sat up in a hurry, scooping my mussed hair away from my face, which was sticky with perspiration. I looked at the driver, who was thankfully by then ensconced in the driver's area separated by a tinted glass partition.

"Who are you?" I asked the woman.

Her face froze, but only for a moment. A generous smile replaced her look of confusion. "You're kidding," she said. "You've always had an offbeat sense of humor."

"I'm not kidding," I said. "I wish I was. I don't know who you or your ogre are." I looked pointedly at the mountain of cheezo bleu operating the SUV.

The woman shook her hair back and laughed. "Gnrok is an orc."

"Sure he is," I said. *He definitely smells like one.*

Her smile faded. "Don't ever let an orc catch you calling him an ogre."

What could I say? It was probably a good tip.

"You're serious," the woman said. "You don't remember me. I can see it in your eyes."

I was going to apologize, but then I remembered that I had just been abducted and I shouldn't be the one apologizing. I glanced at her stilettos again. As far as I knew, I didn't own high heels, but I could certainly see the appeal. A shoe with a built-in weapon like that could come in really handy.

"Asha," she said sharply, and I snapped out of it. "Where have you *been?*"

"Er—"

"My plan was to pick you up and give you hell for going AWOL on us. You owe me three reports and you haven't been answering your phone. You know how much the squad needs you."

"Er," I said again. "Actually, I don't know. I don't know anything. All I know is that I woke up in the hospital a few days ago with amnesia and now I'm trying to piece my life back together."

The woman's red lips fell open. "What?"

"Head injury," I said, gesturing at my temple, as if she didn't understand English.

"I'm sorry, what?" she repeated, leaning forward as if to get a clearer view of me, even though I was right there in the car with her. "What do you mean, a head injury?"

"Someone attacked me. And since getting out I've realized it wasn't a random attack. I'm on some kind of ... hit list, according to my—" According to my what? High priestess? Witch friend? Eccentric yoga instructor? I didn't know how much I was allowed to say. The woman looked like an untouched human to me, but how could one tell? The fact that she had an orc driver/kidnapper made me think she knew all about the Masquerade. It was a minefield.

She didn't take her eyes off me. Deadpan apart from one arched eyebrow, she said: "Hit list?"

I sighed and sat back. I suddenly felt exhausted. It had been an eventful morning. Something in me obviously trusted this woman because my body was telling me it was okay to let down my guard.

"I'm taking you in," she said, looking behind us as if to check that no one was tailing us.

What now? "In where?"

"To the station," she said. "I need to brief you thoroughly."

"Brief me? On what?"

She gave me a hard but slightly amused stare. "On everything you've forgotten."

"It's not that I don't like you," she said. "We get on well. You're one of my favorite agents."

"Okay," I replied. I was waiting for a "but."

"But the reason we're going to the station is to get you caught up on all the cases you're working on."

"So, I work on cases for you."

"For the Scorpions, yes."

"As a—?"

"As one of the best paranormal investigators I know."

P.I.? My head was spinning. According to the coven, I was a cursebreaker. This woman thought I was some kind of detective. According to my own experiences, I was a garden-loving, potion-making, spell-casting hippie-witch cat-mom with a penchant for dead leaf brew. One thing was certain: I seemed to be particularly good at moonlighting.

The woman smiled, as if reading my whirlwind of thoughts. "You always have a lot going on, but they're not separate from each other. You don't need the labels—you never have. One of the reasons you're an effective investigator is because you're able to make great potions, including brilliant glamours for undercover work."

I didn't know what glamours were.

"The reason you make potent potions is because you grow the best ingredients. And the reason for that is because you're a green witch practicing earth magic. It all weaves together."

I blinked at her, remembering the way I had twisted the ivy around the wizard just an hour earlier. Blood rushed to my cheeks.

"Look," she said. "I'm a muggle, so I don't know the ins and outs of your world. But what I do know from you is that earth magic is when you draw on the Void through nature. Nature is your conduit to the magic in the Realm."

Yes, I thought. I could feel that was true. I had felt it the moment I had arrived home after my hospital stay. I could feel the trees and plants in a special way, as if we were all intimately connected. As if we always had been, and always would be.

"We're on the same team," she said. "It's always been your mission to keep the balance of the Realm in check, and the Scorpions' job is to keep the peace."

I watched the trees flash by as we drove. The woman took out her makeup and touched up her lips while looking into the small mirror. While the touch-up was perfect, I could tell she was really checking again to see if anyone was following us. Seemingly satisfied with what she saw, she snapped the lid shut and turned her attention to me.

"So," she said. "Are you ready to get back to work?"

The woman with the London Bus lips took a gold name badge out of her handbag and pinned it to her smart black uniform. Captain Morgan, it said. At least that was easy to remember. After a while, we slowed to a gradual stop outside a gray building.

"*Danka,* Gnrok," said Morgan, and tapped goodbye on the tinted partition. The odious orc gave a half-hearted wave with a hand that looked like a bunch of ham-skinned bananas. I stumbled out of the car, grateful for the fresh air.

"So, you work with orcs?"

Morgan nodded. "It's a relatively new development." She took long strides toward the building despite her spiky heels. "My current budget doesn't allow for human drivers or body-guards. Gnrok is both. And he's a good guy, as far as orcs go. Helpful to have around."

I'd say. He had practically lifted me with one finger.

"Since the Void Fracture the orcs have been in a bad way. People don't trust them after the Hammerskin coup. The elves won't go near them now, and let's face it, they're the ones with all the money. The orcs are facing massive job losses and poverty, even with austerity measures in place. We're working with the Council and the Khargol administration to employ them where we can, outside of untouched people's sight."

I had to hurry to keep up with her. "That's kind of you."

"Not kind," she said, moving a strand of hair that a sudden breeze had whipped across her face. "Just trying to keep things in order. The Void knows the last thing we need are hundreds of hungry orcs on our hands." We reached the building and the captain looked into a small camera, then used her thumb to unlock the biometric bolt, swinging the large glass door open, gesturing for me to go ahead. The receptionist saluted her as we walked past, and soon we were in a transparent elevator, traveling up the glass spine of the building.

Morgan crossed her arms and peered at me. "You don't remember *anything?*"

I shook my head. "I didn't even know I had cats."

She laughed, which made me laugh, too, even though it was more sad than funny.

"My house is teaching me things," I said, leaning against the wall. "And some people are trying to help me remember." *Soleil, Merlin, Sam.* "My psychologist said she thinks it'll come back to me if we work on it, but it might take years."

"We don't have years," said Morgan. The elevator door slid open.

I know that, I thought. *I'm on a magical hit list.*

Morgan didn't break eye contact. "What do you say we try to speed up the process?"

CHAPTER 24

THE AMBITION OF VAMPIRES

ASHA

Of course I said yes, even though it scared me. Morgan, the captain of the Scorpions, was pretty and petite, but I found her quite intimidating. Even though she was only around ten years older than me, I felt like a kid around her, an errant teenage daughter. While I felt vulnerable, she was tough and smart. Plus, she could walk in killer four-inch heels.

We made our way through the chaotic open-plan office, walking past officers wearing casual suits, their black utility jackets hanging from their chairs. When they saw Morgan, they sat up a bit straighter and lowered their voices.

"What's up, you rowdy sons of bitches?" she yelled. They gave good-humored replies and happy salutes. "What are you all so bloody excited about?"

A nice-looking man with blond hair replied. "Linton arrested a vamp downtown. Jeppe Street. He was selling blood."

I kept my jaw clenched so that my mouth didn't hang open.

Morgan stopped. "Blood? Human?"

"The bloodsucker said it was synthetic, but Linton sent it to the lab and they confirmed his suspicions. We're holding him for breaking 408 section B."

"Where's the vamp?"

"He's down in SubT."

"Good," replied Morgan, nodding. "Good. I'll get to him in twenty. Tell Linton to come and see me when he gets back."

"Yes ma'am," said the cop, then smiled at me with all his teeth. "Hey, Asha. Long time."

I was surprised that he knew my name. "Hi," I said. It was immediately obvious that I didn't recognize him, and my greeting hung awkwardly in the air. Morgan saved me by opening her office door. "We've got work to do," she said, and I got the feeling she was tapping her designer shoe, even though she wasn't. I smiled at the man and shrugged in a way that said *I'd better listen to the boss!*

Once I was safely inside, she closed the door. "That's Stuart," she said in a low voice. "He's always liked you." She motioned for me to sit down. Her office was unnervingly neat.

"You really have a vampire here?" I asked.

"Don't worry," Morgan said. "He's locked in the subterranean cells. No one escapes SubT." There was something in her eyes —perhaps a flicker of a memory—which she blinked away. "Well, hardly anyone."

"And he was arrested for selling human blood?" I knew the question had already been asked and answered, but I was still trying to process the information. I realized I must come across as having a room temperature IQ, but I still couldn't wrap my mind around the fact that there were supernatural creatures in the city, especially ones that would siphon your blood for a quick buck.

"We've got every taste of blood you can dream of," said Morgan.

"Excuse me?"

"It's the line on one of the synthetic blood adverts. Plate-let, I think. Warm Velvet Red, pink frappés, red cell protein shakes, scarlet espressos. And yet the creatures still resort to violence." She swiveled in her chair. "They've been too quiet. They're up to something; I can feel it. They're always up to something."

I remembered what Soleil had said. Now that Baldassare was gone, the vampires seemed aimless. But perhaps that's just what they wanted people to think.

"Enough about the bloodsucking miscreants," Morgan said, placing her palms on her desk. "Let's get you up to speed." She opened her laptop and crunched her keys for a while, then turned it toward me so that I could see the screen. "This is your file. Ready?"

"*My* file?" I asked, confused.

"You have a file. Of course you have a file. Do you think we'd ever work with someone without checking out their background? Of course, you're not supposed to know, and you're not supposed to see it, but this seems to be an exceptional case, right?"

"Right," I said, my eyes on stalks.

She pushed the computer over to me. "Go ahead."

I pulled it closer and inspected the screen. There were five files: Gallery; Report; Bio; Surveillance; Miscellaneous. All were locked except the bio and gallery.

Asha Viridian Rook

Female Cauc 5ft8, green eyes

Biometrics captured

Birth certificate NULL

Parents NULL

DOB unspecified, est. early 90s

Social services ward of the state 1996

Incorporated by Copperfield Institute 1998 — Graduated 2010

"That's all?" I asked, not taking my eyes off the screen.

"That's a lot," she replied. "It's a lot to take in. No info on parents, no birth date. In fact, there's no record of your existence prior to '96."

I felt that familiar deep loneliness again—a dark tree sinking its roots into ice. "Doctor Gilbert said I didn't have anyone listed as next of kin."

"You never talked about it," Morgan said. "Your childhood. Or, at least, you never talked to me about it."

"I guess child abandonment makes for awkward conversation."

"It can't be easy," she said.

She didn't have to finish the sentence. *It can't be easy knowing your parents didn't want you. It can't be easy growing up without parental love or comfort.*

"Do you need some time?"

I shook my head. "No, let's keep going." I knew she was busy and that she was doing me a favor by showing me the file. We looked at the gallery next. There were dozens of candid shots of me doing ordinary things—walking, grocery shopping, drinking coffee at a local café—which would seem mundane to anyone else but were fascinating to me. Looking at how I dressed, what I bought, where I went for coffee.

I looked at Morgan. "You followed me?"

"It's protocol. We check out every possible employee."

There was a posed photograph at the end: a graduation picture. I stared at my younger self. Jet-black hair, unnerving eyes. The frame was branded with the Copperfield Institute insignia.

"What is Copperfield?" I asked.

"It's the most accomplished magical academy on the continent. Madame Copperfield vouched for you, so we knew you'd be a good fit."

I didn't know who Madame Copperfield was, but I liked the sound of her.

"We have a couple of urgent cases open at the moment," said Morgan, sliding her laptop away from me. "It looked like we were getting somewhere before you disappeared."

"It wasn't part of the plan," I replied. Although, to be fair, I had no idea if I had ever actually had a plan. My life pre-bludgeoning was still an enigma.

"Well," said Morgan, biting the end of her black pen, "I'm glad you're back."

I felt a wisp of something in my chest. A whiff of hope? A smudge of happiness? All I knew was that I felt grateful that someone had missed me and was glad to have me back, even if it was just to investigate the ambitions of vampires.

"I'll brief you on the top three cases, and you can tell me which you'd like to work on first. We have orc organ thieves, magical animal trafficking, and human children disappearing."

"What's that?" I asked the captain, pointing at the pinboard behind her that was wallpapered with grisly photos and parts of maps.

"Oh," she said. "Don't worry about that. It's an ongoing case I'm obsessed with."

"Looks creepy."

"That it is. There's a vigilante assassin causing havoc. The latest killing was of an orc who was killing untouched humans to collect their teeth."

I must have grimaced, because Morgan nodded and pulled her own spooked expression. Something about the board disturbed me deeply. I cleared my throat. "I ... I don't think I can work at the moment," I said.

Morgan stopped and stared at me.

I shook my head. "My life is completely upside-down. I don't know who I am or what—"

"Bullshit," replied Morgan. "Of course you know who you are. Who you are doesn't get knocked out of you."

"It feels like it did," I said. "It feels like I lost everything." My eyes teared up, and I felt self-conscious about it. Small and weak. I felt like a child, which I realized then was not an unfamiliar feeling. It was the second time in twenty-four hours that another woman had called on me for help, and I knew I couldn't do it. I stood up to leave.

"Don't you dare," snapped the captain. "You have never walked away from a case and you're not going to do it now. Not while there are little girls missing."

I stopped. Obviously I stopped. My instinct to run away dissipated. "Girls?"

"Young girls. Defenseless children. First a couple of them, then a dozen, now they're disappearing night and day, and no one can stop it."

I stared at her. "Why?"

Morgan shrugged, her expression solemn, even bitter. "We were close to finding out, then you went off the radar."

I simmered. I couldn't stop my toes from tapping. "You keep saying it like I wanted to go missing. Like it was a choice."

Her eyes didn't leave mine as she crossed her arms. "Was it?"

"You think I chose to be attacked? To wake up in the ICU?"

"I wouldn't be doing my job if every possible scenario didn't occur to me."

I guess she had a point, but I was irritated nonetheless. I wanted to get out of there, but the idea of the scared little girls made me stay.

"What can you tell me about the children?" I didn't care about the other cases.

Morgan seemed cheered by my question. She opened one of the files on her desk and started dishing out photos like a blackjack dealer. A brown-skinned girl in a powder-blue dress. A peach-skinned girl in shorts and a shirt with a cartoon rainbow. A girl with pigtails, a girl with a messy bob, a girl in a cap. On and on went the pile of pictures. It was heartbreaking seeing their fresh faces and gap-toothed smiles.

"They're so young," I muttered. So innocent looking, so beautiful.

"Between six and sixteen years old," Morgan said. "Nothing to connect them—apart from living in Johannesburg."

I swallowed hard. "Bodies?"

My question shocked me. The casual way I asked it, the familiar way it came out of my mouth, as if dead bodies of little girls were a regular occurrence in my life. A chill went up my spine, and I shivered.

"Nothing," she said. "Not a ribbon. Not a fingernail."

I thought for a while. Morgan said there was nothing connecting the children, but of course there must be. I'd have to find out what.

"Will you help us?" she asked.

I rubbed my eyes. It had been an extremely long day. Did I want to find the missing girls? Of course I did. Was I up to it? Not at all. Besides, I had my own problems, like a debilitating head injury, and staying alive while being hunted by the Dusk Reapers, which at that moment seemed more like a ruinous dream than a reality.

"Every day that passes ..."

She didn't have to finish her sentence. I knew what she meant. Every day that passed meant more children were taken. The captain knew I wouldn't be able to live with that. She knew me better than I currently knew myself.

"I'll call you in the morning," I said. "Thanks for the information from my file."

Even the little I had seen had felt oddly reassuring, like proof that I actually existed before this all started.

"I have more for you," Morgan said. I frowned at her. "I'll pass it on to you once this case is solved."

Of course she would. She was conniving and clever, and not afraid to make use of whatever leverage she had to do her job and keep people safe. I decided I liked her more than I wanted to.

CHAPTER 25

DRUNKEN WARBLE

ASHA

When I walked out of the security door of the Scorpion headquarters, Gnrok was waiting for me. He leaned, casual yet attentive, against the black SUV, watching the pedestrians that crossed the paving between us.

"It's okay," I said when I got into hearing range. "I don't need a lift. Thanks, though."

Gnrok wouldn't take no for an answer. He opened the back door for me. "Captain's orders."

I sighed, gave up, and jumped in. There was no point in arguing with an orc. Once he climbed into the driver's seat and started the car, I pressed the button to lower the smoked glass partition between us. The stink was unholy, but I had questions.

"How come you can stand like that, in full view of the untouched humans?"

"They don't see me," he said.

"You're the size of a mountain," I said. "How can they not see you?"

Gnrok rolled his shoulders, as if they were stiff. "Humans only see what they want to see."

"What does that mean?"

He grunted and then glanced at me in the rearview mirror. "You have a lot of questions for such a small person."

"I'm not that small," I said.

"Humans can only see what they believe."

I frowned at his reflection. "I'm sure that can't be true."

The orc grunted again, this time with more mirth than before. "It's true. And for those who do happen to be open-minded enough to see me, which is rare, we have ways of dealing with that."

"Like what?"

Gnrok scoffed, and that was the end of the conversation.

When we arrived at Tanglewood, I was so happy to be home. I practically jumped out of the car. The cats bolted out from the pedestrian gate to greet me, and I bent down and stroked their vibrating bodies. I was home. All I wanted was a hot bath, a cinnawhisky, and to crash straight into bed, but life had other plans.

Before I could smell him, Gnrok was by my side. He grabbed my arm, squeezing it, eyes trained on my house. "Someone's here," he muttered.

I was about to argue when I saw what he was looking at. A flickering of light through the kitchen windows, a shadow, and then a snatch of a song. A drunken warble. It was a woman's voice.

"It's okay," I said to the orc, but he insisted on accompanying me inside. *What's the worst that could happen,* I wanted to ask him. *An intruder kills me with her bad singing?*

I pushed the front door open, with no idea what or who to expect. It felt odd pushing open the door to my own house and hoping I wasn't interrupting the person inside. Beside me, the mountain that was Gnrok was tense, and I could smell the adrenaline sweat emanating from his rigid body. I refused to retch. Following the awful singing, we approached the kitchen, where we saw a young woman dancing to her own beat. An open bottle of whisky and a single candle glimmered in the dark. Gnrok and I traded bemused expressions. The scene was utterly bizarre.

"H-hello?" I said, but my voice couldn't compete with the swaying human karaoke machine. I inched closer. "Hello?" Still nothing.

"Hello," said the orc. The timbre of his voice, or his B.O., must have carried, because the strange woman immediately opened her eyes and screamed.

CHAPTER 26

GRIN & FROLIC

ASHA

The woman was attractive. She had blonde highlights, a svelte body shown off by her skinny jeans, and proper makeup. The kind of makeup I was sure I'd never be able to apply or pull off. I motioned at her to calm down, that everything was okay, but I guessed that the sight of a strange orc in a dark old house was rather alarming.

When she finally stopped screaming, I asked her who she was, and she blinked at me in bewilderment. "Asha?" she asked, "Is it really you?"

Gnrok was eventually convinced that the tipsy woman was not a threat, and he reluctantly left. I was grateful for his help, but my house has not smelled the same since.

"Savannah!" the woman exclaimed, confusing me further. It turned out to be her name. "You call me Savvy."

"Okay," I said.

"Okay?" she said, and began to cry.

I felt the immediate desire to comfort her, but I was stuck between not knowing who she was and wanting to help her. Instead, I grabbed some glasses, poured more drinks, and we sat down together.

"I don't know if I should," she said, picking up her tumbler and almost draining it. No wonder the woman was listing sideways like an unlucky cruise ship.

"God, I was so worried about you," she said. "This is the fourth Grin & Frolic session you missed. Your phone doesn't even ring. I thought you were gone forever."

"Grin & Frolic?"

"Yes, stupid."

"Um, remind me?"

"Every Tuesday we meet for G&Ts at your place," Savannah said. "We've been doing it for years. Why am I telling you this? Where have you been?"

"It's a long story," I said. I was getting sick of telling it, and now felt sympathy for anyone who had a broken arm or leg and had to tell the same story over and over to curious onlookers.

"You didn't even have any gin," she said, as if this was altogether the worst of my sins. "And I couldn't find tonic, either. Just some pink lemonade in the fridge, which I'm sure you made yourself. Honestly, I don't know what the world is coming to."

"What?"

"Don't worry," she said, waving her hands around. "I didn't touch the lemonade. I know the rules."

Who was this disaster of a woman, and why had she been dancing in my kitchen?

"Why do we meet for drinks?" I asked.

Savannah scrunched up her face. "I don't understand the question."

"Do we work together?" I asked. "Are we ... related? Just friends?"

She almost spat her whisky out. "*Just friends?*"

"I didn't mean it like that," I said. "I just—"

"Yes, Asha, we are *just friends*," said Savannah. "Just best friends since school. Our friendship is just ten years old. Why have you stood me up three weeks in a row? Ignoring my messages? It is NOT like you. I was getting worried."

She didn't look worried, to be honest—dancing and drinking after breaking and entering.

"Which school did we go to?" I asked.

She pulled a face again. "Copperfield, obviously. Why are you acting so weird?"

I told her the story. It turned out that Savannah was a great listener and gasped in all the right places. When I came to the part about the Starfall coven, she rolled her eyes in a wonderfully exaggerated way.

"That group of stuck-up witches," she said. She made the word "witch" sound like an insult. When she caught the look on my face, she quickly sat up straight. "Oh, I didn't mean you, obviously."

"You don't like witches?" I asked, thinking the evening was getting more bizarre by the minute.

She pursed her lips and pulled up the sleeve of her cardigan, showing the Starfall insignia.

"I don't understand," I said.

"Don't worry about it," she said. "All you need to know is that I used to be in the coven, and then I was kicked out. I'm allowed to keep my powers unless I break any rules of the Masquerade, or if I contact anyone from the coven."

"Like me?" I asked.

"Like you," she said, and winked at me. "But you're worth the risk. Always have been. Shall we have another drink?"

"So, let me get this straight," said Savvy. She was almost slurring, but not quite. "You killed someone somewhere in the city—"

"Self-defense," I said.

Savannah waved the fact away as if it were irrelevant. "You woke up in the hospital with no memory. Then some weird things happened."

"I think I sent a tray of instruments flying across the room with my mind."

Savvy nodded. "Nice."

"The psychologist said that my rate of healing was something she'd never seen before, and that I had a history of injuries. I didn't understand it at all. I tried to escape."

"Then a hot cop brings you home—"

"He's not that hot," I fibbed, holding my glass to my face to hide my warm cheeks.

Savvy laughed. "Liar."

I felt like pushing her, gently, like a sister would, and my instinctive body language told me that it was true: we were indeed close friends. "How would you know if he was hot?"

"Because I saw him, dummy. Of course, I couldn't approach him, even when I was desperate to ask about you. But you know, with my record—"

My stomach clenched. "What do you mean?"

"I have a criminal record," she said. "I avoid cops like the freaking plague."

"No, what do you mean you saw him? Where?"

"I've been coming by every Tuesday afternoon, remember? For Grin & Frolics. God, you're not kidding about your sieve of a memory."

"I mean, what was he doing here?" It felt like there was suddenly no breath in my lungs. Armstrong had been *here*?

"Last Tuesday?" I asked.

"Every Tuesday," she said. "Who do you think was feeding your cats?"

CHAPTER 27

DARK ARTS 101

ASHA

"I need you to tell me everything you know about me," I said.

Savannah chuckled. "How long do you have?"

"All night."

"Well," she said, glancing at her watch, "I've got the babysitter till midnight. What do you want to know?"

"Everything."

Savvy adjusted her posture as if she were settling in. "Do you have any snacks?"

The question caught me off guard. I hadn't had an appetite in days. I held up a finger gesturing for her to wait, then raided the kitchen cupboards. I found chips—plain, salted—mixed nuts, pretzels, and dried mango.

"Blessed be," Savannah said. I guess old habits die hard.

"First tell me about my parents." Merlin had said he thought they were dead.

Savannah shook her head. "We don't know. We don't know what happened to you, or why you ended up in the system. When you tried to investigate, they closed ranks. We don't know who your parents were. Honestly, I don't think we'll ever find out, because you're a pretty good investigator and you pretty much gave up. You thought they were dead, so knowing their names wasn't going to change that."

"Why did I think they were dead?"

Savvy shrugged. "I don't know. Maybe because thinking your parents abandoned you is more painful than knowing they are dead?"

"Still abandoned," I said softly, taking another sip of whisky.

Savannah leaned toward me. "What was that?"

"I just said, either way, I was still abandoned, intentionally or not." That explained the hollow heartache that troubled me, the throbbing wound of loneliness.

Savvy scooped up some pretzels and used her upturned palm as a bowl. "Next question?"

"What's the earliest thing you know about me?"

"That you were in some kind of adoption program. But it didn't work out, and finally Madame Copperfield found you. You didn't like to talk about it. You loved the school, though. I used to be a sullen thing and you were always making me feel better about things. I think that the Copperfield Institute was the best thing that had ever happened to you."

"So we met there, and became friends."

"On the first day," said Savannah. "We were both in the witch group. I was this spoiled rich girl and you were the orphan. Perfect match. You weren't the only orphan, of course. Copperfield's always taking them in, sometimes by force. Giving them hot showers and surnames."

"Surnames?"

"Everyone has to have a family name," she said.

"So, Rook isn't my real name," I said. It was the first time it had occurred to me, and it shook me a little bit. My name was one of the things I had latched on to as a fact, as a foundation, but then I realized my name was as illusory as my childhood. It may have been the effect of the alcohol, but I felt like I was walking on shifting sand.

"Don't take it too personally," said Savannah, crunching down on some roasted almonds. "Having a Copperfield name is actually an advantage. Everyone who hears it immediately knows you went to the best magical academy on the continent. Pawn, Bishop, Knight—you're all seen as special."

"What happened after we graduated?"

"I joined my father's business, by which I mean that I got a nice salary every month to do 'yoga' and watch Netflix, and you got a real job. A job that made a difference. I got expelled from the coven, and you became their darling because everyone knows that no one can crack a curse like Asha Rook."

"I wish I knew how to do that now," I said.

"What? Break a curse? It's easy."

"It's easy?"

"Not really," said Savvy, "but you always made it look easy. I'm sure you'll be able to do it again."

"I hope so. The high priestess asked me to help with a case, but I refused."

Savannah's eyes flew open. "You refused Soleil?" She whistled in an amused way, then chuckled into her glass. "Well, now. Things are getting interesting."

"How could I help? I'm completely clueless about curses. About everything! I wouldn't know a wand from a tree branch."

"This is Dark Arts 101, Rook. There are a couple of ways to break a curse. Potions help. You're good at those, too, by the way. You were brilliant at potions at school. Then, if magic doesn't work, you need to kill the curser."

The cinnawhisky launched itself out of my nose and I choked as it burned my sinuses. "Excuse me?"

Savannah didn't seem to even notice that I had almost drowned in my whisky, and not in a good way.

"For stubborn curses," she reiterated. "You need to kill the person who set the curse in the first place."

"Kill," I said. I wanted to be clear.

She nodded as if it were no big deal.

I lowered my voice. "You're saying I used to kill people."

"Oh," Savvy said, smiling. "It didn't happen often. It was the exception more than the rule."

"But I used to kill people," I said.

"Only bad ones. Only those who had it coming. It's a really important job—to restore balance to the Realm."

I reeled so hard that I felt dizzy. I looked at the amber liquid in my tumbler and decided I wouldn't drink any more. The night was surreal enough as it was. Immediately after deciding that, I poured the rest of the fiery drink down my throat. If this was all true, I was going to need all the sustenance I could get.

CHAPTER 28

THE GRAVITRON

ASHA

After Savannah left I crawled into bed, my head filled with slurs and stars. I didn't know what had possessed me to drink so much, but I was certainly going to be paying for it in the near future. Perhaps drinking too much whisky while recovering from a cranial trauma was not the most responsible thing I've ever done. All that said, it was truly wonderful to be able to relax in the company of a friend. It was a gift to know that I had a confidant: I had begun to think that I was alone in the world, but Savannah and even Morgan, Merlin, Armstrong, and the coven had made me realize that I did indeed have people who cared about me. It was no small thing.

As the ceiling spun I tried to figure out what to do next. First on my list in the morning was to call the Scorpion HQ. Deep down, I knew I had to help Morgan. When Savannah—three sheets to the wind and half an hour late to relieve her babysitter—had shown me Instagram snaps of Abigail, her fourteen-year-old daughter, I knew I wouldn't be able to ignore the missing children case any longer. Savvy's daughter looked so innocent, so trusting, it touched something deep inside me and I knew I wouldn't be able to live with myself if I didn't work the case.

Abigail loves you so much, Savvy had said, her eyes shining. *She's been missing you terribly. She calls you her witch godmother. She says who needs fairies when you have a witch in your corner.*

It had been so wonderful getting to know Savvy again. I could see why we were friends. She was cheeky and funny. Despite the great hair and nails, she was authentic and down-to-earth. On the way out, after midnight, she had recognized my pink leopard-print leggings.

"Those are my yoga pants!" she said, and laughed her head off, as if I had told her the best joke of the year. It was then I worked out who the owner of the pink toothbrush was. It was clear that my BFF liked her booze, so it naturally followed that she would sleep over after some Frolic sessions. As it was, I had put a bottle of water into her hands and waved her and the Uber driver off.

～

Of course, if I was going to help the Scorpions, then I would have to help the Starfall coven, too.

I'll help them, I thought, closing my eyes against the spinning ceiling, which reminded me of that amusement park ride where the G-force sticks you to the wall and the floor drops away. The Gravitron. *Of course I will. I'll do what I can to keep people safe, because that's the right thing to do.*

Pictures whirled in my head. The shots of the young girls who were missing. Morgan's red stilettos. Gnrok's blue-veined skin. Then I stopped on something terrifying: the golden tattoo of the wizard who had almost killed me with his voltage spell. A twinkling scythe just behind his ear. I knew instinctively that it was the mark of the Dusk Reapers, and my body suddenly felt cold. I tried to wrestle my thoughts back to Soleil and Morgan.

I'll help them, I thought, *but who will help me?*

CHAPTER 29

NEON NIGHTMARES

NICKY

I woke up to a nightmare.

My pelvis was frozen, trapped in something. My wrists were tied to the stretcher with thick leather straps like something out of a Victorian madhouse. The room was bare and dim. I tried to shift my weight to dispel the numbness in my back, but my spine screeched in pain. I was breathless with the agony.

When the shrill sensation subsided, my thoughts were allowed to surface. I couldn't figure out where I was, or how I had gotten there. And then the memories bobbed up, too. Terrible memories like neon nightmares.

No, I thought to myself. *Nooooo.*

I watched as I hovered above my own body, a body I recognized; actions I did not. I looked on as I stood right in the middle of nighttime traffic and got smashed by a car. I stood up and kept going. I made it to the bridge. I was about to jump, but a man stopped me. A man with a kind face. Someone's son, someone's father. He tried to save my life. Then ... a skirmish. I wish I could close my eyes to it. The body I hovered above reached for the police officer's gun and shot him at point-blank range.

I screamed and screamed, because I knew it was all true. I could feel the dull destruction the car had wrought in my fractured pelvis. I could feel my heart beating, a heart that had surely turned black. I thrashed against my restraints, bringing wave after wave of pain shuttling and swirling through my body.

I wanted to die.

I wished I had jumped off that bridge after all.

CHAPTER 30

PLECTRANTHIL CAPIOLA

ASHA

The doorbell rang, fishing me out of a stress-dream I was glad to escape. The sun shone, bright and hot, without mercy. I couldn't remember exactly what was making me feel anxious in the dream, but my face was shiny with perspiration and my brain throbbed. I tried to swallow the imaginary sandpaper in my throat, which was as dry as a desert mirage. Rubbed-off mascara trailed under my eyes, enhancing the dark moons there. All in all, it wasn't a great look, and I certainly was in no mood to open the door for whoever was ringing the bell. I ignored the second ring, hoping the person would give up and leave. I closed my eyes, willing myself to go back to sleep till I felt human again, but then I jumped in fright when a different ringing sounded right next to the bed.

Confused, I bolted out of bed, looking for the source of the unfamiliar chime. A blue light shone through the bag on the floor. Of course, it was the phone that Merlin had brought for me. I fished the device out and answered it.

"Hello?"

"Good morning, sunshine," came a warm, happy voice. "Did I wake you?"

"No," I automatically fibbed, and then wondered why.

"I brought coffee," he said. I tiptoed over to the window and looked through the blinds. There he was, white beard and mushroom hat, holding up two paper cups from the local café —the one Morgan had shown me in the photos. He really did seem to know me well. His Hawaiian shirt flapped in the breeze as he waited.

"I'll buzz you in," I said.

I splashed some cold water over my face, brushed my teeth, and quickly pulled on some jeans and a T-shirt before meeting him in the kitchen. He handed me a nut milk cappuccino and I wanted to hug him. His eyes twinkled behind his funny round glasses, and he looked happy with himself.

"How did you know?" I asked, gesturing at the coffee.

"Well, it's Wednesday, right?"

I looked at him for further explanation.

"And you always have drinks with Savannah on Tuesday nights."

"Right!" I said, placing my cool fingers on my temples to ease the ache. "I wish you had warned me how much that woman can drink. She's a force of nature."

"*Plectranthil capiola*," said Merlin. "You have some in your tea cupboard."

I did a quick search and found a couple of jars containing small dried mushrooms with long stems. One of them was labelled Plec Cap. When I showed it to Merlin, he smiled and nodded. "Home grown!" he said, approvingly. "Just take one. Chew it. Wash it down with coffee. You'll love me forever."

The fungi was woody and tasted of soil and dehydrated mushroom soup. I scrunched up my face when I chewed it. We sat down at the kitchen counter with our coffees while my hangover receded.

He became earnest again, and stared at me over his cup. "I'll teach you," he said.

"What was that?"

"I'll teach you about mushrooms, like I used to. I'll teach you all over again. I don't mind."

"I can't ask you to do that," I said. It was way too generous. The man had already bought me a phone, a coffee, and magically made my headache disappear.

"I know a bit about herbs, too," he said. "Plant medicine. I'll teach you what I know so that you can get back to making your famous potions. You have all the books you need, I'll just help you on the practical side. I'll remind you about the difference between a mushroom that can harm and one that can heal. It's a beautiful world out there."

I guessed it would be pretty dangerous trying to navigate the tea cupboard, potion room, and wild garden without someone who knew his stuff. I wouldn't want to inadvertently poison someone I was trying to help.

"What do you know about curses?" I asked.

His eyes lit up. "I thought you'd never ask."

"The most important thing," he said, "is finding out who initiated the curse. What kind of magic did they use? What instrument? What was the aim of the curse, and what was the outcome? Sometimes, depending on the curser, these things are very different. If there was a potion, you can make an antidote. If it's a mind-tangling spell, you can break the web. If it's an unwanted transformation, you can reverse the magic. Of course, killing the curser will always reliably break the curse, but manslaughter is generally frowned upon." He beamed at me, his smile brighter than his shirt.

"So, I find out who the curser is," I said. "I start asking questions. Then I decide how to break it."

"Of course, that would be a dangerous position to be in, so it would be best to find out without the magical folk knowing."

"Not so easy," I said.

"Oh," he chuckled. "It's never *easy*. But you are smart, and brave, and you know your stuff—"

"*Knew* my stuff," I said. "Past tense."

"You *knew* your stuff," he said. "And soon you'll be up to speed again. You'll re-learn your potions, your green magic, and your fighting skills. And you'll be a force to be reckoned with, just like before."

I thought of how I had fought off the wizard outside my house the day before. My memory was definitely patchy, but my competence in combat was heartening. My green magic seemed almost up to scratch, but expert potion-making and curse-breaking seemed a long way off.

"You tend to put a lot of faith in me," I said. "I'm not sure it's warranted."

Merlin looked deep into my eyes. "You forget, dear girl, that I know you. And I'll help you get where you need to be." He finished his coffee and picked up his car keys, holding them up to signal he was leaving.

This, I thought. *This is what it feels like to have a dad.*

"Thank you," I said. I felt ridiculously grateful. "You've already been so generous."

"Nonsense!" he exclaimed, walking toward the door. "It's my job! I'm Papa Smurf!"

CHAPTER 31

THE COPPER COG & ALE

ASHA

While I felt comforted by Merlin's visit and generous offer to help, I still felt unsettled. It probably had something to do with the fact that I seemed to be near the top of a supernatural hit list. I fed the hens and the cats, filled up their water, and hit the road with my helmet on. I didn't know where I was going, but my Wasp did. I let my scooter decide the way, and soon I was in a part of town that seemed vaguely familiar, but I wouldn't be able to tell you where it was or why it felt like I recognized it. We took a few gentle turns, and then the Wasp turned into a parking lot filled with fruit trees, which immediately made me feel at home.

Beyond the cars parked in the orchard was the most spectacular building. It looked like a steampunk airship. It had gears on the side and back of the hull, moving metal wings, and a great leathery blimp that was lit from the inside. A garland of copper cogs and bolts seemed to keep the thing moving; it looked like it was flying in the air despite not moving an inch. The copper gleamed welcomingly in the sun, and the front door was open. I took off my helmet and made my way up the cobblestone path edged with daisies and foxgloves. There was activity and talking inside the airship, and clinking bottles. When I arrived at the door, I saw the menu on display and realized it was a restaurant. The Copper Cog & Ale was the name, and it seemed like an excellent time to visit. I was hungry, and for some reason my Wasp had wanted to bring me here. I stepped into the orange glow of the interior, and the scent of caramelized cinnamon pumpkin and buttery roasted potatoes pulled me inside.

It was a glorious place. It was toasty and fragrant, heated by a blazing fire in the center of the flagstone floor. Beside the hearth was a mountain of huge hunks of timber, and each table had its own miniature floating fire in the center. It glowed with these flames as well as the vintage lanterns that blazed on every exposed-brick wall, where a multitude of clocks ticked cheerfully, with shiny copper piping vaulted overhead. I stood at the entrance for a while, taking in the ambience and wondering where I should sit. The pub was packed, but there were some open tables. The loudest group was a rage of orcs in the corner. They all had beer tankards the size of their heads—which was quite something—and were tucking into a platter of what looked like roasted T-Rex legs.

They ate with their hands, with great relish, and threw waves of ale down their throats. Adjacent to them sat some strange slimy creatures drinking green milkshakes. They had wet-looking lips and dirty needles for teeth. About half of the clientele looked human, or human-like, and that gave me the courage to go farther into the space, toward the roaring fire in the center. Before I could find a table, I heard my name being shouted, and I looked up in fear. A very short, stocky woman with flaming red hair braided into pigtails and a copper Viking helmet was yelling my name. I froze as the fiery dwarf rushed toward me.

"Asha Viridian Rook!" she scolded. "How dare you. How very dare you!" She was wearing jeans and had a tea towel draped over her shoulder, as all good pub owners do.

"Sorry?" I said.

"You will be sorry, indeed," she said, and almost flattened me with a hug. She may have been small, but she was as strong as her helmet suggested. She squeezed all the air out of me, then squeezed some more. When she finally let go, I dragged new air into my lungs and found myself glad that the horns hadn't accidentally impaled me.

"I—"

I what? I don't know who you are? My sentient scooter led me here?

"I'm sorry," I said. I decided to cut to the chase. "I don't know who you are, but I know I wanted to come here. I'm still figuring things out."

"Of course you are!" she yelled. "You poor wee thing."

I frowned.

"Asha, dear, I hear everything here. This grapevine is more reliable than CNN, and a lot more entertaining. If you spent a day here pulling lagers and wiping up spilled stout, you'd learn everything you needed to know about the Realm."

I had to admit, it sounded oddly appealing.

"Now, don't you dare sit at that table," the dwarf said. "Come sit at the bar. I have two hundred purple-pearled oysters to shuck and I want to know everything."

I followed the miniature Viking to the bolted copper counter where the beer taps were, and perched on a barstool while she climbed up her steps to be on my level, and took up her oyster knife. I could smell the ocean water on the shells, and the tang of the just-sliced lemons. The dwarf expertly worked her knife into the palm-sized shell, prizing it open and then loosening the creature within. I looked around the bar, noticing the vintage posters, framed on the walls, and the bowls of pentacle-shaped pretzels.

"Ei-LEEN!" she yelled toward the kitchen door, and a young girl who looked almost identical to her came scuttling in.

"Pour Asha here a porter, please, Skunk. And tell Barrigog to prepare Asha's favorite."

The girl went about her business with the same cheer her mother did. Picking up a glass, holding it up to the lantern to make sure it was clean, drawing a dark beer, and serving it on a gold coaster, all in less time it would have taken me to walk around the counter.

"Thank you!" I called, as she shot back through the kitchen door. I took a long and grateful sip of the porter, which was delicious. Vanilla, coffee, velvet. It was downright magical. No wonder this place was so packed. My eye caught a board hanging askew on the back wall.

Your server today is: FERRA

I looked at the dwarf again, still trying to gain my bearings. She returned my gaze, even as her knife glimmered as she worked.

"You're too thin," she said, finishing with one tray and beginning on the next. She wasn't kidding about the two hundred oysters she needed to prepare.

I shrugged. "I haven't been hungry," I said. "Since ... you know."

"Don't you worry, my snapdragon," she said. "We'll fix you up. Barrigog knows exactly what you like."

"So, I'm a … regular?" I hated asking these stupid questions and felt impatient to get my memory back.

"Of course you are!" Ferra laughed, and then stopped and looked quite sad. "You poor thing."

"Oh, I'll be okay," I said, sounding more certain than I felt. "My doctor said it'll all come back to me."

"Och, well, that's good news."

Eileen, the child apparently known as "Skunk," brought out a steaming plate of food and placed it in front of me, along with some bronze-colored cutlery and a linen napkin. I thanked her and she wiped her hands on her apron and curtsied. I looked down at the food and felt properly hungry for the first time since I woke up in that ICU room. The golden potatoes and pumpkin I had smelled earlier were there on my plate, plus a generous serving of sweet potato wedges with parmesan and black pepper. The main dish was a burger with salsa and avocado. What could I say? Pre-head-trauma-me really liked her carbs. I tucked in while I watched Ferra work. Every bite was beautiful. I noticed the burger was made from black beans.

"I'm vegetarian?" I asked.

The orc who had come up to the bar to place an order backed away slowly, as if I had said something truly shocking and offensive.

Ferra leaned in. "Vegan," she whispered, making sure that no one else in the pub overheard.

I frowned. "Vegan?"

"Apart from the hen's eggs, of course," said Ferra, finishing up with the last tray of oysters and wiping her knife before snapping it closed and sliding it into her apron pocket. "You eat eggs as long as they come from your coop. But apart from that, you're a bit strict. Mostly you just eat from your garden. The Void knows that you broke my heart when you told me you couldn't eat my famous roast chicken anymore, but there you go. Now Barrigog loves trying new recipes for you."

I let that sink in.

Ferra looked from left to right before whispering again. "No dairy. Not even chocolate."

As if on cue, Eileen burst through the kitchen door and delivered yet another plate—a bowl of white frozen dessert with toasted pistachios on top.

Ferra winked at me. "No animals were harmed in the making of that coconut sorbet."

After I had eaten, Ferra spun an oat-milk cappuccino my way. While I was drinking it, I felt someone enter the pub, and I turned to look. A strong, slender woman in a leather trench coat strode in, shaking her red hair back. She smiled and waved at Ferra, who beamed back at her. The woman immediately saw the person she was looking for and joined a table where an extremely handsome man sat. He stood, put his hand on her lower back, and kissed her on the cheek.

"Who is that?" I asked. The room had quietened suddenly, so I wondered if she was famous. They certainly looked like celebrities.

"That's Jinx!" said Ferra. "You'll know her as Jax, or Jaquelyn Denna Knight. Vampire killer, Void protector, and overall Savior of the Realm."

"She's got great hair," I said.

Ferra chuckled. "She does, doesn't she? Also, none of us would be here today if it weren't for her."

I wondered what I had done to join the fight against Baldassare's vampire cult and the Hammerskins to save the Realm. It gave me renewed motivation to help on all the cases I'd been briefed on. I thought about that for a while as I finished my coffee, which was just as good as the food had been. No wonder the Copper Cog did such roaring trade.

"I'll introduce you sometime," said Ferra. "To Jinxie. I have the feeling you two will get on."

I doubted we had one thing in common, and I felt out of my league just sharing the same air with her.

"In fact, you must have just missed each other at school. She's a couple years older than you."

I stopped spooning the foam out of my still-warm mug. "What now?"

"You both went to the Copperfield Institute, didn't you?"

"Knight went to Copperfield?" I asked, but before the words were out of my mouth I understood, by the virtue of her last name, that not only did she attend Copperfield, but she must have been an orphan, like me.

"I used to be the matron there," said Ferra. "I used to love the children, but you ferals were my favorite."

First I was an orphan, now it had devolved to "feral."

"Jax was a feral, too, you know. You two really do have a lot in common."

I turned to look at Knight again. She was deep in conversation with her partner, and I envied what looked like an intensely intimate relationship.

Ferra's eyes misted over as she chopped parsley without looking down at the glinting blade, making me nervous. "I squirreled away my salary for years to build this place," she said, smiling widely. I watched her hands work automatically, cutting the fragrant herb. "And here we are."

Ferra was the third person in two days to mention the Copper-field Institute, so I took that as a sign. If I wanted to learn about my circumstances before I was accepted by the school, it seemed like a good place to start. I wondered why I had the desire to begin looking for my parents now, when I had clearly given up years ago. It seemed a doomed mission from the outset, but I had a strong gut feeling that if I wanted to find out who I was, I had to start with them.

From being in a coma a few days before, to having three investigations on the go, there was no time to waste. Best I got cracking. I smiled at Ferra and asked for the bill.

"Coddlewonks," said the red-haired dwarf. "Your money is no good here. Now off with you, and don't be a stranger."

I wouldn't take no for an answer. Not after how warm and welcoming she was, and how sustaining and delicious the food had been. "Of course I'm going to pay," I said. "I'll sneak it in, somehow."

"You do that," Ferra replied, flinging a clean tea towel over her shoulder and getting ready to tackle her next task. She winked at me. "I'll be here, waiting."

CHAPTER 32
A MAZE OF GLOOM
NICKY

It was the middle of the night the next time I saw the nurse. Sister Devka let herself quietly into my room and motioned for me to get into the wheelchair. Groggy from sleep and painkillers, I rubbed my eyes, then she helped me out of bed and into the chair. She let off the brake and pushed me forward, out the door, gliding almost silently through the building. The corridors were dark and empty—a maze of gloom. We wound our way around, following the beam of Devka's flashlight, passing many other cells that looked like mine. My hip bones ached, and a part of me wished that I had stayed in bed under the welcome hypnotic trance the drugs afforded me. When we arrived, she slowed and stopped, her fingers swooping to her chest for her access card, then used it to open a door with glass panels. She put her flashlight on the desk, facing the old landline phone.

"Make it quick," she said.

I rolled forward and snatched the receiver, dialing our home number. While it rang, my eyes searched the room. It looked like a small reception area, and the Riverside logo was printed on the desk pad before me. The phone rang and rang.

"He's not picking up," I said. *Where could he be?* It was the middle of the night.

"Deep sleeper?" asked the nurse optimistically.

"Not usually," I said. But maybe he had taken something to help him sleep. *It can't be easy to rest when your wife is locked up in a bloody lunatic asylum.* Or maybe he was somewhere else.

The nurse looked down at her wristwatch. "Try his cell phone?"

I dialed Derek's mobile. It went straight to voicemail.

"It's off," I said, disappointed.

"Never mind," said Devka. "We'll try again another time."

She pushed me back to my room, my heart heavy. With every revolution of the gray rubber wheels, I understood that a phone call with Derek wouldn't actually solve any of my problems. If Derek had wanted to see me, he would have visited by now. The flashlight swept the scuffed linoleum floors, the chipboard ceiling panels, the heavy security doors. This was my new normal. The prison bars were now my reality. I felt cold imaginary hands on my neck, ready to choke me.

"Why are you being so nice to me?" I asked.

"It's my job," she replied, opening and then locking the security gate separating the cells from the administration offices. "You'll soon see that this is a terrible place to be."

The cold fingers traveled to my heart and compressed it. We spent the rest of the trip in silence.

When we arrived at my cell, Devka helped me out of the chair and back into the cot.

"Then why work here? If it's so terrible?"

"If I didn't, who would look after people like you?"

"People like me?"

What did she mean?

Middle-class white women?

People who weren't insane?

People who weren't serial criminals?

She looked at me with her large brown eyes. "People who don't survive places like this."

I felt my body wilt.

"You're going to start mixing with the general population soon."

I gulped. "I don't want to."

"I tried to keep you isolated for as long as I could, but they don't want you getting special treatment. It looks bad."

I knew what she meant. I was wealthy, and white. It wasn't fair to the others if I received what looked like a superior position.

"I'm scared," I said.

"The most dangerous patients are locked away. You'll never see them."

"And the others?"

The nurse clenched her jaw, making the hairs on the back of my neck stand up.

"You'll need to watch your back."

CHAPTER 33
RUSTY R.I.P.
ASHA

The ride across town on my Wasp felt refreshing after being in the warm pub. I watched the trees and clouds with a new sense of optimism. Now that I had a purpose, life seemed to have more color. Mixed feelings bubbled in my stomach as I slowed to pull into the entrance of the Copperfield Institute. Technically, I didn't recognize the handsome white wall that stretched ten feet into the sky and infinitely across, but deep down I felt it was familiar, like a slippery sense of *déjà vu*. It was an understated entrance for what is regarded as the most accomplished magical school on the continent. A large, handsome electric gate truncated the high walls that glittered in the noon light. A werewolf stood guard in a smart black uniform, sleeves rolled up, his soft ombré fur moving ever so slightly in the breeze. I took off my helmet, and he scrutinized me with his beautiful lupine eyes. I felt a connection to him, but I didn't know why.

He searched the digital screen in his hand. "Name?" His voice came in soft, unlabored panting.

"I don't have an appointment," I said.

"That's a shame," breathed the handsome wolf. "Come back when you do."

I stood there for a while, thinking of what to do. "This isn't how I remember it," I half-fibbed.

"You're an alumna?" he asked.

I nodded.

He flipped the cover back on his tablet and tucked it into his utility belt. "Life wasn't as dangerous, then," he said. "We took a hit last year, when the Hammerskins invaded. Things were lost. We've had to upgrade the security." He looked back at his guard hut, and when I followed his gaze, I saw the large smooth stone on the ground there, painted with the words Rusty R.I.P.

I blinked in shock. "I'm sorry." I didn't know who or why anyone would kill a security guard to break into the school. "I'm sorry to have just arrived like this. I had no idea." I had no idea about a lot of things. The Void Fracture had been a near catastrophe.

The wolf's whiskers wavered. "You said you're alumna?"

"Yes," I replied, "Asha Rook."

But I was put off my plan now. My questions seemed insignificant compared to what the school had recently been through, and I felt bad enough reminding this guard of what awful things he had seen, never mind disturbing the headmistress of the school. "But don't worry, I'll call ahead next time." I was about to put my helmet back on when he motioned for me to wait. He loped to the hut and spoke into a two-way radio. His teeth were sharp, his lips shiny and black. He craned his neck to listen to the reply. All I heard was static, but I guess wolves have, amongst other things, a superior sense of hearing. He nodded and replaced the walkie-talkie, then reached for his tablet again and scribbled something on the screen. He held it up, took a photo of me, then stuck a tracking pixel on my arm. The huge gate rolled open, and the werewolf bowed. "Welcome, Ms. Rook," he said. "You can go straight to Directress Copperfield's office."

I waved thank you and revved my scooter as I whizzed through the entrance and up the long, paved driveway until I came to the giant jacaranda tree that stood before the administration offices. It was full of purple blossoms, and there was a carpet of spent blooms on the ground below. Bees buzzed happily around their sweet-scented payday feast.

"Asha," called a voice from within the building. I looked up and saw a handsome woman with long gray braids step through the arched ingress. They were clipped back with metallic clasps that glimmered as they caught the light. Her cloak was white, edged with copper, and when she smiled at me, I couldn't believe it was Directress Copperfield. I had read that she was eighty or ninety, but her smooth, dark skin didn't look a day over thirty.

"Good afternoon, Directress," I said. I felt like a schoolgirl again.

"Please," she said, "come in." She swept me through the shaded passage, along the hallway decorated with snoring portraits, and into her grand office. Her ebony desk was unnervingly tidy, but the dappled light coming in from the large windows, fluttering on the polished pinewood floors, made the room less intimidating. She gestured for me to take a seat, and she leaned against the front of her desk, facing me.

"Asha," she said again. "I'm so very glad you have recovered."

"My body has healed," I said. "I haven't been as lucky with my memory."

"I have no doubt that it will be restored," she said, which made me feel better. Hope swelled in my chest.

"Funny that you decided to visit today," she continued. "I was going to put in a call to you."

What now?

"I was going to wait a few days. Give you time to recuperate. But I do think you're looking very healthy."

I stroked the scar on my head, but it was almost gone. "You were going to call me?"

She took a breath and smiled, playing with the charm on the silver chain around her neck, zipping it right to left, left to right, then pressing it to her lips and dropping it. "Sometimes I call on my trusted alumni to assist with certain ... challenges we face in the Realm."

"Like last year," I ventured. "The Void Fracture."

"Exactly."

I thought of seeing Jaquelyn Knight earlier, in the Copper Cog, and wondered why Copperfield hadn't called on her. As if reading my mind, the headmistress said: "Ms. Knight is not available to work on this particular case. She is taking care of something else at present. Something extremely precious and delicate."

I nodded for her to go on.

"The Council is deeply concerned," Directress Copperfield began, "about the abduction of female children in the Realm."

"Yes," I said. "Captain Morgan told me about the case."

"While I have unreserved respect for the Scorpion task force, I don't think they are taking this seriously enough, nor does the Council."

"It's their top priority," I said, feeling as if I had to defend Morgan.

"I don't doubt their commitment or efficiency," said Copperfield. "I have seen the captain in action. I just think we need more hands on deck." Her voice changed then. It sounded more emotional. "Girls are now going missing every single day. We can't let this happen."

"Of course not," I said, thinking of Savannah's daughter. My doubts about my proficiency fell away. "I'll do what I can."

"Thank you," said the headmistress, and walked around her desk to sit in her chair. She rubbed her temples, then smiled at me. "You were always a kind girl. Our beginning was a bit rough, but once you settled in, you were a wonderful witch."

I sat forward on the chair, ears pricking up. This was why I had come, after all. "Why was the beginning rough?"

Directress Copperfield chuckled. She seemed more relaxed now that I had agreed to help. "You were ... unusual. Some teachers described you as *wild*." Amused, she stood up again and looked for a file in the metal cabinet in the corner of the room, pulling out a blue folder. She opened it and searched the pages. "Ah, here we go. *Asha Viridian is a tempestuous wildling,* said one teacher. *She refuses to bathe or shower, and squeezes all the toothpaste out of the tube. She climbs onto the roof at night and howls at the moon.*"

I scoffed. "You're joking."

Copperfield's eyes twinkled with mirth. "Not joking."

My cheeks flamed.

She brought the file over and sat on her desk again. "*The Rook child is rude and unmanageable,* said another teacher. *She is a disruption. I refuse to have her in my class. I recommend further psychological evaluation and treatment.*"

"What?" Being wild was one thing, but psychological treatment?

"Don't worry," whispered Copperfield. "I fired her. I don't approve of teachers calling children *disruptions.*"

"But ... psychological evaluation? Was there—is there—something wrong with me?"

The directress shook her head vehemently. "No, Asha. You just had a difficult start in life. We got you through it."

"Ferra Fornak, from The Copper Cog & Ale, described me as feral."

"I suppose you were," she said. "I've always had a soft spot for children like you. Miss Fornak felt the same way. She was forever baking in her spare time and sneaking you and the other orphans extra spice cookies. I turned a blind eye."

I smiled, so very grateful to have a dwarf like Ferra in my life.

"I mean, who could blame you?" asked Copperfield. "Shuttled

from foster home to foster home, destined to fall through the cracks."

Destined to fall through the cracks.

"I was in foster homes?"

"Many," she said. "Too many, until we learned of you and took you in."

"They didn't want me because I was ... badly behaved?"

"Oh, Asha," said the directress tenderly. "You weren't badly behaved. You were just testing your powers. It made the untouched humans nervous, and it threatened the Masquerade. As soon as we learned you were a witch, we took you in."

"Testing my powers," I said, trying to imagine it.

"If I recall correctly, you once set a house on fire."

"No!" I cried, my hands flying up to my mouth.

"Luckily we were already watching you by then and someone stepped in to reverse the spell. Before that you used to spin plates in the air, smash glasses by staring at them, and turn just-landscaped suburban gardens into jungles. You used to scare your poor foster parents out of their wits." She laid the folder down on the table between us. My fingers itched to take it.

"Do you think ..." I ventured. "Do you think that's why my parents abandoned me?"

"Perhaps," said Copperfield, adjusting her stylish bifocals. "I'm afraid I know nothing about your parents or why you parted ways. When the police found you the first time 'round, they guessed your parents had died. From then on we all just went along with that without inquiring into it."

"Could I ... do you think I could look at my file?" I asked.

"Regrettably, that would go against policy," replied the directress, and stood up.

Disappointment cooled my bones. "I understand."

"Now," she announced. "I have to see someone down the hall. I'll be approximately five minutes, so you won't be here when I get back."

"Yes, Directress."

She put an envelope in my hand. "Thank you for agreeing to help us. We'll be in touch."

We said goodbye and I gathered my things. Turning back toward the desk, I saw that the headmistress had left my file behind.

CHAPTER 34
CRACKED PEBBLE
NICKY

A new nurse was on duty, one I didn't recognize. She was taller than Devka, older, and stooped. Gray hair escaped from her hat in untidy loops. My pain medication was wearing off, so I was pleased to see her.

"Hello," I said, sitting up, trying to not groan as the pain in my pelvis flared. Her name badge said SR INGLEBY. "I'm Nicola."

"I know who you are," the nurse said, without making eye contact. She checked on the supplies on the medical cart.

"Of course," I replied. My name was on the door. "I've never seen you before."

The nurse looked at me pointedly, but didn't reply.

"I appreciate everything your profession does."

"Well, don't think you'll be getting any special treatment from me," Ingleby said.

"I don't want special treatment," I fibbed.

The nurse motioned at the wheelchair beside my bed. Her fingers were knobby, the thin skin stretched over the swollen joints. "Get in the chair."

I didn't want to get in the chair. I didn't move. "Where are we going?"

"Ask no questions," said the woman, "I'll tell no lies."

My instinct told me to stay in bed. "I don't need to bathe today," I said. "And I'm not hungry. I think I'll stay here."

The old woman chuckled in a bitter way, and put her gnarled hand on her hip. "You think you have a say? That's the funniest thing I've heard all week. You're not a *guest* here, you know. Your money buys you no privilege here. You're not on vacation. You're a *prisoner,* get it?"

"I just … I just don't feel very well." I gulped down the fear that was rising in my throat. "I'm in pain. I haven't had my painkillers yet."

"No meds for you today," muttered Ingleby.

I felt like she'd thrown a bucket of icy water at me. "What?"

"Doctor's orders."

"Bull," I said through clenched teeth. She was just being sadistic. Of course I needed my meds. I would lose my mind to the pain without them.

"I have broken bones," I told her. "My pelvis is fractured. My organs are bruised. I—"

"Well," said the nurse, in a voice that was so quiet it sounded violent. "Maybe you shouldn't have killed that nice young policeman."

"I—"

"Imagine the pain his family is in. They don't have anything to take their pain away, do they?"

My teeth ground together. "Give it to me," I growled. "Give it to me!"

"Don't you dare speak to me like that," she hissed.

Hot tears sprang to my eyes. My body was blazing at the idea that it would get no relief. I couldn't imagine a whole day like this, and this was just the beginning.

"I demand to see the doctor," I said, swiping at the tears running down my cheeks.

"Really?" the nurse said, a thin smile on her dry lips. "That can certainly be arranged."

Refusing the awful nurse's assistance, shaking and sweating, I gingerly made my way from the bed into the wheelchair. She stood and watched with crossed arms as my skin turned pale and slick. After my breathing returned to normal, I tried again. "It doesn't have to be the strong painkiller Devka usually gives me," I ventured. "I'd be grateful even for some anti-inflammatories. Or paracetamol."

"We'll see how you behave," Ingleby sniped.

"Yes, sister," I replied. I would be good, I promised myself. I would do everything the nurse asked. Making her cross was just going to hurt me more. I wanted to ask when Devka would be back, but didn't want to anger her further.

She wheeled me down the gray corridor I was becoming familiar with, and into a large communal bathroom. Large white tiles grouted with black mold and rust covered every surface. There were no mirrors on the walls, presumably due to safety precautions. I knew I'd certainly be tempted to smash the glass and use it as a weapon. A row of basins lined the wall, and beyond that were showers and baths.

The nurse drew a shallow bath and ordered me to strip. I tried, but was not able. Her nostrils flared in contempt, then she roughly pulled my clothes off, sending wave after wave of pain rippling through my body. Eventually I was naked, every goosebump on display, as I lowered myself into the cool water. I had hoped for a bit of warmth to ease the ache, but Sister Ingleby clearly thought that would be overly indulgent. She watched as I shivered.

"Clean yourself," she said. "Or did you think I was going to do that for you, too?"

I bit my tongue and reached for the cracked pebble of soap.

"I'll be back in five minutes to get you out," she said, and left without closing the door.

I washed myself as well as I was able. The shivering became exaggerated so I turned on the hot tap, hoping Ingleby wouldn't catch me doing it, and was disappointed to find the water was hardly lukewarm. I turned it off again and waited, trying to stop my body from shaking. I was sure she'd be back soon to help me out. I lay back and closed my eyes, trying to disassociate from the ache that had pooled in my limbs. I counted to one hundred and then backwards to zero, then to two hundred, then three. Eventually I heard a movement behind me, and I opened my eyes.

I gasped and covered my private parts, but most of my body was still on show to the man who was standing next to me.

"Get out," I said, but my voice seemed small and unconvincing.

He smiled and waved away my shock. "Don't worry about that," he said, not averting his eyes. "I've seen plenty of naked women in my time." Then he added: "I'm a doctor."

I craned my neck, searching for Ingleby. "I don't think you should be in here."

"Looking for the nurse? I told her I'd let her know when we were done."

My teeth chattered. "I'm not comfortable. I want you to leave."

"Don't worry," he repeated, sweeping his eyes slowly over my entire body from my toes to my eyes. "It's not like I'm in here for thrills."

I had never thought of myself as a violent woman. I had never hurt anyone physically before the incident that put me in there. But at that moment I became so furious that I wanted to scratch the doctor's eyes out. I wished I could punch him in his smug and condescending face. Instead, I lay in the cold water, still covering the parts of my body that I could, and tried to tone down my quaking.

"I just came to introduce myself," he said.

He didn't acknowledge what an odd time and place it was to make an introduction. I wondered if he did this to all his patients—a patronizing power trip to signal who was in charge.

"I'm Doctor Adrathar."

It struck me as an unusual name, and I didn't think he looked like a doctor. He had dark hair and a matching beard, and wore a charcoal-colored lab coat.

"We'll be starting therapy today," he said.

My limbs felt colder still.

"Physical therapy?" I asked.

"No," he replied, smiling. "I'm not that kind of doctor."

CHAPTER 35
SMACK
NICKY

It was a relief to get dressed at last. Ingleby gave me what was to be my uniform for the foreseeable future: chunky white underwear and gray flannel sweats. Still feeling vulnerable after Doctor Adrathar scrutinized me in the bath, I was grateful for the warmth and modesty the fabric offered. I hoped that I could climb into bed and warm up, but the nurse had other plans for me. I didn't want to anger her, but my body was exhausted from the pain and the shivering.

"Please," I begged. "I need to rest."

The nurse's mouth was a hard line. "You know what they say about rest for the wicked."

I closed my eyes and inhaled. I didn't know if I had the strength to get through this day. I longed for Devka to be back on duty.

"It's breakfast time," said the nurse.

"I'm not hungry."

"It's breakfast time," she said again, louder. "And it's time to meet your fellow patients."

"I don't want to," I said.

"Of course you don't want to," sneered Ingleby. "Because you think you're better than them."

The truth echoed in the room. "Once you realize you're one of them, your stay here will become easier."

Once I accept that I'm criminally insane? I couldn't see that happening.

"Get back in the chair," she commanded, and I began to weep.

The nurse forcibly pushed me along in the wheelchair, bumping into corners and doors every now and then as punishment for my stubbornness and tears.

"You're weak," she muttered to me, her swollen knuckles glaring as she gripped the handles. "You're despicable."

She said it so softly, I wondered if it was my imagination. I couldn't decide which was worse: to be called despicable by such a terrible person, or to be leaning toward crazy and imagining the insults.

"You're revolting," I thought I heard her say.

I didn't want the other inmates to see me crying, but I couldn't stop. I knew I was being weak, just as Ingleby had said, but I just couldn't accept that this was now my life: pain, humiliation, suffering. I realized without a doubt that I'd rather be dead. I made a mental note to search for a knife in the dining room. Even a regular butter knife would do. What it lacked in sharpness I would make up for in force.

The small dining room smelled like rancid cheese and oatmeal, and I felt my stomach contract. I was sure I'd vomit if I put anything in my mouth. Ingleby parked me at an empty table covered in a yellow plastic sheet and strode to the kitchen hatch to collect food. I kept my shoulders rounded and eyes downcast, not wanting to cause trouble.

"Psst!" someone hissed. I ignored them. "Pssssst!"

I kept my gaze on the yellow plastic. I was beginning to perspire again. A plastic fork skittered across my vision, and I watched it land just to the left of me.

"Hey!" said the owner of the fork.

I looked up. A young woman grinned at me. She had blue eyes, freckles, and long dark hair in a middle part.

"Hi, newbie," she said, waving. "Don't be shy."

I gave her a superficial smile. I didn't want to be friends, but I also didn't want to make enemies of crazy people and end up with a plastic fork in my back.

"Hi," I whispered back.

"I see you've got the old battle-axe today," said the woman next to her, motioning at Ingleby with her eyes. "Bad luck."

"Tell me about it," I said. "She won't even give me my pain medication."

The women looked pointedly at my wheelchair and then frowned at the nurse, who was chatting with the kitchen staff behind the counter.

"That's not cool," said the young woman, and the other woman nodded and swore. "But Alison and I can get you some."

My ears pricked up. "Some medicine?" I asked.

They both kept their eyes on the nurse while they nodded. "Whatever you like," Alison said. "Cocaine, heroin, tik. Cigarettes, booze, books. Just tell us what you need."

"I need whatever they usually inject me with. Morphine?"

"Pethidine," they said together.

"Pethidine," I repeated. Then I remembered the butter knife. "And sleeping pills. As many as you can get."

Why were these women in here? They seemed sane. As sane as I was, anyway. I quickly scanned the rest of the dining room. The other prisoners all looked sane enough, apart from the woman staring out the barred window and talking to herself.

Another woman glared at me from across the room as if I had mortally offended her. I avoided eye contact.

"Alrighty, newbie," said the older one. "We'll get you your smack."

"I want to pay," I said. I didn't want to owe anyone favors. I'd watched prison movies before. Then I realized I didn't have any money.

The dark-haired prisoner, Fikile, eyed my wedding ring. The casualty staff had taken my engagement ring for safekeeping but left my gold band on. I looked down at it. Derek and I had been happily married for fifteen years. I couldn't remember the last time I had taken it off. I didn't understand why he hadn't come for me, or why he wouldn't answer his phone. My throat swelled, but I blinked back the tears.

"Okay," I said. "Deal."

No matter how much I loved the ring or my husband, the searing pain in the core of my body took precedence. I knew I couldn't live in this kind of agony, so in a way, the ring would be saving my life.

"Good," she said, and they looked pleased. Ingleby had now turned around and was walking back toward us. The women stood to leave.

I wished that I still had my special silver raven necklace. It had been a gift from Derek on our seventh wedding anniversary. It was another item I hardly ever took off. It always seemed to bring me good luck, which I could have done with right then.

"Don't eat the porridge," the older woman murmured. "It's always full of weevils."

Bile surged in my throat. I nodded gratefully and they moved away, taking their empty trays with them. I swallowed the bitterness and urged myself to keep it together. I'd have relief soon. I'd be in less pain. I'd rest. I'd have therapy. Devka would be back on rotation soon. Maybe Derek would find me. Or maybe the court would reconsider my case due to good behavior. I could do it. I could pull through. *Baby steps,* I told myself. *Baby steps.*

The nurse placed a yellow tray in front of me. The cutlery was, as I had guessed, flimsy plastic. There was cold, soggy toast, margarine, and a generous helping of porridge with suspicious brown flecks. I glanced up at Ingleby, and before I could stop myself, I threw up all over her shoes.

CHAPTER 36

GLACIAL

NICKY

Ingleby rushed off to change her shoes and socks, and I couldn't say I was sorry. Of course, the knot in my stomach told me that I would pay for it later, but there was a small part of me that was glad to have revolted in some way. One of the net-haired kitchen staff took over the stewardship of my wheelchair and drove me in silence to a part of the building I'd never seen. She left me in the passageway, outside a door, and scuttled back to the kitchen.

"Where am I?" I called after her, but she didn't reply.

I spent the time staring at the floor, the ceiling, the other doors. Of course, I was in no condition to escape, but I wouldn't always be incapacitated. In the meanwhile, I could formulate a plan.

With no warning, the silver handle next to me twitched suddenly, giving me a fright. Doctor Adrathar darkened the door.

"There you are," he said in a friendly way, as if he were a perfect professional and hadn't intimidated me earlier. "Please, come in."

Dread spilled into every part of my body. I hesitated, then wound my wheels forward, slowly edging my way into his office. I hated the idea of being in there alone with him. Even Ingleby's hateful gaze would have been better than being alone with the doctor. I wondered if I could simply refuse his help and accept whatever punishment ensued, but it was not to be. I heard the lock click closed behind me. My heart began to sprint, and I felt cold all over. I was back in the frigid bath water, and he was trailing his predatory eyes over my skin. The world went blurry.

Doctor Adrathar was clicking his fingers in front of my face. "Earth to Nicola," he said. When I blinked and finally focused on his face, he smiled. "Hello. You disappeared there for a while."

I blinked again and sighed. "Sorry," I said, confused. "I'm not myself."

"Of course you're feeling odd," said the doctor.

I thought it was an incredibly strange thing to say to a patient who was incarcerated for murder and being deprived of pain medication. "Odd" wouldn't have been the word I would have used.

"I haven't been given painkillers today," I said. I could still taste the vomit in my mouth.

"Yes, you have," he said.

"No," I said, my vision blurring again. "Sister Ingleby said no meds. Doctor's orders. You're my doctor."

He smiled at me. "You're confused. You've had your shot. I checked your file."

"You want me to lose my mind," I said. "You know I'm sane, but you want to keep me here. You're trying to make me crazy."

"We don't use the term 'crazy' in here, Mrs. Landau. And I'll tell you why we know that you are, in fact, mentally ill. Sane people do not walk across highways and shoot policemen at point-blank range. You are a danger to society."

"It wasn't me," I said.

He lifted his pen. "It wasn't you?"

"I would never do something like that."

"And yet, you did. We have camera footage and the reports of many eyewitnesses. I've watched it multiple times and there's no mistaking the killer's identity."

"No," I said, covering my face.

"You pulled the trigger like it was nothing to you," said Adrathar. "Your expression was glacial."

I felt despicable then. Just as Ingleby had said. I couldn't help rubbing my face, like a nervous tic. I told myself to lower my hands—to put them in my lap—but they wouldn't obey. On they went, rubbing my cheeks and forehead, like I was trying to erase myself.

"It was my body," I said. "I know that. But my mind was ... I don't know. It was like I was under a spell."

The doctor raised his eyebrows and licked his lips. "Interesting."

"It was like I was hypnotized," I said. "I had no agency over my own body. All I knew was that I had to get onto the bridge and spread the message. The message was the only thing that was important."

"The message?" Adrathar was scribbling in my file.

"I had to tell everyone that death is not the end," I said. "I had to let everyone know."

"Death is not the end?"

"Yes."

"And that's why you were going to jump off the bridge?"

"Yes."

"There's no record of you having prior mental illness," said the doctor. "Or suicidal ideation. Had you ever felt suicidal before this incident?"

"No," I said, shaking my head. I didn't think mentioning my current suicidal thoughts would be a good idea.

"Let's go back to that night," said Adrathar. "Why would you feel the need to spread that message?"

"It felt important at the time," I replied.

"And now?"

"And now it feels empty. The message never came from me, not really. So it's empty."

"Do you believe that there is something after death?"

I shrugged. "I don't know. I don't think so."

"Your tox screen was clear," he said. "So you weren't under the influence of any kind of mind-altering drugs."

"I don't do drugs," I said. At least, I never used to. Now my body was screaming for them.

"How would you explain what happened that night?"

"I can't," I said. "I told you all I know. It was like I was hypno-tized. But it was more than that."

Doctor Adrathar watched me as I spoke. His eyes were cold.

"It's difficult to explain." I shook my head. "Hypnosis refers to consciousness and suggestion, right?"

Adrathar nodded.

"This didn't feel like a small modification of the mind. It was a full-body feeling. A body annexure."

He narrowed his eyes and scratched his jaw. "Your whole body was mesmerized."

"Yes," I answered. "It was like being on puppet strings. I tried to stop it. I couldn't. I didn't know how."

Doctor Adrathar gave me a starched cotton gown to change into, and an adult diaper. "Time for your treatment."

"What is this?" I asked, but he didn't answer. "I need help putting it on."

When he turned to help, I spun my wheels backwards. "A nurse," I said. I thought I could actually manage changing, but I wanted a nurse in the room for whatever the doctor had planned.

He narrowed his eyes again. "The nurses are busy at the moment."

I wanted to argue. I wanted to tell him that we could do the treatment later then, when there was a nurse free, but anxiety flooded my abused body. I needed the pain to stop. I would do anything to make it stop.

"What kind of treatment?" I asked. "Will it help with the pain?"

"It should," he replied.

I slowly wheeled myself behind the partition and sat for a while. I waited, not sure what to do. I didn't want to change. I certainly didn't want any treatment Adrathar wanted to inflict on me, but we both knew that I didn't have a choice in the matter. I began the agonizing process of pulling off my gray sweatsuit and pulling on the thin gown and the diaper.

CHAPTER 37

STRANGE THINGS HAPPEN WHEN SHE IS IN THE ROOM

ASHA

Directress Copperfield had signaled that I had less than five minutes to look through my file before she returned. I grabbed my new phone. I hadn't yet figured out how the camera worked, so I wasted valuable seconds fumbling with the device. Once I figured it out, I snapped pictures of the pages as fast as I could. Phrases stood out, even when I was trying not to read.

Abandoned.

Uncontrollable.

Undernourished.

Dirty.

Had to shave child's hair off due to matting and lice.

Strange things happen when she is in the room.

I had to read that one twice.

I whispered curse words at myself to hurry up, which didn't help. I finally got to the end of the file just as I heard voices in the passage. I neatened up the pages and placed the folder back in the middle of the desk, thanking the directress silently, and stealth-danced out the door. I jumped on my Wasp and accelerated down the long driveway. The black werewolf opened the gate for me and waved as I sped away. It had been an interesting day, indeed.

I was utterly relieved to get home. All I wanted to do was have a bath, wrap myself up in a huge soft blanket, and go to sleep. Remembering the wizard who had attacked me outside my house made me think the garage door wouldn't open. I assumed he had cut some connection. But when I pressed the button on my remote, the door lifted and groaned all the way up. Confused but relieved, I rode in, not seeing the shadow in the corner of the garage.

"Don't get a fright," said a man's voice. The suddenness shocked me, but it was a voice I recognized, so I didn't order the ivy outside to swallow him.

"Armstrong?" I asked.

"Guilty," he replied. He had his toolbox with him.

My heart beat faster than normal. "You fixed the garage door."

"It was nothing," he said. "Easy job."

I was going to ask him how he knew, then remembered that he got an alert from my security company when there was any kind of breach in the system.

"Thank you very much," I said.

Detective Armstrong shrugged it off, then lifted his eyes to look into mine. "You look like you've had quite a day."

My hands flew up to my helmet-shaped hair, my smudged makeup. I felt self-conscious, and stupid for feeling so. What did I care about what this man thought of my appearance? I didn't! But my darkening cheeks insisted otherwise.

"Sorry," he said. "I didn't mean it that way. You just look tired. No! I didn't mean that either. Sorry. I'll be on my way."

"No," I said. "The least I can do is offer you a drink."

He shook his head. "It's not necessary."

"I'd like you to stay." The words were out of my mouth before I had time to think them through. Now he was going to get the wrong idea. "I mean, I learned some things today. We can catch up."

Armstrong blinked at me, then nodded. "Okay," he said. "That sounds good. As long as it's not tea."

I smiled. "What? You don't like old sticks boiled in water?"

"What? No! I love boiled sticks! God, I love them. I'm just in the mood for something less exotic."

We walked through the house and into the kitchen. I began searching for a new bottle of Ferra's cinnawhisky, hoping that Savvy hadn't drained my entire liquor cabinet. I rubbed my neck, which was aching, probably from fighting the wizard earlier.

"I don't want to be presumptuous ..." said the detective.

I spun around, my stomach tingling. I arched my brows at him to go on.

"I'm just wondering if you'd like to have twenty minutes to yourself. To just lie down or take a shower or something. I can keep myself busy. I'll pour drinks and feed the cats. Do a bit of vacuuming."

"Really?"

"Yes. Apart from the vacuuming. I was kidding about that."

"Ha," I said.

"As long as you don't feel weird about it," he said.

"I don't," I said. "If you don't."

"It's settled, then. Be gone. But before you go, tell me what you'd like to drink."

I had a bath. It was quick, but it did the job, easing my sore muscles. My bruises from the morning's battle were already fading. I climbed into fresh clothes: casual linen pants and a T-shirt with floral graphics, and pulled a cardigan around myself. I decided to skip the makeup, but remembered to put on some lip balm, because I'm not a complete slacker. When I arrived downstairs, the kitchen was lit by candlelight, the drinks were on the table, and Armstrong was reading one of the books from my shelf.

"Be careful with those things," I said. "You never know what you'll find in them."

He closed it thoughtfully and looked at me. "Indeed."

I sat down with him, and we clinked glasses. Pretty much every moment since I had woken up from the coma in the hospital had felt surreal, and this was no different. After a day of "yoga," fighting for my life, being abducted, and investigating my childhood, here I sat drinking—by candlelight—with a not-unattractive man who happened to be the cop who had tried to arrest me at said hospital.

"I can't figure you out," I said.

"The feeling is mutual," he replied.

"You tried to arrest me."

"It was a tactic to get you to talk. You killed a man."

I winced. He made me sound cold and vicious. "It was self-defense," I said.

"I know. That's what I put in the report."

"What changed your mind?" I asked. "A few days ago, you were ready to handcuff me."

"That's before I knew you."

"You don't know me," I said. "I don't even know myself."

"Ah," he replied, taking a generous sip of his drink. "But we're both working on that."

CHAPTER 38

A CONSTELLATION OF SCARS

ASHA

That made me remember the photographs on my new phone. I opened the camera album and showed Armstrong the visuals of the documents in the Copperfield file. I had to share it with someone.

"Strange things happen," he repeated, rubbing his jaw slowly, thoughtfully, "when she is in the room."

"Never mind that," I said. "Look here. No birth certificate, no parents, no evidence of a childhood whatsoever, until the police found me that day."

Frustrated, I tossed the phone down. It landed in the middle of the table and spun as if we were playing spin-the-bottle.

Armstrong watched it until it came to a stop, pointing at him. "I'll see what I can find out on my side," he said. "But I'm not promising anything."

"You won't find it," I said.

"Why not?"

"It's not on the official record, as far as I know. It all seems to be shifting shadows."

He reached for the phone and began looking through the snaps again, pinching in and out to read the text, as if he were arranging puzzle pieces in his head. He looked especially handsome in the warm light. "Let's start at the beginning," he said.

I nodded. It would be good to have him talk through the events and details with me. I was supposed to be a good investigator, but the case of my birth and subsequent abandonment overwhelmed me. Like a spider in a web, I was too close to it to see clearly.

Armstrong scratched his head and swiped past a few pictures. "So, the first knowledge the world had of you—as far as we know—was when the Nottingham Road police officers found you in a midlands forest. When I'm at the station tomorrow I'll check that report, see if there's any more information there. Perhaps they would have tried to press charges against your folks. Maybe there'll be something there."

"Thank you," I said.

"So," he continued, rubbing his chin. "The squad alerts social services, who pick you up and take you for the usual checks.

You were in bad shape. Malnourished, wild, generally neglected."

"Not much has changed," I joked, but he didn't laugh. I suppose child neglect wasn't joke-worthy unless you're the child and you're trying to deflect.

"Social services tries to place you with one foster family after another, but none are successful."

I imagined sitting at a lovely dinner table in a cozy home, surrounded by the perfect family. Then all the glasses would start floating in the air and they'd all turn to glare at me, a bruised child of five years old, and I'd be sorry and drop the glasses, accidentally smashing them as they fell, simultaneously ruining dinner and any chance I ever had of having a loving family.

"They said I was spooky," I told Sam. "I was practically feral. They had to shave my hair to get rid of the lice. There was nothing they could do about the scars. So you can imagine that my presence didn't make for easy dinner conversation."

I saw by the look in the detective's eyes that he had seen the page I was referring to, annotated by the medical doctor who had checked me out after I was discovered. The skin on my arms, legs and torso had been covered in small scars of indecipherable origin. No wonder I had decided to get so many tattoos; the beautiful inked flowers flowed over the mysterious cicatrix.

Armstrong rubbed his cheeks and looked at me in a tender way. "How are you not certifiable? After all of that?"

I laughed and downed my drink. "How do you know I'm not?"

His eyes twinkled, and I looked away.

"You end up at this … academy," he said. "They train you in … what?"

"Life skills," I replied. I didn't want to lie to the detective, but I had agreed to preserve the Masquerade. I could tell that this balance was bound to get trickier, especially seeing as I was growing quite fond of the man. Dishonesty is a sure-fire way to disrupt balance. If you add a vibration of lust to the equation, you know you're asking for trouble.

He was amused. "Life skills."

"Yes," I said. "Clearly you don't know me well enough, Detective, or you'd know that I have superior life skills. In fact, my life skills are known to be exceptional."

"I see," he said, swirling his glass as he looked at me. The smile didn't leave his face. I wondered what it would be like to kiss him. "All right. So you graduate, and then what?"

"I don't know," I said. It was partly true. Somewhere between leaving school and being attacked by a Dusk Reaper, I had managed to find a perfect house, adopt two cats and too many chickens, be sworn in by a coven of witches and recruited by the Scorpions, all while growing a perennial food jungle in my back yard and mixing sorcerous potions. He gave me a hard look then, as if he were waiting for me to tell the truth, but I had nothing to offer him.

He exhaled and tapped his fingertips gently on the table, playing a silent piano tune. "Have you ever considered the possibility that you never found your parents because you never wanted to?"

"What?" I replied. "No!"

"I'm just saying, you're intelligent, you're curious, you're committed. If the Asha you were before the accident wanted to find her parents, I'm sure she would have."

"That Asha stopped looking," I said. "She thought they were dead."

"Or maybe she just wanted to think of them as dead, after how they had abandoned her. Maybe she was—you were—happy to leave them in the past."

"You think I'm dredging up unnecessary drama," I said.

Armstrong shrugged. "I don't think anything. I'm just here to ask questions. It's what I do."

"I need to protect myself from the people who are intent on doing me harm," I said. "To do that, I need to figure out who I am, and why they want me dead."

Armstrong watched me for a while, and I returned his gaze. There was no denying the chemistry between us. Eventually, the detective shrugged. "Fair enough. Shall we have another drink?"

Detective Armstrong and I were on our third whisky, and the small amount of awkwardness that had plagued us from the beginning had been replaced by a large dose of craving. I knew it was reciprocal, because the light in his eyes mirrored mine. We wanted each other's company, mind and flesh. The core of my body began sparking with excitement at the idea of pressing myself up against his. I imagined him pulling me into a deep kiss that thrilled my whole body and set my skin alight.

Then I noticed his wedding band, flashing in the low light as if signaling to me that he was out of bounds. Of course he was married. I had known that, just conveniently forgotten. I stood up suddenly, causing him to ask me if I was okay. I would drink a cold glass of water and go to bed. I would not lie in bed thinking of the man in my kitchen.

"Yes," I said. "I'm just—"

He waited.

"I'm just tired. It's been a long day."

"Of course," he said, standing up. "I've overstayed my welcome."

"No," I shook my head. "Not at all. I was so glad for the company."

The awkwardness came crashing back, and I was sorry to see it. I much preferred the languid lust between us, the slow burn of unhurried desire. But he was married, and I had sheep to count. I unlocked the front door and we walked outside, the sky bright with stars.

"That's Venus," I said to him, pointing. "That's Sirius."

The moon was luminous, and it made me think of the werewolves in the city, good and bad.

"Will you be okay?" he asked. "On your own?"

"I think so," I said. Hadn't I always been on my own? What I really wanted to say was: *I wish you could stay the night. I wish you weren't married. I wish you were the owner of the pink toothbrush.*

I was truly exhausted, but of course I couldn't sleep. I had pre-empted my hangover by taking some *Plectranthil capiola*, but it turned out to be a bad idea. Bright visuals of everything I had experienced that day flashed in my mind like a badly edited slideshow, and it wasn't helped by the rapt longing I felt for Armstrong buzzing in my pelvis.

You are not going to become emotionally involved with a cop, I told myself. *Or any kind of involved.*

Too late, came the reply.

The images racing through my brain were all mixed up and confusing: a beautiful tree; a dead wizard's body; Armstrong's strong frame; his tender touch; someone screaming; darkness; blood in my hair; an orc named Gnrok; a cluster of sugar snap peas; a hen scratching for grain; a missing girl; a pack of wolves racing through a forest; a coven ceremony by candlelight.

I saw pictures of my childhood body: matted hair, emaciated frame, a constellation of scars. It hurt me. The pain I had kept at bay in front of the directress and Armstrong crashed over me now as I processed the information I had seen in my file. My sinuses began to sting, my throat ached, and intense weeping took over my body. *How could anyone do that to a child?* I wondered. How cruel it seemed, how careless. How could a mother abandon her daughter? It was a nagging question I was sure I'd never have the answer to. I sobbed for the child I used to be. I sobbed for all the affection that was lost, a lifetime of unconditional love that other children have the luxury of taking for granted—as they should. I cried and cried until my eyes were swollen and my stomach muscles ached. The skin on my nose was raw. When there seemed to be no tears left, after I had exhausted myself, I took a paracetamol with a glass of water and tucked myself into bed wearing well-worn

Spongebob Squarepants pajamas. Tomorrow would be better, I assured myself, and finally drifted away.

At three a.m. I sat up in bed: my missing parents, the missing children. It was a sign. My parents may be dead, but there was still a chance of finding the abducted girls and sparing their folks a lifetime of heartache. I needed to get those girls home safely.

CHAPTER 39

A BARELY BREATHING CORPSE

NICKY

Doctor Adrathar appeared behind the partition just as I finished changing. Not waiting for me to tell him I was ready before coming around the divider was another mean grab for power, just like it had been when he invaded the bathroom earlier while I was naked in the bath. He would do what it took to thrust his power on to me, and he wanted me to know it.

"Everything okay?" he asked, a superficial smile plastered on his face. I didn't smile back. He helped me limp toward the other door, which I guessed was the examination room. My skin was slick with pain- and stress-sweat.

It felt like ever since the accident I had been propelled into this totally surreal life, and there was no way of escaping it. Everything about it felt wrong. I missed Sebastian, our Labrador. Sometimes I cried when I thought of him, knowing he'd be confused, wondering where I was, thinking I had abandoned him. I missed our beautiful, comfortable house, and plants and books. I missed food—proper food. Food you'd *recognize* as food. And coffee! And, even though it seemed that my husband had forsaken me, I missed Derek. I longed for him more than I wanted to, more than I would have expected. He worked such long hours that I was used to living a rather solitary life, but this nightmare brought things back into focus. I had been so lucky to have everything I had. Had I taken it for granted? Would I ever get it back?

Doctor Adrathar helped me onto a sturdy hospital bed in the center of the plain room. A camera watched us from the corner of the ceiling, showing a steady green light. The room had gray walls, florescent lights, and the scent of disinfectant. It seemed like every other room in the asylum apart from the awful communal dining room, which was made more awful by its rancid yellow color scheme and *eau de oatmeal.* Lying down on the firm bed set my pelvis on fire, and I gasped and cinched my eyes shut. I only noticed the straps around my wrists once he'd closed them, followed swiftly by the ankle restraints.

"You don't have to do that," I said. I wanted them off. I didn't want to be strapped down, alone in a room with him. "I won't struggle," I promised. "I won't fight."

"Oh, don't worry about them," he said, seemingly entertained by my anxiety. "It's for your own safety."

My skin and scalp itched with new perspiration. "I don't need them. Please take them off." Tears rushed to my eyes. And then, hating myself for playing a little girl, I said, "I promise I'll be good."

He looked pleased, but did not remove the restraints. "They're for your own safety," he repeated. He busied himself with turning on one of the machines. "The treatment causes seizures, and we don't want you falling off the bed and hurting yourself again."

My whole body felt instantly chilled. "Seizures?" I asked. "You can't do that. I don't give my permission!"

Adrathar smiled again. "I don't need your permission. You're a ward of the state now, and it's my job to treat you."

"Not like this," I said. "If you touch me, I'll scream so loudly. I'll tell everyone. I'll go to the press. My lawyer will be after you. When my husband finds out about this place, he will eviscerate you!"

The doctor waited for me to finish my tirade, then looked me in the eye. "Your husband wants you here. Who do you think signed your admission documents?"

A small bomb went off in my brain. I lashed out and wept. I tried to fight and kick despite the cuffs and the searing pain. I wanted to kill Adrathar. I wanted to kill myself. He moved around me, talking quietly as he placed the electrodes on my temples, ignoring my threats and pleas. Once I had exhausted myself, I began hearing snippets of what he was saying.

"... in cases of severe depression ... patients who don't eat ... uncooperative ... suicidal ... electroconvulsive therapy causes seizures which seem to reset the brain."

"I don't need it," I said. "I'll be good, I promise I'll be good."

Of course, Adrathar didn't care that I was sane. I wondered how many patients had come in with their mind intact and then were subjected to Adrathar's eager ministrations. Fear scraped my wrists raw, and the exposed flesh burned under the sweat-salted leather.

The doctor looked up at the camera in the corner and subtly flicked his wrist. The green light turned off.

"What's happening?" I asked.

The doctor looked at his watch and dimmed the lights, ready to begin.

"Anesthetic," I said, my voice hoarse from crying and yelling. "You're supposed to give me anesthetic."

"I know," he said. I could see his white teeth in the subdued light. "But, in my experience, I think it works better without."

Adrathar forced a rubber bite-plate into my mouth and turned a dial before I had time to brace myself. Electricity surged through my skull, which in turn sent furious lightning bolts through my body, forcing every muscle to seize. My organs were on fire. My fractured pelvis lost its familiar ache, giving way to a brand-new agony. My jaws wired themselves shut with such force I thought my teeth would break despite the rubber shield. Even if I could have talked, I wouldn't have made sense, because words lost all meaning. There was just terror and pain and a blurry, dark dizziness. When the current finally let me go, my body slumped down, dead weight. A barely breathing corpse.

The first round was new and utterly horrific, and I just wanted to die. The second round was worse, because I knew what was coming and I knew I didn't have the strength to withstand it. I was wrong. I survived the second, and the third, and the fourth electrocution. When the fifth started, I thought I was dying. The pain subsided along with my consciousness, and I flew into the darkness like a wild raven let out of a cage. I hurtled into the dark, dark night, and then I was gone.

CHAPTER 40
WASTELAND
NICKY

"Nicky." It was a familiar voice, feminine and kind. "Nicky."

I kept my swollen eyes glued shut. My body was a wasteland that I didn't want to return to. Why wouldn't these people just let me die?

"Nicky," Devka said again.

I groaned. I had no tears left; the emotions had been sucked out of my body. Despite that, a sudden sob racked my brokenness. My jaw muscles felt torn, and I had dried blood on my lips.

"It's okay," she uttered. Her voice sounded emotional. "You're going to be okay. I'm sorry they did this to you."

I groaned again. If my mouth was working, I would have said, *It wasn't your fault. Even guardian angels need a day off.* I would have begged her to never leave me again.

The weeping returned. It was nonsensical; I was empty of feelings, tears, and words, yet my wounded body convulsed with sobs.

Sister Devka held my hand while my body worked out its post-terror grief.

"I knew it," she said at last. "I knew that Adrathar had set his sights on you. I don't know why he chooses who he does. Perhaps it's some kind of ... attraction."

I heard some tinkling of metal or glass. I finally opened my eyes and saw the nurse applying a clear liquid to a cotton pad. She used it to clean my burned temples, and my lips, which I had bitten to bleeding. With a new pad she cleaned my chafed wrists, then applied antiseptic and bandages. She was quiet while she took off my adult diaper and sweat-soaked gown. The smell of urine wafted toward me, as did waves of shame. Devka gave me a quick sponge bath and dressed me in a clean sweatsuit. My body, half asleep, no longer listened to commands. I blinked at her in gratitude.

"I don't know why he's singled you out," she said, once she had tucked me in for the night. "But it's clear that he's made his decision. He's chosen you as his pet."

I thought the fear had been shocked out of my body, but then I felt it again: a flame on the horizon.

Devka squeezed my hand. "We need to get you out of here."

I jolted out of my stupor. *Out? How? Surely that wasn't possible.*

"I've seen what he does to women," Devka said. "It's always the same. He'll do it to you, too."

I took her arm, weakly. I needed to know how to escape.

"It's never been done before," she said. "You'll probably be killed."

I blinked at her.

"But believe me," she said, "it'll be better than what he has planned."

She packed up her supplies and I reached for her arm again.

"Pain," I managed to say.

Devka frowned at me. "You've already had twice today. Ingleby signed them off in your chart. With the anesthetic you received, you should be good until morning."

I shook my head. *No painkillers,* I tried to say. *No anesthetic. My body is a bonfire.*

Devka stopped, her usually nut-brown skin pale under the artificial light. "You're saying they didn't give you anything? At all?"

I nodded, my face crumpling.

Devka was paler still. "Adrathar administered ECD without anesthetic?"

I nodded, not letting go of her arm. The nurse had become my world, my salvation.

She looked worried. "I don't have access to that cabinet till morning."

I let my hand drop.

"Because your chart was signed as completed."

Adrathar and Ingleby's cruelty was calculated and comprehensive. I couldn't stand a whole night like this, writhing in pain, in the dark. Waiting only for the sun to rise on another day of torture.

I want to die, I tried to say, but the words escaped only as groans. My grip on Devka's arm stiffened as my eyes pled with her. *Please help me die.*

The nurse leaned down and whispered in my ear. "I know where I might get some."

Devka left the room and returned shortly with the familiar-looking vial and syringe that I had grown to love.

"Thank you," I slurred, while I tried not to cry.

The nurse made quick work of it, and soon there was the pinch of the needle going in, and the cool sting as the drug flowed into me. A minute later—warm relief in rivers, and the dissipation of utter desperation. Three minutes later, I was out.

CHAPTER 41

WONDERWITCH

ASHA

I spent the next morning working in the food forest. I don't know if it was my imagination, but after the ivy and soil absorbed my assailant the day before, the garden was blooming better than ever. The apricots that were the size of marbles when I arrived back from hospital were now swollen and blushing, the rosemary was flowering—whipping the bees into a frenzy—and the sage was heavy with flowers and butterflies.

I pruned and harvested as I went, filling a bucket for the hens and compost heap and a basket for the kitchen. My hands knew what to do, so I let them shear and pick and collect seeds while I thought of how on earth I was going to find the missing children. I guessed I could start by interviewing the parents, but I wasn't keen on that idea at all. Besides being traumatized, they would have already been bothered by the police and press on multiple occasions. The last thing I wanted to do was add to their pain. Of course, the other side of the coin was what if I could find their daughters? If I had a daughter missing and there was even the slimmest chance of someone finding her, I'd agree to an interview in an instant.

One of the hens pecked at my toes, looking for grubs. "Hey," I said in mock annoyance, and threw her a few peas. This caused chaos in the rest of the flock, who sensed my favoritism from a mile away. They squawked and clamored toward me, running on their little yellow wax-warty feet. I sprinkled the entire pea bounty on the ground, as well as the rocket, spinach, and marigolds, and watched them gobble it up. Suddenly there was a movement deeper in the garden, and I froze. Another hen? One of the cats? A goat I'd never known I'd owned?

I took a step in that direction, breathing shallow, heart hammering.

I needn't have worried. It was Soleil, sitting happily on the pretty wrought iron garden bench. The arch around and above her was heavy with roses, and she looked perfect sitting there, a carpet of wild grass and daisies underneath her fashionable boots.

"Hello, dear," she said, smiling. "I do hope you don't mind me popping in."

"Er," I said.

"I used *nebulam ianua sit* to spirit myself directly here. I hope you don't mind."

"Nebula—?"

"*Ianua sit* is portal magic. *Nebulam* is a vaporizing spell. It's quite a comfortable way to travel, if you perform it correctly."

I stood there and blinked at her, stupidly.

"Now, usually I would have driven the Land Rover and rung your doorbell, but I'm afraid I'm in a bit of a hurry. Do you have your magical arsenal ready? Are your spells up to scratch?"

"Negative," I replied.

"That's funny," the high priestess said. "I heard a report of you taking out a Dusk Reaper yesterday. I thought you were back."

How had word reached her so quickly? I thought I'd be able to keep that particular secret.

"Where is your wand?" she asked. "Your sword? Amulet?"

"You don't understand," I said. "I was just defending myself. I didn't have anything on me. I didn't plan to do it."

"So you're still in the dark?" Soleil seemed a bit tetchy. Perhaps she was disappointed that I hadn't turned into WonderWitch overnight. "You're still not working?"

"I'm ready to start working," I replied. "I want to start, but I'm worried that I don't know what I'm doing."

"Fair enough," said the witch, her irritation fading. "I suppose I can't expect too much of you, yet. I just—" she scratched her forehead. "I just ... we're in a hurry to help this woman, you see. It's become rather urgent."

"Which woman?" I asked. "What can I do?"

I fetched Soleil a glass of pink lavender lemonade and sat down beside her. She took it gratefully and had a good gulp. "There's a psychiatric institution called Riverside."

"Sounds like an expensive retirement village," I said. Or a summer holiday destination. I pictured a cheerful elderly crowd drinking gin and playing cards.

Soleil eyed me. "It's the opposite of that. *Psychiatric institution* is the spin. It's actually an inviolable house of horrors disguised as an asylum for the criminally insane."

"Okay," I said, immediately sorry that I had made light of it.

"There are some terrible people there. Psychopaths, sadists, mentally unbalanced—and that's just the staff I'm referring to."

I looked into her eyes, waiting for her to continue.

"There is a woman incarcerated there who needs our help."

I angled my head. "A criminally insane woman in an impenetrable prison needs our help?"

"We have reason to believe that she is innocent. She didn't even stand trial due to what looked like her incapacity."

"They can't get away with that," I said.

"The court-appointed psychologist diagnosed her. The only problem is that the same doctor works for Riverside, and if they don't keep their numbers steady, their funding dries up."

"I don't know," I said. "It seems a little far-fetched, doesn't it?"

"Some of the most convoluted conspiracy theories are true," replied Soleil. "But that's another conversation. Believe this: an innocent woman named Nicola Landau is locked up in that wretched asylum as we speak. She is a woman like you or I, and her sanity is in danger. She has no one on the outside. No one to fight for her or challenge the court's ruling."

An odd sensation flared in my chest. "I'll help her," I said. "Of course, I will. Just tell me what to do."

CHAPTER 42

THEY DON'T ALWAYS FIND THE BODIES

ASHA

"You'll need to get in, of course," said Soleil, thinking out loud. "That will be difficult, but not impossible."

"Couldn't I vaporize myself, like you did to get here?"

The high priestess's eyes widened. "Goddess, no. It's far too dangerous for someone of your ..."

Lack of experience? Out-of-practice spell-slinging? General mediocrity?

"It's just that it's an extremely delicate spell, and if you can't manage to re-materialize..."

"Never mind," I said. "I understand." I gestured for her to continue.

"Once you're inside, you'll have to find a way to break her out."

"Sounds easy enough," I joked. "With the impenetrable security and all of that."

Soleil ignored my attempt at humor. "She doesn't have long. She'll be dead in a few days if we don't get to her."

"How do you know?"

"Let's just say that Riverside doesn't have a very high survival rate—there are always odd deaths happening there. Prisoners jumping out of windows or into the rocky river. They don't always find the bodies."

I thought of Morgan, the missing daughters, and their anxious parents. Somehow, Nicola Landau's case seemed easier to close than the vagueness of the kidnapped girls. I knew who and where she was, and I had a ticking time bomb of a deadline. I could get her out, then catch up on the abduction case as fast as possible.

"Now," said the high priestess, looking me over. "We need to get you ready."

We started with physical exercises. Soleil reminded me how to jump, lunge, and squat. I had to practice over and over again until my thighs burned like a dying phoenix. Next came swordplay, without the sword. The movements were grounded and elegant, and as I did them I felt my muscle memory kick in. My body knew how to do this, even if my mind was still trying to catch up. Soleil had seamlessly turned from a stylish yogi witch to a martial arts sensei.

"Up!" she yelled when I wasn't holding my imaginary sword high enough. "Faster. Smoother. Go in for the kill! You're a hornet. A cobra. A scorpion."

After an hour of practicing in the garden, Soleil finally let me rest in the cool kitchen.

"Have some water," she ordered. "Just because we have super-powers doesn't mean we don't have to stay hydrated."

We washed our hands and glugged down some tap water. Next on the training schedule was the re-introduction of magical items.

"Right," said the high priestess, rubbing her palms together. "This is the fun part."

I took out the necklace with the small vial attached to it, the tanzanite ring, and the wand that I had been too nervous to wield, and set them all out on the kitchen tabletop. We stared at them together.

"I don't know where you got that ring, but I can feel the energy coming off it. Like a glow. Can you feel it?"

I shook my head. It looked like an ordinary ring to me. Soleil picked it up and studied it. "It has a potent protection spell on it."

"To protect the ring?" I asked.

"No, to protect the wearer." She handed it to me. "Best you just put it on and hope it comes in handy. The vial is obviously for your excellent potions. You are the best mixologist Starfall has ever known."

"Good to know," I said. "But I'm clueless about potions now."

"Spend some time in your tincture room with your Book of Shadows. You'll soon figure it out."

Last was the wand. "Now, you don't specifically need a wand, but it does serve the purpose of concentrating your magic and allowing for focus. Think laser gun as opposed to shotgun. But if you don't have it on you, don't panic. At the same time, do NOT let anyone else take your wand from you. It will immediately make you more vulnerable. Think of your wand as a precious part of your body."

"Got it," I said. My thoughts were scattered. There was a lot of information to process, and my thighs were still aching from the martial arts refresher training.

"Good," said the high priestess, who looked pleased. "There is one more thing."

She placed her pale hand into a handbag I didn't see her bring with her and brought out a large giftbox wrapped in blue paper and bound with a gold-colored ribbon. The illustration on the paper—copper cogs and pistons—whirred and ticked away in her hand. I had never seen illustrations on paper move like that, so I frowned at the animated graphics.

"Take it," said Soleil, wagging it at me. "It's a gift from Ferra Fornak."

The copper cogs! Of course it was. How generous the dwarf was, and how lucky I was to have her. I started fiddling with the beautiful gold ribbon but the high priestess got impatient with me and clicked her fingers. "*Monstras*," she uttered, and the ribbon untied itself, the blue paper fell away. The lid floated above the box, revealing a beautiful ritual knife inside. I picked it out from the box and studied it. It looked exactly like the one the police had found, but it was shiny and new. The phrase RUPTOR MALEDICTUM was engraved neatly on the metal.

"Ah," I exclaimed. "I love it!"

"Don't forget the spice cookies," said the witch. I looked at the bottom of the box, and there lay a packet of Ferra's famous sweet and spicy cookies—with a scribbled card assuring me they were the vegan version.

It had been a long day and I was craving a shower, a cup of dead leaf brew, and bed. Unfortunately for me, the coven boss had other ideas.

"Are you ready to go?"

"Go?" I asked.

"To Riverside," Soleil replied, and tapped her watch with two fingers. "The longer we wait, the more damage they will do to her."

My body was stiffening up. Surely she didn't want me to go right away? I needed at least one night to recover from this morning's impromptu martial arts class, and if I didn't shower, the guards at Riverside would smell me coming.

"I need to practice my magic," I said. "I need spells and potions. I need to learn how to use this—" I gestured at the knife. If nothing else, I needed to change clothes. There was no way I was breaking into a mental asylum in my Spongebob Squarepants pajamas.

"You've got ten minutes," declared the high priestess. "I'll lock up."

CHAPTER 43

TRICK-OR-TREAT

ASHA

The Uber was waiting for us outside. The driver looked cagey, probably worried that one of us was one hot salty French fry short of a Happy Meal, seeing as we were heading for the most notorious asylum in the city. It probably didn't help matters that I was wearing what looked like a futuristic witch's cloak. Strong, clean lines, smooth cut, with a subtle flare from the hips. Beautiful, generous black satin hood. Best of all, it had pockets.

"Got your wand?" the high priestess asked. I nodded. I was also wearing the tanzanite ring, but I had left the necklace at home, as the vial had been empty. I wore the knife on my thigh, in a soft faux-leather thigh holster. Despite looking prepared, I was terrified. I felt like a child dressed up for a particularly dangerous round of trick-or-treating.

"Don't look so worried," Soleil said. "This is the easy part."

I gave a nervous laugh.

"Think of this meeting as a recce," said Soleil. "Check the place out, look for vulnerabilities in the security system, and talk to Landau to find out everything you can. Once we know what we're dealing with, we'll get her out."

This made me imagine Hollywood scenes of men dressed in black suits and balaclavas throwing grappling hooks over high walls, and bodies being snuck out in laundry hamper trolleys.

"Ivy, our expert hacker, pulled some strings and had the visitor request pass approved for you. You are to be Landau's sister, in for a fifteen-minute visit. They don't allow more than that."

"Okay," I said, relieved that I would be able to walk in—this time—instead of swinging those tricky grappling hooks.

We arrived at Riverside as the sun was setting. The building looked like it was straight out of a horror movie. Sure, it had a modern, tasteful facade and neat landscaping, but that somehow made it even creepier than if it had been a moldy concrete block festooned with barbed wire. It was like I could feel the evil emanating from the place, a pink-skinned peach about to burst open, torn apart from the inside by hungry worms. I shuddered and looked at the witch beside me. "I can feel it," I whispered.

She gave me an understanding look and held out her forearm so that I could see the goosebumps on her skin. "Be careful."

I took a breath and climbed out of the car.

The sun was slowly melting the view, turning the pavement the color of marmalade. I was glad I only had fifteen minutes with Nicola Landau, because I didn't want to be inside the building after dark. The huge security guard at the gate grunted at me in greeting and proceeded to search my handbag with his supersize hands; it was like watching a bunch of bananas dipping into the bag. He was clearly human, but his physique made me wonder if he had any orc DNA running through his veins. After walking through the metal detector, he took my phone, wand, and knife, but not before inspecting the weapon and looking me up and down, as if he couldn't imagine why a petite little sister of an inmate would be carrying a ritual knife. I didn't want him to think I was trouble and turn me away.

"It's my gardening knife," I said.

"Gardening knife," the guard repeated, blinking slowly.

I nodded.

He didn't break eye contact. "You always bring your gardening knife to psychiatric correctional facilities?"

I don't always visit psychiatric correctional facilities, but when I do, I bring my gardening knife.

"Yes?" I replied.

"Cute," he said, and let me through, watching with beady eyes as I moved through the next stage of access. A woman behind a counter barked at me to look up, then blinded me with the flash of a camera.

"Sign here," she said, passing me an electronic clipboard. I signed Landau's fictional sister's name, and she motioned with her head for me to keep walking. The next guard smiled at me, then picked up the card that the machine beside him spat out. He clipped it to a lanyard and I put it around my neck. Hot off the press, the visitor's pass was warm against my chest. All three of the employees had guns in their holsters and pepper spray in their utility belts. They also had walkie-talkies. Suffice to say that if we were going to ever break in, I doubted we'd come through the front entrance. As I was congratulating myself for getting through the first three stages, a gray-haired nurse strode up and peered intently at me.

"Sharon Metcalf?" she enquired. "Nicky Landau's sister?"

I cleared my throat. "Mm-hmm," I murmured, nodding. Something told me I wasn't very good at deception, or perhaps it was just nerves.

The nurse didn't smile. "I'm Sister Ingleby. I'll take you through."

Sister Ingleby was exactly as I had expected. When you think of a nurse in an asylum for criminally insane people, what do you picture? I was thinking a heavy-set body, thick flesh-colored stockings, and sensible gray shoes. Steel-colored hair, varicose veins, bunions.

"She's not in a good place right now," said Ingleby. "We have her sedated."

"Sedated?" How was I going to speak to her when she was asleep?

"We had no choice," said the nurse. "She's a very troubled woman. She was about to hurt herself."

I dropped my voice. "Can you tell me ..."

She spoke over me. "Your sister arrived in an extremely bad condition. After the incident at the bridge, her pelvis was broken, she had internal bleeding, and she was incoherent. The police drove her to the local hospital where they operated and stabilized her. As you know, she was judged unfit to stand trial, and she was transferred here, where we keep patients suffering from various degrees of psychosis."

"Psychosis?" I repeated. "She was mentally fit before the incident."

At least, I thought she was. That's what I had gathered from what Soleil had told me.

I concentrated on the way we walked into the building so that I'd know how to find Landau's cell when we broke in. From the front entrance we walked straight down a corridor, past four doors, then turned left as we hit a T-junction. I wondered how I was going to get any real information out of the nurse. We turned right. The corridors and floors were gray. There was neither artwork nor a plant in sight. I was sure I would be suicidal if I had to spend time there, never mind show up for work every day.

"How long have you worked here?"

Ingleby shrugged. "A lifetime," she replied, turning left and making me feel disoriented. How many turns had it been? How many doors? Damn it, I was a terrible spy.

"Can't be easy."

She slowed down and looked at me. "No," she said. "It's not. But Doctor Adrathar needs me."

The nurse had stopped completely, and I wondered if we were going to have a quick heart-to-heart, or if she was going to cover our mics and whisper something to me, but instead she brought out her access card, the door beside me clicked open, and we went inside.

CHAPTER 44
LANDAU
ASHA

The black plaque on the cell door read *LANDAU*.

There was a motionless shape on the medical cot pushed against the concrete wall. The room was small, dark, and mean. I shuddered. Sister Ingleby closed the door and switched on the light, which flickered half a dozen times before emitting a cold, unwavering glare. Under the unforgiving luminance the nurse looked even older than I had previously guessed. I could see the capillaries on her eyelids, and her lips were dry and pale. My eyes darted to the unmoving body. I guessed I should go over and hug her, but her body was so still that I hesitated.

"As I told you, we had to sedate her. She was fighting with the doctor."

"Does that happen often?"

"When she came in, it was like she was possessed. It wasn't human, the way she was screaming. It's like there was something ... inside her."

Alrighty. I wasn't qualified to be a spy in an asylum, and I certainly wasn't qualified to exorcise demons. I felt like backpedaling in a big way, all the way back through the depressing gray maze of the institution and to the marmalade sidewalk outside. Why had I agreed to this, again? This whole building was rotten. I could feel the evil emanating like smoke from a burning wall.

I stepped toward the cot.

"As you can see, the patient is resting. I'm sorry your visit is wasted. Perhaps next time you can give us more notice and we'll make certain she's awake to see you."

"Of course," I said. "I understand."

I shifted the blanket down from Landau's face, and I had to swallow my gasp. She looked like a wax sculpture, a day-old corpse. I grabbed Landau's wrist, searching for a pulse. It was weak. What the hell had they done to her? While her heart was beating, the coolness of her skin startled me, and I took a step back, tripping over something I hadn't seen was there. I lost my balance, but the nurse lunged forward and caught my arm in time. She was stronger than she looked. When I recovered, I looked to see what it was I had fallen over. It was a wheelchair.

"Mrs. Landau has a broken pelvis," Ingleby said.

This was going to make the break-out a lot more complicated. It's not like I'd be able to just grab her hand and run up the stairs. Honestly, the whole plan was starting to look more and more impossible. I stared at Ingleby's access card, which she had left on the side table.

"The doctor has been treating her violent episodes with electroshock therapy," the nurse said.

I tore my eyes away from the access card, hoping she hadn't seen me muttering. White-hot rage ignited at the base of my skull. "What?"

"Nonmedical people think it's an outdated therapy, but it's actually been shown to have positive results when done in the correct circumstances."

I couldn't help clenching my fingers into a hard fist.

"I didn't see any other visitors in the book," I said.

"Yes," said the nurse. "Unfortunately, no one has come to see the patient until you arrived."

"You don't think that's strange?"

The nurse sighed. "Not really. No one likes to come here."

I frowned. "What about the people whose loved ones are in here?"

Ingleby shrugged. "No one loves the people who are in here."

Perhaps realizing that she was coming across as prickly, the nurse made a show of checking on Landau, plumping her pillow and sweeping stray strands of hair out of her face. Checking if she had water in her hospital-issued jug. While the sister had her back turned, I quickly swapped the card I had just conjured with hers.

"Her husband hasn't been to visit once," said Ingleby. "Not even a phone call."

"That's odd."

She stopped fussing and turned to face me. "Is it? Can you blame him? It must be a shocking thing to have to process. Imagine your partner shooting an innocent person at point-blank range. A person who was trying to help them."

Landau groaned softly, as if she had heard that fragment of conversation. The nurse motioned that time was up, but I wasn't ready. I had to survey the place, look for a way in; a way out. But we had used up our fifteen minutes, and it was time for me to leave. The wheelchair and bare concrete walls told me all I needed to know. There was no way to get Nicola Landau out of there.

I received my confiscated items back from the suspicious security guard and hopped back into the purring Uber vehicle. Relief swept over me as the driver accelerated away from Riverside.

"Have I aged?" I joked with Soleil, even though the mood was decidedly unfunny.

She gave me an understanding look. "It was that bad?"

"Worse," I replied. "I wouldn't last a day in there. I'd rather kill myself. I'm being serious. I'd rather die."

I leaned back in the seat and took a deep breath. I was rattled, and I didn't mind Soleil seeing it.

"On the plus side, I managed to conjure a copy of the nurse's access card and swap it for the original."

Soleil's lips hitched up at the corners. "Excellent," she said. "How's Nicola?"

"They told me she was sedated. She looked half dead to me. Pale as a corpse. Ligature marks on her wrists, burns on her temple ..."

"Where's the cell?"

"I was totally lost in there," I replied. "But then just before we turned into Landau's room—number forty-seven—I saw the orange light of the sunset painting the wall ahead. So it's ground level, on the southwest side. No windows in the cell, no doors apart from the main one which requires a staff access card to open. No trapdoors in the corridor ceilings from what I saw. Plenty of security cameras."

I felt almost surprised by my monologue. I hadn't realized I'd been taking mental notes in there, but I guess I had been. Maybe I wasn't such a terrible spy, after all.

"Basically, I saw no way in. And getting out will be even more difficult, because Landau's in a wheelchair."

What I didn't say out loud was that it probably wouldn't matter in the end that we couldn't break in or out, because by the looks of Nicola Landau, she wouldn't last the night, anyway. The high priestess's eyebrows shot up at this, as if she had been listening in to my thoughts. She pursed her lips and looked away, spending a while scanning the blur of trees we passed on our way back to the city. "We'll find a way," she said at last. "We always do."

"I don't know about that," I said, crossing my arms.

The high priestess smiled at me. "That's because you've forgotten that we have magic on our side."

CHAPTER 45

DEAD BLACK BUTTONS

NICKY

I slept for fourteen hours and was disappointed when I woke up. A part of me had wished for an easy nighttime death, peaceful and pain-free, but it was not to be. I lay there for a while, contemplating the complex nightmare my life had devolved into, then decided there was no use in wallowing when I could be trying to figure out an escape plan.

Neither Devka nor Ingleby seemed to be around, so I hauled myself up and into my wheelchair. My pain was at a tolerable level, so I guessed that Devka had injected me again once she was allowed access to the medicine cabinet.

I knew I should go to breakfast, now that I was supposed to be dining with the other inmates, but even though my stomach was gnawing itself in hunger, I couldn't face a meal in that place. I didn't want to be seen as stuck-up, though—I knew what kind of bullying that would encourage—so I decided to go, show my face, and pretend to eat a piece of toast. The last thing I needed was more enemies.

The guard at the door unlocked it for me, and I wheeled slowly down the corridor. I noticed that my biceps, which had always been unremarkable, were now a little defined. I could feel my shoulders were stronger, too. It was the one upside of being in a wheelchair. It made me think that if I ever hoped to escape, I'd have to work on building my strength. Easy to say when you've had your morning pethidine; not so easy when you're racked with pain.

The cafeteria was as odious as I remembered it from the day before, and I swallowed the sudden tightness in my throat as I slowly rolled in. The smell was enough to put anyone off their food, even if the food itself looked okay—which it didn't. The scrambled eggs were caked up and gelatinous, the sauce of the baked beans was congealed, and the "toast" was warmed-up cardboard. It was a far cry from the low GI seed bread I used to eat at home. I took some, anyway, and poured myself a cup of gray tea from the communal urn. When I turned back to face the dining area, I didn't see the women—Alison and co.—from the day before. Most of the tables had people sitting at them, who I was nervous to join. There was a counter with only one inmate toward the back of the room. I gritted my teeth and decided to join her.

Balancing my tray on my lap, I slowly wheeled toward her. I pulled my lips into an awkward smile as I approached. Her eyes were dead black buttons. Her greasy hair hung like a despairing weeping willow around her blank face. By the time I realized I was making a mistake, it was too late to turn around.

"Do you mind if I sit here?" I asked.

Without looking up at me, she shrugged.

I put my tray down and automatically looked at hers. It was similarly empty. Synthetic juice watered down to within an inch of its life, a slice of chewy cardboard, and some unidentifiable orange jam. I sat down.

"Not hungry, either?" I asked.

I didn't think she'd answer me, but when she did finally turn her face to me, I was able to look at her eyes properly, and my body flooded with ice water. Her irises were vacuums, spiraling black holes that threatened to suck me in. I felt something inside my chest rising as if to leave my body. I tore my eyes away from her and stared at my tea, blinking, trying to calm myself. My cheeks grew cold; it was an odd feeling—the opposite of blushing. I realized that this was the woman who was rocking and talking to herself the other day. The only one in Riverside—so far—who seemed to live up to the crazy label.

With a trembling hand, I took a sip of lukewarm tea. Out of the corner of my eye I could see the woman still staring at me. It was irrational, but I felt that if I turned my gaze upon her again, I'd lose a part of myself to her ravenous eyes. I hunched further over my tray feeling stupid and sick. She kept staring.

"He chose you, too," she said. It was a low whisper; guttural.

My body stiffened. I kept my eyes on my sad excuse for toast. "What?"

"He finished with me, then he chose you," she said. When I finally lifted my gaze toward her, she moved her hair away from her temples, revealing a thick mass of burned skin. I dropped my plastic mug, and the tepid tea ran all over the yellow plastic tablecloth. I swore loudly and grabbed at the thin paper towel on my tray, wiping up the spill and failing, so small and mean the napkin was. Just as the tea was reaching the edges of the table, ready to trickle onto the woman's and my lap, a wad of paper towels landed right in front of me. I grabbed a few and managed to shore up the spill, and when I looked up to see who had delivered the napkins, I saw Alison and her friend.

"Careful of this one," said Alison, flicking her eyebrows in the direction of the woman across the table. "She's as mad as a basket of snakes."

I didn't answer. It seemed cruel to acknowledge what was plain to see.

"Fikile," she said to her partner. "It looks like Emily needs some salt on her food."

Fikile reached across and grabbed the salt cellar, then poured it over Emily's breakfast, including into her cup of juice. I wanted to stop her, but I let my cowardice get the better of me. I didn't want to make waves. I didn't want trouble. I wanted to disappear.

"That's enough," said Alison, and Fikile stopped pouring and dusted off her hands. They both looked at me.

"Be careful of her," Alison reiterated. "She'll haunt you."

I didn't know what that meant.

"Tell your new friend what you did, Emily."

Emily shook her head.

"Come on," Alison needled. "Tell the newbie what you did to land up in here."

Emily's mouth twitched.

Alison wouldn't let it go. "She killed her whole family."

My whole body went cold. Emily stared at her ruined breakfast.

"See you around," said Fikile.

I nodded.

Alison gave me a kind of friendly two-fingered salute, and they exited the room. Without looking at Emily, I finished cleaning the table and readied myself to leave.

Emily set her dark eyes on me, forcing me to return her awful gaze. "They're right, you know."

I felt a phantom ice cube slide down my back. I wheeled backwards and left as quickly as I could.

CHAPTER 46
ESCAPE OR DIE
NICKY

I was worried when I didn't see Devka. Bad things happened when she wasn't around. I went straight back to my cell and wheeled myself into the corner, trying to tame my anxiety. I closed my eyes and focused on my breathing for a few minutes, until my thoughts came under control. The burned skin on my temples throbbed. How many times had that woman undergone Adrathar's torture? Had she been relatively sane before then? I had the feeling she might have been. I had the unreasonable thought that the doctor had sucked the soul out of her body, and that was why her expression was so hungry, and so desperate.

A shiver raced down my spine. I felt torn between trying to end my life and planning an escape. Life here was so horrifying that I wouldn't hesitate to end it. Sitting there in the corner, I decided I'd never go through with another therapy session with Adrathar; I'd literally rather die. On the other hand, escaping seemed impossible, and I couldn't imagine expending the energy it would take to make it successful. Constant pain steals your energy and your ability to think decisively. Also, I had to be practical. I was in a wheelchair, for God's sake.

Then I thought of the prisoner's scarred skin, and her terrifying words. *He finished with me. He chose you.*

My chat with Devka came to me again. *We need to get you out of here,* she had said. *I've seen what he does to women. It's always the same. He'll do it to you, too.*

No, I thought. *No! I'd rather die than become Adrathar's pet.*

The pain from my fractured pelvis began to surface. I looked at the clock. I wasn't due my next shot until lunchtime, and it was only ten a.m.

I would have to find something to distract me. I reversed out of the corner and turned around to face the cell. We weren't allowed music, books, television, snacks, or any communication with the outside world. Not for the first time, I wondered if the Riverside Asylum caused insanity more often than they cured it. What did the other prisoners do with themselves all day? I would ask Alison and Fikile. Maybe I could get some books and chocolate smuggled in along with my smack.

I observed my cell. It was bare and boring. I wondered how many days I had lain here, semi-comatose, after the accident.

In my head I had to call it "the accident," because as confused as I was about what had happened that night and the fallout thereafter, I knew one thing for sure. I would never knowingly shoot an innocent person, never mind an innocent person who was trying to help me, at point-blank range. Don't get me wrong—I knew I pulled the trigger. I remembered the sensation of my finger pulling back on the cold metal while the dark night and twinkling cosmos swirled around us. The muted shouting in the background, most likely calls for me to put the gun down, to climb back down off the bridge, to calm down while they could figure out what I was doing and how they could help me. But it was all background noise to me. All I knew was that I had to get the message out there, and I had to move into my next phase of existence.

Death is not the end. It was a chant in my brain that reverberated in my whole body. It had seemed so important at the time. Life or death, except that death seemed to be the obvious choice. I had never been suicidal, not even close. If anything, I was blissfully out of touch with my needs and feelings as I led the life I thought I had always wanted to live. The life my parents had lived and had wanted for me. They both loved Derek and were thrilled when we moved in together. After the big white wedding, they had waited patiently for the grandchildren they had expected to appear, only to be told that I preferred dogs. I chose a Labrador over children, and while they vocalized their acceptance of my decision, I don't think they ever forgave me. It was hard to tell, because we never spoke about it, and then one day it was too late.

It seemed odd to me that I was living what I could only then identify as a pretty out-of-touch life— homemaker, book club member, pilates practitioner, chardonnay drinker, loyal wife and dog-mom—only to suddenly have this vision and feel the need to spread the word to complete strangers and then dive off a bridge and land in oncoming traffic on one of the city's busiest highways.

It would be a different story if I had been "spiritual"—if I were the kind of person to go on mountain mediation retreats, read tomes written by white-haired gurus, and drink ayahuasca. Then maybe I'd be the kind of person who would feel compelled to share a message and then jump off a bridge. But I was just not that person.

Even though I now wished I had jumped, the story just didn't add up, and I was more than surprised that any court would have forgone a trial and instead ordered a direct psychiatric institution admission. How was that legal? It was the first time I was able to think about the case rationally, because before that day I was so consumed with guilt over what I had done that I couldn't face thinking about it. I started to scrape away the useless emotions—the guilt, the heartache over a husband who never visited—and began to see a bigger picture, and that picture just didn't make sense.

I wasn't going to sit there and sulk. I wasn't going to wait to become Doctor Adrathar's victim again. I would fight if I needed to—and I was guessing that I would need to. Ultimately, I'd have to escape or die, and to do that, I'd have to get myself out of the wheelchair. I looked around the cell again, this time with fresh eyes. There was a clothing rail that could perhaps take my body weight. I could do pull-ups. I could do push-ups and sit-ups, and when I healed more, I'd be able to do squats, and run on the spot. There were strength-building pilates exercises that I knew by heart that didn't require any equipment. Once I needed weights, I could try to lift the bed, or the wheelchair. I would do stretching and strengthening and core-building until I was a strong as I needed to be. And I was ready for it.

I wriggled out of the chair—easier said than done, with a broken pelvis—and landed hard on the concrete, smacking my cheek against the cool solid floor that was to become a familiar friend. I caught my breath, straightened my stiff body out, and began doing push-ups. I could only manage three before I collapsed. I rested, then tried again. Four. The next time I could only do two before my arms gave way. Two hours until my painkiller shot. It was agony. But this time, choosing between life and death, I chose life.

CHAPTER 47

MADE OF SHADOWS

ASHA

I sat down at the polished mahogany bar and ordered a dirty martini. The androgynous bartender slid a coaster toward me and began mixing the cocktail. I was wearing the slinkiest dress I had found in my closet—a shimmering metallic shift that showed off my boobs—and some geometric earrings that floated under my freshly styled hair. Of course, I hadn't done the makeup or hair myself. That would have been asking for trouble. Instead, I had put in a call to Savvy and she had been thrilled to help.

"You remembered," she had gushed on the phone. "That's fabulous!"

I paused. "Remembered what?"

"You remembered that I always do your face when you've got a date!"

"I don't have a date," I said.

She ignored me. "Is it that hot cop?"

"No!" I said, but it did make me think of Armstrong, and I felt a flash of something through my body. Longing? Before I could name the emotion, it was gone. "No," I repeated. "It's not the hot cop."

"Pity," Savannah murmured. "I'll be right over."

An hour and a half later I looked like a much younger, sexier version of myself, and the bartender was placing a triple-olive martini in front of me. I thanked him and reached for my card, but he waved it away.

"First drink is free," he said.

"Really?"

"It is when you look like you do," he replied. "Boss's orders."

"It's a good policy," I said, raising my glass to him and taking a sip. It was a bloody good martini. Edison tucked his towel into his smart black apron and left me to attend to another customer. When he came back, he was smirking.

"What's up?" I asked.

He slid another martini my way. "It looks like you're not going to be paying for any drinks tonight."

When I knitted my brows, he lifted his chin toward a group of men farther down the bar. They smiled and raised their drinks to me, and I returned the gesture while mouthing "*thank you.*"

"Thanks," I said to the bartender. "But please don't accept any more drinks on my behalf. Two martinis are about as much as I can handle."

"Yes, ma'am," Ed replied, and took the empty glass away.

"Before you go," I said. "You see that man in the crisp white shirt? Maroon tie?"

The bartender looked across at the group of men, who seemed engrossed in a story. The maroon tie was glancing over at us even as he listened to his friend talk.

"Affirmative," said the bartender.

"Can you tell him I'd like a word?"

If Edison was confused by my sudden turnaround, he didn't show it. "Yes, ma'am."

He made his way over to the group of men, waited for the end of the story, which erupted into peals of laughter, then had a quick word with the man in the maroon tie, who looked over at me again and excused himself from the crowd.

He sauntered over, and I immediately disliked the arrogance in his body language. My knife tingled against my thigh, reminding me that it was there should I need it.

I offered him the seat next to mine and he took it, putting his golden lager down next to my cocktail, as well as his car keys and phone.

"Thank you for the drink," I said.

"Oh, it wasn't from me," he shot back. "It was Andrew. The blond guy."

"It doesn't matter," I said. "I wanted to talk to you."

He smiled. "I've never seen you here before. You new at Bergdahl?"

I shook my head. "I'm not an investment banker."

"That's what I would have guessed," he said.

"Why? Because I'm a woman?"

"No. Because you're young and beautiful. You look too healthy to be on the floor."

I laughed. "Is that why you lot are all so pale? Too much time on the floor?"

He rolled up his sleeves and rubbed his face. I had unintentionally struck a nerve. "Yes," he said, after a long sigh. "I guess so."

Some of the men glanced over from time to time, no doubt wondering how high maroon tie's hand was progressing up my skirt. They were destined to be disappointed.

"It's a stressful job," I said.

"Ah, it's O.P.M."

"Opium?"

"O.P.M. Other People's Money."

"But it's still stressful."

"I've had two cardiac episodes in the last couple of years."

"You ever think of switching to something less demanding?"

"No."

"No?"

"My job is the easy part. My home life is the demanding part." He showed me the pale band of skin from where his wedding ring used to be.

"Ah," I said. "Getting rid of the old ball and chain?"

"Trying," he replied. He tried a rueful grin, but didn't pull it off. As much as he pretended to be unconcerned with his marital status, there was still a shadow in his eyes. He downed the rest of his beer.

A notification came up on his phone, and he looked down and dismissed it. Behind the message I saw his wallpaper: a picture of a blonde woman, close up and laughing. A bird—a silver raven—hung suspended from the delicate chain around her neck. The woman was Nicola Landau, although you'd never draw that conclusion if you had only met the patient in the Riverside cell. The notification itself had informed him that he had a WhatsApp message from "Chione." The man picked up his phone and put it face down on the bar counter, and signaled for another round of drinks. Edison lifted his eyebrows at me and I shook my head almost imperceptibly. He understood and surreptitiously mixed me a cold water in a martini glass, with olives. I wanted the maroon tie to carry on drinking, but I needed a reasonably clear head to get the information I was after.

Edison watched us unobtrusively while he polished wine glasses. He held each glass over a steaming teapot until it was misted over, then rubbed the glass with a clean white napkin. I watched my drinking partner empty pint after pint while his phone vibrated with messages. The other patrons began to clear out, some of them giving us a wave and a yell of encouragement as they left. Derek Landau told me about the stresses of his job, his family, his marriage. He poured his problems out to me as if I were nothing but a vessel. He was acting exactly the way I had expected him to. As he brought me close to tears with boredom, I realized one small but important thing. Derek didn't have a magical bone in his body. Not one; not even a hint of one. He may be arrogant, boring, and unfaithful, but Derek Landau had not cursed his wife.

Still, I wasn't about to let him off the hook completely.

"Tell me about your wife," I said.

He shook his head. His movements were slower now, his speech becoming more slurred. "I don't want to talk about her." He rubbed where his wedding ring used to be. Did he miss her? Or was it just out of habit?

"The nurse at Riverside told me that you haven't visited her once. Not once since she's been there."

Derek's eyes snapped open, and he seemed instantly sober. "What? Who are you?"

"A friend of Nicola's," I replied. "And I'm wondering how a husband could leave his wife to rot in a terrible place like that. Do you know what they're doing do her? Do you know? While you're out drinking with your buddies and pouring your heart out to strange women at a bar."

He gave me a hard look and reached for his keys, but they were gone. He looked around for support from his colleagues, but they had gone home.

He smacked the bar counter. "Edison!"

"Sorry, sir," said the bartender. "You've had more than five drinks. Boss's orders. I'll keep your keys for you till tomorrow. I'll call the cab. We'll take care of the charge."

Landau glared at Edison, and then at me. "You can both go to hell."

"Funny you should say that," I replied. "I'm freshly escaped from hell. I was visiting Nicola at Riverside today. And you know what? I'd rather be dead than be stuck in there. They tie her up. They run volts through her brain. It's a torture chamber."

Derek held his head as if he felt the electroshocks himself. His expression was desperate. "She killed people," he stammered. "She shot a man—"

"You know that Nicola wouldn't do that," I countered through gritted teeth. "You know your wife."

"That policeman had children!" he said.

"Is that what you tell yourself? Is that what makes you feel better when you're trying to fall asleep at night? That she deserves to be locked up in that hellhole because the policeman had children? Wake up, Derek! You know that Nicola would not do that! Something happened to her!"

"I know!" he yelled, beside himself. "Don't you think I know that? We've been married for fifteen years!"

I sneered at him. My disgust was palpable. "Well," I said, standing up. "Congratulations."

I waved goodbye to Edison and hung around outside the bar until Derek Landau stumbled out. I put on my helmet and revved, ready to follow the cab he climbed into. The taxi drove for just over ten minutes, until we reached an expensive-looking apartment block on the outskirts of Sandton. I killed my lights and rode quietly in, tailgating, and parked my Wasp in the shadows.

I took out my wand, nervous to try a spell. I had done well with magic when I was fighting off that wizard, but that was life or death. I had no idea how this would go, and worried I'd make a small mistake with big consequences. I didn't have much time, so I just had to get on with it. I squeezed my eyes shut and recalled the cheat sheet of spells I had read over before heading over to Riverside. I held my silver wand purposefully and focused my energy on it. I breathed in and out, until I could feel the magic swirl from all around me, and directed it inwards until I had a whirlwind of green sparks flying around and into me. I felt the power, and it was good.

"Invisibilis factus," I whispered, and my wand vanished.

"Hex!" I swore, thinking I had just made my wand disappear. But then I looked at where my hand should have been, and my feet, and I realized my spell had worked. I was invisible, made of shadows. Heart hammering, I padded over to where Derek was waiting outside a front door. It opened, and the light from inside the house poured out, dramatically framing him as if he were the main actor in a stage play.

"You took your time," said the woman who had opened the door. She seemed more amused than angry. She grabbed his tie, which was by then looking worse for wear and probably smelled like lager, and used it to pull him inside, and into a passionate embrace. The door slammed shut and then thunked and rattled as their bodies slammed into it. I assumed the svelte, smoky-voiced redhead was doing most of the work, as Derek was pretty far gone by then.

I had guessed that there was another woman; that part seemed obvious. What I hadn't expected to see was that the mistress was wearing Nicola Landau's necklace—the one with the silver raven charm.

Okay, "Chione," I thought. The plot has certainly thickened.

CHAPTER 48

PRISON CURRENCY

NICKY

Exhausted, in agony, and soaked in sweat, I decided to bathe myself for the first time since being at Riverside. It would be distracting, and the warmth would be good for the pain. Devka was nowhere to be seen, and I didn't want Sister Ingleby or Doctor Adrathar deciding they would take me for a bath, so I thought I'd beat them to it. I grabbed my toiletry bag and a fresh sweatsuit, and put them on my lap. My biceps burned when I wheeled myself along, but for once, it was a good pain.

The communal ablution facilities were rather empty, and I was grateful. I avoided eye contact with the few women who were in there, ready to shower. I chose the bath right at the end of the hall, and squeezed my chair in the small space next to the small, stained porcelain bath. When I had done so, I realized the door couldn't close, so I had to maneuver my way out of the wheelchair again—I was getting good at it, but my arms were tired from my workout before—and push it out of the bathroom, then close and latch the door. I was going to get strong, I promised myself, whether I liked it or not.

Soaking in the lukewarm tub I closed my eyes and tried to imagine I was somewhere else, if only for a few minutes. I tried to pretend I was at home. Deep, salted water, as hot as I wanted it; classical music; scented candles ... but pain and fear kept bringing me back to the gray-grouted room, nagging at me. Every now and then I'd open one eye just a little to check that Adrathar wasn't standing there watching me. His eyes gliding all over my body, and my scars.

Soon the water was cold, and I began to shiver. That's when I realized that I hadn't brought a towel. I whispered curse words, called myself a useless child. I hauled my body out of the bath and dried it with my soiled clothes. It took ages to put the fresh sweatsuit on, and get back into the chair, but when I had done so, I felt triumphant. Not only had I worked out and pretended to eat breakfast, I had also just bathed myself. I did a little wheelie in the chair to celebrate, and then felt foolish for doing so. I couldn't help thinking that life was going to improve.

I was almost out of the white-tiled ablutions hall when I heard footsteps outside. I stopped. There was something about the sound of the steps. You can hear it when women are walking freely, perhaps chatting, without mission or malice. These footsteps were the opposite. I waited for them to pass, trying to keep my breathing quiet, but no such luck. My instinct told me to run for it, which my legs didn't find very funny.

This is why you're supposed to wait for Devka. This is why you're not supposed to go to places on your own, I told myself, but it was too late for a scolding. I sat dead still, waiting. Hoping they'd pass, but they didn't. I watched as five women in sweatsuits walked in. I was so relieved when I knew two of them—Alison and Fikile—that I sighed audibly.

"Jeez," I said. "You gave me a scare."

They didn't smile as I expected they would. They didn't chuckle and say *You need to chill* or *Why are you so on edge?*

Instead, they all stood and looked at me as if I had taken the last chocolate chip cookie.

"What?" I asked. It struck me then as odd that all five women had decided to come into the shower block at the same time. They weren't carrying toiletry bags or towels. One of the women closed and locked the main door.

"What is it?" I asked again, my heart doing the rumba.

"Don't worry, honey," said Alison. "There's nothing to be scared of."

That made me nervous as hell. "I'm not scared of you," I lied.

"You should be," said the woman who had locked the door.

"Just tell me what's going on," I said. "We can come to an agreement. No one has to do anything stupid."

One of the women eyed me aggressively. I guessed she thought I had just called her stupid.

"As I said," continued Alison, "there's nothing to worry about. We're just here to collect payment."

"Oh!" I said, relieved. "Of course."

They didn't move or say anything.

"So how does it work? I pay you and you get the pethidine for me?

"You've already taken the peth," said Fikile.

"What? No, I haven't."

I remembered the nightmare that had been the night before. I hadn't been given painkillers all day, and Devka didn't have access to the med cabinet. She had magically conjured up some opiates, and now I realized it hadn't been by magic.

"Of course," I said. "Thank you. Are there any … more?"

I knew I couldn't count on Ingleby to dispense the correct amount of analgesics, and I hadn't seen Devka that morning. I was going to need a shot soon.

Alison reached into her pocket and showed me two more vials.

"I thought ... I thought that maybe I'd get more for my ring," I said.

"I'm going to need more than that and my ring is the only thing I have to trade. "I don't know how I'll get more money."

"There are ways," said Fikile. "We'll teach you."

"Okay," I said. Who could argue with that? Although it was clear that I was being fleeced, it looked like the choice was to either take the two vials or get my head smashed in. I knew which scenario I preferred. "Okay."

I put the vials in my back pocket and then looked at my left hand, admiring the ring for the last time. Would Derek be upset that I was pawning my wedding ring for drugs? Would he even care? How much life had changed in the last few months. I quickly made peace with the exchange and pulled at the ring. The problem was, I hadn't removed it for years and years. It was pretty much part of my skin and skeleton. I pulled again, but it wasn't budging.

"Hang on," I said.

"Don't mess with us, Landau," said Alison's friend. All the other women threateningly advanced.

I pulled some more. It hurt my skin, but didn't move a millimeter. "I need to put soap on it," I said. "It's stuck."

The most intense woman sucked her teeth. "She's faking. I'll get that ring off."

I imagined her pulling the ring off and taking all my knuckle-skin with it.

"No!" I said. "I'll get it off. I just need a bit of soap. I have some here." I motioned at my toiletry bag.

Alison instructed one of her minions to check the bag, perhaps suspicious that I was harboring a weapon in the tiny transparent bag. The aggressive one passed me the small cake of prison-issue soap and I moved slowly to the row of basins, wet my hands, and rubbed the soap on my finger. The ring loosened nicely, but still wouldn't move past my swollen knuckle. I realized with rising dread that it wasn't going to budge.

"I'll get it off," I said, not with much certainty.

Alison crossed her arms. "You agreed to pay with a ring you knew you couldn't remove."

"No! I ... I haven't tried to take it off in years."

"It's a pity," she said, "that you can't be trusted. We could have looked after you."

I pulled and pushed at the slippery golden ring, wishing the stupid thing would just break in half. I could perhaps force it over the knuckle and lose that skin.

"I'll lose weight," I said. "I'm not eating, anyway."

The women scoffed and pouted. "Lose weight? From where?"

"I'll stop drinking water," I said. "That should do it."

"No," said Alison. "I want the ring now."

"Or," I said, reaching into my back pocket for the vials, "you can have these back until I can get it off. Then we can do the transaction in a few days once I've managed it."

"No," said Alison.

"No?" I asked. I didn't see another way of solving the problem.

"You've already had one, and we need to get paid."

"Fine," I agreed. "Just tell me how."

"I want the ring," she said. "That was the deal."

I felt like rubbing my face off in frustration, but I resisted. Also, I didn't want to make any sudden moves in front of these crazies. Instead I wet my hands again and scraped more soap onto the ring, forcing it with all my might. Still, the ring remained in place.

"Bring the bolt cutters," Alison said to her henchwoman.

They had bolt cutters? Why hadn't they said so? We could just cut off the ring and the problem would be solved. Then I realized there was no way that the bolt cutters were going to fit between my skin and the metal. When Alison had called for the tool, she hadn't meant for it to cut the ring.

CHAPTER 49

WET WITH MAROON

NICKY

I started moving backwards in my wheelchair, but it was all useless. With five able-bodied women against me, I knew that I didn't stand a chance.

Alison enjoyed watching me squirm. "Where are you going?"

I was out of options. All I could do was back into the corner. Within minutes, the short-haired woman was back, proudly brandishing a pair of bolt cutters. Just looking at the blades made my lungs wheeze, my heart shrink.

Alison wriggled her hand at me as if I were a toddler. "Come on," she said. "Come here."

I frowned at her. Did she really think I was going to volunteer to have my finger cut off so that she could have a bloody ring? So much for me thinking that most of the women at Riverside were sane.

I clenched my jaw and waited, hoping a nurse would pass by in the corridor, or another prisoner would come in and scream, or something.

"Come here," said Alison again, her eyes bugging out because I hadn't obeyed her first command.

"I'm going to keep trying to get it off and I'll give it to you as soon as it budges." As I spoke, I was forcing the band onto the knuckle, cutting the skin there. I didn't care. I had decided that knuckle-skin was no longer a priority. Still, the metal wouldn't come free. Alison, realizing the lamb wouldn't come willingly to slaughter, gestured to Fikile that she should take the cutters and come to me.

"Get it," she ordered.

The others flanked Fikile as she held up the bolt cutters. They were backing her up, knowing that I would struggle.

"No," I said. "No." Even though I knew that nothing I said would stop them from taking my finger. "No!" I shouted, and my voice echoed in the hall. I panicked, and inside the panic there was a small calm space, a kind of *déjà vu* knowledge that I had been here before, perhaps in a nightmare. Or maybe I had seen this coming, these women with their wild, shiny eyes and set brows. These patients who thought nothing of taking someone's finger so that they could get their payment on time. That strange, calm, familiar space existed, but it was soon overruled by panic. I started screaming as if my hair were on fire. I lashed out. I was a wild animal. Having lost my fear of death made the struggle easier.

"Shut her up!" shouted Alison.

I had the feeling that some—if not all—of the guards were on Alison's payroll, because someone should have heard the scuffle by then. I was screaming my lungs out. It made sense that the guards were the ones who got her the contraband she sold to the other prisoners. I wondered what she had to do for them to make it worth their while.

Fikile lunged toward me, and I made a fist for the first time in my life and rammed it into her jaw. It was the first time I had ever punched someone, and it hurt like hell. I was sure I'd done some damage to my hand, but at least I still had the ten fingers I was born with. She let out a yell of surprise and listed to the side, but stayed on her feet. The woman next to her grabbed me by the throat, strangling me so that I could no longer draw oxygen. My hands still free, I tried to push her away, tried to reach up to scratch her eyes, but because of the lack of oxygen and my awkward position, I could do neither. Although it was painful to move my legs, I tried to kick her knee in, but that didn't work either.

My vision was slowly fading, and I saw stars. My face was throbbing as I slowly lost consciousness. Soon the other women were there, all putting their hands on me, and then Fikile approached, the tool's arms open and the glinting blades ready to amputate. Things were fading, but I could tell that two women were holding my struggling body down while another held my left hand, forcing it open and splaying the fingers to make space for the teeth of the cutters.

No! I tried to shout, but the strangulation had cut off my voice. I tried one last time to throw them off, but it was no use. Despite being mostly in darkness, I heard the crack of the vials in my back pocket, and felt the cool spread as their precious liquid spilled out. I felt the cold metal biting down on my ring finger and I tried to scream, but nothing came out.

One of the women attacking me grabbed my hair and pulled it back while the others continued to restrain me. A sharp current of pain shot up my hand. Just before she managed to finish the job, I saw a blur of dark hair and pallid skin, and suddenly I was able to grab my hand back, and draw in enough air to cough and splutter. Emily stood there, a terrifying sight in her dirty gown and stringy hair, paper-pale skin and holes for eyes, like something out of a horror movie. She launched into Fikile, viciously punching and clawing until Fikile let the bolt cutters fall to the ground with a metallic clank. Emily picked the tool up and the women scattered. She hissed at those who hadn't yet disappeared, and they retreated. Alison sneered at me, promising vengeance, then left. The hall became quiet.

I felt a warm puddle on my lap. When I looked down, my sweatsuit was wet with maroon. I lifted my hand to inspect it. My ring finger was spurting blood, but it was still attached. I was scared of Emily, but my gratitude was greater than my fear. Her back was to me, her spine stooped and knobby.

"Thank you," I ventured. My voice—barely a whisper—echoed in the vast space.

Emily slowly turned around to face me, and the lights overhead flickered. When I saw her face, I tried to scream, but no sound came out.

CHAPTER 50
CUT THROUGH BONE
- CUT THROUGH BONE -
NICKY

A guard came running into the shower block, a baton in one hand, the other resting on her pepper spray. When she saw me, her eyes flew open in shock. The blood had spilled over my lap and the chair, and was forming a crimson paint spill on the white tiles below. She reached for her two-way radio and called for help. After she clicked it back on to her belt, she approached me with caution.

"What happened?" the guard asked, looking around for the perpetrator.

I gazed at her freckles and blinked slowly, gradually escaping the trance I was in.

"Who did this to you?" She grabbed my face with a muscular hand and spoke right into my face, trying to get me to answer her, but it seemed that my mouth was not in functioning order. "Are you all right?"

I was sitting in a puddle of my own blood and my body was marble. I didn't know how long I'd been there like that, stiff and blue, but it was clear that I was not *all right.* I assumed above-average IQ scores were not in the top prerequisites for getting a job as a guard at Riverside Asylum.

The guard checked my pupils and my pulse, then kicked open all the toilet stall doors. Empty. Shower block and bathrooms were similarly unoccupied. When she was satisfied that we were alone, she checked on me again and wheeled me out, leaving a trail of blood behind us.

I was still in a silent stupor when I arrived at the nurse station, and one of the sisters I didn't recognize gasped at my state and took me from the guard. She pushed me into a nearby room with first aid supplies, dressed me in a clean gown, and tended to my finger. After looking at her name badge, I saw she was in fact a resident doctor. Aoife Byrne spoke gently in a subtle Irish accent as she worked, telling me what she was doing.

"Local anesthetic," she said, as the needle went in. Once it was numb, she cleaned and stitched it, stopping only briefly to blaspheme about how deep the cut was, and how fortunate I was that it hadn't cut through bone.

"Nerve damage for life, I'm assuming," Doctor Byrne said, in an upbeat way. "So maybe you're not that lucky, after all."

Her humane way and tender touch made me feel emotional, but my body language was still blank. I wanted to thank her, yet my body felt paralyzed.

As she was fastening the bandage, a shadow fell across us. Sister Ingleby stood in the doorway. "I'll take her from here."

I didn't want to go with Ingleby, but I didn't resist. My body was drained of energy.

"She's still in shock," said the doctor. "She should go straight to bed with a cup of tea."

Sister Ingleby crossed her arms, apparently offended by the suggestion she act kindly to one of her patients. "No time for dilly-dallying. She has a session with Doctor Adrathar."

When I heard his name, my throat closed up and my lungs burned. I tried to refuse, but all I could manage was a succession of fast blinking.

Doctor Byrne picked up on my anxiety and shook her head. "Her therapy can wait a day. I'll call Adrathar and let him know. Right now, she needs to rest."

Ingleby forced her lips to turn up at the corners. Her eyes almost disappeared in the superficiality of the smile. "Of course."

The doctor turned to me again. "I'm going to have a quick tidy up here, then I'll come to check on you in ten."

I felt Ingleby's body tense up. Now she would have to take me back to my cell. She may even have to make me a cup of tea. All I could think of was how grateful I was to Doctor Byrne for getting me out of a session with Adrathar.

Thank you, thank you, thank you, I whispered in my head. I managed to lift my bandaged hand a few inches off my lap. The doctor saw my gesture and waved back.

I was comforted by the worry in her eyes.

Uncharacteristically, Ingleby let me rest for the remainder of the day. The next morning, I felt vaguely human again. I was able to move, and to think with relative clarity. I was up at sunrise, working out before anyone could notice or stop me. Push-ups were harder with my throbbing finger, but I breathed through the pain. Every time I felt like giving up, I forced myself to think about being in Adrathar's room again, or being pinned against a wall by Alison's minions, or being alone in a room with Emily.

Emily had without a doubt saved me the day before when she showed up in the ablution block and scattered the gang of inmates intent on taking my finger. I was indebted to her, especially after the way I reacted when she had turned to look at me after dispersing my attackers. I kept pushing the image out of my mind, so disturbing and confusing it was. The problem was that I hadn't understood what I had seen when she turned around. It didn't make sense to me. Now that I was out of that immobilizing stupor, I realized it must have just been a shock response, and my eyes had played tricks on me. When Emily had turned around to face me, the lights overhead had coruscated, and it felt like I had been sliced right into a jump-cut of a monochromatic horror movie. The filth-grouted tiles took on a more sinister look, and the hall was silent apart from the flickering bulbs. Emily's face was an exaggerated mask: ivory skin with gray capillaries pulsing underneath, wide-open black lips baring a dark pit and too-sharp teeth. Her eyes were the familiar dark spirals that threatened to suck me in.

I had screamed, but the sound didn't escape the room. Emily sucked it in through the dark holes in her face.

I shivered, and took a break from the push-ups. I used the fear from the memory to pull myself out of the wheelchair and stand on my own. Pulling my body out of its usual sitting position to stand up straight was agony. Pain reverberated through my backbone and hips, and my thighs burned with the effort. My lower body muscles had atrophied; I needed to build them up again if I wanted to walk on my own. I stood there, shaking and sweating with the effort, for as long as I could, then collapsed into the chair. The next time I would do it—I'd take a step forward. The time after that, two steps. Then back to arm strengthening and core exercises. Who knew that my pilates experience would come in so handy? I hauled myself up again. There was no time to waste.

CHAPTER 51

RESIDENT WRAITHS

ASHA

Twenty-one minutes after Derek staggered through her doorway, his mistress opened the front door and rather stealthily left her apartment. I guessed that Derek was out for the count, most likely snoring in drunken postcoital slumber. I watched the woman close the door quietly and stride toward the entrance of the complex, eight-inch heels hitting the paving in perfect rhythm, as if she were born in them.

This is interesting, I thought. I understood why spouses might perhaps sneak out in the middle of the night, but not paramours. I was glad she hadn't waited five minutes more, or I would have missed this fascinating development. I suppose I owed my thanks to Derek, who hardly seemed like the most considerate beau—or generous lover.

A black Aston Martin pulled up. I expected the woman to quicken her pace, but instead she took her time. The driver, who wore a dark suit, greeted her and opened the back door. This was no regular Uber ride. By then I was on my Wasp, and as soon as the luxury car pulled away, I negotiated my way between the boom and the well-lit security room, narrowly escaping scratching my Vespa.

"Hey!" I heard from inside the small room. When I automatically turned my head, I saw a guard in a khaki uniform fumbling for his pistol. As quick as a whip I kicked out my stand—so I wouldn't have to balance and sling a spell at the same time—and I grasped my wand. Our eyes connected, and we both got hold of our weapons at the same time. He had only to pull a trigger, while I had to remember a spell and utter it correctly. The odds were clearly not in my favor.

He hesitated. Perhaps it was the odd sight of a woman dressed in black riding a scooter in the middle of the night, or maybe it was the glint of moonlight on my wand. Whatever it was, it gave me the two seconds I needed to protect myself.

"Protendo!" I declaimed. It was a basic safeguard that—mostly—didn't harm the other party. Perfect for a situation like this when the person attacking you was well within their rights to do so, or if there was any other reason you didn't want to harm them, like the framed photo I spied in his booth of him holding a baby up to the camera, or the healthy-looking potted plant on his desk.

It wasn't enough, though. I didn't want him calling the cops on me, and I certainly didn't want a security camera video of my tailgating making the rounds on the neighborhood security network.

"Fiat fulgur!" I yelled, pointing my wand at the circuit box at the back of the room. A bolt of lightning surged through my veins and stormed out of the wand, zapping the electrical casing and, with it, the security company's video feed and radio signal. Not only did the lights in the guard room go out, but so did every bulb around the entrance and in the parking lot. As the man was plunged into darkness, I kicked my stand back, thanked the goddesses, and accelerated into the witching hour.

I managed to pick up Derek's mistress's trail by using a *monstras* spell. Despite how it sounds, the magic is not used to summon monsters, but to show something that is hidden, as in *demonstrate*. In this case, my vision went from a dark suburban street to a neon trail of blue lights, indicating the path the Aston Martin had taken. As I followed the track I couldn't help wondering where all this magic was coming from. It seemed that the more magic I performed, the more I remembered. Magic muscle memory. There was no way I could have thrown up a protection spell a few days before; I was clueless. But now I was beginning to trust myself more, and was learning that the more I did, the more I remembered. Soleil was right—I just had to remember who I was.

I kept a good distance from the fancy car and traveled with my headlight off. The roads were empty, so it was safe enough. Around fifteen minutes later we were in the glittering city center, and the car pulled into the entrance of a huge building that took up the whole block. Two men with automatic weapons guarded the heavy front gate as it closed. I had no idea how I was going to get in.

Something odd happened. I felt all at once as if I were surrounded by a spiritual support system. The sensation was coming from the building and the grounds, as if the very soul of the establishment was rising up to help me. I started to shake, not knowing what was happening. It felt like a benign, even beneficial power, but what did I know? It could well have been a spiritual spiderweb inviting me into its lair. The resident wraiths—or whatever they were—beckoned to me. *Come in,* they were saying, *all will be well. You are one of us.*

The last bit frightened the bejeezus out of me. I pinched myself to make sure I was alive. It hurt, so I took that as a good sign. I knew I had literally died on the operating table, so it could have gone either way. I was relieved to confirm that I had in fact made it back in one piece.

I knew I couldn't just breeze in on a scooter and high-five the guards, so I rode a little farther on and ramped up the pavement, parking it against the wall and turning it, as well as myself, invisible. By the time I walked back to the heavily armed security, I had a plan. Holding my breath, I tiptoed toward the first man in uniform and whispered something in his ear. He stiffened and looked right through me, searching for the thing that had just grasped and tugged at his imagination. The souls vibrated the ground.

I spoke again. *"Evoco et excito, nunc et semper, res ac mortales."*

For a second, it felt like his gasp was inhaling me.

"Ignis!" I hissed, so that only he could hear me.

He blinked hard, snapping out of his momentary hypnotic state.

"Fire!" he yelled into my face—although he couldn't see me—making me jump, despite the fact that I was the one who had inserted the conjuration in his mind. "Fire!"

I could see the flames in his eyes, the reflection of the phantom catastrophe he was seeing unfold before him.

The other guard rushed forward. "Hector," he shouted. "What are you talking about?"

Hector ignored him, pushing past and buzzing the huge gate open to appraise the fire he thought was approaching the old building. I slid through the gap and ran into the dimly lit property.

"There's no fire," said his partner, shaking him. "Hector!"

I let go of the conjuring spell then, and the imaginary fire disappeared, probably leaving Hector doubting his sanity—and his colleague, his sobriety.

Sorry, Hector.

There was a tingle of magic in my fingers, like I had on the day when I'd dispensed of the Dusk Reaper who had tried to kill me. Just as I turned the corner, I saw the Aston Martin pull away from what looked like a side entrance. I checked that I was still invisible, ran up, and then slipped through the gap she had left. More guards with more weapons lurked on either side of the door. If they sensed me in any way, they gave no indication. Once I was inside, I sighed quietly, and Derek's mistress looked back, wondering what she had heard. I froze and held my breath again, waiting. She narrowed her eyes like a cat, sniffed the air, then turned back and continued forward.

I followed Chione's svelte form over the crimson carpet and into the building, which turned out to be some kind of old rich boys' club. The structure itself seemed to be over a hundred years old—which I guessed explained the spirits who helped me get in—and had the décor to match. Ancient marble pillars and grand staircases, pressed ceilings and chandeliers. We climbed two levels. I admired the mistress as I followed her, watching her stilettos and fascinated by the way she sprang so easily up the steps, knowing that I would have certainly broken an ankle by then. Finally finished with the climb, we sped along a long corridor carpeted in Persian rugs.

As we walked, I caught sight of various rooms. An old oak-paneled library, a green cigar lounge that reeked of stale tobacco. An armory room, a huge dining room, an old-fashioned water closet. *What is this place?* I wondered. *And why are we here?*

We reached a slim door at the end of the passage, where the woman finally pulled off her shoes. I felt relief for her. And just as suddenly as her heels were off, she disappeared, and the door swung closed.

Hex! I cursed, under my breath. To have come all this way just to lose her at the very end. I gritted my teeth while anger warmed my cheeks. I knew what had happened. I had become too confident, too quickly. Just because I could muster a couple of spells did not mean I was ready to dive into this dangerous magical world. Not even close.

I flailed for the swinging door, trying to rush after her, but as I stepped through the frame I yelped and grabbed on to it. There was nothing beneath me but the night sky. I scrambled backwards and slammed the door, reversing onto the building's balding red carpet and falling to the floor as I did so. I noticed my arms, which no longer appeared invisible. I uttered the invisibility spell again, but it didn't work, perhaps because my body was in shock. I could feel the adrenaline washing through my body, painting it cold.

I was sure that my yelp would bring unwanted attention, so I had to get out of there. I didn't know how I'd do it if my magic wasn't working, but I had to try. I was about to stand up when Derek Landau's mistress stepped into my light, casting a long shadow over me. I looked up at her silhouette, holding her heels to my chest. I couldn't read her expression, but I was pretty sure she was unimpressed.

She whipped a silver cord around my body and pulled it tight. "Not so fast," she said.

Landau's mistress pulled the silver cord that she had lashed to me, and with a whip of her wrist we were transported from that musty corridor to a cozy piano room, where she sat in a large wingback, staring at me. The melody was haunting. I looked over to see who was playing, and saw the keys dancing on their own. Despite us being the only ones there, a cocktail with crushed ice appeared in front of the woman, condensation running down the glass as if it had been waiting for her. I smelled bourbon and mint. When she crossed her legs, I saw that her shoes were back on.

"Who are you?" she asked, taking a sip of her dripping drink.

"I barely know the answer myself," I replied.

Her lips pouted in irritation. "I could use a truth potion on you, you know."

I sat up straight, the bright cord pulling at me. "Could you? I have so many questions."

"Insolence." She slammed down her drink. "Do you know what those guards will do to you? I could call them right now."

"But you won't," I said. "Or you would have already. Tell me your name, and I'll tell you mine."

She gazed at me with her green eyes, a close match to mine. "You can call me Chione."

Key-own-knee, I thought. It sounded vaguely exotic.

"Chione," I repeated.

"It's Egyptian."

The piano came to the end of its tune. I looked down at the cord tethering me.

"*Rumpis,*" I whispered. It snapped off, stinging my skin in the process. I tried not to wince, but I couldn't help rubbing my arms where the rope had abraded my skin. Chione was looking at me intently. I clicked my fingers and her cocktail appeared in my hand. A lighting-speed *volas* spell did the trick. I raised the glass to her and took a sip as the next melody began. Despite the ice, the bourbon burned my throat. I put it down with more confidence than I felt, and we locked eyes once again.

"Hello, Chione," I said. "I'm the Cursebreaker."

CHAPTER 52
GRIMALKIN
ASHA

"What is this place?" I asked.

Chione looked entertained by the question. "You've never been to the Auric? I'm not surprised. It's by invitation only."

She snapped her fingers, and her drink flew back into her hand. It was so fast that I didn't see it fly through the air, and so smooth that it didn't spill.

Good riddance, I thought. I didn't like the taste, anyway.

"Let's not waste each other's time," I said. "What are you doing with that untouched human?"

"Do you mean Landau?"

"Of course I mean Landau. Which other untouched people are you messing around with?"

Her eyebrows shot up for an instant, making me more certain that perhaps Derek Landau wasn't her only iron in the fire. *Poor humans,* I thought. *They don't stand a chance around someone like Chione.* Seductive magic radiated off her like incense smoke.

"It's just a business transaction," she replied.

I thought of how she had pulled him into her apartment and kissed him. "What kind of business?"

"I've been patient with you," Chione said, her eyes traveling to the diamond watch on her wrist. "But I'm tired now. It's very late."

"I need to know what your plan is with Derek Landau," I said. "I don't care about him, but I'm trying to free his wife."

Chione froze. "What?"

"His wife. I don't expect you to care about her, but she's in trouble. I'm trying to help her."

"She deserves to be in that place."

I angled my head. "I don't think she does."

"You need to stay out of other people's affairs," Chione said. She didn't smile at her unfortunate term; perhaps the pun was lost on her. Perhaps it was deliberate. I felt she was growing impatient to end the conversation, but I still had questions. Nicola Landau's silver raven necklace dangled from her neck.

"What did Landau do to his wife? Why did she snap? Is it because she found out about his relationship with you? Why do you call it a business transaction?"

"I've had enough of this," she said. "Your questions are like bullets."

"I apologize," I said in a way I hoped was scathing. "It's not every day I interview a home-wrecking gold-digging sorceress."

Chione chortled. "Is that what you think I am?"

"You've clearly cast some kind of spell over Derek. Only the Void knows what you did to his wife. She'd be better off dead than in that terrifying place. Never mind the people who did actually die in that bridge stunt. I'm still waking up to this world, but I know evil when I see it."

"It's what he wanted," Chione said, barely suppressing a yawn.

"I doubt it!"

"I wouldn't have been able to bind him, otherwise."

"You're saying Derek Landau wanted his wife locked away in an asylum. Why?"

"So that he could be with me," she purred. "Why else?"

"That's what divorce attorneys are for," I said. "You didn't need to ruin her life."

"Derek didn't want a messy separation. He didn't want his clients to find out about his personal problems."

"You mean he didn't want to pay a divorce settlement?"

"Well," Chione drawled. "He is an extremely wealthy man."

The piano stopped playing.

"So, that's why you did it." My distaste was clear.

She shrugged. "There are worse reasons."

"I can't think of any."

Chione shifted in her seat and put her empty glass down. "Look, you want someone to blame? Go see him. He was the one who was unfaithful."

"You mesmerized him!" I yelled.

"You know just as well as I do that if his love was pure this never would have happened."

"Sorceress," I hissed, feeling the magic tingling in my finger-tips again.

"Not sorceress," she corrected. "Grimalkin."

Grimalkin? Her feline movements made sense. She was a cat mage.

I sat back with a sigh. *Holy hex.*

You know the superstition that says you should never cross paths with a black cat? Let's just say that Derek Landau had done more than that, and now he and his wife were paying the price.

CHAPTER 53

BREATHING CADAVER
NICKY

I wondered where Sister Devka was. I hated it when she wasn't on duty. My stomach ached and rumbled. I was doing plenty of physical training and I hadn't eaten in what felt like days. It wasn't because I couldn't stand the food —although it was truly awful—but rather because I couldn't risk running into Alison's gang or Emily. I batted thoughts of cold cardboard toast away as I padded across my cell to the opposite wall. I touched the cool plaster, then limped back. It was getting easier. Perhaps Devka would bring me a sandwich, or a couple of crackers from the nurses' station. I wanted to show her how much progress I had made in my mobility. I felt that small, hard glint of hope. It was what kept me going through the aching gray days.

When I heard movement outside my cell, my heart lifted. It would be so wonderful to see a friendly face again. I also looked forward to the relief of the painkillers she would bring. I moved as quickly as I could to my wheelchair and sat down just in time. Unfortunately, the face was less than friendly. It was Ingleby—empty-handed—and my stomach contracted.

"It's time," the awful woman said, pulling the front of her uniform down to straighten it, even though it was perfectly straight to begin with.

"No," I replied. "I'm not going back there."

"Doctor Adrathar is waiting."

"I don't care," I said, holding tightly on to the handles of the chair. "I won't go."

The electroconvulsive therapy was so terrifying and painful that I would rather die fighting than be subjected to it again, especially under the sadistic hands of Adrathar.

Ingleby dropped her cheerful façade and sighed through flaring nostrils. "Now, Mrs. Landau. Don't make this harder than it needs to be."

I spoke through my teeth. "I. Am. Not. Going."

I watched as the nurse's jaw muscles worked furiously under her skin. The artificial light from behind her gave her a more menacing appearance than usual, and I watched those twitching muscles in monochrome as she stood her ground, while I did mine.

She advanced slowly, a vulture approaching a half-dead thing.

"Leave me alone," I said. "Don't come any nearer."

"Do you think you have a say?" she whispered in a hard voice. "You lost your rights when you killed those people."

"It was a psychotic episode," I said. "I didn't mean to kill anyone."

"And that is why the doctor is being kind enough to help you."

I thought my head might explode. Did she really believe in the therapy, or was she just as sadistic as Adrathar?

"In my opinion," the sister said, "the state should get rid of people like you."

"People like me?"

"Sick people. Murderers. Why should we have to deal with your kind? You should all be put down."

Put down. I should have flinched, but I didn't.

"How would you do it?" I asked.

She seemed genuinely surprised at the question. She didn't realize that I'd rather be "put down" than face a future at Riverside.

"Stoning?" I ventured. "Guillotine? Hanging?"

"Of course not," she muttered. "A humane way. Lethal injection."

"Would you know how to administer such a thing?"

Sister Ingleby frowned at me. "I beg your pardon?"

"I would arrange to pay you, somehow. If you could organize a vial. You wouldn't have to inject it. I can do that on my own."

She stood there for a moment, staring at me without blinking. "If I helped to end your life, Mrs. Landau, then how would I be any better than you?"

You should all be put down, she had said. I think she just answered her own question.

Sister Ingleby called the guard to help escort me to Adrathar's rooms. She knew she would have a fight on her hands, and I delivered. I struggled all I could to avoid leaving my cell. I kicked and bit and punched till my wrists and ankles were forcibly trussed and I was tied into the wheelchair. My injured finger throbbed. Once I was safely tied down, the nurse stood up and brushed a strand of hair out of her eyes, as if she had done nothing more aggressive than tie her shoelaces. I noticed a scratch on her cheek, and was glad.

"Thank you," she said to the guard, out of breath. "I'll take it from here."

"You're bleeding," said Doctor Adrathar.

"Oh, it's nothing," said Ingleby, putting her hand up to cover her lacerated cheek.

"Let me quickly see to it," he said, and set about patching her up while she pretended not to enjoy the attention.

"She's feisty today," said the nurse, looking at me. "She's getting stronger."

"We'll soon sort her out," promised the doctor, and Ingleby's mouth twitched into a smile.

The rest of the session was a blur. Adrathar called two guards from the passage and they untied me and levered my struggling body from the wheelchair to the bed in the treatment room. I tried to get away, but one of the guards backhanded me, sending my cheekbone fizzing. My knees gave way, and stars filled my vision. My mind began to dissociate; I felt like I was floating above the bed looking down while they stormed my body, ripping my sweatsuit and underwear off and replacing it with a diaper, and then, as an afterthought, a paper sheet to cover my nakedness. I watched my body loll like an open-eyed corpse, all vitality vanished.

This is the last time, I promised myself as I drifted above, as Adrathar set about placing the electrodes and the needles, and forced the rubber bite plate into my mouth. This was the last time I'd let the doctor get me in his clutches. I looked on as he turned the evil machine on, sending a current through that breathing cadaver below. I watched as my body tensed and arched, and my eyes rolled back. I swore to myself that it would never happen again.

CHAPTER 54
BEWARE THE CAT
ASHA

I woke up in my own bed, in my own home, and could only imagine that the Grimalkin had used her magic to portal me there. I still had the taste of that awful cocktail in my mouth, and realized it had been a Catnip Julep.

I was grateful to her, begrudgingly so, especially when I saw my scooter parked neatly in the driveway. She could have locked me up, or killed me. She decided instead to deliver me safely home, even though I had enough information on her to report her to the Council.

Smudge-eyed, I made my way down the stairs, through the house, to the kitchen. I fed Circe and Odysseus, made tea, and took it through to my potion room, where I opened the book *Magickal Creatures.*

Grimalkin

Beware the cat!

Cat mages are not to be trusted. If you happen to cross paths with a cat mage, do not engage the feline. Let them go on their own way and hope that they will leave you in peace. If you have to connect, do so with utmost care. Cat mages are notoriously sly and will always have one up on you because, as the old saying goes, they have nine lives.

Cat mages, also known as Grimalkins, will snub good values if they have to choose between those and creature comforts like good food, warmth, and coins. Beware of this tendency, and do not be surprised if the mage betrays you for a single sardine or a simple gold coin.

These mages are deft at seduction, and will use their powers to lure partners for material gain.

Do not believe a Grimalkin who tells you they will change. The only thing they are talented at changing is appearances—their own, and others'.

STRENGTHS: Longevity; seduction; transformation; beauty.

WEAKNESSES: Greed.

TIP: Every Grimalkin has a talisman which focuses their power. It could be a piece of jewelry, a weapon, or a garment. If you are able to separate the mage and their talisman, their power will be greatly reduced.

The tea tasted terrible, but I knew it would make me feel better, because Merlin had recommended it. I wondered what he'd have to say about meeting up with Grimalkins in secret clubs in the middle of the night. I felt the urge to see him, as well as Savvy. After a day like yesterday, it would be nice to have some friendly faces around. Apart from moral support, I knew I needed help, but I was terrible at asking for it.

It seemed to me that if you are abandoned as a child, that sense of rejection stays with you for your whole life. When you finally make friendships, you hold off on asking for help, for fear of being rejected again. Perhaps it makes you think that your relationships aren't as solid as they could be, and that asking for help could somehow strain them, so you don't dare. Whatever the case, I felt lonely and muddled up. If the Grimalkin was so evil, why had she allowed my safe return home?

I craved spending the day in my garden, but I knew that Nicola Landau was suffering every minute she stayed in Riverside. Her face haunted me. I had wasted enough time. I had to get her out of there.

CHAPTER 55

THERE BY THE GRACE OF THAT GOBLIN I GO

ASHA

I practically jogged into the Copper Cog & Ale. As usual, it was pumping. The clocks ticked away on every exposed brick wall, and the fire roared in the hearth.

"Rookie!" called Ferra. "Let me get you something to eat."

"No time," I replied.

"No such thing," she said, her halo of red hair and ruddy cheeks aglow. Within seconds she delivered a small golden-crusted pie and a glass of cinnacider.

"Thank you," I said. I couldn't remember the last time I had eaten, and the aroma was delicious. The pastry was rich and flaky, and the saucy mushrooms inside were fragrant with garlic, thyme, sage, and black pepper. For a second after I took the first bite, I forgot why I had come.

"What's your question, then?" asked Ferra, slinging her tea towel over her shoulder.

I quickly finished chewing and took a sip of the cider, which was fresh and spicy. "How did you know I had a question?"

"Why else would you be here, no time for food and all?" She finished pouring the espresso I hadn't known she was making and sent it spinning on its saucer in my direction.

I quickly grabbed it and smiled.

"Ei-*leeeeeeen!*" Ferra called toward the flapping kitchen door. A child came scurrying through to the pub. "Get Asha another pie, will you? Take away. And some cookies."

"No, really," I said, putting my hand out to refuse.

"Nonsense," replied Ferra. "You're too skinny!"

I shot her a look of gratitude. You couldn't feel lonely when you were in the Copper Cog. Ferra waited for my question.

"Um," I said. "I need to figure out how to portal. Urgently."

Ferra shook her head and crossed her arms. I watched her muscles flex in her well-developed forearms. "Absolutely not."

"It's not a choice," I went on. "I have to do it. I need to get somewhere and portal magic is the only way in. Or out."

"Look," said the dwarf. "Portal magic is a very specialized branch of spell-work. If you don't get your incantation at least

99.9% correct, you could end up anywhere. And if you don't know where you are, you can't portal back again."

I put my coffee down without taking a sip.

"Or, worse," she said with wide eyes, "you could mistakenly portal only certain parts of your body."

I almost choked. "Seriously?"

"It's been known to happen," she whispered, looking around. "No one likes to talk about it. And, no offense meant, lassie, but you're still remembering your craft. You are the last person who should dabble in portal magic. It's just too dangerous."

My shoulders drooped. Ferra's daughter rushed back with the supplies and handed them over shyly.

"Good work, Skunk," said Ferra. "Now back to work."

I winked at the girl and covertly handed her a two hundred koin note. She looked up and beamed at me.

"Ah, but don't take it too hard," said Ferra. "You just need to find someone who will help you."

"I don't know anyone like that," I said.

"Och, that's the easy part. You're in the right place! Listen here, Rookie. There's a goblin I know. Now, don't get me wrong, she's just as frightful as the rest of her breed. She's slimy, sneaky, rude, greedy ... and she has the most terrifying dirty-needle teeth you've ever seen."

I must have pulled a face, because Ferra grinned at me.

"She is also by far the best portaler in the history of ever."

Hope jumped. "You *know* her?"

"Know her! I've been cooking her Sunday lunches since the Void Fracture." She looked around then, and lowered her voice. "It was all because of Nilve SaltySnap that we were able to get into that pocket realm and confront Baldassare. Without Salty, I just don't know. It scares me to think. There by the grace of that goblin I go."

I had heard whispers about goblins, and wasn't quite sure they existed. They seemed to belong in fairy tales, along with unicorns and fae.

"Where would I find her?" I asked. "Nilve SaltySnap?"

Ferra took my empty coffee cup away.

"Goblin City," she replied. "Where else? And tell her you're a friend of Jax."

"That would be lying," I replied.

"I'll introduce you in the future, so it's not quite a lie. It's a future truth. Besides, they're hardly the most honest creatures you'll meet. You know that quip about goblins."

"What is it?"

"How do you tell if a goblin is lying? His lips are moving."

I smiled and stood up, ready to find my way to Goblin City.

"Before you go, Rookie. I have a little something for you." The dwarf motioned for me to join her behind the bar. Thinking of Nicola Landau stuck in the nightmarish institution, I felt anxious to get on my way, but I trusted Ferra, so I took a breath and followed.

I had to duck to avoid hitting my head on the dwarf-sized doorway that led into the hobbity kitchen where a whole tribe of Fornaks were busy roasting, basting, grilling, and baking. Despite my full stomach, it smelt heavenly. By the looks of things, the dwarf culture had no problem with child labor. At least a dozen children who had Ferra's gold-flecked nutmeg eyes and Scot-red hair worked happily on their culinary tasks, whistling, chatting, and singing, including a teenager using a steampunk-inspired bolted-together blowtorch on a tray of creme brûlée, and a toddler rolling out pastry dough like play dough.

"Matthew, easy on the salt in that stew!" yelled Ferra. "Francis, keep your eye on that boar bacon!"

"Yes ma'am," the kids replied.

"Looking good, skunks," she said, and the children smiled.

Ferra pulled me along to the opposite end of the kitchen. "Idle hands," she said, with a wink. I couldn't believe any member of the Fornak family was ever idle, including her husband, who I spotted drilling holes in metallic sheeting outside.

"A new invention," she said, rolling her eyes. "He's got a right bee in his bonnet today."

At the opposite end of the kitchen there was an arched door which led to Ferra's tiny office. Inside the nook there was a heavy security door. A brass, gold, and copper version of what you might find at a bank vault. It had a combination lock and a turning wheel, like a ship's helm. Ferra wiped her hands on her apron, and while the dwarf punched in the twelve-digit code, I looked at the framed embroidery swatch hanging on the opposite wall. It was an Arthur C. Clarke quote. Stitched in copper wire, it said, "Any sufficiently advanced technology is indistinguishable from magic."

"*Patentibus,*" she said. The seal released with a hiss, and we went inside.

CHAPTER 56

ILLUMINO
ASHA

When the heavy door opened, I stared inside. Ferra's workshop couldn't have been any more different from the warm, fragrant restaurant she was so well known for. This was a cutting-edge high-tech lab that would get any engineer drooling. I had imagined the dwarf's workshop to be flagstone-walled, dimly lit, low-ceilinged, with a fire in the corner for smelting the ore she was so fond of using. Instead, it was spacious, with clean lines and white light, and touch-sensitive storage space under every available surface. I had imagined the dwarf's workshop to be flagstone-walled, dimly lit, low-ceilinged, with a fire in the corner for smelting the ore she was so fond of using. The steampunk theme was great for the pub, but for her lab, Ferra seemed to prefer a more scientific approach.

"We'll just be a moment, Rookie," Ferra said. "I know you're in a hurry." She marched over to an immaculate counter and touched the surface. A drawer slid seamlessly out, and inside a beautiful new ritual knife was nestled in black satin. My hands flew up to my mouth. Was it for me? It was so very beautiful. I blinked at her, feeling emotional.

Ferra grinned at me. "Well? Aren't you going to pick it up?"

I moved toward the drawer and scooped it up. "It feels … perfect," I said. The handle felt like it was molded especially for my hand, and the feeling of the grip was extremely satisfying.

"Let go," said Ferra, confusing me.

I let the knife go, expecting it to clatter on the pristine floor, but it stayed glued to my hand.

I smiled. "Oh!"

"Just a simple magnetic *velcro impedio* spell," she beamed. "When you do want to let go, just throw it at someone."

"What?"

Her eye glinted with mischief. "Or just pop it in your holster."

I tried slipping it into the faux leather pocket, and the knife came away. When I reached for it again, it stuck to my palm.

"Now!" the dwarf said, clapping her hands. "Let's see what your aim is like."

"Er," I said. I wasn't sure about my knife-throwing skills.

"Och, go on," she said, and pressed a button under the counter. A target appeared at the other side of the workshop. The poster featured an evil-looking skinhead orc with prison-quality tattoos.

"Who is that?" I asked.

"It's a Hammerskin," said Ferra. "The group of Neo-Nazi orcs who burnt the Copper Cog to the ground this time last year."

"Fair enough," I replied, and took aim.

Apparently dwarfs knew how to hold a grudge, and I couldn't say I blamed them.

I held my left arm out in front of me, closed one eye, and threw the knife as hard and straight as I could. It missed the orc's head by an inch.

"Hex," I swore, but Ferra seemed quite happy. She walked up to the poster and prized the knife out of it, handing it back to me.

"*Illumino,*" she uttered, and the Hammerskin's body lit up with warm pixels of light.

I tried again. I used the same stance and aimed as best I could, but I knew as the knife left my hand that it was too high to hit the target. Oddly, the knife righted itself in midair and pierced the orc right between his eyes.

"Excellent!" said Ferra, more to herself than to me—rightly so. "It's heat-seeking," she said. "I worked on the tech last year for Jax's crossbow bolts."

As grateful as I was for the weapon, I couldn't help feeling a stab of envy when Ferra mentioned Jax. I knew it was a useless emotion, but I couldn't help it.

I hugged the dwarf. "Thank you so much." I knew for certain the knife would save my life. Ferra waved away my thanks as if the gift was no big deal, and handed me a copper-colored gift bag.

"It's nothing," she said. "Just a new outfit."

I pulled out black leggings—*mostly bullet-proof, but they do get a bit hot in Summer,* said Ferra—a long black top—*same kevlar-lycra fabric with a built-in bra!*—and a new witch's cloak. My mouth fell open when I shook the cloak out and tried it on; it was magnificent. Like my original cloak, it fitted snugly around my torso and flared slightly at my hips. The graphene fabric felt light but sturdy.

"It's beautiful," I whispered. More importantly, it was mostly bullet-proof.

Ferra clicked another button, and a full-length mirror appeared in front of me. For the first time since waking up in the hospital, I felt like a real witch.

The genius dwarf frowned and fussed, making sure she was happy with the stitching and pockets. She came away looking satisfied, then clicked the mirror button again. The mirror turned into a red velvet curtain. I was puzzled until she told me to stand in front of the curtain.

"Now put the hood on," she said.

When I did, my cloak went from smooth black to red velvet. I looked at Ferra, who smiled and clicked again. This time the background was elaborate maroon wallpaper with gold pinstripes, as was my cloak.

"How?" I asked.

"Ah, it was easy, really. Plain old biomimicry. I had the idea one day when I took the skunks to the Realm Reptile Park and we saw one of those disguise dragons. You know those ones who change their scales to blend in with their surroundings? I thought, how hard could animating camouflage be? All you need to be able to do is replicate a feat of nature using magic and technology. It wasn't rocket science."

Although, to be fair, I thought Ferra was perhaps too smart for rocket science.

"It's epic," I said. I held up the ritual knife again, and the blade glinted in the white laboratory light. On one side, the now-familiar phrase was engraved: RUPTOR MALEDICTUM. The other side, which was blank on my original knife, was now stamped with an insignia. I looked closer: it was the Fornak coat of arms.

"That's to remind you that you have family, no matter what," said Ferra, making tears spring to my eyes. When she saw the emotion in my face, she hugged me so hard it felt like a Heimlich maneuver.

CHAPTER 57

STEPS FOR MY ENEMIES
NICKY

When I woke up in the darkness of the cell, I was back in my body. How I wished I wasn't. I squeezed my eyes shut and cried, the saltwater running down and stinging the burnt skin on my temples. Why couldn't I have just died? I thought I might have been close, the way I had left my body like that. I hoped that I could have somehow swum away in the air, so light I was, while my fleshy skeleton was being tortured below. Once my weeping abated, I realized I wasn't in my own cell. Although I couldn't see anything, it smelled different. The walls felt different. And the cot I was lying on was not my bed. I lifted my aching body slowly and moved to sit on the edge of the bed, and blinked until my eyes became accustomed to the dim light.

From what I could see, the cell was tiny, probably two by four meters. There was a basin-toilet in the corner, but nothing else. I sat there for a long time. Was the cell to be in perpetual darkness, or was it just nighttime lights out? Most importantly, would Devka know I was here? After a while I grew tired again and lay down, hoping that the next time I woke up, I'd be in my regular room.

The cell was slightly less dark when I woke again. The only light in the room was the washed-out morning sun that filtered through the tiny horizontal window high up on the wall. It wasn't much, but I was grateful for it. I sat up again, feeling stiffness in every part of my body, and forced myself to stand. It felt like I had crushed glass under my skin.

I will master the pain, I told myself. It was the only way. I would stop lamenting the agony and use it to push myself instead. I would use it to strengthen my body and to fight. I would make pain my friend.

I took a step, and pain shot up my leg, making me stumble and fall onto the hard, cold floor. I grunted and forced myself to stand up, dragging my body weight up by using the bed for support. Finally, I was standing again, and tried another step. That time, I did not fall. I took a step for Devka, a step for Derek, a step for Sebastian. A step for my unborn children who I now knew I'd never conceive. I even took steps for my enemies. A step against Adrathar, one against Ingleby, one each against Alison, Fikile, and the rest of the gang. I took a step for Emily, although I wasn't sure if she was a friend or foe. A step for the policeman I had killed; ten steps for his grieving family. When I ran out of people, I took steps for the memories I had. My wedding; my parents' funeral; adopting my beloved Labrador. My first overseas trip; my first boyfriend; losing my virginity.

This became my game, my reason to live. I could train all day if I put my mind to it.

When the diluted morning sun shone brighter, there was a rapping on the metal door.

"Hello?" I called. The small letterbox aperture clanged open, and a yellow tray was shoved through it. I grasped it just in time. It was maize porridge, as cold and congealed as old blood. I would force myself to eat it anyway, because my body needed the energy to heal and build muscle.

"Hello? Can you please tell me where I am?"

The cover crashed shut.

CHAPTER 58
MILKYWAY
ASHA

I tapped "Goblin City" into my maps app. A quick history came up alongside the directions, which I quickly skimmed over. Apparently, Goblin City was in the east of Johannesburg, in what used to be a popular amusement park, but was abandoned when a rollercoaster unaccountably left its rails, hurtling into the sky and then down again, killing over a dozen untouched people. GO CITY theme park was the perfect place for the goblins to set up shop. SA GobCom, the South African goblin committee, bought the dilapidated theme park for next to nothing since the humans didn't want it, saying it was cursed, painted an extra BLIN onto the billboard—so that it read GOBLIN CITY —and called it home. The goblin race went from being spread out all over the province to having their own playground at the outskirts of the city. The original child-friendly restaurants, toddler-sized bathrooms, and kiddie rides were all ideal for a species their size. The fair-themed snacks were perfect for their sweet tooth, and the tragic history of the rollercoaster accident and subsequent urban legends suited them, too, because it meant humans stayed out of their territory.

I walked past some of the amusement rides, including a three-loop rollercoaster, a rocking pirate ship, and a swirling platform of giant seashells with shrieking goblins strapped inside. It was totally surreal to be there and see the odd creatures living their best lives. They looked half human, half Slimer from Ghostbusters. Their skin was a gross tint of green, with blue veins snaking below, their eyes were big and bulging, and their long dirty-needle teeth and rubbery lips glistening with saliva were difficult to look at. Even the gob children, who you would think would be cute, were worryingly fierce-looking little drooling ankle-biters. As I avoided crossing paths with a large family eating cotton candy, I hoped that my rabies shot was up to date. I soon found an information stall and asked for Nilve.

"Is she expecting you?" asked the suit-wearing slimeball. His eyes were slightly squinty, giving me the uncomfortable feeling that he might be talking to the person behind me.

"No?" I said, then wanted to kick myself. According to Ferra, you didn't strictly have to tell the truth when you spoke to goblins. Apparently they didn't take honesty as seriously as we uptight human folk.

"No?" he said, my question mark hanging in the air between us. He squinted at me pointedly.

"I mean, yes?" I was clearly not good at lying. *Damn it.*

"Yes?" his wiry eyebrows, like black fish gut threaded into silicone, moved up and down as he inspected me.

"We have a mutual friend who ..."

The goblin's long-fingered hands tapped impatiently on the counter of the info booth. The color of his skin gave me an idea. Ferra had given me a tip as I left. I should buy Nilve Salty-Snap her favorite treat, a lime milkshake.

"I'm here to buy her a lime milkshake," I said, then felt ridiculous.

The goblin's body language instantly relaxed, and he showed me all his dirty needles. "Why didn't you say so?" He wiped some errant drool from his chin and spoke into his toy walkie-talkie. When he turned to me again, he smiled. "She'll be waiting for you at the MilkyWay."

The goblin's directions weren't very easy to follow, but I reached the ice cream bar eventually, after tripping over a miniature railway line and almost having a small train plough into me. *What an unfortunate headline that would have been,* I thought.

Witch survives numerous Dark Wizard bounty attacks only to be run over by cheering goblins in Lilliputian locomotive.

Ferra would not have been happy, nor would Nilve SaltySnap, who was expecting me to pay her bill and had already had, by the looks of it, two lime milkshakes and a plate of waffles. No wonder the goblins all had potbellies and stained mouth-prongs. They ate fairground junk for every meal. Just in the last five minutes I had seen rainbow popcorn, *koeksusters*, cotton candy, hot dogs, and deep-fried donuts drizzled with chocolate. As if to illustrate my point, Salty burped loudly and gave me a food-drunk look, then ordered another plate of waffles.

The restaurant was painted in a way that I assumed was supposed to look like our galaxy—a deep black and purple background dotted with planets and stars. The moon was the top view of a glass of milk. Only after you figured out what the moon was, you saw that the galaxy was really a tablecloth, and the planets and stars were cookies and silver dragées on the table. It was quite mind-bending, and I was glad to sit down.

"You're paying, right?" she slobbered.

I nodded. "Yes," I said. "Thank you for agreeing to see me."

"My ex would tell you that I'd do anything for a lime milkshake," she said, and laughed.

Ugh, I thought. I didn't need those images in my brain. I rubbed my forehead as if to erase the last few seconds, but it didn't work. A new plate arrived for the goblin, and she tucked in, but not before soaking the waffles in maple syrup. I think I must have been staring at her wolfing down the food, because when she looked up, she pointed her fork at me.

"Want some?" Soggy crumbs sprayed the table.

I hid my shudder. "No, thank you."

"You're very polite."

"Am I?"

"Most humans treat goblins like garbage. You use your manners and everything."

"Er…"

"Loosen up," said Salty. "Do you want a beer? We can go to the Cowboy & Coyote Corner for a beer. They've got great snacks there. Peanuts."

I shook my head. "I need your help. I need to hire you for a portaling job."

She wiped her Goodyear lips with a paper napkin, scrunched it up in her hands, then threw it down onto her syrup-smeared plate. "It'll cost you."

"I can pay you," I said.

"I want your coat," said the goblin.

"I can't give it to you. It was a gift."

"Gimme," she said, her hand making grabby movements in front of my face.

"No," I said. I was starting to understand why humans had to be firm with the creatures. You give them a lime milkshake and they'll take the clothes off your back. "I'll pay you with koin," I said. "You can buy your own coat. One that fits you."

She pouted. I wondered if, by giving a goblin an item of your clothing, it gave them some kind of power over you.

"Fine," she said. "Ten thousand."

"Ten thousand! You haven't even heard the details."

She took her last sip of lime milkshake and swished it in her mouth, then gargled and swallowed. "It's my flat rate."

I didn't know where I was going to get so much money, but I had no option but to agree. I wondered, rather optimistically, if perhaps the Starfall coven had a budget for this kind of thing. Then I remembered how wealthy Derek Landau was, and understood where I'd be getting the money. I reached over to shake Salty's hand and instantly regretted it. Her skin was clammy, sticky, and cold. It was like holding a frog. I forced myself to not spring away in revulsion.

"Deal," I said.

"I'll need the cash up front," said the goblin, picking her teeth. "Plus expenses."

"Expenses! What expenses? All I need you to do is show up when I tell you."

"And a bonus afterwards, but only if you're satisfied with my work."

I gritted my teeth. "Fine," I said. It wasn't my money, anyway. And Derek deserved to pay. "If you get us there and back successfully, I'll pay you double."

CHAPTER 59

DAYLIGHT PRIVILEGE
NICKY

Every time a meal was delivered, I would ask the same question. Eventually, I got an answer.

"Desolation," the masculine voice replied.

I wasn't used to male guards, and I wasn't sure I'd heard correctly. "Pardon me?"

"Desolation," replied the guard. "It's what the inmates call solitary confinement."

"How long am I here for?" I asked. "When can I go back?"

"They didn't say."

After days of being locked in a dim room, the conversation seemed precious to me. I wanted him to keep talking.

"Can I go shower?"

He hesitated. Perhaps talking to prisoners in solitary confinement was against the rules. "You can use your basin."

"It doesn't have hot water," I said. "Or soap."

"You can use your basin," he repeated.

I decided to try another track. "How long have I been here?"

"I don't know," he said. I could feel the shrug in his voice.

"A week?" I asked. "Two weeks?" I had no concept of time anymore, not that it mattered.

"Less," he said.

"Okay," I said. "Thank you."

There was a long silence, so I thought that was the end of that, but he surprised me.

"I'm Dillon," he said. It was more than an introduction: it was an invitation to keep talking.

"Nice to meet you," I said. "I'm Nicky."

Dillon, the solitary confinement guard on the Desolation level, became my new best friend. It turned out that he found guarding cells an incredibly boring job and lacked the toxic masculinity required to take pleasure in seeing sick women locked up. We began our conversations cautiously—gradually establishing that I was not, in fact, a psychopath—but soon we were discussing everything from Netflix series, to books, to dinner recipes. He was married, and enjoyed cooking for his wife, but often ran out of inspiration and ended up cooking the same dishes again and again. I gave him ideas and explained how to prepare certain things. I would write out recipes for him, from memory, on his little Riverside-issued notebook. He would report back on his next shift. Sometimes, when it was a success, he'd give me his packed lunch: leftovers from the night before. I teased him, saying that once he mastered cooking, I would teach him how to crochet.

When Dillon finished his shift, it was my cue to exercise. While the wheelchair accumulated dust in the corner, I progressed from walking to running and jumping an imaginary skipping rope. It didn't matter how exhausted or in pain I was: I did push-ups, pull-ups, squats, jumping jacks. Soon, the pain faded. I fantasized about escaping almost every minute of the day.

"My wife didn't like the idea of us talking," Dillon said one day.

"I don't blame her," I replied.

"But now she likes you. She said I must say thanks to you for teaching me how to cook."

"Oh," I said, feeling suddenly emotional. "She's very welcome. Does she know that you've saved my sanity?"

"Have I?" he asked, sounding surprised.

I swallowed the lump in my throat. "Whatever was left, anyway."

There was a pause.

"I have good news," said Dillon.

"The lasagna was a success?" I guessed. "You got the béchamel right?"

"No," he replied. "I mean, yes. But that's not the good news."

"Spit it out, man. Don't you know that you shouldn't keep a criminally insane woman waiting?"

"There's a new update on your file. Rubber-stamped yesterday."

"What is it?" Were they letting me out of Desolation?

"You've been granted daylight privilege. You're allowed outside for an hour every day now."

"Daylight?" I said. "At this stage I feel like I'll go up in smoke if this pale skin sees sunshine."

"Ha," he said, but didn't laugh.

When Dillon finally opened the door to my solitary confinement cell, we looked each other up and down.

"So that's what you look like," he said, smiling.

All of our conversations had taken place through the aperture in the metal door, so we only had a vague idea of what each other looked like. He had a nice face, and beautiful light brown skin. He looked puzzled at my wheelchair, which I had dusted off for the occasion. He motioned at it and said "I didn't know."

"Pelvic fracture," I said. He nodded and took the handles. Once he started pushing me, our conversation felt awkward. We weren't used to the new dynamic.

"The lasagna was good," I said. "Really good."

"Thank you," he replied. "Joanne liked it, too."

"She's lucky to have you," I said.

He stopped to rub his cheek. "Nah. She could have married up. She should have. She could have married an engineer or something."

"Rubbish," I said. "I was married to a successful investment manager, and look where it got me."

We both smiled, even though it wasn't funny.

I wondered later why I had said that. Why I had made it sound, even in jest, that Derek was the reason for me being committed. Even after shrugging it off, the idea kept floating to the surface.

"So, this is it," Dillon said, pressing his access card to the sensor, which automatically opened the double doors. "The great outdoors."

I shielded my eyes. I had dreamed for weeks about being able to go outside again. I had pictured fresh air and trees, a vision colored by freedom. This was different. The air wasn't stale, which was a bonus, but the glare from the white gravel and concrete and the glittering razor-wire fence hurt my eyes. The air was so hot that it took me a few breaths to get used to it, and the only plant life was a few straggly bushes in the corner, battling to cope with the incessant heat.

"You weren't kidding about the daylight," I said.

"There's more shade in the communal garden," he said. "But it's not really a garden, and Desolation patients aren't allowed to socialize with the general pop. So this is what you've got, for now. Until they decide to let you back."

"Let me back?" I said. "I think they've forgotten about me."

Dillon looked at me. "They haven't forgotten about you."

We sat for a while, trying to enjoy the change of scenery.

"It's nice to have a break from the cell," I said, eyes smarting.

"Yes," said Dillon.

I looked up and took in the promise of the sky.

"You see that?" asked Dillon, pointing at the razor-wire fence.

"Yes."

"That's the reason us guards can't leave Desolation prisoners here on their own."

"What?"

"A prisoner could climb over that fence. It's not like, say, a smooth wall that surrounds the rest of Riverside. That's why prisoners always have to be accompanied out here."

"Okay," I replied.

"It's scalable, right?"

I looked at him. "Right. But there's razor wire at the top."

"*Ja,*" Dillon said. "But it's just a bit of razor wire."

While Dillon wheeled me back to solitary, he told me that the other guard would take me outside the next day.

"Why?" I asked. "Where will you be?"

"Doctor's appointment," he said shyly. "Joanne took a pregnancy test last night. It was positive."

"Oh! Why didn't you say anything? That's wonderful."

"If it's a girl, we'll call her Rose. That's my mother's name. But we're not going to tell anyone about the pregnancy. Till we're sure."

"Yes," I said. But he had told me.

CHAPTER 60
EDISON'S
ASHA

It had been a long day so far, and it was getting longer. I arrived at Edison's with a thirst no water could slake.

"I know that look," he said, placing a coaster in front of me. "Martini? Three olives?"

I thought fondly of Savvy and thought I should call her. Our drinks evening would be soon.

"I'd love one," I replied. "But I need a clear head."

He nodded. "Single? Gin and tonic?"

"I'll have a beer, please. A lager."

"You got it," he said, and I watched him pour a perfect pint from the chilled tap.

The first swig was golden. "Thank you," I said.

Edison began cleaning the worktop near me, as if availing himself for conversation if I wanted it, but at the same time happy to work in silence.

"You're good at this," I said.

"Good at what?"

"Good at owning a bar."

He shrugged. "I've worked hard for it."

"I don't doubt it." I took another sip. "I've only been here twice but you remembered what I liked to drink."

"It's my job," he said, polishing silver teaspoons for the coffee station.

"You have a good memory," I said.

He stopped working and looked at me, concerned. "Is this about the other night? Did something happen to you?"

"No," I replied. "Yes. I mean, nothing happened to me. But I'm here to ask you about that man."

"Derek Landau," said Edison. "You don't get more of a regular than that guy."

"He's in here often?"

"Most afternoons. Some evenings. Sometimes till closing time. Often, *ja*."

Edison hadn't asked for Landau's address when he had hailed a cab the other night.

"Often enough for you to be able to tell the Uber where to take him after he's had too much to drink."

"Yes," said Edison. "Well, we use the same cab service every time, so I don't even have to know the addresses. They take care of that."

This sounded promising. "The same cab service?"

"Uber is great," he said. "But I prefer a service we know and trust. I don't want to send a patron home in a—let's say a vulnerable state—with a stranger. Especially if the patron is a woman. There's more accountability with a designated driver."

"I don't suppose you'd be willing to give me the name of the cab service?"

Edison shrugged. "You're welcome to it, but don't go thinking you'll get any personal information from them. In fact, if you do, I'll terminate our contract tonight."

I put fifty rand on the counter. Enough for the pint and a generous tip. "Please call me a cab."

He hesitated, trying to work me out, then nodded. "Yes, ma'am."

The driver arrived in the same car he had the night before when he had picked up Derek Landau. Reluctantly, I left my scooter in the parking lot and climbed into the taxi.

"Evening," he said. "Where are we off to?" He tilted the rearview mirror so that he could see me, and as soon as I got a good visual of his face, I locked eyes. As far as I knew, I had never tried mesmerizing anyone before. It was usually a talent of vampires, if the fantasy books were to be believed.

"Monstras animo," I uttered. *Reveal your mind.* Worst case scenario, he'd think I was a tourist and ask me to speak English. Best case scenario, he'd tell me what he knew. He blinked at my reflection, and I held his gaze. The engine was still running. After a long, painful pause, he spoke. "What do you need to know?"

CHAPTER 61

WEDDING RING
ASHA

I got him to drive around the block as we chatted.

"You often take Derek Landau home," I said.

"Yes."

"You also take him other places."

"Not often."

"His mistress's home."

"Yes."

How could I ask him when I wasn't even sure what I was asking? I decided to keep it broad. "Tell me about the time with Derek Landau that sticks in your memory."

He was quiet for a while, and my hope faded. Then he started talking. "It was late. Edison's was closing."

"You collected Landau."

"Yes," said the man.

I exhaled, still maintaining eye contact. He moved mechanically, changing gears and turning corners. The car purred under his experienced operation.

"You didn't take him straight home, or to his girlfriend's house."

"No. He was in a strange mood. It was late, but he wanted to go out."

"Where did you take him?"

"Rosebank," he said. "There's a club there that stays open late."

"Okay," I said.

"You can buy drugs there."

"Landau was after drugs?"

"Not always. Not usually. But that night he wanted to party. That's what he told me. He gave me one of his credit cards and asked me to hang around. He didn't want to get stranded somewhere."

"And did you?"

"It was after one in the morning. I didn't expect any more

pick-ups, so I agreed. Also, I felt a sense of loyalty to the guy. He was a regular, and I could tell he might get into trouble."

"Get into trouble?"

The driver shrugged. "I don't know. He had this weird energy. I thought he might overdo it."

"You didn't think of phoning his wife?"

"That's the last thing I thought of doing. He said they were close to getting separated. I didn't want to make things worse. I decided I'd just hang around as agreed and make sure he came out okay."

"So you went to this club. You stayed in the car?"

"No. Landau wanted me as a wingman. Besides, I had his credit card."

"So, you watched him party."

"He was in a bad place. I could tell he was hurting. You know, about his wife. I think he loved her. It was hurting him."

I rolled my eyes. "He was cheating on her."

"It happens," he said. "It doesn't mean the love is gone. Not always."

I decided then was not the appropriate time to have a debate about loyalty in monogamous relationships.

"I mean, I saw him talk to his wife on the phone before things got bad. Pretty sure he loved her, but what the hell do I know? I'm on my third unhappy marriage."

"So you watched him drink. Swallow some pills?"

"No pills that I saw. But he'd definitely taken something. I wasn't comfortable. After an hour or so I decided to take him home, but he wouldn't come. He kept saying *one more drink*. The club closed at around two, but Landau wasn't finished yet. I told him it was time to get home, but he wouldn't listen. I had agreed to watch over him, so I couldn't leave him there. He'd be mugged and shoeless by sunrise."

"You stayed in Rosebank?"

"I was trying to get him to walk it off, you know? We were just outside the club and we were walking. There was a burger place, but it was closed. I was talking to him, trying to get him to calm down, to get sleepy and want to go home, but he was buzzing. He wanted to go to the next place. I told him there was no next place. But then—it was weird, man—suddenly there was this door that I'd never seen before. And a bouncer. And he told us we were welcome to go in. Landau and I argued. It looked as dodgy as hell and I didn't want to go inside. I don't know what happened inside there, man. All I know was that Landau went in with a wedding ring and came out without it. I only noticed because he kept rubbing his finger on the way home. I said we should go back for it but he said it was too late. What was done was done. The whole thing gave me the creeps. You know when the hair on the back of your neck stands up? That's how I felt outside that place. You wanna know the weirdest thing?"

"Yes." I definitely wanted to know the weirdest thing.

"I went back the next day. I thought I could get his ring back for him. Felt bad for his wife."

"And it was gone," I said. "The door, the bouncer, everything."

"As if it had never been there," said the driver. "I couldn't make sense of it. It bothered me. The next night, his wife tried to jump off that bridge."

CHAPTER 62
WHEN THE MISTRESS IS A MAGE
ASHA

I lay in bed that night with the day's events hurtling through my brain. This curse-breaking job, I realized, wasn't the path to peaceful sleep. I had very little time to work out what kind of curse had been put on Nicola Landau, and there was no way of guessing without being able to spend time with her. I felt guilty lying there, warm and comfortable, while Nicola Landau was being abused at Riverside. I wished there was a quicker way to get her out, but Salty's magic would only be ready the following night. I looked at my watch. It would be sixteen hours or so before we set off to free her. My body was taut; my stomach, hollow. I tried to relax into the mattress, which worked for a few minutes— until I started worrying again, and my limbs would stiffen and my insides contract.

I was desperate to get Landau out, but there were so many things I hadn't prepared for. If the mission failed because of something I had failed to do, I would never forgive myself. At the same time, if I didn't sleep, I wouldn't be on top of my game. I had a serious case of imposter syndrome. It boggled my mind that people were counting on me to *save someone's life* when I had so little to draw on. I was practically a baby witch, yet someone like Soleil had faith in me to put things right.

"It's what you do," she had said to me two days before. "Restore the balance. It's what nature does."

With that in mind, I sat up and meditated. I turned my worries away and thought of my forest, my hens, my cats, and felt fortified by them. If what Soleil said was true, then Nature was on my side. I must have fallen asleep then, because that's the last thing I remember.

The sun was already up when the doorbell rang. I groaned and wished there was someone around to make me tea. *I must teach Circe and Odysseus,* I thought. Surely a witch's cat was capable of that kind of thing? The last of my dreams faded— stress-mares of prison cells, pain, and dark magic. The rays of golden morning sun burnt away the last of the visions, and I could hardly remember what the dream had been about.

When I opened the front door, I heard Soleil calling cheerfully from the front gate. "Good morning, sunshine!"

She was holding something. When I opened up, I saw it was a steaming cup of takeaway coffee.

"You are my favorite person right now," I said, eyeing the cappuccino.

"I'd love to say it's from me!" she said, hitching up her skirt to cross the threshold. "It was delivered just as I arrived. The man rang your doorbell, but I didn't see who it was."

I took the warm vessel from her. On the side of the brown recyclable cup there was a scribble in black marker. "Asha! Had to run. X, Papa Smurf"

I smiled. "Ah," I said, feeling warm. "I know who it was." We walked into the house and I poured the coffee out into two mugs and handed one to Soleil. "I'm so glad you're here," I said. "I need your advice."

I told the high priestess about everything that had happened since we had last seen each other when we visited Riverside.

"You think this Grimalkin cursed Nicola Landau?"

"Yes," I said. "Derek Landau is extremely wealthy, and they're married in community of property."

"So the mistress wanted Nicola out of the picture, but a divorce would have cost too much money."

"Yes."

"What bad luck," she said, tutting. "To be cheated on is one thing, but when the mistress is a mage ..."

"You know what they say about black cats," I said. Circe gave me a withering look. I winked at her to show I was only joking. I knew that, if anything, black cats were very good luck. "The question is, how do I break this curse?"

I felt like a bit of an idiot asking her, seeing as I was supposed to be the curse-breaker and all. It was a bit like a comedian asking how to tell a joke.

"There are three main ways to break a curse," said Soleil. "If you know the exact spell, you can reverse it if you have an equal amount of power—or more power—than the curser."

"That seems easy enough."

"Not really," sighed the witch. "It gets dangerous if you don't know the precise wording."

I looked at her, trying to understand.

"Think of it like a fishing hook going into your flesh."

I grimaced.

"If you are able to remove the hook reversing exactly through the original path, it will only cause a little pain. But if you try even the slightest angle, not only do you cause more problems, but chances are, you won't get the hook out."

"Got it," I said, nodding. I didn't need any more discouragement than that. "So, there's an easier way?"

"That is the easiest way," she said. "The second way requires theft, and the last, murder."

My throat felt constricted and I had to swallow. I remembered my conversation with Savvy. "Go on," I squeaked.

"The second way to break a curse is to find—and by that I mean *steal*—the payment given to the curser and transfer it to the one who is cursed."

"That would be easy enough," I said, "If I knew what the payment was."

"Ah-ha," said Soleil. "Time for you to do some investigating."

I don't have time to investigate, I thought, looking at the clock on the wall. *I'm meeting Salty in a few hours and I've got so much to do before then.*

Of course, we both knew the third way to break a curse.

Soleil drained her coffee and set the empty mug down on the counter. As she looked at me, her eyes were piercing. If I didn't find that payment, I would have to kill the curser.

CHAPTER 63

GOOD WEATHER FOR BREAKING AND ENTERING

ASHA

The high priestess trained me for an hour under the apple tree in the garden and then left, telling me to call on her when I needed to. Nervous, sweating, I fed the animals, took a long shower, and pulled myself together. Words echoed in my head.

Kill the curser. Kill the curser.

Is that what I had done in my previous life? Killed people? It made me feel extremely uncomfortable in my skin. Strange; dark; unredeemable. No matter how much I tried to relax my body, my stomach remained a tightly stitched leather ball.

Live.

Die.

Kill.

It's what Nature does, said the voice in my head. *Things live, and things die.*

All that burns will soon flourish

and all that flourishes must burn

Death is not the end, no, no—

The world just turns and turns.

I shuddered while I toweled myself off, trying to keep my breathing even to keep my anxiety under control. I would decide on my plan, and execute the plan. Worrying about it wasn't going to help anyone, including Nicola Landau.

My phone rang, shattering the silence. I jumped. So much for not being nervous.

"Asha," said Directress Copperfield. "I hope I'm not catching you at a bad time."

"Er," I replied, wishing I were even half as eloquent as she was.

"I'm just ringing to enquire if you've made any progress on the missing daughters case."

I was so consumed by the Landau case that the mention of the missing children made my head spin faster than the possessed girl in *The Exorcist.*

"Er," I said again, hating myself.

"I don't mean to put pressure on you, Ms. Rook. I'm sure you are well aware of the urgency of this case. You've no doubt been informed that another three girls have been taken since our last meeting."

I didn't want to lie to her, but I couldn't bear saying I hadn't even started, either.

"It's terrible," I said. "I don't have any news yet, but I hope to have some soon."

"Thank you," said the headmistress. "I'm so grateful to you for making this a priority."

My cheeks burned with shame. I still had the envelope bulging with cash that she had given me as an advance payment, and I hadn't done a thing. I swore to myself I'd begin working on the case the moment Nicola was safe. Once we had said goodbye, I put on the new clothes I had received from Ferra and tied my hair back tightly. The clothes fitted perfectly, and when I looked in the mirror, the witch gazing back at me looked sleek and strong, and ready to break the Landau curse.

To portal to Nicola, Salty needed a personal item of hers, so first up on the list was to collect one. In a rare moment of forward thinking, I had gotten the address of the Landaus from the cab driver the previous night. I felt sorry for the man; he was clearly spooked by the case. I got his number, too, in case there was a happy ending to the story, so I could put his mind at rest. I hoped he wouldn't suffer too many ill effects from the long session of mesmerization I had subjected him to.

I glanced once more at the mirror, then jogged downstairs and jumped on my scooter, plugging the Landau address into my GPS.

I knew Derek Landau was wealthy, but hoo boy! I did not expect the mansion I arrived at when I raced up Dresden Drive. Number 61 was utterly magnificent, and if I weren't wearing my helmet, I'm pretty sure my jaw would have dropped. The estate was ensconced behind a high security wall—as was the fashion/necessity in Johannesburg in 2022 due to the high levels of mostly human crime—but I could see through the front gate and up the generous winding driveway that led to the house. The driveway was expertly laid red paving that matched the shingles on the roof, and it was edged with hedgerows of fragrant jasmine and blooming antique tea roses with large thorns. The house itself was a grand two-story affair painted white, which stood out against the clear blue sky.

Good weather for breaking and entering, I thought as I crept up to the gate under the watchful eye of a security camera. Johannesburg might be besieged by criminals, but at least we had the best weather in the world. Small victories, and all of that. I took out my wand and pointed it to the camera.

"Fiat fulgur," I uttered, and a little zap of electricity short-circuited the device. I repeated the spell on the motor of the gate, allowing me to open it enough to slip through and close it behind me. Feeling a little more confident, I tucked the wand back into my flowing coat pocket as I strode up the driveway. Fear ebbing, I thought, *I can get used to this.*

As I walked farther up the drive, I heard a loud argument in the distance. I had assumed that Derek would be at work, but I had been wrong. It was strange to hear him shouting, but stranger still was the feeling I got as I neared the mansion.

It was difficult to explain, but I felt like I was seeing through a mirage. From the street, the house looked perfectly maintained and managed, and the garden beautifully manicured, but from halfway into the property I started to see what was like little glitches in the matrix. I caught sight of weeds pushing up from between the pavers that had just moments ago seemed perfect, but when I blinked and looked again, they were gone. The expertly trimmed jasmine hedges suddenly looked straggly and overgrown, but soon snapped back to their previously neatly trimmed state. The house was the same: beautifully painted and clean walls flickered to damp-stained and dirty, then back again. I didn't know what was going on, but it felt like magic. As I approached the house the shouting got louder, and my nerves scratched my insides. The Landau mansion looked too perfect to be true, and it was.

CHAPTER 64

THE SILVER RAVEN
ASHA

"How could you do that?" shouted Derek. "How could you!"

"I can't believe you're fighting with me over this. Do you care about a *dog* more than you care about me?"

The woman's voice sounded familiar. I sneaked along the side of the house and found a small window to peer through. Derek was wearing an expensive-looking suit, but the tie was pulled to the side as if he had needed access to extra oxygen while arguing with his lover. Chione was as svelte and feline as ever in a figure-hugging black dress. The more heated their argument, the more glitches appeared. The carpet they were standing on went from clean to grubby, the parquet flooring peeking out changed from perfectly smooth and varnished to matte, and lifting from the concrete screed below. The houseplants were thriving, then wilting, and back to thriving, then played dead. I blinked harder. What was going on?

"Derek!" shouted Chione. "Derek! It's a bloody *dog!*"

"It's not just a dog!" he yelled back. "It's Sebastian! It's *my* dog! And I loved him!"

Loved him? I thought. *Past tense?*

"You mean Nicola loved him!" shouted Chione.

"*I* loved him! *I* loved him!"

Chione folded her arms. "More than me, it seems!"

Derek's body was stiff with frustration and fury. "Don't be ridiculous," he said.

"Oh! So now I'm *ridiculous.*"

Derek collapsed into a chair, his hands in prayer position in front of his face, his nostrils flaring. He lowered his voice. "I'm not saying you're ridiculous."

"That's what it sounded like!"

"Chione. You are the love of my life."

I was hurt on Nicola's behalf; I felt like I had been pricked by one of the rose thorns. They had been married for thirteen years. Loyalty was clearly not one of Derek Landau's strong suits.

"Then act like it!" she snapped, her voice like a razor.

He dropped his hands. "My love. Have I not done everything you have asked? Have I not given you everything you wished for?" When she didn't reply, he added: "Of course I don't care about Sebastian more than you."

"Fine," she said.

"Fine?" he stood up again, his body as tense as a violin string. "It's *not* fine! That's what I'm saying! You had no right to do what you did."

Only then did I spot an old dog collar and leash on the coffee table.

"You asked me to live here," said Chione. "You had me move in. You know I'm allergic to dogs. What did you expect?"

"What did I expect?" he said incredulously. "I expected you to take some bloody antihistamines until you got used to being around her!"

"You're too soft, Derek," she sneered. "You've always been too soft. That's why you were with Nicky for so long. You didn't have the balls to leave her."

"I loved her," he said softly, gazing at the empty dog collar in a defeated kind of way. "That's why I didn't leave her."

This seemed to infuriate Chione, who picked up a nearby glass and flung it at the wall. It smashed into small pieces and landed on the floor that flashed from varnished to damaged, and back again. The broken glass seemed to galvanize Derek, who stood up with resolve and grabbed his car keys.

"Where are you going?" she demanded.

"Where do you think?" he sniped. "To earn money to pay off your credit card bills."

I watched as she swallowed her reply, not wanting to bite the hand that clearly fed her jewelry habit. "Fine."

"It would be nice to have some dinner on the table when I get back," he said.

She looked offended. "I'm not your personal chef."

"Fine," he said. "I'll grab something at Edison's."

"Fine," she replied.

"Fine," he repeated.

I couldn't help but join in. *Fine,* I said to myself.

There was a loud roar from the garage, and the door lifted. Derek's angry-sounding sports car sped down the driveway. Luckily for me, he didn't look in his rearview mirror as I slipped into the garage before it closed again. When the gate motor wouldn't work, he climbed out of the car, swearing, and wrenched the gate open. I noticed that he hadn't yet fixed his tie.

Chione spent the next few minutes pushing over furniture and smashing things as if the house were an expensive hotel room and she was the lead singer of an '80s rock band. When she had finished, she looked at the damage she had wrought and clicked her fingers, restoring it to its previous state. It was fine as long as you didn't look too hard; if you did, you'd see that nothing was fixed at all. She was obviously using some kind of magic to keep up a façade while the real thing crumbled around her. I assumed Derek didn't see the flickers of devastation or surely he would have known that his mistress was no ordinary woman. I couldn't stop looking at the mournful-looking dog collar on the table. The woman seemed to have no conscience whatsoever.

It helped me, because I had no reservations at all about what had to do next.

I stepped from around the corner, wand extended, and pointed it at her. She was too busy finishing her tantrum to notice me. I didn't have the finer details of my plan worked out; I didn't know what to do next, so I let my instinct take over. I was relying on my magic muscle memory to kick in. Unfortunately, it didn't.

I waited for something to come out of my mouth, and then out of my wand, but both remained quiet, as if they had been short-circuited like the security camera outside. Chione felt my presence and whirled around like a dervish.

"Witch," she sneered. "What are you doing here?"

My wand trembled. "I've come to get what belongs to Nicola Landau."

"Ugh," she said, flicking her wrist. "You can have him."

"What?" I said. "No. I need the silver raven necklace."

Wide-eyed, she clutched the necklace as if it were suddenly strangling her. "No."

"I need it," I said. Salty had said the more attachment Nicola had to the item, the better. As the necklace was an anniversary gift from Derek, and one she was wearing in so many photos around the house, I guessed it had sentimental value to her. It would be perfect. If I could get it off the Grimalkin.

"Give it to me," I said, but I knew it wouldn't be that easy. I grasped my wand tighter and said a silent prayer to The Wild. I moved closer to her, and she hissed at me with her perfect white teeth.

I should have brought catnip from my garden, I thought, as I held my wand higher. Before I could issue a spell, Chione launched herself at me. In midair she changed into a black jaguar; I smelled cat skin and blood. I fell under the weight of her, her paws on my chest, banging my head on the floor and narrowly missing the edge of the coffee table.

As she was preparing to sink her teeth into my neck, I grabbed for the dog collar and quickly whipped it over her head, then pulled it tight around her neck. She roared in anger as I tugged the leash, trying to bite me as I tied it around the leg of the table. She tore at my arm, drawing blood, and I screamed. I pulled the leash tighter. She growled and tried to get away, but her jaguar form faded almost immediately, as if she had exhausted all her energy and her magic for the attack. She was left in her human form, panting on the floor beside me, lips smeared with blood. I leaned forward and pulled the necklace off her neck, leaving just the grubby dog collar there.

"Suits you," I said, and crabbed away from her before she bit me again.

CHAPTER 65

FIAT FULGUR

ASHA

I made sure the leash was securely lashed to the stone coffee table, then scrambled backwards to lean up against the legs of a sofa and put the necklace into my coat pocket. I had something of Nicola's to use as the portal key. Now I needed to locate the payment Chione had received to set the curse.

"I need you to tell me the specifics of the curse," I said.

She laughed, then spat some blood onto the carpet. "I can't think of one reason to tell you."

"To save Nicola Landau's life," I said. "You had her sent to that place. Do you have any idea what it's like?"

I saw a shadow flit across her face, which surprised me. I had begun to think she was soulless. She looked away from me, not wanting to betray any emotion.

"I didn't mean for that to happen," she said, and sneezed.

"Sure you didn't."

I noticed then that the skin touching the old dog collar was red and inflamed. She scratched it and grimaced, clearly uncomfortable. I thought about loosening it, but I didn't. Soon her eyes were watering and swelling shut, and she began wheezing.

"Look," she said, wiping her lips on the back of her hand and then making eye contact again, even though she had to strain to do so. "It was supposed to be a temporary psychotic break—"

"Oh," I said. "Well, that's not serious at all."

Chione sneezed again, and her eyes were almost swollen shut. She wasn't lying when she had told Derek she was allergic to dogs. "I thought she'd be sent to a fancy sanatorium for rich people just long enough for me to clean Derek out. It would be like a nice holiday for her."

I gave her an incredulous look. "Are you serious?"

"I didn't even know Riverside existed. It sounds infernal."

"And yet you've done nothing to help her."

Chione shrugged and wheezed. "It would implicate me."

"You can make it right," I said. "It's not too late. Just tell me the exact spell you used to curse her and I'll be able to reverse it." She cleared her throat and tried to look at me, but her eyelids were squeezed shut. I was worried about the intensity of the allergic reaction, so I loosened the collar. She was wheezing so hard that I began to panic.

"Chione?"

I wondered if it might be a devious trick, but then she lost consciousness and slumped to the floor with a dull thud. Her tongue lolled, looking worryingly purple and swollen.

"Hex!" I swore. *That escalated quickly.* I tore off the collar and leaned in. She was hardly breathing at all. I didn't know CPR. Or did I? Would mouth-to-mouth even work for someone whose airways were swollen shut?

Ye gods.

I leaned over her, pinched her nose shut and blew into her mouth. Her chest rose and fell, which I took as a good sign. At least the air was going in. My lips came away bloody. I did it again, and again, but she didn't seem any more alive than she had when I'd started. If anything, her mottled skin had paled to match the carpet. I decided to do some chest pumps, and alternated that with the mouth-to-mouth. The closer she got to death, the angrier I got.

"Damn you," I said to her, though gritted teeth. "You vixen. You selfish hellcat. I should be out helping Nicola and instead I'm trying to save you!"

I put my ear to her chest but heard nothing. Her heart had stopped, along with her breathing. Without hesitating, I put my palm over her heart.

"Fiat fulgur," I whispered. A bolt of electricity shot from my hand into her body. I hoped my aim had been okay and I hadn't just fried an essential organ. Just as I began to think the worst, Chione gasped and her back arched. She spluttered, then hauled air in on her own in labored lungfuls.

I crossed my chest as if in a backward prayer of thanks, despite the fact I had never, to my knowledge, been Catholic. Maybe it was a witch thing. Her air passages seemed to be opening. Unfortunately, she still couldn't move, see, or talk, which made it difficult for her to tell me which spell she had used to curse Nicola.

"Which curse did you use?" I asked. "I need to know the exact spell." Soleil's image of the hook stuck into flesh came to mind, and I knew I couldn't afford to get it wrong.

Chione just gurgled. She couldn't tell me, even if she wanted to. I had to go with plan B.

"Tell me what payment you received from Derek to set the curse," I said. Of course, she couldn't answer that either, but she did pulse the fingers on her left hand. I looked in the direction of where her hand was pointing, but it was just an empty corner.

"The *payment*," I said. Then I saw that her thumb was tapping her ring finger, and I got it. The driver had said that Derek came out of that strange club without his wedding ring on. The next day, Nicola was on that bridge. He had given the disguised mage his wedding ring as payment to get rid of his wife, a premium worth more than the simple gold it was made of. No wonder the curse had been so potent. A symbol of unconditional love and commitment. Derek had, in his drunken stupor, sold the soul of his marriage.

I began hunting through the house for the ring. It was made more difficult by the fact that Chione's magic was depleted, so the handsome façade she had put in place faded. Now the temporary glitches I had seen before were permanent, revealing moldy walls, water-stained ceilings, framed family photographs shattered in jealousy or spite. It was clear that the Grimalkin's malice had leaked into everything around her, tainting it, making it crumble. What a shame it was. I also couldn't help noticing that Nicola's things were all packed up, stored in boxes in the garage, while Chione's things were spread about everywhere like cat hair.

I, on the other hand, was stalking around like a mad woman, visiting every room, holding my wand up and saying, "*Monstras! Monstras! Monstras!*" asking the wedding ring to reveal itself to me. Unfortunately, it did not. Had the mage stored the ring elsewhere for safekeeping? I tried to interrogate her again, but she was comatose. I looked at the time, and my stomach twisted. I only had a few more hours till I was due to meet Salty. After turning the house upside down in a flurry of panic, I sat down and thought about it. If I were Chione, where would I put the ring? Chione only cared about new, shiny things. The last thing she'd want was a scuffed gold ring, especially if it signified the Landaus' marriage. It could also be used as proof that she was involved with the bridge disaster.

Of course it wasn't in the house, I thought. Most people would wipe their fingerprints off something like that and throw it into a river, but not Chione. Despite her elegantly orchestrated windfall, she couldn't throw it away. She had sold it, and I realized with rising hot dread that now it could be anywhere.

CHAPTER 66

PSYCHEDELIC EXPLOSION OF CURSES

NICKY

The door to my solitary confinement cell clanged open the next day, and a new young guard stood in the doorway. He was perfect.

"Daylight privilege," he said, as if it were an order.

I adjusted the blanket on my lap and pushed my wheels forward. "I'm Nicky," I said, but he didn't answer me. He wheeled me out into the glare, and I pretended to be grateful.

"So good to get outside," I said, but he turned his face away.

I noticed that it had not rained, and the plants were more wilted than the day before. We sat in silence for five minutes while I stared at the fence. The razors glittered as they had the day before, warning of their keenness.

I tried to gather my courage but look perfectly sedate at the same time. I didn't want the whippersnapper getting suspicious and reaching for his gun, which hung at an arrogant angle from his belt. I closed my eyes and leaned back, pretending to enjoy the sun, wondering when the right time would be.

When the eardrum-piercing siren pealed, I almost jumped out of my chair. The young guard looked startled, too, and looked backwards at the building, and then at me, and then at the building again. I was a deer stuck in headlights. The guard decided that I wasn't a threat—being in a wheelchair and all — and rushed back into the building to see what the emergency was. Was it a fire? A fight? He needed to know what the problem was before following the protocol he had been trained in. As soon as he was out of sight I launched out of the wheelchair and sprinted toward the fence with the blanket I had brought with me. I took a quick preparatory breath when I got there, nervous about climbing, and threw the blanket over the razor wire. I was only successful on my third attempt, wasting precious time. I scaled the wire easily, even though I had adrenaline coursing through my veins and making my hands and feet feel numb. I reached the top, heart smashing my ribs, and climbed over and down the other side. I could hear yelling from inside the building, and I wasn't sure if they were shouting about me or about the "emergency." All I knew was that this would probably be my one and only chance to get out of Riverside, and every risk I took was worth it. I landed on my feet on the hard ground below, and felt a jolt to my old pelvic injury. I had taught myself to use my pain to propel me forward, so despite the sharpness in my hip, I began a limping jog away from the asylum property.

The siren seemed even louder, perhaps because my senses were heightened. There was nothing to hide behind, just knee-length golden grass. I kept up my limping jog. I was about a hundred meters from the building when I felt a snapping sensation in my shoulder blade, as if I had dislocated something. The force sent me stumbling, and only when I hit the ground did I see the guard running behind me—the whipper-snapper—with his arms reached out, his gun in his palms. I ate dirt. I tried to jump up; I was desperate to keep running, but the pain in my hip now radiated through my legs, and whatever the guard had shot me with had frozen my back. I groaned and scrabbled forward, not caring if he shot me again, but my arms had lost sensation. My brain was a psychedelic explosion of curses.

All that work. All that pain. And I wasn't going anywhere.

CHAPTER 67
MELTING
NICKY

The whippersnapper had hit me with some kind of tranquilizer. My whole body became warm and numb, as if my organs were melting. It felt good, because it dissolved the pain. He picked me up and slung me over his shoulder as if he were a prince rescuing a princess—although that could have just been a warped fantasy of mine as the drug clouded my reason. My prince carried me back to my razor-wire tower, and before the doors closed behind us, I had succumbed to the drug.

I woke briefly to see beautiful, kind Devka, who I hadn't seen in weeks, and I told her I loved her and missed her. I saw Ingleby's sneer, and Emily's fangs. It was like being in a warm river. I could feel the movement of being swept downstream without having to make an effort. I wanted Devka again, but saw Alison instead, and I groaned. I was on the guard's skinny shoulder again, and I thought I might vomit. Then there was Dillon, who I wanted to apologize to, and Derek, who I didn't. When I saw Adrathar's face above mine, I knew he was real. I could hear his machine humming in the background, warming up before it sent its next bolt of lightning into me. I drunkenly grasped at the electrodes he had already stuck to my skin, and he frowned and scolded me, calling for help again from the guards. The needles slid into my temples, and I stopped struggling. It was over, and I was relieved. My only regrets were not being able to hug Sebastian one more time, not being able to thank Devka, and wish Dillon well with their firstborn. As soon as I was able to let those things go, I was whipped out of the room and slung into the dark vacuum of space, and it was a crushing relief.

"It's not your time," Devka said to me.

I looked around, confused. I was pretty sure I had died, so where was I?

"You have to go back."

"No," I said, shaking my head. "Never going back."

"It's not up to you," she said.

"It can be," I replied.

"You don't understand. There are things you need to do."

"No," I said. "My life is empty. Even before this happened. No meaning."

"You'll see when you return," Devka said. "You will serve a purpose."

"I don't want to go back," I said. "I don't want to rot in that place."

"You won't," promised Devka.

The electric current cracked my body in half; or at least, that's what it felt like. I think I was screaming, because Adrathar injected me with something—a sedative—and I was calm again, despite my body feeling hollowed out and burnt. My limbs seized, and my whole being shuddered. I could feel my eyes rolling back and my diaper filling with warmth. *This is death,* I thought to myself. *It is finally here for me.* But I was wrong.

CHAPTER 68

STEPPED THROUGH THE WALL

ASHA

I walked back into the living room where Chione was splayed out on the carpet. Unfortunately, she was still unconscious. To break the curse, I needed to either find out the exact nature of the spell she had used, find the ring, or kill her. The final option was becoming more and more attractive, because I was running out of time, but I knew I couldn't do it. The Grimalkin wasn't evil, nor was I. It didn't stop me from being extremely annoyed with her, because now I had to find the bloody wedding ring, and it was going to be like trying to find a diamond in a bag of glass with a clock ticking in my ears.

I spent the next five minutes scowling at the mage lying on the floor while I thought about what to do. Eventually, an idea came to me.

I pushed a pillow under her head and left Chione lying there, but not before calling an ambulance and watering the dying houseplants. I opened one of Nicola's storage boxes in the garage and grabbed a scarf, tucking it into my pocket for later. I hurried down the long driveway, slipped through the wrought iron gate, and hopped onto my Wasp. Fifteen minutes later I arrived at the block in Rosebank the driver had told me about. It was late afternoon, so I wasn't expecting the portal door to be visible, but I needed to find it. The driver had said it was between the late-night club on the corner and the dodgy burger joint.

I paced between the two, searching for some kind of sign of the portal but not seeing any. I checked the cracks in the wall, touching the bricks to see if any of them were magical. Pedestrians who passed threw me quizzical and suspicious glances. Suddenly self-conscious, I wondered if I had dried blood on my face from giving Chione CPR. I must have looked to them like a sloppy vampire who had lost her keys. When I didn't find anything promising, I stepped back. I had just over an hour to get to Salty or our mission would be cancelled.

Stepping back gave me the perspective I needed to know what to do next. I inhaled deeply and grasped the wand in my pocket. I kept it inside my coat as not to scare the people passing by, but wrapped my fingers firmly around it. I took in the afternoon sun, the cirrus clouds against the blue, and the fluttering of leaves around me. Birds flew overhead. Even there, in the city, with traffic rushing by, honking and polluting, Nature was still queen. I breathed in the Void's power and felt her grace swell inside me. Standing on the sunbaked concrete I was reminded of her abundance; her magic was everywhere.

"*Adversum invisibilis,*" I uttered, reversing the invisibility spell I suspected was hiding the otherworldly gateway. At first, I was disappointed, thinking it didn't work, but as I watched a little sparkle appeared on the wall I had previously inspected. It was as if the wall had become slightly translucent, and someone was holding a sparkler on the other side. Soon the single spark became a line, and then a rectangle in the shape of a door. As soon as the shape was complete, I looked from side to side and stepped through the wall.

The passage was dark and smelled of stale beer. There was indie rock playing in the background. I sealed the doorway up behind me with my wand and walked tentatively toward the sound of the music. Despite the sun being up in the land of the untouched, this establishment's clocks all read midnight, and the arms didn't move. I had the feeling you could trip in here at six in the morning and it would look exactly the same. There were some old neon signs on the walls that flickered, adding to the general unease, and the tables looked like they hadn't been wiped down since Count Dracula was alive. The bartender looked up at me, ready to take my order. I flinched. I didn't want anything this seedy place had to offer. Instead of grimacing, I thought of Nicky and plastered a fraudulent smile on my face while I approached him.

"'ello darlin'" he leered. "Welcome to Grackle's. Not seen the likes of you in 'ere before."

"Hi," I said, as friendly as I could fake it.

He looked at me with undisguised carnality. He was missing a few teeth and reminded me of a pirate. "You meeting someone?"

"Yes," I lied, hoping it would stop him from hitting on me.

I looked around again. Now that my eyes had adjusted to the dim light, I could make out who was sitting at the tables. There was a stink of semi-conscious orcs in the corner, with beer-stains down their vests. A lone goblin sat on his own, nursing a bottle of whisky, and a dwarf couple sat nearby, holding hands while whispering over their jugs of cider and cold chips. The Grateful Undead's "Love Deep or Die" drawled from the speakers above.

There'll be a time

When you'll say goodbye

It'll hurt so hard, love deep or die

No one wants to feel the low

But when you know, you know

It's time to end the show

Love deep or die

I looked back at the pirate and gestured at the bar. "Do you mind if I sit here while I wait for him?"

"Be my guest!" He picked up a rancid-looking cloth and wiped the counter where I sat down, looking pleased with himself. "Now, don't get upset, but we don't do those magical cocktails that girls like yeh drink. Those smoking hemlock-tinis and black ice daiquiris."

"That's fine," I said. "How about coffee?"

It was his turn to hide his grimace. "I wouldn't recommend the coffee."

Something sealed would be good. "Sparkling water?"

"Nah, sorry."

"Beer? Any beer."

He smiled, showing me his antique piano key teeth. "Yeh've come to the right place!" He set about getting the bottle from the clinking fridge and proudly opened it for me with a bottle opener in the shape of a small monkey's skull.

"Much obliged," I said, pretending to take an appreciative swig. I looked at the clocks on the wall. Still frozen. This was already taking way too long.

"I was wondering if you could help me," I said, playing with my hair a little in what I hoped was a mildly flirtatious way. It was a delicate balance to strike—I had to interest him enough to answer my questions, but not enough to get me into trouble, because the last thing I needed was to be in an awkward position with a pirate.

CHAPTER 69

ILL-GOTTEN GOLD

ASHA

I took another pretend swig of the beer and looked over the counter at the piratical pub owner.

"A few weeks ago there was a man in here. Business suit. Drunk. Looking to party. Early hours of the morning."

"Yeh've just described every shift," he grinned, his gold teeth and oily skin catching the garish lights.

"This guy was untouched, so I'm not sure how he got in."

"Easy enough if yeh know someone."

"Know someone?"

"Yeah, if you're meeting someone here, they'll open for yeh, won't they?"

"So someone in here opened for him."

He shrugged, and as he did so, the navy-ink tattoos on his neck crumpled.

"Okay," I said. "That makes sense. This guy would have met with his mistress. A mage. Probably in a dark corner."

"Again, not unusual," he said.

"She's a Grimalkin."

"I don't know anythin' about Grimalkins," he replied. I didn't think he was lying, but I couldn't tell.

I tried a different tack. "Is there a regular who trades goods? Like a pawnbroker, or a fence?"

There was a hard glint in his eyes now. "I don't get involved with stolen goods."

"I'm not a cop," I said.

"So yeh say."

"I'm not a cop. I'm just looking for a wedding ring that man lost that night. I don't expect to get it for free. I'll pay for it."

"What's so special about the ring?"

"Sentimental value. As I said, it's a wedding ring."

The man gazed at me. "Careless of the man, to lose something like that."

"Yes," I replied slowly, trying to read him. It sounded like he knew something. "I'm guessing the mage sold the ring right here."

He looked at me for a while, possibly wondering how much to say. "Your guess would be correct."

"Really? To who?"

"Let me give you a clue," said the pirate. "What kind of creature likes gold and shiny things?"

I blinked at him, and he raised his eyebrows in the direction of the solo-drinking goblin.

"She sold it to a goblin?"

"'Not any goblin. *That* goblin."

I left money on the counter, enough for the drink and a large tip, and took my beer over to the goblin.

"Hello," I ventured.

"Ah, bugger off," said the grumpy goblin, not even looking up.

"Er ..."

He slammed his fist on the table, looked up at me with spectral eyes, and hissed through his dirty needles. "I said get lost! Witch!"

I looked around the dark pub, not wanting to cause a scene, but the orcs were snoring loudly in the corner and the dwarf couple had eyes for no one but each other.

I sat down. "Look here, slimeball," I said with aggression I didn't feel. "You've got something I need."

His wide, shimmering white eyes were disturbing to look at. How had he known I was a witch?

"I have money," I whispered, not wanting the orcs to hear. "Just tell me what it costs, I'll pay you double, we'll do the transaction, and I'll never bother you again."

He ignored me, and spoke to his whisky bottle. "That's what they all say. It's never true."

I sighed, looking at the frozen clocks. My frustration was mounting.

He tapped his long, green-tinged fingers on the table top. "My mother, may her soul rest in peace, taught me that you shouldn't sell if someone offers to pay you double."

I acquiesced. "Wise woman." *I never had a mother.*

"You never had a mother," he said, and I dropped my beer, catching it just in time to stop it from shattering on the dirty floor. "You have her protection, though."

"What? How do you know?"

"It's a curse," he said. "Lost my eyes, gained something else. Let me tell you, it's a real bitch to hear people's thoughts all day long. That's why I took to the bottle."

Holy hex! This blind goblin could read people's thoughts?

"Blah blah blah," he said, making his fingers go snap, snap, snap, like a crocodile. "SO boring." Then he motioned at the pirate behind the bar. "It doesn't help that Crusty Jack plays the same album on repeat every night."

"Goblin," I said, sitting up straighter. "I really need your help."

"My name is Boris."

"Boris," I said. "Please. You know what I'm here for. Please help me."

He hawked and spat on the floor. "Why should I?"

"There's a woman in trouble."

"I know. Why should I care?"

"You know?"

"I heard the whole conversation. They were in that corner, whispering." Boris flicked his fingers in the direction of the darkest corner of the pub. "They thought no one could hear them above the music. They were wrong. Their emotionally-charged thoughts were like electric mosquitoes in my brain even though I tried to wave them away."

"The man, Derek Landau, met his mistress here."

"Yes," said Boris. "But Landau didn't know that."

"What?"

"He stumbled in and found a table. A man in a dark coat sat with him and plied him with a drink, getting him to open up about his troubles. May the Void endure, that man had a lot of problems."

Boris finished the last of his drink and I signaled to the pirate to bring another bottle of whisky.

"He lost his clients' money. All of it. He'll be fired as soon as they find out. He was already behind on his loan repayments, about to lose the house. Couldn't bear to tell his wife, and definitely wouldn't tell his mistress, who sounded very demanding."

"He told all of this to the stranger?"

The goblin shook his head. "No, no, I could just feel the thoughts swirling around him, like black smoke. He was consumed by them. He only told the man about how his mistress wanted him to leave his wife. I guess he thought it was a relatable problem. Less shameful."

The bartender arrived and slammed down a new bottle of whisky, then winked at me.

"Did Derek Landau want to divorce his wife?"

"He seemed undecided. He felt his life was falling apart and he didn't want to drag her through it. He loved her, I could tell, but he was in a real mess."

"But his mistress was pushing for a divorce."

"Not a divorce, *per se*. Divorce costs a lot of money, and she wasn't in the mood for sharing."

"Okay," I said, pouring Boris a generous glass. "So, Landau tells this man he needs to get rid of his wife."

"Basically, yes."

"But he was torn. He even had this silver necklace in a box, all polished up. A silver raven charm. He had gotten the clasp repaired. Was going to surprise his wife with it."

The necklace pulsed in my pocket.

That doesn't sound like a man who has given up on a marriage, I thought.

"Exactly," said Boris. "But the man in the cloak had a way about him, stroking the man's ego, agreeing with him that he worked hard and deserved to get what he wanted in life, including a mistress. It was like he was mesmerizing him."

"Hmmm," I said. That sounded familiar.

"They came to an agreement. The mage would remove the wife from the picture, and Landau would be able to get on with the life he wanted. Landau made him promise that he wouldn't harm his wife, and the mage agreed. *I won't harm a hair on her head,* he said."

"He had to hand over his wedding ring as payment," I said, and Boris nodded. "And he later gave the necklace to his mistress."

"Of course, the man in the cloak *was* his mistress. She used a glamour to trick him."

"Of course," I said. That Grimalkin was a wily bitch.

The goblin took a sip of whisky, then ran a hand over his balding head. "After Landau left, the mage drops her glamour and moves to another table, where a wizard is sitting. He had been watching the whole thing."

My blood ran cold. "Which wizard?"

"She never said his name, and he never thought it, so I don't know."

This was getting way too complicated for me. "They're in on it together?"

"That's what it seemed like to me. But what do I know? I'm just a blind old goblin with a drinking problem."

I sighed and sat back. "Chione is smarter than I thought."

"Yes," said Boris. "Smart girl. Personally, I wouldn't go within spitting distance of her."

"But you did that night," I said. "She sold you the ring."

Boris shook his head. "I wouldn't go near her. I certainly wouldn't trade ill-gotten gold with her."

My body slumped. "You don't have the wedding ring?"

"I never touched that ring," he said, casting his white irises at me. "I'd advise you to do the same."

I marched up to the bar again. "I'm about to lose my mind."

"Don't do that," said the pirate. "You're too pretty to end up at Riverside."

My insides froze. "What do you know about Riverside?"

"I know a doctor who works there. Nasty piece of work."

We stared at each other, the neon lights flickering on our faces. How much did he know? What part had he played in it?

He hit a button on the cash register and the tray sprang open with a *ting*, vibrating the coins in the bottom. He scratched at the back of the tray and pulled out Derek Landau's gold ring.

CHAPTER 70
A HUNDRED FLOATING FIRES
ASHA

The pocket realm was getting more and more surreal. I felt as if I had shared that bottle of whisky with Boris the blind goblin, even though I'd had nothing to drink.

I suspiciously eyed the wedding ring that Crusty Jack was holding. "How did you get that?" I asked.

The bartender shrugged again. The more I looked at the tattoos on his neck, the more they looked like prison ink. Apprehension clawed at my gut.

"The mage with the glamour ordered drinks all night, but when it was time to pay, she didn't have any cash. She gave me this. I haven't had time to pawn it."

I squeezed the bridge of my nose. "Please, can I buy it from you?" I knew the answer would not be straightforward.

"Sure yeh can," he replied.

"Really?"

"Really. Shall we say five thousand koin?"

"Seems a little steep."

"I'll throw in that bottle of whisky Boris is drinking."

He knew I wasn't there to haggle. "Okay," I said. "Deal."

I was about to count out the notes when he said, "Not here."

I looked back at the orcs in the dimly lit corner and saw one of them was watching us. *Damn it. Foul creatures.*

"Come to the back," he said, and motioned for me to walk around. I felt the orc's eyes on me as I did so.

We entered a poky room piled high with boxes of booze and teetering stacks of files. Papers littered the desk and a dusty-leafed plant wilted in the corner. The pirate closed the door behind us, which I didn't think was necessary, but I didn't argue. I needed that ring and I needed to hightail it out of there if I wanted to get to Salty on time. I looked down at my wallet and took out the cash, quickly counting the hundred-koin notes. That was when I felt Crusty breathing on my neck. It made me shudder. He took it as a good sign and grasped me from behind. I dropped all the cash, and the ring went flying.

"No!" I yelled, wrenching myself out of his sweaty grip. I swung around to face him. "You got the wrong idea."

"Did I?" he sneered.

I honestly didn't have time for this. "Look, I won't hold it against you. We got our signals crossed. I'm just here for the ring."

"Well," he said, adjusting his belt. "I don't feel like selling it to you anymore."

I felt magic tingling in my hands, but tried to keep calm.

Do not send a lightning bolt into the pirate, I told myself. *We need the pirate on our side.*

"I'm going to find the ring," I said in as calm a voice as I could muster, "and I'm going to leave the cash for you."

The bartender's voice was bitter. "I know your type. Pretty, rich city witch, coming in here and expecting to get your way. Well, tonight, I'm going to get my way."

He advanced, and I reached for my knife. It was gone. So was my wand. The portal entrance must have removed them. I swore under my breath. *Bloody sophisticated magic tech security portal doors. A hex on them!* I resorted to using my fists and feet. He had a barrel of a chest, so I didn't fancy my chances there. Instead, I right-hooked him so his face smashed one way, then did a roundhouse kick to smash it the opposite direction. He looked stunned, but he was still standing. I kicked him again, this time full-on in the chest, then dropped to take out his knees. Despite the brutal hits, he remained standing. I searched for something I could use as a weapon, but somehow, I didn't think a stapler would do it.

"Come here."

His voice made me shake. He lunged at me. I just escaped his touch and scrambled over the desk. I quickly scanned the floor for the ring, but I couldn't see it. Realizing he had me cornered, he smiled and kept advancing.

"Leave me alone," I said. "I'm warning you."

He laughed.

I put out my tingling hand and thought of the sky and birds and trees that waited for me just outside. "*Ventum exquiris,*" I chanted, whipping up the stale air into a whirlwind that lifted all the papers in the room. I desperately looked for the ring. The pirate looked confused for a moment, but quickly leaned forward to grab me. "*Impedio!*" I yelled, and he froze in his tracks. I knew the spell would only hold for a few seconds. It's not good practice to split your magic between two different spells at the same time, but desperate times, etc. etc.

I dropped to the filthy floor. I had hoped that the ring would be too heavy to be swept up in the wind but the floor would be cleared of papers. I had been half right. Even though the papers cruised around us like mad sailboats, I still couldn't spot the ring. For a maddening moment I felt like giving up. And then I saw it. It must have rolled when it hit the floor, because it was upright and half hidden behind a filing cabinet. *Yes!*

Just then the man was on me again. I had dropped my guard. He pulled at my clothes with clumsy hands and rough fingers.

"No!" I shouted again, but my voice was lost in the whirlwind. His grip on me was unrelenting as he grabbed me, trying to bend me over the desk. "*Ignem exquiris,*" I said, setting fire to every piece of paper in the office. I thought that would distract him, but he wanted to finish with me before attending to the flames. Now we were surrounded by a hundred floating fires. He tugged at my pants again, but they wouldn't budge. I remembered I was wearing the leggings that Ferra designed. She had obviously layered some extra magic in the design, one of which seemed that no one could force your pants off. Literally, no one could get in your pants but you.

Blessed be, Ferra Fornak!

Before I could celebrate, the smoke filled our lungs and stung our eyes. I blinked back the first tears, but it got worse. The pirate let out a roar of frustration and fury at not being able to further assault me and clobbered me on the back, winding me. When I could breathe in again, it was a lungful of smoke. He grabbed my shoulder and wrenched it back, forcing me to face him, and drew his fist back, ready to smash my skull. He had letters inked on his fingers, but I couldn't make them out. My brain stumbled on a spell, and nothing came out. His fist came hurtling toward my face and then there was a loud bang and the lights went out. His fist never made contact. The room was only lit by the dying embers of the paper, but I saw the pirate crashed out on the floor. When I looked to the entrance to see what had happened, a large shape grabbed me. I knew by the smell, even past the acrid smoke, that it was an orc. The orc who had been watching me. He tossed me over his shoulder easily, as if I were a doll. As he strode out of the office, I put out my hand for the last time and pointed it at the floor by the filing cabinet.

"Contendis!" I choked, and the wedding ring rose and floated toward me. I snatched it from the air just in time as the orc carried me out of the pocket realm and into the fresh air.

CHAPTER 71

DERANGED, DUPLICITOUS

NICKY

"Mrs. Landau," said Sister Ingleby, shaking me. "Mrs. Landau. Nicola! Wake up." She snapped her thick-skinned fingers in front of my face.

I blinked at her. It was the only muscle in my whole body that seemed to be working.

"Stop feeling sorry for yourself and sit up."

I stared at her. If I had a body at all, I couldn't feel it. I had eyes, and maybe a mouth, but I wasn't sure about the rest.

Ingleby seemed furious at me for being paralyzed. She squeezed her eyes shut, then opened them again. "Will you stop being such a drama queen! We need you up and about."

I wasn't sure why the nurse was so desperate for me to get up, but I couldn't, even if I wanted to. A part of me was glad that I couldn't obey her, but the sensible part of me realized that this was the worst thing that could have happened. Being in a vegetative state made me extremely vulnerable to the dark elements of the asylum. I imagined Adrathar darkening the door and immediately felt ill. He would be able to do whatever he liked to me and I wouldn't be able to report him. Then there was deranged, duplicitous Alison and her ilk, and white-fanged Emily.

"I knew you were trouble," the nurse seethed. "I knew you were trouble from the day you arrived here."

I didn't remember having met her in the beginning. All I remembered was Sister Devka and the four walls of the cell— but I couldn't reply, even if I wanted to. I blinked lazily at her.

Don't you see? I was saying. *Don't you see none of it matters anymore?*

The nurse seemed genuinely agitated. Part of me enjoyed seeing her squirm. The rest of me mourned the loss of my muscles, and with that loss, any chance I had of escaping. Being in this insensate condition ruled out breaking free, or suicide. I wanted to weep, but my face was so numb that even that was denied me.

CHAPTER 72

SMOKED EYEBALLS

ASHA

I had no energy to fight the orc. If he killed me, at least I wouldn't be subjected to the pirate's greasy grip. My body swung like a deadweight on his huge shoulder as he strode out of the office, down the dank corridor, and through the sparkling-edged supernatural doorway. I held on to the ring as if I were Gollum traversing Middle-earth. The orc carried me outside, where the fading sunshine hurt my smoked eyeballs, and quickly into an alley, presumably to mug me out of sight of the untouched. It was just that kind of day. I didn't fight him when he lowered me onto a windowsill and stared into my face.

"You okay?" he growled. "Witch girl?"

I sniffed the air. Yes, I had ash on my skin and fumes up my nostrils, but I was pretty sure I recognized the stench of this one. Rotten pumpkin, skunk smoke, and raw onions.

"Gnrok," I heaved.

He grunted in assent.

I felt faint with relief. "Thank you."

"I'll take you to Boss Morgan," he said.

"No." I shook my head. "I don't have time."

"I'll take you to Boss Morgan," he repeated, and threw me over his shoulder again.

Morgan took one look at me and pulled down her Scorpion-issue first aid kit. "What the hell happened to you?"

"I really appreciate the concern," I said, giving Gnrok an enthusiastic thumbs-up and smiling with all my teeth, "but I really have to go."

"What's the rush?"

"I was supposed to meet Nilve SaltySnap at the old train station at six p.m., and it's already quarter-past."

Morgan looked interested. "Let me just—" She motioned at my face and performed a circular washing pantomime. She sprayed some cotton wool and began wiping my face. The cotton came away gray. After slinging three used-up balls into her trash can like an NBA pro, she said, "That's slightly better, but you still look like you've stepped off a *Predator* film set."

"I don't know what that means."

"It means that at least you'll be well camouflaged for the rest of your evening. What are your plans?"

I told her that I was meeting Salty to portal into Riverside.

Morgan's smile vanished. "You can't portal into Riverside!"

"We don't have a choice."

"Asha," said Morgan shaking her head. "We've had reports about that place." The captain looked spooked.

"Nicola Landau," I said. "She's in a bad way."

Morgan frowned. "I heard of the case. It hit the headlines a few weeks ago. She had a psychotic break and killed people."

"Yes. Except that it wasn't a psychotic break. It was a curse. She was cursed by a mage, a Grimalkin. It's up to me to break the curse and get her out of there."

"But what use is breaking the spell now? Surely the harm is done?"

"Because she's imprisoned by her guilt as much as those cell walls. She deserves to know the truth. That she didn't do anything wrong, and she doesn't deserve to be in there."

Morgan tapped her stilettos. "I want to help you," she said. "But I can't. I'd be risking my job."

"Of course. I understand."

"But there is something I wanted to tell you. Something else," said Morgan.

"All ears," I replied.

"I feel bad about withholding that information from you as incentive to work for us."

I blinked at her. "About my personal file?"

"Officially, it's not in your file. I was able to find out your mother's name."

"What? What is it?"

"I mean, I'm not sure if it was her legal name, but it's what she was called."

"Land the plane, Morgan!"

"Maleficum."

"What now?"

"Belladonna Maleficum."

"Maleficum?" I repeated. "It sounds ..."

"Like an evil Disney queen?" said Morgan.

"Right," I said.

"Anyway, I thought you should know."

"Thank you," I said, my thoughts swirling. I looked at my watch. "Hex it, I'm so late. Twenty minutes and counting."

"Goblins are pretty grumpy creatures," Morgan said. "My guess is she'll be gone by six thirty. You'll never get there in time."

"Ugh." My energy leaked out of my bones. I felt defeated.

"You'll never get there in time ... unless you have a police escort."

I looked up at her.

Before I had time to reply, she nodded at Gnrok. "Make sure she gets there before half past six."

CHAPTER 73

SCORCH MARKS AND SADNESS

ASHA

The ride over to the train station was hairy as hell. Gnrok had his lights flashing and siren wailing, and jammed his foot down on the accelerator as only an orc can. More than once I felt the car balancing on two wheels as he took a corner too quickly. A safe following distance did not apply. Turn signals were a distant memory—perhaps orc fingers are too big to use them without snapping them off altogether. I stopped counting after the third red light we sailed through and sat back into the seat, closing my eyes against the squeals of tires, trying to prepare myself for what lay ahead. I attempted to clear my mind of the day's events, which was easier said than done. Traumatic images flashed in, especially of giving Chione CPR and fighting off the assault by Crusty Jack, the piratical bartender.

For some reason, I also had a thought-loop going around in my head that I was still not free of the dark sect of wizards who were working against me, nor had I recovered from my amnesia. Yes, I was remembering spells as I went along, and my muscles and bones knew how to battle and how to heal, but my memory was still a static television screen. I tried to tuck all those images and thoughts away for a while inside a box inside my brain—just until tonight's mission was over. I would need distraction-free focus if I was going to get Nicola out of Riverside safely. I made a quick call to the Edison's cab driver. When he answered, I reminded him who I was.

"I need a favor," I said.

Soon, we screeched to a stop, and my door automatically opened.

"Thanks," I said to Gnrok, happy to be on *terra firma*. He grunted and sped off, leaving me standing in the dusk at the abandoned train station. No one ever accused him of being a gentleman. I heard bats flying overhead and imagined their leathery wings flapping in the cool evening air. I took a breath and started moving toward the old hall.

The building was dilapidated. Scorch marks and sadness graffitied the concrete floor where vagrants often made fires to keep warm on winter nights. Window frames were empty and rusted black. With the broken-down train cars outside, the broken railway lines, and the pollution-pumped sunset colors streaming through the smashed windows, the scene looked like something out of a dystopian landscape. Most troubling was the fact that Nilve SaltySnap was not there as my watch struck six thirty. I swore under my breath, and when that didn't make me feel better, I yelled out curse words into the ramshackle hall, and they echoed back at me.

I heard glass cracking on the floor behind me and spun around, ready to grab my knife.

"Asha," said Detective Armstrong, rubbing his hair as he slowly came toward me. "I'm so glad you're okay."

It was good to see a friendly face. I wanted to hug him, to draw him in close, but my paranoia twitched. I stayed where I was. "What are you doing here?"

"I came to find you. I was worried."

I knew deep down and without reservation that Sam was a good guy. So why was he making me feel nervous? The shadows of the rusted steel distorted his face. "How did you know I was here?"

He laughed. "It's a long story."

"I like long stories."

Sam's smile melted away. "You weren't at home last night when I went to check on you, nor this morning. I started to get concerned. Then there was a witness report of a large man carrying a woman who matched your description into an alley in Rosebank."

"That was me," I said.

"I know. I went there and found your scooter. But you were gone. I checked your GPS and saw that this was to be your next destination, so I took a chance."

"Turns out you're a pretty good detective," I said.

"I don't know about that."

I smiled. I trusted him, right? I trusted him. I shouldn't let my paranoia destroy the few allies I had. "I'm supposed to be meeting someone here."

"I know," he said. "I've been keeping her company while we waited for you. I brought doughnuts."

I imagined how happy Salty must have been to see doughnuts. I was just happy she had waited.

"Come on," he said, and walked out the way he came. "We're just around the corner, here."

Despite my nagging trepidation, I followed him.

There's a reason you should always listen to your instincts, especially if you're a witch. Even more especially if you're hanging out at an abandoned train station as the sun sinks behind the skyline. Detective Armstrong led me to his car, which he had managed to park inside the property, next to a palisade fence. A breeze blew sand across my path, an omen saying *go no farther*. Still, I went.

The back door was open, but the car was empty, apart from the aforementioned box of doughnuts.

Sam scratched his head. "She was here a second ago."

Suddenly, Salty launched herself into the air from behind a rusted container. Using both hands, she held a glinting emerald-glass dagger. She was behind Sam, so he didn't see her. A scream caught in my throat. He saw my expression and tried to turn, but it was too late. The goblin had plunged the dagger into his back. He fell forward, onto the dry sand between us, and convulsed. An electric current of shock shot through my body. He continued seizing, his shirt blooming red.

"No!" I screamed, crouching down to help him, then looking up at the treacherous goblin. "What have you done?"

"Stand back!" yelled Salty.

"What?"

"Stand back, witch!"

I stumbled backwards and fell over a rock. *What the hell is going on?* Blood leaked from Sam's body, forming a dark puddle in the sand. The goblin reached forward and wrenched her dagger out of his back. I grimaced and turned away, my mind whirring with all the good things the detective had done for me. As soon as the emerald glass left Sam's flesh, something odd happened. His body changed shape, his hair changed color. The dead man went from a six-foot-something muscular frame to a flabby man a foot shorter with curly hair.

Still on the ground, all I could do was watch in horror—and relief. Salty wiped the dagger on her victim's shirt and put it back in her scabbard, then with great effort, she turned the body over to show me who it was.

"How?" I asked, but really what I meant was, *tell me what the hell is going on, I'm so confused.*

The dark curly hair, the golden scythe tattoo. The dead man lying there was the Dusk Reaper who had broken into my house the week before to kill me.

Seeing his face was too much for me. I stayed on the ground, feeling pressed down by fear and confusion. I looked at Nilve SaltySnap. "I don't know what is real anymore."

"Nothing has changed," said Salty matter-of-factly. She may be slimy, but she was practical.

"Nothing has changed?" I yelled. "Does Sam Armstrong even exist?"

Salty searched his pocket and found what she was looking for. She pressed a button on the remote and the trunk of the car sprang open. I stood up to inspect what was inside, expecting the worst, but there was the real Sam Armstrong, gagged and bound, looking at me as if I had just saved the world.

CHAPTER 74

MISTER COP

ASHA

I pulled down Detective Sam Armstrong's gag and reached for my ritual knife to cut away his bonds.

"Thank you," he said. "My knightess in shining armor."

"More like a witch having a panic attack," I said. Once he was disentangled, I levered him up. He groaned; his muscles were stiff from being stuck in the car. "Salty's the one who saved you. I'm just here for the doughnuts."

Nilve SaltySnap could see I would ask questions all night if she didn't tell me what had happened, so she gave me a quick rundown. Basically, everything the fake Sam had said was true. The real Sam had tracked me down via the police report and the scooter's GPS—and brought doughnuts. Unfortunately, the Dusk Reaper had also been following my trail via Sam, and when they had arrived at the train station, he decided to use a glamour to impersonate him to win my trust and make for an easy kill. Unluckily for him, he had underestimated Salty, who could spot a glamour—and a dark wizard—from a mile away. Sam watched her with bulging eyes as Salty approached the wizard bounty hunter's body. I felt for him. Imagine not believing in magic, then seeing a goblin for the first time, especially one with bloodstained hands, rifling through a corpse's pockets.

Sam cleared his throat in an uncertain way, his body language tense. "Who's this?"

The sight of a goblin on his side of the veil must have been surreal indeed, especially when she was fleecing a corpse. He kept staring.

"This is Salty," I said. "The one who just saved both of us. She's a goblin."

"Goblin," he said slowly, then looked at me as if to say, *Are you seeing what I'm seeing?*

"Look," I said. "There are some things you don't know."

"You can say that again."

I knew that the high priestess had instructed me to keep the veiled Realm a secret at all costs, but Sam had already seen Salty. My options were to cast a spell to make him forget all about the strange encounter—which wasn't without risk, particularly given my current lack of remembered experience

—or take him along for the ride and deal with the consequences later.

The detective was still gaping at the creature, speechless. It wasn't just about coming across a random goblin, of course. It was the worldview-shattering realization that magical creatures existed, which opened up a whole new exciting and scary dimension of possibilities and problems in fantasy technicolor. No wonder he looked pale.

"Thank you," he finally eked out. "For saving my life."

The goblin didn't have time for etiquette. She spat on the ground and said, "Let's get moving."

"Wait," said Sam, his head still spinning. "Where are we going?"

"You're not going anywhere, Mister Cop," she said. "You've caused us enough trouble tonight."

"He can help us," I said.

The goblin scoffed. "Human police? *Help?* Which realm are you living in?"

"We're portaling into Riverside Asylum," I said to him. "There's a woman there who needs our help."

"You're breaking into a government correctional facility?" he asked. "You can't. You won't be able to get in. And if they catch you trying, you'll be arrested."

"I have to," I replied. *Balance the universe, it's what I do.*

"Look," Sam said. "You've had a hell of a hard day. Let's go home and discuss the case. Come up with a strategy."

I shook my head and put my knife back in the holster. "There's no time for that."

"We can approach this the legal way. Get a court interdict. Get her out of there legally, permanently. I know lawyers who will help us. Good people."

"Where were these so-called good people when Nicola Landau didn't even get a trial?" sneered Salty.

"Honestly, I don't know," he replied. "But we can fix it. Legally."

"*Legally*," scoffed the goblin.

I looked into his eyes. He was a good man; I'd known that all along. Probably too good for me.

"This is crazy. Dangerous. Let me take you home." He gently took my hand, and the feel of his warm skin on mine was extremely distracting. "Let me take care of you."

Oh. My. Hex. That was so tempting. I imagined a bath, a comforting meal, a whisky—or three—with Sam. It was exactly what I needed. But I couldn't do it, not with Nicola languishing in that hellhole.

"You're making this difficult," I said, smiling. "I'd love for you to take me home. But I need to do this first."

"Then let me come with you," he said.

I shook my head. "You'll lose your job."

"I'll get another one."

I looked over at Salty. I noticed she had managed to eat all six doughnuts. She had rainbow sprinkles on her lips. "Can Mister Cop come with us?"

The goblin shrugged. "Does he have a gun?"

Sam showed her his holster, which snugly fitted his police-issue Beretta.

The goblin smiled, showing us the doughnut crumbs she had in her sharp teeth. "Then Mister Cop can come with us."

CHAPTER 75
THAT WITCH
ASHA

The reason Nilve SaltySnap wanted to meet at the defunct train station was because the energy there —even though it was now in ruins, with rusted train cars dry-melting into the ground—was about transport and travel. *It's a tricky assignment,* she had said. *We need all the help we can get.* We were going to harness the potential energy that the property held—of all the frustrated trains—and use that to propel us into the Void, to be sucked along the vortex, and land where we wanted to, inside the asylum.

We stood in a circle.

"Ready?" asked the goblin. She still had rainbow sprinkles on her lips.

"Ready," I replied on behalf of myself and Sam, who still looked profoundly puzzled by the whole thing. I could tell he wasn't expecting the spell to work. Salty stuck her tongue out and curled it over the side of her top lip as she concentrated. She wagged her hand at me, and I emptied my pockets. I had the Copperfield envelope, the silver raven necklace, Derek's wedding ring, and Nicola's scarf. I handed the necklace to the goblin, who looked at it approvingly.

She clutched the jewelry and closed her eyes. She rocked on her heels and began her incantation. Her voice gradually got louder, and when her eyelids fluttered, I saw the whites of her eyes. Sam gave me an uncertain look. I squeezed his hand and closed my eyes, letting go of the earth beneath me and allowing Salty's chanting to transport me.

The next second, we were whipped into the air where we floated for a bit, then just as we got used to that feeling, we were flung along time and space as if we were ping pong balls in a lottery machine. The landscape became stars and space, rain on our faces, and the smell of rocket ships and ozone. Cold lightning made me gasp, and then rushing, rushing, rushing in my ears, which faded to a total and utter silence that I had never experienced before. Then came the unpleasant part: a crushing pressure that seemed to bear down on every cell and organ in my body, until my skin was stinging and my skeleton crumbling. I lost my grip on Sam's and Salty's hands. I groped for them, but they were gone. My cheeks were pressed in so hard that I thought my face would implode; my teeth were pushed farther into my gums. And just as it got to be too much, and I felt like I couldn't take it anymore, the Void gave me one last squeeze and expelled me like a newborn baby, raw, shocked—and possibly crying.

I landed hard on the tarmac. I could still smell the afternoon heat coming off it. That didn't feel right. I had expected a concrete or tiled floor, but I had been dumped outside somewhere. On a road. I opened my eyes and blinked a few times, trying to figure out where I was. Neither Nilve nor Sam were with me. What had happened? There was a light, and a movement, from a shack nearby. No, not a shack. It was a security guard hut. And a huge white wall. I was outside the Copperfield Institute. I looked down at my hand and realized with alarm that I had been holding onto the envelope that Directress Copperfield had given me. I had inadvertently used it as a portal key, and now Salty and Sam were inside Riverside, and I was stuck here.

I was so furious with myself for being so stupid. If I could have turned myself to ash in that moment, I would have. I didn't have the curse words in my vocabulary to adequately express how I felt.

"Hey," came a voice made of velvet. I wrenched myself away from my damning thoughts and looked at the werewolf, letting out little puffs of white vapor as he panted. "You're that witch."

"Yes," I said, getting up and dusting myself off. "I guess I am that witch."

The witch who messed everything up. The witch who didn't break the curse and didn't save the woman in need.

"You came to see the directress the other day," he said.

"Yes."

I hadn't solved that case, either. I'd managed to spend the generous advance, but didn't have one lead to show for it.

The witch who couldn't solve a case if little girls' lives depended on it. Which they do.

The werewolf pulled on his black leather jacket, ready to leave. "Why are you here?"

I understood then that it hadn't been a mistake, because the universe doesn't make mistakes. I had been inelegantly deposited here for a reason.

"You're knocking off?" I asked him.

"*Ja*," he nodded. "It's the end of my shift."

"How would you feel about portaling with me to an asylum for the criminally insane?"

He laughed. When he saw that I was serious, he stopped laughing. "Um, no? I was just about to head out for something to eat and then go home."

Even in the dark I could see the evening breeze rippling through his ombre fur. He was beautiful.

"I knew Rusty," I said. "May the Void ensconce him."

"May the Void ensconce him," repeated the guard.

"There's an innocent woman locked up at the Riverside Asylum who needs our help. If Rusty were here, I know he'd come with me."

It was a terribly manipulative thing to say, but I stood by it. The werewolf looked at me carefully, sizing me up.

"Helping people out got Rusty killed," said the guard.

We stood in silence for a while. Feeling cold, I tightened my cloak around me.

"There is an innocent woman in trouble," I said slowly and carefully. "She has no one but us. Please, will you help me?"

He stared at me for a while, then sighed.

"When you put it that way," he said, zipping up his jacket. "Who needs dinner and rest, anyway?"

"I don't know your name."

"I'm Stoker," he said. "Rusty was my uncle."

"I'm Asha Rook."

"Oh, I know that," he said. "We'd better move it, Asha Rook. My next shift starts at eight a.m."

CHAPTER 76

SLUNG THROUGH SPACE

ASHA

I didn't tell Stoker that I didn't know if I was any good at gateway magic. We had no option but to try. I took Nicola Landau's scarf out of my pocket and Stoker and I held it, together. I took a deep breath to settle my nerves. I closed my eyes and tried to conjure up the picture of Riverside as clearly as I could in my mind. I thought of the friendly landscaping that hid the truth of what went on inside. Once I got a clear image, I breathed deeper, trying to pull the magic up from the earth and through my body. I felt it warm my feet, then creep up slowly through my legs. Once it reached my face, I knew I was ready. With renewed confidence, I held on to that power and expelled it as I spoke.

"Ianua sit!"

The spell worked immediately. My body—that had just recovered from being slung through space—was once again slingshot through the Void. We flew and tumbled together, feeling exhilaration and fear as we rushed through space and sparks toward our destination.

One of the reasons I had wanted Salty to portal me into River-side was that I knew she had a reputation for the best gateway magic in the province. Her landings were not only soft, but precise. I wanted to land in Nicola's cell. Of course, my portal spell was nowhere as good as the goblin's, so there was no telling where in the asylum we'd show up, the idea of which made my anxiety spike. We landed with a bang in what looked and smelled like a cafeteria. Cockroaches scurried over us, making us jump up and dust off our limbs in an impromptu dance. Even after getting rid of them, I imagined them tickling my scalp and scuttling over my skin.

"Give me the scarf," Stoker whispered.

I did, and he put it to his nose.

"Okay. Follow me."

We skulked out of the dining room and down a dark passage. Stoker quietly sniffed as we went, trying to pick up Nicola Landau's scent. The look on his face was not comforting.

"A lot of bad things happen here," he said, which made the hairs on the back of my neck stand up like they had on my first visit. We moved quickly forward. I jumped at any sound, which I'm sure irritated the werewolf with his senses so finely tuned. After a while, I felt like we were going around in circles.

All the passages looked the same, all the cell doors seemed identical apart from the patient's names scribbled on them.

"Are you picking anything up?" I asked.

"Patience," he hissed. "The owner of the scarf is here." He slowed to a stop and showed me the door. LANDAU, it said on the outside.

"You beauty," I said to the werewolf, and I meant it. I pulled out the copy of Sister Ingleby's access card I had conjured when I had visited a few days before. I held my breath as I pressed it to the chip reader. It beeped softly, and the light turned from red to green. I exhaled in relief, and we quickly slipped into Nicola's cell. I searched for the light switch, but Stoker's night vision was superior to mine, and he beat me to it. As the artificial light glared down into her cell, Stoker and I looked at each other unhappily. It was Nicola's cell, but it was empty.

Not only was Nicola not there, but Sam and Salty were gone, too. Was it possible that they had rescued Landau and had already left? *That would be amazing,* I thought, *but not very likely.*

"Can you smell a goblin?" I asked.

"That sounds like the beginning of a bad joke," Stoker replied.

"Seriously," I said.

I saw the werewolf's black nostrils flare.

"No," he said. "No goblins here."

"How about a cop?" I asked. "Human, untouched?"

"This place reeks of humans," he said. "Do cops smell different?"

I didn't have an answer. Why would the multiverse send me to collect Stoker if Landau wasn't even in her cell? I guess not even the multiverse could predict every slight development.

"Can we start again? Looking for Landau, using the scarf?"

Stoker nodded. "That's why we're here."

"Bonus points if you can track down the goblin and the cop," I said.

"Oh, good," he said, and smirked. "Bonus points."

CHAPTER 77
WORSE THAN LOST
ASHA

The werewolf and I left Landau's cell and prowled around the dark corridors, dodging nurses and guards as soon as we sensed them. Stoker seemed to be confident in the direction we were going and I thanked the Void for him. I would have been worse than lost without him. When Nicola hadn't been in her cell, I had felt utter despair, thinking there was no way we'd find her in the spooky labyrinth that was Riverside Asylum. But, thank the goddesses, within minutes of feeling that hopelessness, Stoker nodded at me and said, "We're close."

My heart beat faster, and I began to feel the energy tingling in my hands. If I had to fight—*when* I had to fight—I'd be ready. We stalked past a dozen or more locked cells and turned into yet another passage. I was grateful for portal magic for many reasons, one of which was that I was sure I'd never find my way out of there on foot. Another corner, and then down some dark stairs, and just as I started to feel claustrophobic Stoker slowed down and stopped. Someone in the next room was talking. As we waited, ears on stalks, I could hear Stoker's faint panting and smell his lupine musk. When I heard Salty's voice, relief eased my shoulders down. She was speaking softly and calmly, which made me think they were not in danger. Stoker and I nodded to each other and entered the dark room, startling the others, including Sam, who had reached for his gun with lightning speed and was aiming it at Stoker.

"Easy, tiger," I said.

The detective rolled his eyes in relief and put his safety catch back on. "Don't you know you shouldn't sneak up on people with loaded guns?"

"I don't know," I replied. "My memory isn't what it used to be."

Despite our mock bickering, I felt a huge wave of warmth come from him, and I felt the same way. I hoped we all survived the night.

"How are you?" I asked him.

"Adjusting to life with goblins in it," he said, and smiled.

I took out my wand. "*Illumino,*" I said, lighting the tip just enough for us to see each other.

"You took your time," said Salty. "Did you stop to adopt a dog on the way?"

"Not a dog," growled Stoker.

"This is Stoker," I said. "He's Rusty's nephew. Head of security at Copperfield. He helped me find you. It's a long story."

Sam was doing that goggle-eyes thing again, reminding me that he'd never seen a werewolf before. Stoker stopped snarling and tucked his fangs away. Armstrong and Salty stepped aside to reveal a motionless body lying on a hospital bed. This looked more like a hospital ward than a cell, with machines lining the walls and a thin curtain on a steel rail around the beds, of which there were four.

"We have a problem," said the goblin.

Nicola Landau looked in much worse shape than she had two days before. I wouldn't have believed it possible, because when I had seen her, she had been virtually comatose. Now she was thinner, paler, and the marks on her temple were worse. She looked as close to a corpse as I had ever seen. How was I going to help her when she couldn't even hear me?

"Hex," I said, rubbing my face. Was she even alive? I watched her chest rise slightly and fall, which I took to be a good sign. We would take our small victories, and this was one of them. I looked at Salty. "We have lots of problems. Which one would you like to discuss first?"

"The Council Law and Regulatory Act 204, part 6," she said. I thought she was joking, but she continued. "Because of the rise of kidnappings in the Realm, the Council took away part of our portal magic."

"What?"

"We can't portal anyone without their consent."

I looked at Nicola again. "Oh. I see the problem."

"And it'll be tricky to get her out of here without portaling," said Sam. I thought of the maze of corridors swarming with the red ant guards and I agreed. It seemed like an impossible situation. They all looked at me as if I should have the answer, but I didn't.

A voice spoke from the other side of the ward, and it made us all jump.

"It's too late," said the voice, then the curtain rings scraped against the rail, revealing a young woman with long dark hair. She was wearing the same cotton shift as Nicola. Her face was white, and she had dark circles under her eyes. Without trying to be uncharitable, she reminded me of the girl in *The Ring*.

When I managed to get my breath back, I wheezed, "Who are you?"

"It doesn't matter," she said.

"You're a patient here?"

She smiled, revealing sharp brown teeth. It was a terrifying sight. "Isn't it obvious?"

I shuddered, and I could see Stoker's fur rise. Armstrong, whose hand had been strumming his holster, stopped moving.

"My name is Emily," she said. "Not that it matters."

"Of course, it matters," I said. *What has this place done to her?*

"It's too late for your friend," she said, motioning at Landau's listless body. "She's just a meat sack now. Bag o' bones."

"What happened to her?" I asked.

She dropped the maniacal grin. "Doctor Adrathar had his way with her."

Dread boiled my insides. "Do you mean—?"

"I mean he used his lightning machine on her. He stole her mind, just like he tried to steal mine. That's what he does with the lightning machine. He takes all of you till there's nothing left. You're here to save her, but you're too late. There's nothing left to save."

CHAPTER 78

YOU NEVER GET OUT
ASHA

"We can't get her out of here in this condition," said Salty. "I did my bit to portal you here, but I can recognize a lost cause when I see one. I vote we abort the mission."

"No!" I cried. "We can't leave her here."

"Well, I'm the one with the portal magic, so I have the only vote," said the goblin. "I'm not risking my life for a breathing skeleton."

"How can you be so cold?" I demanded.

"I'm a goblin," she replied, as if that answered my question. She spat on the floor, then wiped her rubbery lips with the back of her slimy arm. "Why are you so obsessed, anyway? You don't even know this woman."

Because I know how it felt to be abandoned, I thought.

"Please," I begged Salty. "Can we just try?"

She crossed her arms on top of her round belly.

"Please," I repeated. I was not above begging a goblin.

She bared her needles at me.

I turned to the odd girl, Emily. "Do you know how to get out of here?"

She laughed. "There's no way out. We're all mad here, and that's part of the madness. *You never get out.*"

I closed my eyes for a second, trying to think. There must be a spell that could help us escape. We were, after all, on the right side of justice, so the Void should bend in our favor. I racked my brain and once again felt frustrated at my lack of magical knowledge, the wisdom I had lost in the attack. The only magic I seemed to know now were the spells that spilled out of me when I was in danger.

As if summoning said danger by accident, we heard voices in the corridor outside.

"Hide," I whispered, and everyone flew for cover. I snuffed out the light on my wand. The footsteps slowed outside the door, and the women walked inside. There were two of them, dressed in gray sweatsuits, and I knew immediately something was off. These weren't nurses to check on Landau, they were prisoners seeking her out for some other nefarious reason.

Damn it! As if this wasn't hard enough.

"Do it quickly," said the one inmate.

In the dark, there was a glint of blade.

"No!" I shouted, and jumped out from behind the nearest bed. As soon as the word came out of my mouth, I knew it was too loud. The guards would be on their way. My wand was pointing at them. "You leave her alone."

"Who the hell are you?" asked the inmate. Her face was screwed up in confusion and disgust. The other one bobbed her shiv at me. I heard sounds in the building, hurried footsteps. It seemed the red ants had been alerted.

"Get her," said the bossy prisoner, and her partner came at me with the hand-fashioned blade.

CHAPTER 79

THE DARK MAZE

ASHA

A great deal happened in the next moment, and it was difficult to tell exactly what, there in the dark with two psychos, a goblin, a werewolf, a witch, a cop, and a criminally insane character from a blockbuster Asian horror film.

The loudest event was the explosion of magic that came from my wand, a spell I don't even remember casting. A huge wall of flame shot up between the women and me, setting fire to two of the screening curtains, including Nicola's. I'll never know why I didn't go for a quieter, less damaging spell, but there you go. Two flimsy screens roared quickly into ashes and petered out, but not before dropping flames on the linen of both beds and starting fires there. The woman giving orders seemed entranced by the blaze. The smoke detectors sniffed the carbon and immediately the fire alarm sounded. I blinked in slow motion, regarding my stupidity, then leapt into action.

"*Volas*," I whispered, whipping my wand like a fishing rod in the direction of the shiv, and grabbing it from the prisoner's hand. It came darting toward me, and I caught it—luckily, by the handle. It could have done a lot of damage. My anger toward the women rose inside me, strengthening my magic. Equally furious, they both advanced on me. While this was happening, Armstrong and Salty managed to put out the flames on Nicola's bed and lever her body into the adjacent wheelchair, ready to wheel her out. Emily stayed hiding in the shadows, and Stoker waited until the prisoners were an arm's length away from me before pouncing. He hit the one who had been holding the blade square in the chest and knocked her down to the floor. The sound of her skull cracking against the floor was horrific; she didn't move after that. The other woman didn't seem to care about her friend and took another step toward me. I heard footsteps rushing in the passage.

"We're on the same side," I said, breathlessly, to her, holding out my wand should she get any closer.

She smiled. "No, honey, we're not."

"We're here to break Landau out. You must come with us."

She laughed. "There's no getting out. Don't you think we've tried? It only gets us thrown into Desolation."

The last thing I wanted was to have this woman walking free, but sometimes you have to make a deal with the devil.

"Help us," I said. "And we'll help you."

She calmly rubbed her cheek, as if she had all the time in the world to think it over. My nerves were jangling all over the place. I knew we had seconds until the guards found us. "Okay," she agreed. "Why the hell not?"

All the breath left my lungs. "Thank you."

She pointed at Nicola. "But we have to leave that chair behind."

I was about to argue when Emily appeared like a specter, shaking her head. "Can't trust Alison," she said. "Can't trust her."

Alison pulled a face again. "Not you."

"Can't trust her," repeated Emily.

"This one is as mad as a box of frogs," said Alison. "Best leave her behind, too."

Emily kept shaking her head.

"Where is Desolation?" I asked.

"You don't want to go down there," said Alison. "Some people who go down there never come back up."

"We'll take our chances," I said. We needed somewhere not swarming with red ants; somewhere quiet enough for our spells to work, to break the curse and to portal out. The guards were right outside.

"Take up your weapons," I said, tossing the shiv to Emily.

Sam grabbed his revolver, and Salty, her emerald glass-shard dagger. I chose my wand over my ritual knife. Stoker creased his snout, baring his fangs.

The first of the guards ran in with batons and tasers. Armstrong immediately disarmed his opponent and used the guard's own taser on him, then his colleague, dropping them both to the floor like tired puppets. The next pair ran in, and as Sam picked up a dropped taser and tased the one closest to him, Alison head-butted the other one, knocking him out cold.

Okay, I thought. *We're a team. We can do this.*

"Desolation," I said to Alison. "If you want to get out of here."

"Can't trust her," echoed Emily.

"Follow me," said Alison, and we headed out into the corridor, fighting guards off as they approached.

Again, we were in the dark maze. Left, right, right. I had no way of knowing if we were going the right way. Emily pushed the chair while I and the others fended off the ants. Sam got struck on the head with a baton, and Salty was punched, but we managed to make it to the stairs.

"*Contendis,*" I said, touching my wand to the arm of the chair. I felt the anxious energy rushing through me and into the steel and rubber of the wheelchair, lifting it up, precariously balancing Nicola Landau as we moved down the steps. It got darker and darker as we descended. I did not feel in control of the situation.

CHAPTER 80

DESOLATION
ASHA

You could tell from the evil stink in the air that only the most criminal of the patients were kept down in Desolation. The doors were heavier, triple bolted, and the color of despair. We could only just see where we were going, and kept bumping into each other. Anxiety lurked in our steps. Desperate moaning leaked from beneath the cell doors and the letterbox tray openings. Prisoners' names were scratched into makeshift labels on the walls. Insanity shuddered all around us, and I felt extremely disturbed. I wanted to go back upstairs, even though the guards were there with their batons and tasers. I wanted to get back to the light and knowing what was around the next corner instead of the sinister reek in the seemingly solid blackness. It was like treading dark water, not knowing what monsters the abyss held.

Armstrong grabbed my arm and I flinched.

"Asha," he said. "Are you okay?"

I nodded. "Fine." *Just scared out of my wits.*

He returned my nod and held his gun a little higher. He had yet to use it.

We kept wading into the midnight maze of corridors, a ragtag army of supernaturals and humans—and a squeaking wheelchair—looking for a way out. The groaning and banging resounded off the walls around us.

Alison was murmuring to Salty as they passed the name badges. "This one axed her grandparents. This one drowned her kids." I winced. "This one ate her—"

"Shut up!" I whispered. "We don't need to know. Eyes on the prize."

But I couldn't help reading the names myself. *Rogers, Mbalula, Witepski. Viljoen, Greensmith, Naidoo.* I wondered how they came to be in such a terrible place, and how different their lives might have been if just a few more things had been in their favor. Different DNA, a loving parent, the absence of a traumatic event. How many were here for what they had done, and how many were here for what had been done to them?

"Stop!" came a masculine voice from the darkness. We all whirled toward him, weapons drawn. I blinked against the darkness, unable to make out any form there.

"We won't hurt you," I said. "Just let us go."

Salty was a little more direct. "Turn a blind eye, and keep your eyes."

The man stepped into the dim pool of light between us. He was a Desolation guard, dressed in a black uniform. There was no aggression in his body language, and he showed us his empty palms. When he caught sight of Nicola, his face contorted in worry. "Nicky? Nicky! What have you done to her?"

Alison spluttered. "What have *we* done to her? What the hell have *you* done to her?"

"What? I would never hurt her."

As if to agree, Nicola finally moved. She held her arm up in his direction and tears rushed into her eyes, only to be matched in his. He moved closer to her and took her hands, searching her eyes. "What did they do to you?"

He was close enough for me to read his name badge. *Dillon.*

Nicola tried to say something. We all listened, but couldn't make it out.

I was relieved to see evidence of at least some brain function. When I had first come across her an hour ago, I thought we had indeed been too late.

"Dillon," I said, and he looked up at me. "We're getting Nicola out. We need your help."

He didn't hesitate. "Of course. What do you need?"

We needed a quiet room where we could reverse the Grimalkin curse and then portal back to safety.

"There's an empty cell at the end of the corridor," Dillon said. "You'll be safe in there."

My first reaction was *AH, HELL NO!* No way I would agree to be locked down here. But, really, was there any other option? The man was offering exactly what we had asked for. We followed him. We hurried past more cells, but I paid less attention to the names. That was, until we got to the third cell from the end, and the name plate said *Maleficum.*

What? I thought. *What are the chances?* Conflicting thoughts tumbled in my head, confusing me. It couldn't be. But it made sense. But, no.

Salty slapped my leg. "Stop daydreaming, witch!"

I shook my head and tried to focus on the job at hand. I could think about the name later. I could wonder why my mother's name was on a door in the cold black bowels of an asylum later.

Dillon used his access card to open the door of the last cell as we heard the red ants clamor down the stairs. There was nowhere else to go; without him, we would have been trapped.

"Blessed be," I murmured to him. He looked slightly confused. Perhaps when something really lucky happened to him in the near future, he'd remember the odd utterance and connect the dots. We all shuffled into the cell and switched on the light, causing the cockroaches that had taken up residence to scuttle away, into the corners and the cracks in the walls.

Dillon began closing the door.

"No!" I yelled. "Stay in here, with us."

He seemed like a good man, but I'd known him all of two minutes. He could easily lock us up and win the day for the Riverside authorities.

He shook his head. "I'll keep the others away. You do your thing. Knock three times when you want me to unlock."

This plan made me feel supremely uncomfortable, but we didn't seem to have a say in the matter. Anyway, it was true. The other guards would bust right in if there was no one standing guard outside. Nicola Landau's expression told me we could trust the man, so I let him go. He locked the door from the outside, and there we stood, crowded in a claustrophobic concrete room, no doubt all wondering which of our unfortunate life choices had led us there.

Alison crossed her arms. "So, you got us locked up in Desolation. Congratulations. I hope you have a plan."

CHAPTER 81
RUMPIS ANIMO
ASHA

Stoker was not happy to be in such a small space. "Time to go," he growled. I heard the clicking of his nails touching the floor as he paced.

Salty stared at me. "What are you waiting for? Do you know how easy it will be for them to get in? We've got minutes."

Yes, I thought. *Yes. Time to break the curse.*

The problem was, I felt like a total imposter. How was I supposed to break a curse when I had never—in living memory—broken one before? I knew of my history and reputation, but that meant hex all when it came to the bunch of us standing around a broken woman in a wheelchair, my mind as blank as an overcast sky. I gulped as quietly as I could as everyone looked at me.

"Right," I said, urging my voice to not shake. "Everyone, stand in a circle. Sam and Stoker, please lay Nicola out on the floor, in the middle."

I urged myself to keep it together. Even with my limited memory I knew that nerves and spell-slinging were not a good match. The best-case scenario would mean your adrenaline made the spell stronger; the worst—and more common—case resulted in mixed up magic, which was often difficult to reverse. I closed my eyes and took a deep breath.

You can do this, Asha Viridian Rook.

Still, my heart ping-ponged around in my ribcage. There was a sudden noise outside the door; a struggle, crashing, then gunshots. I urged myself not to think about who shot whom— I hadn't seen a gun on Dillon's belt. I suspected Nicola came to the same sad conclusion, because I saw a fresh trail of tears race down her cheeks. It was clear that Dillon had been a friend to her, and I felt her sorrow keenly.

We stood in the circle, with Nicola Landau spread-eagled in the center wearing her charcoal sweatsuit. Despite her eyes being open, her body lolled, making her look like a doll, apart from the burn scars on her temples. I didn't know the exact curse the Grimalkin had used, but I guessed it was something along the lines of *Rumpis animo*: break the mind. Guesses weren't good enough, though, as Soleil had taught me, so I'd have to stick with giving Landau her necklace— and her bastard of a husband's wedding ring—and hope for the best. First, I needed some energy swirling in the room.

"I need you all to hold hands and chant," I said.

"You have got to be joking," said Alison. "What is this? Team building?"

"We're breaking a curse," I replied. "The curse that landed Nicola in here."

The prisoner rolled her eyes. "Can we just cut the BS and get out of here? What's your plan?"

"This is the plan," I said. "Break the curse, then portal out. We can't portal Nicola out in this condition. She needs to be stronger to survive the trip, and she needs to consent."

"Curse? Portal?" she said, then whistled. "Why did I think you guys had a legitimate plan? You're just as crazy as the people locked up here."

"Stand in the circle," hissed the goblin. "Hold hands. Shut up."

Alison did as she was told. Perhaps setting eyes on the strange-looking creature reminded her that there was indeed magical energy around us, not to mention the werewolf who had been pacing the cell.

They stood as requested. I pulled out the small piece of chalk from my coat pocket and reinforced the circle, chanting as I did so. I started off feeling self-conscious, but it soon faded as I felt the magic sparking in the air around me. When the chalk circle was complete, it began to glow.

"Holy sh—" said Alison, but Salty squeezed her hand to hush her.

Emily's pale face looked lunar. Armstrong's jaw was set, his eyes wide. My chanting became louder without any effort on my behalf, and I felt a strange, wonderful bliss as the magic moved through me, as if the glow was inside me as much as it was in and of the circle. It was an intense sensation of well-being and purpose, and I understood then why I had chosen to become a curse breaker—or why it had chosen me. When I felt the energy had reached the correct resonance, I moved over to Nicola and we made eye contact in an intense way that felt like it was melting our bodies. I took out the silver raven necklace and fastened it around her neck, then pressed Derek's gold ring into her flaccid palm and folded her fingers over it. The ring grew hot. So hot that I feared it would burn her, but it didn't. The necklace glowed in tandem.

"It's working," I said, relief ballooning my lungs. I topped it off with a healing spell, hoping to get her mobile enough to portal.

Despite my previous moment of bliss, I waited for something to go wrong.

CHAPTER 82

FLORENCE NIGHTINGALE

ASHA

Nicola Landau's body tensed up. She screamed and held her hips as if she were in agony. I got a fright, thinking I had hurt her, but then I realized the pain was the bones knitting together. I could almost see it happening, as if I could look into her body. I also "saw" her arm being mended, as well as a cracked rib and a deep cut on her ring finger. Her scream faded, and she was left glassy-eyed and panting. I had healed her body, but what about her fractured mind? We all waited in silence, despite the frightening noise outside the door.

"Nicola?"

Nothing.

"Nicola?" I said, louder. "Can you—?"

This time when she looked at me, it was with clear eyes. I could read her fear and confusion, but the addled stupor she had previously been in was gone.

"What is happening?" she asked

"Count your luckies," said Salty. "The witch just uncursed you."

"What?"

"Do you know where you are?" I asked.

Nicola sat up. Her body looked strong. She looked at the circle of people surrounding her and shook her head. When she caught sight of Alison, she flinched. "I know her." Emily stepped forward, and Nicola recognized her, too. "I'm at Riverside."

"You were imprisoned for something you didn't do," I said.

"I did do it," she said. "I remember doing it."

"You had no choice," I told her. "You were cursed. You were made to do it."

"Cursed?" Nicola said. "I don't understand."

"You don't have to. We're out of time and we need to get you out of here. Would you like to come with us?"

"Dillon is outside," she said. "He helped me."

"It's too late," I said.

Her brow creased. "We can't leave him here. His wife is expecting."

"Sorry," I said. "It's too late for him. But it's not too late for you."

Nicola's eyes were wild and blinking. "What about Sister Devka? We need to take her with us."

Emily began shaking her head and didn't stop. A nervous tic. "Sister Devka's not coming with us. Sister Devka stays here."

"She needs to get out," said Nicola, growing agitated.

Alison cast her annoyed eyes at the ceiling again. "God help us."

I frowned at her, and she sighed. "Sister Devka isn't real."

"Liar!" shouted Nicola. "Liar! Devka has helped me every day I've been here. I wouldn't be alive without her."

Emily piped up. "Sister Devka is real. She's just not alive anymore."

When everyone stared at her, she moved back into the shadows.

Salty was sweating. "We need to go. Our window is closing."

"I'm not going without Devka," said Nicola, moving toward the door.

Alison stepped in her path. "Listen to me, Landau. Everyone knows. Sister Devka used to work here … a hundred years ago, when this place was a Victorian madhouse."

"Nonsense," said Nicola, but something in her face changed, as if some things were beginning to make sense.

"Devka worked and died in the asylum in the 1900s. She was like, I don't know, Florence Nightingale. But she died here. You got me? There's no Devka to rescue."

"You're not the only one who sees her," said Emily. "Patients often talk about her. Sometimes takes treats from the nursing station and leaves them under patients' pillows, and that kind of thing. Even the nurses know she's real."

Nicola's shoulders sagged, and her face was grief-stricken. I understood that for the weeks she had been incarcerated here, Devka and Dillon had been her family, and now she was losing both of them.

"We need your permission," I said. "To help you escape. We can't take you against your will. But the portal window is closing, so if we don't leave quickly, we'll all be stuck here."

She sniffed and looked at me. "Yes, of course. Thank you. Let's go."

I nodded at Salty. There was more gunfire outside the door. *Hurry,* I mouthed.

My adrenaline was cascading again, knowing how close we were to escaping, and how near the red ants were outside. This time they were carrying more than batons and tasers.

"Everyone in the circle again!" I shouted. They snapped to it, including the stiff-bodied Nicola, who could now stand and walk on her own. I felt Salty's magic swell around us, getting ready to spin us out into space. I closed my eyes in relief. It was almost over. Mission almost accomplished.

The goblin spat on the floor and began to chant. I didn't know if the spitting was part of the magic or not, but I went with it. I wasn't going to argue with one of the best portalers in the Realm. I felt her words wash over me and the space in the room. We all lifted our faces and closed our eyes, levitating ever so slightly, the sign that we were about to be plucked out of the room. I had Sam to my right and Emily to my left. Just before Nilve finished her spell, I quickly backed out of the circle and joined Sam and Emily's hands, fixing the circle where I had broken it before it lost any power. Sam's eyes snapped open and he looked at me, puzzled, wondering why I had left. I moved farther back, making sure I was out of the portal aura, and watched as everyone else swirled away in a giant whirlwind of multi-colored spirits. I smelled the ozone, saw the sparks, and silently wished them a safe journey as I stood alone in the small dark cell.

CHAPTER 83

DESOLATION WAS DEFINITELY AWAKE

ASHA

This part wasn't going to be easy.

I was pretty sure Dillon was dead, but I knocked three times, anyway. Perhaps it was for closure, or for luck. Either way, it didn't work. I had to wait until one of the red ants finally found the requisite keys and cards to open the door and drag me out. I blinked at the bright lights that now streamed down from the buzzing bulbs above. I could hear the prisoners in solitary confinement shouting, crying, and banging things. Desolation was definitely awake. The lights were on, and two guards in maroon uniforms forced me forward, out of the cell that was now empty apart from a spent chalk circle on the floor. I did a quick headcount and got to around eleven or twelve. One tired witch against a dozen armed guards; I didn't fancy my chances much. But if I got what I stayed for, it would be worth it. I centered myself and gathered my energy, drawing it up inside me. I lamented the fact that there was not one live growing green thing as far as the eye could see—so I couldn't draw on the abundant power of nature as I had in the past—I just hoped I had enough to keep me alive for the foreseeable future. Inside my body, I brought together the magic I could feel coming from the earth. The cold slab of concrete seemed impenetrable, but it was no match for earth magic, which regularly smashed through rocks and roots. The ink tendrils and flowers on my skin shifted and bloomed and grew. I felt the magic gather in my bones, muscles, and veins. I was nature. I was The Wild. I was everything I needed to be to defeat evil.

I roared, and the guards let go of me instinctively to cover their ears. I pulled my hood over my head, and the cloak went from black to camouflage. Violence took hold. I began to fight the way Soleil had trained me, the way my muscles remembered to move. The moves came easily as I punched, chopped, gouged, and kicked the men who were trying to grab me again. The guards all looked the same to me, as if they were a computer virus or a glitch in the Realm, reminding me of the Landau's crumbling mansion. I thought of everything Nicola had lost and felt fury for her. I right-hooked a man to the jaw, shook out my hand, then roundhouse-kicked his colleague. My graphene cloak deflected their bullets, but I felt every one of them like a punch in the ribs. One of the bullets almost took my knee out. I flattened five guards before the rest of them came for me. I took my ritual knife from the sheath and spun it at the red ant approaching me. Despite a dodgy throw, the knife corrected its trajectory and embedded itself in his chest. He choked in surprise and moved to grasp the knife, but I was too quick for him.

"*Contendis!*" I called the knife back and it obeyed, landing smoothly back in my hand.

"*Augescis!*" I yelled, and the knife grew into an elegant sword the size and shape of a samurai warrior's. Miraculously, I remembered the actions the high priestess had taught me and was able to cut a few of the guards down. Out of breath and close to exhausted, there were three more guards left to fight, and I didn't know if I had it in me. The sword was becoming too heavy to wield, and my movements had become clumsy due to the muscle fatigue. I dropped the sword, and it clattered on the hard ground beside me. The guards had their guns pointed at me.

"Come with us," said the tall one. "We won't hurt you."

Now, where have I heard that before?

I didn't answer them, so they rushed at me. I quickly drew my wand.

"*Fiat fulgur!*" I shouted. Despite the chaos that was playing out right before me, I couldn't help noting the irony of using the very same spell I had on the Grimalkin just hours before to save her life. A white-hot bolt of lightning shot through my forearm, concentrated in my wand, then sang though the air and smashed into the tall guard's chest. He shuddered from the electrocution and crumpled to the floor. The other two looked less certain. I was an easy height to tackle, but they didn't like the look of what I could do with a wand. I thought they would do the smart thing and back away, but, alas, human nature is not always that bright. They came at me just as they had before I had barbecued their friend, and I had to choose which moron to defuse first. My arm was still burning from the electricity spell, so I had to get creative.

"*Glaciem exquiris!*" This time, instead of unbearable heat shrieking through my muscles, ice flew through my veins, freezing my hand to the wand, but not before sending out a powerful surge of ice toward the man grabbing for me. He froze immediately, and his skin turned from peach to purple, encased in an abominable-snowman-shaped case of transparent ice.

I lost sensation in my wand-hand and was sure I'd done some permanent damage. Burning—and then freezing—one's hand is probably not the healthiest thing to do if one would like to keep one's hand. You live and learn.

I turned to face the last guard. He had a gun. I had nothing left, and he knew it.

CHAPTER 84

MALEFICUM
ASHA

This wasn't how I wanted to die. Not in the ominous basement of an asylum, not killed by a man in uniform. I heard his gun click. Safety off, finger on the trigger.

Damn it.

"Damn you," I said. I didn't often curse people, but my bitterness got the better of me.

"You don't have to die," he said. "Let me take you in."

"I'd rather die," I said.

Eleven bodies littered the ground around us. I doubted very much they would let me live, whether I surrendered or not. He pulled the trigger, and the bullet bit into my left arm, shattering the radius. I shouted out in pain and lifted my wand. There was another explosion, another bullet, and my wand went flying, sparks showering my face and shoulders. Both hands were out of commission, which wasn't good news.

The red ant stepped closer and beckoned to me. "Come on. I'll take you up."

My teeth were clenched. "No."

Closer.

I could no longer pick up my sword or lift my wand, even if I could find it. Judging by the triumphant look on his face, I could see he knew this. He was already imaging the medal he would get from the correctional facility organization for bravery. Out of a dozen guards, he was not only the sole survivor, but he had brought in the Evil Witch.

"Not gonna happen," I said.

"What?"

"I'm not going anywhere."

The man shrugged. "Fine," he said, and raised his gun to my head. He had figured out that the cloak was bullet-proof, but my skin wasn't. I watched as his finger slowly pulled the trigger, and there was an almighty *bang*.

I could smell the gunpowder and the blood, but there was no pain. I was temporarily blinded by the bright explosion.

Small mercies, I thought, as I fell down onto the hard concrete. No pain. No regrets. Or, at least, hardly any regrets. Which was more than some people could say.

"Witch!" said a male voice, the owner of which was bent over me. I opened one eye.

My mouth was so dry I could hardly speak. "Dillon?"

"Yes, ma'am."

"We're both dead?"

He snorted. "No, ma'am. Still breathing."

Dillon helped me up, and I saw the last guard lying in a puddle of blood. "You shot him?"

"Only because he was about to shoot you."

The pain returned to my arms, especially my left, which I could tell was badly broken. Dillon passed me my wand and the sword, which had shrunk down to its original size. I thanked him, and noticed his bloody handprint on my wand.

"You're hurt?" I asked.

"It's nothing," he said, but I could see the worry on his face.

"You need to leave now," I said. "Your family needs you alive."

"I need to stay to help you."

I thought of his pregnant wife. "You've helped me, now go."

He hesitated.

"Goddess help me. If you don't go right now, I'm going to hurl a mighty fireball at you." I lifted my wand to show him I was serious, but it dangled lamely from my injured hand.

"I'll just hang in the background," Dillon said. "Just until you're safe. You won't even notice me."

I sighed in frustration. Of course, I was secretly relieved, but I didn't want him to know that.

I didn't have a choice but to capitulate. I limped toward the door I had noticed earlier. "Please open this door for me." I showed him the cell that read *Maleficum*.

Dillon looked perplexed as he unlocked it for me. The heavy metal door creaked and swung open into darkness. "This cell has been empty for years."

The light went on, and a man in a dark cloak stood in the center. He smiled in a sinister way that made the hairs on the back of my neck stand up. "It's not empty now."

CHAPTER 85

PET PROJECT
ASHA

"Welcome, Ms. Rook," said the man in the dark cloak. "I must thank you for coming. This is just perfect."

"Doctor Adrathar," said Dillon, narrowing his eyes to shield them from the bright light. "I didn't know you were down here."

"You're bleeding," the doctor said. "Sister Ingleby will take care of you."

"I'm fine," said Dillon, shrugging off his concern.

An older woman dressed as a nurse became visible. She was neatly dressed, and her gray hair was pinned tightly under a white nurse's cap. "Nonsense," she said. "You're dripping blood everywhere." We all looked down at the floor, and it was true. When we looked up again, the nurse quickly removed the syringe she had stealthily injected Dillon with, and he collapsed. I moved to catch him, but Doctor Adrathar grabbed my arm, his fingers digging into my already aching flesh.

"Don't worry about your friend," he said. "Sister Ingleby is an excellent nurse. She'll have him sorted out in no time."

I heard a clicking sound where Adrathar gripped me, and I saw that he had handcuffed me. When I looked at his face, I saw the dreaded golden sickle tattoo behind his ear.

"I wasn't sure you'd fall for the name on the door," he said. "I'm so glad you did."

"How did you know my mother's name?"

The doctor's eyes sparkled. "I did my research. I had to work hard to get this plan to succeed. But now it's all paid off."

I wished that I could fall through the floor. I wouldn't be meeting my mother, after all. I looked at the dark wizard. "How much are they offering for my life?"

"It's an extremely handsome sum. As a rather reluctant Dusk Reaper, I haven't seen such a large bounty ... ever. No wonder there's been so much excitement around you. You've got all the Reapers positively frothing. Personally, I don't chase the smaller bounties. But this one was difficult to ignore. It's certainly enough to keep my little hobby going for years."

My tired and overwhelmed brain worked hard to put the pieces together.

"Your little hobby?"

"This," he said, and gestured grandly at the room. "My pet project." This was no little cell. It was large and filled with medical equipment and machines I didn't recognize. "I treat patients here. Patients with intractable mental illness. The equipment is not cheap."

I got that spooked feeling again. "You mean you experiment on your prisoners here."

Adrathar pulled his face into a purposefully fake smile. "How can you progress medical science without experimentation?"

I felt sick enough to vomit. "You think they belong to you. You do as you please without anyone's critical gaze."

Sister Ingleby returned to the room. Her previously snow-white uniform was smeared with Dillon's blood. She triple-locked the door behind her.

"What did you do to him?" I demanded.

"No need to shout, dear."

"Is he alive?"

"It won't matter for much longer. Let's get you onto the machine."

"Hex that," I said. "No way." *Not going to happen.* I'd rather die fighting than get plugged into one of those horrific machines.

"Don't make this harder than it needs to be," the nurse said. "Everyone fights it, and everyone lands on the machine." There was a hard glint of depravation in her eyes.

"No," I said, stepping backwards. It was only then that I noticed I had cuffs on my ankles, too. I couldn't reach any of my weapons, and my new cloak wouldn't protect me from Adrathar's high-tech torture chamber.

Ingleby and Adrathar nodded to each other. They swooped for me, scooping me up while I impotently kicked and thrashed. It just made them clutch me tighter. They carried my jostling form to the biggest machine in the room: a bed with its own cuffs, many monitoring screens, conductors, and needles.

"No!" I yelled, fighting with all my might. "No!"

I could feel my body panicking as if it were a separate entity. It thrashed almost of its own accord. My mind retreated, thinking fast. I had trained myself through meditation to be able to focus in frightening times, but I don't think I'd ever been this fearful. Dying was one thing, but to be tortured by a Mengele-esque wizard was a fate far worse than death. I needed a plan, even if escape seemed impossible. Ingleby clicked the machine's robotic cuffs on my wrists and removed the steel handcuffs, then did the same to my ankles. Adrathar was preparing some sort of injection. A sedative, perhaps, or something mind-altering. I held out little hope for anesthetic because it was clear to me that the man was a sadist. If anything, he would inject something that enhanced pain instead of easing it.

"You can't do this," I said. "You're a bounty hunter. If you kill me, you won't get paid."

"Wrong," said the doctor. "They're not interested in a kicking and screaming prisoner. In fact, the bounty is only payable on presentation of your corpse."

CHAPTER 86

MEMORIES INTO MAGIC

ASHA

"The bounty on your head was announced last month. The reward was so high that even the most eremitic dark wizards crawled out of their crevices to see if they stood a chance. You seemed like an easy hit. A young witch ... feminine, petite, alternative. They didn't understand who you were."

"And you did?"

"More than most," he said. "I knew your mother, after all."

This took the air out of my lungs. "What?"

"The other Reapers hit out at you like blunt instruments, but you fought them off. I knew that if I wanted to capture you, I had to have an excellent strategy."

"Who is offering the bounty?"

"You'd be so heartbroken if you knew. Let's not make this harder than it needs to be."

He stepped closer to me and began assembling a needle and syringe. Seeing the large needle made my stomach burn.

"Your strategy worked," I said. Without making it too obvious, I wanted to stroke his ego enough so that he'd brag about how he had done it. My thoughts were still swirling and I couldn't quite piece it together. I needed time to think.

"It was perfect," Adrathar said. "When it started coming together, I realized that I would have a pet project and a lure at the same time."

"What do you mean?"

"You're the cursebreaker. I knew I needed to lure you in with a curse that you couldn't resist untangling. When I met Derek Landau, I understood that his wife would be perfect. Everyone in the Realm knows that a cursebreaker can't resist a spell like the one Nicola was subjected to."

"So there I was, having a fire whisky at Grackle's in the Rosebank pocket realm, trying to figure out who I could curse and why you'd care. I couldn't believe my luck when Derek Landau walked in three sheets to the wind and spilling his guts all over that poor bartender with the eye patch. Crusty

Jack Teach. I was drinking alone and couldn't help but overhear him complaining about how his mistress wanted him to leave his wife, but he didn't have the money for a divorce. I took him aside and bought him a final drink. Told him that I could make his problem disappear. He was shocked at first and refused, but his rubber arm didn't take too much twisting. Soon, we had a deal. I'd remove his wife from the entanglement without hurting her. He still loved her, he said, but she deserved better. He paid me what I asked—his wedding ring—and we went our separate ways. I left the ring with Teach for safekeeping, but now I see he is a better dispenser of ale than he is a protector of magical artifacts."

"You cursed Nicola," I said. "I thought it was Chione."

"The Grimalkin played her part."

That's why Chione couldn't tell me the exact curse used on Nicola—because she had never cast it. I felt an immense wave of guilt for the suffering Nicola Landau had endured for the sake of my bounty.

Ingleby spoke up. "Once we had Mrs. Landau here, I called the leader of your coven and said I suspected something was awry with one of our patients. She agreed to send someone. Of course, because it involved a curse, we knew she'd send you."

My insides were rushing in panic. "What are you going to do to me?"

Sister Ingleby's face twitched in anticipation.

"I've been working on a new machine," the doctor said. "It's really rather unique."

I couldn't think straight; pure panic ran in my veins. I took a long, deep breath, and told myself to calm down or die.

"It feeds off your mind, drawing power from your thoughts and converting it to energy. Specifically, it turns your memories into magic."

I shook my head. It sounded like a fantasy.

"The test results so far have been outstanding," he said. "The energy I was able to draw from a patient here maximized the magic I used for the curse on Nicola."

I remembered the empty look on the face of one of the prisoners. Emily. She seemed hollow inside.

"And that was just testing on nonmagical humans! I'm thrilled to be able to try it out on you."

"Too bad for you that you're too late," I sneered.

Adrathar frowned at me.

"I don't have any memories. One of your Reaper friends made sure of that."

The doctor became agitated. "I've heard of that," he said. "Hand-held devices that siphon and store memories."

"It wasn't like that," I said.

"Well, my machine is more sophisticated."

I gave him a superficial smile. "Of course it is."

Doctor Adrathar tapped his syringe and stepped closer to me.

"Don't you come near me with that," I said.

He smiled in an indulgent way, a parent disciplining a small child. *It's for the best.* "There's no point in fighting," he said.

I writhed and kicked, but my injured arms flared with pain, and the cuffs bruised me, despite being made from some kind of hard rubber. I screamed for help. Again I tried to calm my thoughts, knowing that panic made for terrible decisions and even worse magic. Fear clawed at any clear thought, a snarling catfight in my head and chest. Ingleby placed electrodes on my head and chest while Adrathar began flicking switches and checking screens. My anxiety spiked with every button he pressed.

"Don't do this," I pled. "Please."

CHAPTER 87

ARC OF AGONY

ASHA

octor Adrathar leaned over me, and I felt a pinch in my upper arm where he drove the needle in. If he had been close enough, I would have bitten him.

"What was that?" I asked. I assumed it was some kind of sedative to stop me from struggling.

"Just a little psychoactive medication," he replied. "It helps the machine work its magic."

Before he'd even finished his sentence, the room began to spin. I forced my eyes to stay open, but felt sick and dizzy. When Adrathar spoke again, his words no longer made sense, as if he were speaking in a language I didn't understand. I was seeing double, in different colors. My terror reared up. I thought I had been incapacitated before, but now I couldn't even see straight. I knew for certain that I wasn't going to be able to fight them off; that they'd have their way with me under these cold fluorescent lights. I stopped thrashing around, but it was not of my own accord. My limbs were no longer obeying instructions. I stared at my hand, willing it to move, but every finger remained still. Adrathar clicked a small flashlight and shone it in my eyes.

"Good," he said. "She's ready."

Ingleby unlocked the rubber cuffs from my wrists and ankles and replaced them with a large weighted blanket that she pulled around my body from below, fastening the belts to keep it in place. It would be easier to break out of than the cuffs, but as I was paralyzed, it no longer mattered. Adrathar was adjusting dials on the machine as it powered up. I could hear a faint buzzing as it came online.

Soon I felt completely limp, unable to even lift my head. I was probably drooling. Just one blink seemed to take a century. The apparatus got louder. He nodded at the nurse, who pulled down from the top of the machine what looked like a helmet, placed it over my head, and clicked it in place. My petrified face stared back at me from the shiny underside of the roof of the machine, my heavy-lidded eyes bright with fear. My whole body was slack and now locked in place while the room swirled around me. I was the proverbial sitting duck, and a drunk one at that.

I tried to think of a spell, but words were jumbled in my head. Even if I could find the phrase I needed, I didn't have the energy to put behind it, like having the key to a car but no fuel. The contraption started whirring and clunking, and then two needles from either side of the machine moved toward my temples.

No! I tried to shout, but it came out as a moan. I tried to move my head out of the path of the needles but not a muscle obeyed. The needles moved closer and closer, then moved through their respective holes in the helmet and pricked my skin.

No! I shouted again, feeling the sharp metal penetrate my flesh. The drugs were making my brain malfunction, and I began to see the pain as a giant flying insect curling his thorax over me and stinging my head, which made me panic even more. The whirring of the machine was the beating of its wings. I choked on my fear, losing precious breath as I lay there being killed by a gigantic psychedelic wasp with a thousand eyes. The needles traveled deeper, pushing against my skull. I screamed inside my head as the pressure mounted. I felt like my whole skull would crack under the force of it. Warm liquid trickled down, tickling my scalp, staining the pillow red. I watched all of this in the horror show that was my reflection. The pressure built and built until finally there was a shrill noise—like a dentist's drill—and I realized the needles weren't just needles as they drilled easily through the thin skull bone. I was intensely relieved that the pressure abated, and horrified that they were through the skull. How long would this take? How much would I have to suffer?

"Okay," said the doctor, sounding pleased. "We're ready. Stand back."

Ingleby forced a rubber bite plate between my teeth and moved away from me.

The wizard did one last check, pulled down a lever, and turned a dial. His eyes were aflame.

At first I didn't feel anything, but gradually a heat traveled through the needles. Adrathar adjusted something else, and the pain went from one straight to ten, in a second. It was a flash of heat inside my skull so intense I thought I would die. I hoped I would die. It was too much to bear. After the flash of heat, it reverted to a warm sensation, my brain simmering on a galactic stove. One more adjustment by the doctor and the real work of the machine started: I could feel as the appliance slowly siphoned what it could from my memories. There weren't many available, and I watched in a kind of indifferent way as the wizard frowned at his invention and ground his teeth in frustration. He spun a dial, sending a lightning bolt through me, lifting my body into an arc of agony. I bit right through the rubber in my mouth. I was in too much pain to cry, but tears rushed to my eyes and spilled down my temples. I looked at Adrathar, pleading with him with nothing more than my shocked face, begging him to stop the torture. He ignored me and, apparently still unhappy with the amount of juice he had extracted, turned another dial.

I screamed and screamed into the dark, spiraling vortex that was my mind, sure that I would be insane by the end of the treatment. How many women had come in here with relatively minor problems—or none at all, like Landau—only to be tortured into insanity? How many lives had this wizard stolen for his own enjoyment and magical enrichment? I hated him more than ever. It felt like my blood and soul were being drained from my limp body. I kept screaming as I tumbled through time, losing the few memories I had left.

CHAPTER 88
POPPYCOCK
ASHA

The session felt like it had taken an eternity; I no longer had a concept of time. I lay slack-jawed and close as hex to death. The drug was beginning to wear off. I knew that because I was able to understand Adrathar and Ingleby again.

"How is she still alive?" I heard the nurse ask.

"No idea. Never seen that before. But look at that tube. We definitely got what we were looking for."

"Patients have died at less than half of that voltage."

"Well, remember where she comes from ... who she comes from. She's no ordinary witch."

"Still."

Adrathar gave his invention one last affectionate glance, then snapped out the tube of memories he had extracted and put it in his pocket.

"At least she won't fight back anymore. Won't give us any trouble before we hand her over tonight."

"Yes. I think we've had enough trouble for one night. I'll be glad to be rid of her."

"To say nothing of the bounty," said Adrathar. *"Have you got the Plan B shot?"*

"Right here," said Ingleby, and showed him an injection ready to be administered.

They were right. There was no fight left in my body. I knew it was over.

I was grateful that I was able to break Nicola Landau's curse. Grateful that I was given an extra week left to live after I should have died in the first Dusk Reaper attack. Everything else was a fog. Had there been a werewolf? A goblin? A cop who made my heart beat faster? It all seemed like a far-fetched fairy tale.

You did well, I told myself as my eyelids closed. *You finished the job. You righted the universe, if only just a little bit.* I would welcome that final lethal injection. It was time to rest, time to leave this world and enter the next dimension. I closed my eyes and let my spirit drift.

Oh no, you don't, I heard Directress Copperfield chime in. The drugs must have still been in my system, because she wasn't in the room but her voice was as clear as a school bell. *You can't leave yet. You haven't solved the case of the missing girls.*

I sighed, long and slow. The little girls.

They are somewhere, Copperfield said. *Lonely and frightened half to death. You need to save them. We're counting on you.*

I can't, I replied in my thoughts. *I don't know where they are. I don't know where to start. Also, I'm dying.*

Poppycock! exclaimed the directress in my half-baked dreams. *Your heart is beating, isn't it?*

That, I agreed, was true. I tried to move, but my body remained paralyzed.

How do I get up? I asked her. *How do I break this state I'm in?*

I opened my eyes, but the directress was gone.

I watched the dark wizard and his henchwoman clear up their equipment. They were gearing up to take me in and claim their reward. The fatal injection lay in a steel pan on a side table at the base of the bed. I tried to sit up, but not even one muscle took my command seriously. I couldn't talk; I couldn't move. How did Copperfield expect me to fight my way out of there?

Of course, as soon as I thought that, the answer was clear.

As a child I was abandoned by my parents, but the one thing that had never abandoned me was my magic.

CHAPTER 89
FLAMES CARPETED THE FLOOR
ASHA

I needed to be able to think clearly in order to sling a potent spell. The drunken thoughts sloshing in my head were not incisive enough to power the kind of magic I needed to fight off the two monsters in the room, but the effects of the drug were fading. I tried to bring my erratic breathing under control, tried to steady my heart, which was flip-flopping in its ivory cage. I attempted to clear my head of everything that wasn't the focus of the magic I needed to save my life.

Surreal sound effects leaked into the room. Police sirens, and a wailing ambulance. Would they be able to find me in time? I couldn't take that chance. Adrathar and Ingleby's brows creased. Their eyes met. *Hurry,* they both seemed to intone. The wizard's medical bag was packed, the nurse picked up the injection that was meant to end my life. I realized the blanket that was belted around me was actually a body bag.

"Time to go," said Sister Ingleby, leaning into me. I tried to lift my arm, but knew it was pointless. I needed help. I summoned every molecule of energy I had and stared into the nurse's eyes. I couldn't talk out loud, so I uttered carefully in my heart—

Evoco et excito, nunc et semper, res ac mortales.

I don't know why I chose a conjuring spell. It seems like an odd choice, looking back. Maybe I had some spectral guidance, or an unusual premonition. Perhaps I knew I didn't have enough energy to defend myself with fire, ice, or electricity, so I instead chose to conjure someone who could defend me.

Suddenly, there was another presence in the room. Not flesh and bone. It was more of a breeze, a scent, a silhouette of silver shimmers. The other two didn't even notice, so intent they were on making me flatline and rolling me out of there. I blinked as I watched the spirit come closer. She took on more substance, and I saw a young woman wearing a Victorian nurse uniform.

Devka.

She smiled at me, then reached for the fatal injection, grabbing it out of Ingleby's hands and stabbing her in the neck with it.

Too late, Adrathar cried out some kind of stuttered warning. Sister Ingleby's eyes bulged, the veins on her neck snaked as she realized what had happened. She didn't have to endure the shock for long, because the toxin worked almost immediately. Ingleby's skin flushed red as she made a choking sound and collapsed to the floor. Twenty seconds later her seizures stopped, along with her heart. Devka seemed pleased.

Adrathar had reversed, and his back was now pushed up against the wall. Devka picked up a scalpel from a silver tray.

"No," he said. "Please."

She advanced on him despite his plea, blade raised, ready to strike.

"Don't," I said, my voice hoarse. "Don't kill him."

Devka whirled around at me. *"Do you not know what this man has done?"*

"I know," I said. "I know. But let the Council deal with him."

"He was about to kill you," the ghost said. *"Sell your body like a burnt-out carcass."*

"I know," I repeated. "But we're better than him. We don't have to kill to show our power."

"What about justice?" Devka asked. *"What about the women he has tortured and killed? I've held their hands, nursed their wounds."*

"He'll receive justice," I said. "I'll make sure of it." When she didn't seem convinced, I added, "He doesn't deserve an easy death. Let him face up to what he has done."

The ghost wasn't happy, but she acquiesced.

"Thank you," I said. "For saving my life."

"Oh," she said. *"You saved your own life."*

Suddenly I was standing in the middle of the room in place of Devka, hand outstretched. Ingleby lay dead on the floor. Adrathar was hunched in fear, waiting for me to strike with the scalpel. When I looked at my hand, I realized I was holding my wand instead of the scalpel. I took a step forward. I didn't understand what had happened, but my ring was glowing.

"Give me the tube," I demanded.

"No," the wizard shook his head. "I need it."

"The game is up," I said. "The police are outside. They know what you've done, Adrathar! It's over."

He looked weaker than he had before, as if he had aged ten years since Devka appeared.

I clenched my teeth. "Give it to me."

Adrathar clasped his pocket, refusing. I clutched my wand. "I'm giving you one more chance."

Without warning, I got hit by a bolt of lightning. Adrathar had pulled out his wand under his cloak and sent a spear of electricity through me, sizzling my already seared brain. I doubled over in pain, my injured body crumpling easily before him.

"Bastard!" I whispered.

He stood up and raised his wand higher.

"*Glaciem exquiris,*" I uttered, before his spell spilled out of his mouth. I aimed the ice spell at his wand-hand, freezing the metal as well as the magic that was about to erupt. He glanced down in annoyance and shook it, but the wand was stuck fast to his palm. Taking the opportunity while he was distracted, I sprang up and flung another spell his way.

"*Fumum!*" I yelled, and focused my power on his frozen wand. We watched as it dissolved into vapor.

Adrathar narrowed his eyes at me, sneering. "You little—"

"*Ignem exquiris!*" I shouted, and a stream of fire launched out of my wand and blasted the wizard.

Adrathar raised his hand and blasted the fire back at me. "*Effectus adversum!*"

I felt the flames singe my hair. The heat literally took my breath away. The flames landed on the machines, the bed linens, and his desk, where there was plenty of paper to catch alight. We were surrounded by thin plumes of smoke.

The doctor was furious. *"Rumpis!"* he yelled, blasting the floor where I was standing. It was as if he'd thrown a grenade at me. My whole body was lifted by the force of the explosion and thrown aside. I landed sprawled on my back. The fire got hungrier. Flames carpeted the floor. We didn't have much time. We were locked in, and I didn't know how to open the door.

CHAPTER 90
MORE THAN A CURSEBREAKER
ASHA

I focused on his cloak pocket, the one I knew had the memory tube in it.

"*Volas*," I whispered, whipping my wand up, and the glass cylinder came hurtling toward me. Too fast.

Hex! I thought, but it was too late it slow it down. I tried to catch it, but it bounced off the heel of my palm and crashed to the floor, shattering. The colored smoke escaped and dissipated before I could do anything about it. Fury raged in my chest, hotter and taller than the flames that seemed about to engulf us.

Then a very strange thing happened.

I could no longer see the purple smoke that disappeared from the tube, but I could sense it and smell it, despite the black fumes that swirled around. It was as if the smoke found its way to me, and I was able to inhale it without choking on the hot air that surrounded us. Perhaps it came to me because it was part of me, or perhaps I was just lucky. I breathed in the memories and magic that were taken from me, and immediately I remembered what had happened in the last week.

Stranger still, more visions were presenting themselves. Thoughts and images from *before* the first Dusk Reaper attack. I remembered the attack in detail: the wizard in a black cloak who tried to kidnap me. I screamed and fought back. He smashed my skull in and tried to drag me to his vehicle, only to be scared away by something. Perhaps a noise or a siren. Leaving me to bleed on the dirty pavement. Then I remembered Savvy, and our beautiful friendship. I remembered adopting Circe and Odysseus as tiny black kittens and spending hours with them on my lap as I mixed potions in the Shadow Room. I remembered the Starfall coven and how supportive they had always been. Captain Morgan enlisting me for my first job for the Scorpions. The Fornaks! Ferra and her tribe. My heart. Getting my bike license and buying the Wasp. Copperfield.

Adrathar's machine was indeed powerful. My life came rushing back to me. Every memory I had lost returned. It was exactly what I'd been wishing for, but the timing was tricky. Adrathar and I were now surrounded by a wall of fire.

Then I remembered something else. I had a dark secret that no one but Soleil and Savvy knew: I was more than a cursebreaker.

I felt overwhelmed by the memories that rushed in. The memories matched those crime scene photos that were pinned up on Morgan's board.

The vigilante assassin who the Scorpions were searching for was me.

I remembered killing the vampire who took out an entire untouched family; the witch who killed every husband she managed to ensnare; the orc who collected the teeth of his untouched human victims. I remembered taking their lives, and I remembered it in stark detail, because that's what happens when you kill someone. You remember every scent and searing sensation.

In a normal environment, in a calm space, the memories probably would have sent me reeling. But stuck in a locked room with Adrathar, with flames licking the walls and smoke filling our lungs, it had the opposite effect. The knowledge that I moonlighted as a vigilante assassin under the high priestess gave me a focus and strength I hadn't previously felt. If I could kill those terrible people, then I could defeat Doctor Adrathar. I wasn't just a green hippie hedge witch who happened to stumble upon an evil man. I was the one who was meant to take him down, to seek vengeance for the vulnerable women he had abused. As a witch, a cursebreaker, and an assassin it was my job to restore balance in the Realm. I was there for a reason, and I would fulfill my destiny.

CHAPTER 91
A GOOD DAY
ASHA

"*Rumpis!*" the wizard yelled, sending another invisible hand grenade my way and blowing up half the room so that concrete fell from above. I rolled away just in time, before a massive chunk crashed down right next to me. I rolled straight into the fire. Fortunately, I was wearing my graphene cloak which offered me some protection. I batted at my hair, which I could smell burning, and jumped to my feet, ready to deal once and for all with Adrathar.

"*Rumpis!*" I sent back to him, blowing up the wall where he had been standing.

"If you kill me," he said, "you'll never find out who signed your death warrant."

"If you live," I replied, "it won't matter."

I knew that Adrathar wouldn't rest until he handed my corpse to the one who was offering the reward.

The smoke was getting thick, and we were both tearing up and coughing. We'd die of smoke inhalation if we didn't get out, ASAP. My lungs felt like pieces of coal.

"*Rumpis!*" I shouted again, and sent another explosion his way. It knocked him off his feet. He still had his wand, which was now pointed directly at me. I flicked up the collar of my cloak, which turned the color and texture of the surrounding fire and smoke. Adrathar frowned and cast around, wondering where I had disappeared to. His eyes were watering, and he coughed.

I'm a vigilante assassin, I told myself. *Killing bad people is what I do.*

I padded up to the dark wizard and pointed my wand at his heart. I could almost see it beating through his chest, as if I had suddenly developed x-ray vision. He could not see me as I touched it to his breastbone.

"*Impedio,*" I whispered. *Halt.*

Adrathar stopped coughing. He realized what I had done, and grabbed his chest where I'd touched it with my wand. He tried to say something. Maybe it was a reversal spell, or a line of attack, but the words did not manage to escape his lips.

His heart had stopped beating. He keeled over, dropped his wand, and died.

Exhausted, injured, and oxygen deprived, I collapsed, too. My hood fell down, rendering me visible once more. I didn't know how to escape the furnace, and I didn't have the energy to try. The concrete beneath me was baking hot; I felt it on my cheek that lay glued to the floor, waiting for oblivion.

There was a blast. My eyes flew open, but all I saw was more black smoke. What was happening? I grabbed Adrathar's wand off the floor. Was he alive after all and throwing *Rumpis* spells around again? No. I could still see his motionless body. The blast wasn't magical. It had the real heft of dynamite or Semtex. I lost consciousness as the shadows crept in.

Someone with muscle lifted my body. He half carried, half dragged me out of the burning room. I dreamt it was Sam, and had a short-lived fantasy that the detective had come to rescue me. I would kiss him, of course, and we'd live happily ever after. Except that as he was carrying me, I realized that what I could smell was not the lovely citrus scent of Sam's aftershave, but rather the skunky raw onions that I had come to ... appreciate.

"Get her to the ambulance," said Morgan.

I forced my eyes open to look at the captain of the Scorpions. She looked beautiful. The emergency vehicle lights backlit her hair, giving her an amazing multi-colored halo, which she totally deserved.

Gnrok laid me gently onto the stretcher inside the ambulance. Immediately a paramedic got to work, taking my vitals, slipping an IV line in, and covering me with a foil blanket.

"You said you couldn't come," I said to Morgan, my voice all but lost in the screaming and the smoke. "You said you'd lose your job."

"Well," she said, with a skew smile. "If I get fired for doing this, then it's not a job I want."

She opened a bottle of water and passed it to me. It was the most beautiful thing I had ever tasted in my life.

"I remembered some things," I said. "Most things."

Morgan looked surprised. "Good! Does that mean we can start work on the other cases soon?"

I smiled, thinking of my singed hair and seared lungs. "Yes. Tomorrow. I'm going to prioritize the missing girls."

"The missing daughters," Morgan said. "That's what we're calling the case."

"Okay," I said. "I'm on it."

"Oh," said Morgan. "I almost forgot. Your boyfriend is here."

My stomach leapt. "What?"

"The muggle cop, right? Armstrong? We had to stop him from running into the burning building to save you."

"Oh," I said.

"We told him that it was too dangerous for a human. I told him that I knew you, and you could save yourself."

"Damn right," I said. "Especially when there's an orc to drag me out."

"Rook," she said, sternly. "You've done a good thing. Armstrong called his cop bosses and they're all arriving, ready to shut this place down."

"He does things the right way," I said. "By the book."

"Looks to me like you also do things the right way," said Morgan. "Maybe sometimes you need to burn stuff down to get people to pay attention."

"Maybe."

"Anyway. I thought your boyfriend would leave—"

"He's not my boyfriend," I said.

"I thought that the hot cop would leave, but he decided to stay and help evacuate the other patients. He's still pulling people out of the fire. So ..."

"So?"

"I don't know. He seems like a good guy."

"*Ja*," I replied. "He does."

I saw some odd movement behind the captain's head. I sat up straight.

"Talking of paying attention," I said, and looked pointedly at some silhouettes in the distance. They were walking toward us intently. Morgan reached for her gun, and I, my wand. Everyone on the scene was busy with evacuating people and putting out the fire. No one had even seen the crowd coming toward us. I pulled my fresh IV out. Morgan and I both stood up and got ready to fight.

CHAPTER 92
GHOST SONG
ASHA

As the crowd advanced, I realized they were not human. At least, they were *no longer* human. I recognized the silver shimmer they carried, exactly as Devka had done. I shook my head at Morgan, motioning that she could put her gun away, but she looked spooked and kept it in her hands.

It was a crowd of around two dozen ghosts, and they had come to get what they wanted. Or, rather, *who* they wanted. They walked in calm and silence, padding over the dew-damp black grass. Most of the untouched humans did not see them. When they got closer to us, I heard them humming something very quietly.

There'll be a time

When you'll say goodbye

It'll hurt so hard, love deep or die

No one wants to feel the low

But when you know, you know

It's time to end the show

Love deep or die.

It was the song from the Grackle Plague Pub. The soundtrack to which Derek Landau had sold out his marriage and his wife for a trickster mage of a mistress.

The cab driver had brought Derek here, as I had asked him to. I don't know what he had told him, but whatever it was, the ruse had worked. Derek stood outside the taxi, not knowing what was happening. Despite being untouched, he saw the choir of ghosts coming for him. That's when I understood who they were. Leading the fright was the ghost of the cop from the bridge on the night of the curse. Beside him floated the phantoms of the people who had died in the resulting pile-up on the highway, including some sad, marble-eyed children. I couldn't drag my eyes away. The singing sent shivers down my spine, and Morgan looked pale. She holstered her revolver.

I saw on Derek Landau's face that he had also worked out who the spirits were as they approached him, and he was terrified. Too terrified to run. Or perhaps he accepted then and there that this was what he deserved. The choir linked arms with him, and without using force they took him away, singing all the while. With Derek in their company, they unhurriedly returned to where they had come from, leaving Morgan and I feeling completely unsettled.

Death is not the end.

It turns out Nicola Landau's message had been right, after all.

EPILOGUE
WHAT I REMEMBERED DURING THE FIRE

"Welcome to the Starfall coven," Soleil said, gesturing with open arms and a generous smile.

Nicola Landau smiled back. She still had scars on her temple, but she looked much stronger than I had ever seen her. I was relieved to be safe and surrounded by my witch folk in the pseudo-yoga studio. I had my memory back, Merlin had brought me a coffee that morning, Savvy had called, Nicky Landau was safe, and I finally felt that everything was right with the world.

"Thank you for everything you've done for me," said Nicola.

I wished we could do more. The poor woman had had her life destroyed mostly because she had been a pawn in the Dusk Reaper's plan to deliver my corpse. She had lost her husband, house, and dog, and she had almost lost her mind. I admired the way she was still able to drag herself out of bed and meet with us, a coven of eccentric strangers. I felt slightly disingenuous accepting her thanks. None of this would have happened if it weren't for Adrathar's master plan ... or would it have? There was no telling what the multiverse wanted. Weren't we all pawns at the end of the day? The Wild will have its way with us no matter what we have planned.

"It's always a treat to have a convicted felon join our meeting," said Boston. Everyone fell silent at first, until they realized she was joking.

It was true that Nicola Landau was still wanted by the law. It seemed ridiculously unfair, but she had never been cleared of the crime she had been cursed to commit. They were treating her case as an escaped prisoner, to be apprehended on sight. There were also further crimes pending against her, because along with Emily and Alison—a convicted arsonist—they had been the only ones to escape the Riverside fire and remain unaccounted for. It followed, according to the investigation team, that they had been the ones to start the fire that killed so many guards, a nurse, and the head doctor.

Nicola Landau would always be on the run, which seemed grossly unfair. With that in mind, Soleil had arranged a new identity for her. She called it *The Witches' Protection Program*. Forsythia, the travel agent, had arranged a new passport as well as a ticket to New Zealand, where Landau would be able to set up a new life. We presented the passport to Nicky in the farewell ceremony. She was so grateful that she began weeping. We gathered around her and hugged her, murmuring that everything was going to be okay. She was nodding and crying, and she just seemed desperately sad.

When Chione slinked in, I tensed up so much I almost cracked a clavicle. I wrenched her aside, out of view of the others.

"What are you doing here?" I demanded in a harsh whisper. "Haven't you caused enough harm?"

"That's *why* I'm here," she said. "I brought something for her. For Nicola."

The Grimalkin sneezed.

"You didn't have her dog put down?"

"Of course not," said Chione. "I'm not a monster." She scratched at a rash on her arm. "I'm on a near-lethal dose of antihistamines at the moment, so if I pass out, you'll know why." She whistled loudly, and Sebastian came running at a full clip.

Nicky, hearing a dog running, looked up from the crying and hugging and looked in our direction. When she saw her dog, she yelped and fell to her knees, and Sebastian ran straight into her arms, licking her face and barking. Astonished and delighted, Nicky laughed and cried and kept telling Sebastian what a good boy he was.

"That was a kind thing to do," I said to Chione.

"It was the least I could do," she replied, and I couldn't help but agree.

"Thank you," she said to me.

"Me?"

Chione nodded, albeit reluctantly. "You saved my life. I owe you one of my nine."

"That's not necessary," I said.

"It is," said the Grimalkin, then stole away from me, toward the coven.

"Landau," said Chione. Nicola looked at her, clearly unaware who the mage was, and thanked her profusely.

Chione held up her hand to stop her. "I'm Chione. You need new fingerprints," she said.

"No," said Soleil. "We're setting her up in New Zealand."

"Oh, no," said Nicky. "I'm sorry. I can't. Not now that I have Sebastian back."

"We can send him to you," said one of the witches.

Nicola shook her head, not taking her hand off her dog. "No, I'm sorry. I know you've gone to a great deal of trouble. But I'm not leaving him again."

The Labrador panted and barked.

"Also, Dillon's wife will be giving birth in April, and I'm going to help them with the baby."

Soleil looked worried, but accepted her decision.

"As I was saying," said Chione. "If you're going to stay in Johannesburg, you'll need new fingerprints."

"That would help," said Nicky. "Yes."

"I can cut and dye her hair," said the beautician.

"Okay," announced the high priestess. "New plan. Chione, you start work now on Nicola's fingerprints. Lucy, go and buy scissors and dye. Esmerelda, some dog supplies. Forsythia, can you get your people to produce an ID and driver's license in Landau's new name?"

"Sure," she said. "What is it?"

We all looked at Nicola, who blinked rapidly as she thought it over. "I don't know," she replied. "Maybe ... Devka? Rose Devka?"

Sebastian barked, and she hugged him.

"Good." Soleil rubbed her fingers to get a golden spark in her palm, then laid it on Nicola's head. "Welcome to The Witches' Protection Program. I now bless you and your future as Rose Devka."

I jumped on my Wasp and negotiated my way through the morning traffic, my head spinning with what had happened in the last few days. To a certain extent, I felt the weight was off my shoulders knowing that one case was solved, but I knew that the feeling wouldn't last for long. I was ready to tackle the case of the missing daughters. I knew it was going to be a tough one. The sky was clear, and there was a slight breeze. It was absolutely perfect weather. I was off to buy a big lunch for Nilve SaltySnap at The Copper Cog & Ale to thank her for her excellent portaling magic. I was planning on giving Ferra the wand I had taken off Adrathar. I hoped she could melt it down and do something useful with it. But before I did that, I had someone to see.

Detective Sam Armstrong was in the Morningvale Hospital, getting medical attention for his smoke inhalation and minor burns. It turned out that he had pulled twenty-two people from the burning building, and was to receive some kind of medal of honor when they discharged him. In the meantime, I was going to visit. If he was interested, I'd tell him a little bit about what I remembered during the fire.

Of course, I wouldn't be able to tell him everything. I couldn't even tell Morgan everything. No one knew that dark secret except for Savannah and the high priestess, and I had to keep it that way.

I parked my scooter and headed straight for the hospital gift shop, where I bought something for Sam, paid for with the last of my Copperfield envelope cash. I walked into the elevator, clutching the transparent clamshell container of green grapes to my chest, and couldn't help smiling as the doors closed to take me up to Sam.

YOUR NEXT ADVENTURE AWAITS

Thank you for joining us on this caper!

Grab the next book in this 6-book series now
to read more about Asha's mission to find the missing
daughters, all the while dodging violent vampires and
psychopathic elves.

~

ALSO BY JT LAWRENCE

FICTION

WHEN TOMORROW CALLS

• SERIES •

(Futuristic kidnapping thriller)

The Stepford Florist: A Novelette

The Sigma Surrogate

1. Why You Were Taken

2. How We Found You

3. What Have We Done

When Tomorrow Calls Box Set: Books 1 - 3

(complete)

URBAN FANTASY

BLOOD MAGIC

(complete 6-book series)

1. The HighFire Crown

2. The Dream Drinker

3. The Witch Hunter

4. The Ember Isles

5. The Chaos Jar

6. The New Dawn Throne

CURSEBREAKER

(complete 6-book series)

1. The Dusk Reapers

2. The Haunted Portal

3. The EverShade Ring

4. The Obsidian Castle

5. The Pick Pocket's Curse

6. The Eternal Betrayal

STANDALONE NOVELS

The Memory of Water

(steamy psychological thriller)

Grey Magic

(witchy magical realism)

EverDark

(urban fantasy)

SHORT STORY COLLECTIONS

Sticky Fingers

Sticky Fingers 2

Sticky Fingers 3

Sticky Fingers 4

Sticky Fingers 5

Sticky Fingers 6

Sticky Fingers: The Complete Collection:
Books 1 - 6: 72 Short Stories

NON-FICTION

The Underachieving Ovary

(memoir)

The Indie Author Game Plan

www.ingramcontent.com/pod-product-compliance
Lightning Source LLC
Chambersburg PA
CBHW020345220726
48290CB00014B/1025